The Fortune Follies

Catori Sarmiento

Initially Published in 2018 by Double Dragon Publishing
Copyright © 2020 Catori Sarmiento

Cover art "Bionic Robot Female" by Johann Bret Bautista

ISBN 978-1-77115-484-0

This book is a work of fiction. Names, characters, places
and incidents are products of the author's imagination or are
used fictitiously. Any resemblance to actual events or locales
or persons, living or dead, is entirely coincidental.

This book is dedicated to my husband and my daughter, without whom I would not have the support and inspiration to write.
A further appreciation goes to a family I knew well while living in Japan.

Author's Note

This book contains several alternate events that diverge greatly from our own, the foremost being the use of Operation Downfall in World War Two as opposed to the bombing of Hiroshima and Nagasaki. During the war, there were two options to be considered when it came to the Allies fighting the Japanese Imperial Army. In the world of *The Fortune Follies*, President Roosevelt chose to follow Operation Downfall in a plan to invade Japan near the end of 1945. This plan involved several sub-operations, including Operation Olympic, and relied on cooperation from Allied powers, concluding with the historic study done for the Secretary of War by William Shockley, the invasion of Japan by Allied Forces estimated that fatalities could range anywhere from 300,000 to 720,000 with casualties between 1.7 to 4 million. These numbers are lessened in the book due to the existence of the Sinclair Industries manufactured Iron Boys and their use during the invasion.

While numerous events and locations in this book are fictional, the historical systematic internment of 110,000-120,000 Japanese-Americans from 1942-1946 occurred with the onset of President Franklin D. Roosevelt's Executive Order 9066. The 442nd Regimental Combat Team that is mentioned in the text was indeed the most highly decorated unit in the history of American Warfare. Similarly, there was indeed a great earthquake that occurred in Seattle on April 13th, 1949. The locations of King Street Station and The Black and Tan Club are also factual. Several of the folktales are taken from their real counterparts from the Yamanashi, Kanto, and Nikko regions of Japan with slight changes to reflect the fluid nature of oral tales.

The Fortune Follies

Sarah
Escaping the Bond
March 1949

It was a terrible thing that she did and it had been necessary. Rippling before her mind are the long white envelopes that she tore open. As expected, there were great amounts of cash in each. She took them all, making sure to take the envelopes with her, hid them deep in her purse, and snuck out the back exit of the church as the chatter from the party faded. She knows that she should feel a rousing despondency, but it hangs like a silver lure in a saltwater marsh.

Sitting by the porthole window, Sarah makes sure she can watch the shore of Alaska fade into the distance, watching the clouds and the sea. At times a splash and the bobbing heads of seals rise and dip back against the glass. A cheap room by the standards of a luxury ocean liner. Hers is the bottom bunk. An older woman naps on the top, snoring loudly; in the adjacent bunk is a young boy traveling alone who left his luggage so he could eat his lunch in the restaurant upstairs. The bed above his holds a luggage case that belonged to a "P.L. Weathers" who has yet been unseen. Revving in the sky causes her to glance up to the tiny window to spy a grey airplane passing overhead. There have been more military airplanes these last few years for reasons she hardly considered. Their presence as concerning as a flock of geese passing overhead; noticeable but not affecting.

She steadies her feet to the movements of the ship as she ascends the steel stairs and past the racket of churning engines, higher and higher, all the way to the fourth floor.

The narrow hallway is plastered with bulbous yellow
wallpaper that had once been white, changing drastically to a
newer, more lustrous, gilded, floral design when she passes
the second floor. On reaching the great mezzanine, there is a
wide-open space with a central lounge surrounded by a
curved wet bar where tuxedo-clad bartenders stand at
attention with their hands resting stiffly at the small of their
backs. Each face bears a kind grimace that can be mistaken
for resolve. Tall windows on each wall guide her eyes to an
enormous stained-glass ceiling where Scarlet Peacock
butterflies dance across a clear surface to let in overcast
sunlight, brightening the intricate floral designs in the carpet.
White and pink roses interweave with bluebells to form a
repeating circular pattern separated by pudgy-cheeked
cherubs. So detailed are the woven threads that each petal is
distinguishable from the others and every angelic body seems
poised to flutter up from the threads. Two sizable wooden
doors engraved with harp-playing angels stand between the
comfortable warmth and the sea winds on the veranda.

Absorbing the surroundings of wealth, it seems wrong
that some should have so much and others so little. A glance
at her own threadbare clothes handed down by her older
sister easily displays her class, made all the more obvious by
those walking the upper deck, particularly a man in a black
suit escorting a small girl, no older than five, across the room
and to the outside deck. As the little girl skips, the length of
the bright orange fox fur wrapped firmly around her neck and
clasped in the front with a bejeweled oval broach bobs up and
down the front of her azure wool coat. Why should a girl
have more money hanging on her shoulders than Sarah had in
her life? The girl reminds her of her cousin. A fickle girl with
an overwhelming inheritance. Overwhelmed by the scene,

2

she returns to the deck where a handful of passengers admire the scenery, some with children who are left to play freely. Clear blue above her where she expected rain and a wafting heat from which she was already moist. A ribbon of green is the sea. Unending. In the midst are parcels of lands in lines too straight to be made by nature. From white shores to spikes rising into a milky sky. Settled on these are square, flat topped buildings painted white. From behind are four large square pillars with electrical towers on either side. Jutting out from the shore, steel arms pump and pull the water. There were three of these such islands. A speck of white wearing a yellow cap moves like an insect along the shore next to one of the arms. She realizes then that it is a person. A click from the speaker set above the doorway makes her flinch in surprise, and then a commercialized voice emerges:

"Ladies and Gentlemen, as we approach the docks, please marvel at the electrical engineering that powers everything in the city, from radios to trains. It is so unique that it is the only such feat on the entire West Coast. This, of course, is a creation of the great Mr. Robert Sinclair. Yes! Robert Sinclair: the man, the visionary. You've heard of his automatons, now see what he can do with an entire city! During your stay on shore, be sure to visit the many sights made possible by Mr. Sinclair's extraordinary imagination, including the one-of-a-kind sky train."

The announcement ceases abruptly. Who had not heard of the man, Sinclair? Not only are his businesses ubiquitous, but it was his invention of the Iron Boy automatons that helped win the war. Perhaps the announcement had influenced her, but she too becomes excited to see what such a man has done to a city. Though

3

she had passed by here years before, the circumstances of that arrival cloud any clear memory she has of Seattle.

Even in the day, lights flash from towers so it can be seen in the clouds. Far to the right, past the port and buildings stands a tower rising higher than the others and a red brick factory below it where black clouds erupt from smokestacks and a sign atop reads "Sinclair Industries". The approach to the port reveals fisheries, docks, sailboats pulled into the wooden docks and fishing boats unloading their catch. On the pier stands a Ferris Wheel where on the spoke a giant clock of silver and gold might glimmer if the sun ever emerges from behind the clouds. Her eyes are drawn to a system of tall, wide pylons with gaps in the center connecting rail lines. Through the towers, a sky train winds about like a snake through corn stalks. As the liner glides into port, a statue comes clearer into view.

A mermaid nearly one hundred feet tall, the top of her head rising far above the mast of the ship. Sarah looks down to see that the statue had been driven down into the seabed where the mermaid's tail bends under the water, barnacles latched on to the lowest part, dark lines marking past tides. The statue, long hair running slick down her back, is bare-breasted and reaches her arms into the air, welcoming sailors into her bosom with a motherly smile. As the liner settles in, bells ring from below. Her head towards the sky, Sarah finds colorful hot air balloons floating at different levels, each one with alternating stripes of red, white, and blue. Where the basket should be is a steel box fitted with megaphones on each side. The sea invades her senses with a murky salt so strong she coughs. Cawing seagulls fly every which way. Three come down to land their orange feet on the edge of the pier to screech at her, begging for scraps. She shoos them off with a flick of her hand as she focuses carefully on her steps down the ramp while the carpet bag slaps at her side. Walking on, she startles when a gruff voice addresses her. She snaps her head up to see a blue-uniformed man whose brass rank makes her squint.

"You have to go out of the INS exit."

"Pardon?"

"The INS exit." He points to the port side where men were already unloading baggage from a ramp, one at the top sliding down suitcases to another who catches them and places each in a roller bin. Other passengers are already filing down the ramp and into a white square building with one large wooden door, a glass window and gold letters saying, "Immigration Service."

"Down there?" she asks, pointing, sure that there must be some mistake.

He nods. She knows better than to resist authority and toes carefully along the ramp with the others to the plain building, where inside there is an even plainer room. A bench with worn varnish where those before sat. White walls to match white floors. The only decorations are framed posters. Above the bench, a blue star with a standing eagle in the center on a white background. Next to this are words all in capital letters saying "Freedom to Work at Sinclair Industries" with a happy-faced white woman in blue coveralls working on a machine Sarah does not recognize. The others waiting before her are addressed and dismissed to sit or to wait in a far room.

A voice calls, "Yes?"

Sarah turns to the sound where a woman in a grey blazer with a buttoned-up high collar sits behind a reception desk. Sarah walks forward, keeping her bag with her.

"I'm here visiting my cousin," Sarah says.

The woman flicks thickly lashed eyes to her, commenting, "Your English is very good."

Sarah gives a sarcastic smirk and nods.

The woman lifts her eyebrows while taking a long slip of paper and a pen from behind the counter and setting it before Sarah.

"Fill this out, and I need some form of identification." Sarah rifles through her pockets for a thin billfold to present her brown Alaskan residence card, which is quickly taken, then stands, writing answers to the simple questions. Putting the pen down, she slides the paper to the woman who takes it wordlessly. Skimming it, she glances back up.

"I see. Please sit down in the room over there." She motions to a closed door marked "Intermittent" in painted black letters. "Until a relative can vouchsafe for you, you'll have to wait."

"How long will that be?"

She meets the young girl with a revealing glance before covering it with an insincere smile.

"As soon as your cousin arrives, and you are issued identification, you may exit."

"I'll just wait here," Sarah says, pointing to the bench.

The woman nods once and begins punching the keys on a typewriter hidden from view. After four hours waiting, she moves into the resting room where a woman not much older than herself sleeps with a baby snuggling against her chest. She might know. Sarah taps her, asking how long she has been there. The woman's heavy eyes open. She tuts, says some angry words in what Sarah suspects is Chinese and

shuts her eyes once more. On a stool sit three homemaker
magazines and a single paperback titled *The Trolley Car
Family* by Eleanor Clymer with the back cover torn off. She
is not that desperate for entertainment yet, but after staring at
the blank walls, she picks up the book and skims the pages,
reading words that flit about in her mind as other thoughts
whirl, grabbing her attention. Staying with her cousin will
solve her current predicament, giving her time to decide what
to do and a place to remain safe in an otherwise unknown
city.

A rustling from the woman gets her attention. The
baby grunts like a sleeping pig and soon it is suckling. Sarah
remembers a similar noise from when her mother fed her
baby brother. Her father, when he was joyful with drink, told
her stories that redeemed his brusque, sober qualities. The
Chinese baby, she thinks, looks like *Issun Boshi*. She
remembers the story, her father's voice relaying it over her
own.

"*Mukashi, mukashi*," he said, "there was a sweet old
couple. Childless, but wanting one very much, they went to a
shrine and prayed, 'Please, please let us have a child, no
matter how small.' Soon, a son was born to them. But the
child was so small—no larger than a man's fingertip. So, the
couple raised the child, and he became a bright young boy
but did not grow any taller than when he was born. That is
why he was called Issun-boshi. One day, he told his parents
that he wanted to have an adventure in the city. Trusting him,
they sent him off with a sword made of a sewing needle, a
sheath made of straw, and a boat made from a rice bowl with
a chopstick for an oar. He walked along until he came upon a
river. There he put his rice bowl in the water and paddled
with the chopstick for days until at last he reached the town.

7

Along the way, two ogres suddenly jumped out onto the road and blocked his path." Here, her father would stop to make a monstrous growl to mimic the ogres. "He took out his needle-sword and came upon their attackers. But then suddenly one of the ogres swallowed him up in one gulp. He stabbed the insides of its stomach and the ogre was so overcome with pain that it threw Issun-boshi up. Free, he jumped up on the other ogre's eyebrow and stabbed its eye. Defeated, the ogres fled away, crying."

*

Sarah wakes to the screeching babbles of the child and a pulsing headache with her flat shoes still firmly on her feet. The Chinese mother stands, holding her son's hands as she steadies his balance while teaching him to walk. He lifts a foot, wobbling on his other leg, puts it clumsily in front of him before setting it down. They continue walking in circles around the room. Clicking heels signal the receptionist's arrival. She appears by the door, careful not to touch so much as the framework. Seeing her, the woman perks up, eyes hopeful.

"Ms. Igarashi," she says to which the woman turns back to her child, burying disappointment, "your cousin is here."
Eager to leave the room, Sarah pops up and quickly follows. Waiting outside to greet her is Penelope.

"There!" she exclaims and embraces her too quickly for Sarah to refuse.

Her skin a perfume of faint sweat, cigarette smoke, jasmine, and Dial soap. Pulling back, Sarah scrutinizes the face that is clearer in the daylight. In the absent years, her once subtle Scandinavian features have become sharper with

8

the Japanese recognizable in her almond-shaped eyes and the smoothness of her aquiline nose.

"I came as quickly as I could do. I'd just got in and, you know, Mom is gone so there was no one there to answer the phone. What a night it was. But look at you! What a country girl you are. How's *oniisan*? Doing well, I hope?" *Oniisan*. A sweet name Penny always used to refer to her uncle, Sarah's father. She pushes away the image of his scarred face, of the body that breathed from a room she avoided.

When no answer comes, Penny says, "Never mind" and folds her smooth hand over Sarah's calloused skin, "we'll get right home."

Penny grabs Sarah's hand and pulls her toward the door. As they turn to leave, the woman shouts after them, "You aren't permitted!" to which both young women return to the desk.

"I'm sorry, Ms. Morgan, but there is one more item before your cousin may leave."

In a swift fashion, she flips a paper from under the desk, smoothing it out on the top. Taking a pen from its place in her front jacket pocket, she hashes several blank lines with Xs and lays it perpendicular on the top of the form.

"Sign and initial by the marks," she says, "you *can* read English?"

"Of course I can," Sarah says, picking up the pen, skimming over the agreement; A standard identification form entitling the cardholder to ninety days of residency and revocation of assistance in the event of arrest or tax evasion. Once the form is signed, the INS woman slips it to her, muttering "Just a moment," and whisks to a machine press with a type keyboard attached. A *calunk, calunk*, echoes in the vacant room while she presses the buttons. After enduring

9

minutes of racket, Sarah feels the springing pulse of premature tension at the base of her skull. The woman stops the machine and immediately slides two cards in Sarah's direction. One is her original Alaskan identification and the other is a blue plastic card with a white star on the top and her personal information below. She slipped them in her pocket.

As the two relations exit through the terminal gates, vendors line up on either side of the docks. Some shout towards the streets, trying to sell their wares. Black taxis along the curb, waiting for disembarking passengers. There are advertisements pasted across the sides, screaming "Eat Lactaid Chocolate Today!" and others asking "Feeling Tired? Try Sinclair's Famous Firelite Cigarettes." She spies at the edge of the pier closest to the mermaid a small stone alcove with the same figure nestled inside. Hanging from its outstretched arms and fingers are blue ribbons—so many that it seems she wears sleeves. Coins lie at the base. Above the old factory that used to be Hartford Manufacturing before Sinclair ran them out stands a billboard advertising: "Pocket Pets: A pal you can take anywhere! No food. No water. Just fun!" A young boy gawks at the varieties of pets and insects contained in a case small enough to fit in a pocket. Noticing her cousin staring at the advertisement, Penny nudges her with an elbow.

"Never seen that in Alaska, have you? The most popular now are these dwarf chameleons inside glass. Most kids I've seen have them in what looks like a watch. Spoiled kids have two or three different ones and wear them like jewelry. I was thinking of getting one for Timothy. You know George's son, don't you? Don't know *how* they stay alive, though."

As they wind through people passing in front on the street, Sarah looks out at the commotion. With so many people in one place her eyes become exhausted, leading her to see a man with metal legs and face. Blinking to reset her vision does nothing to remove the mechanical man walking through the street. Weathered metal figures with police badges on their chests, each one equipped with a lightning weapon; a rod where a left hand ought to be that sparks with blue bolts. Noisy mechanisms that sting her ears. Passing by the metal men are young girls in day dresses with bejeweled gear wheels fused to the skin around their eyes, rounding the mobile machine as if it is a boulder on the sidewalk. At the flat harbor steps are a small crowd of people. A long banner reading "Fair Wages for Fair Work" written in blue paint and capital letters is held high by two people who wear matching uniforms of white blouses tucked into blue work pants. They shout speeches about the evils of Sinclair's business, about the unfairness of their employment practices while thrusting fliers at passers-by. Some take them out of courtesy, but most walk past.

A bulky figure that looks much like a steeple roof with arms and legs catches her attention. She wanders away from Penny's side to get a closer look and sees inside the steeple roof covered in glass an old man with a balding head. Just below the center of the glass, a chrome mesh speaker. His hands and arms are covered with a rubber material that feeds into the box-like contraption, similar to his legs. Surrounding the inside of the glass are little white lights that illuminate his face. He patrols up and down the street slowly as people let him pass. Some glance back to see the neon sign glowing on his back. A loud twinkling song erupts from the spouting speaker on the top, announcing his approach and a

11

group of schoolchildren stop before him, chat, and then leave with convenience items in hand—a candy bar, a cool drink, a sandwich. Curious, Sarah goes up to him, struck that he is not a man at all but another machine. His face from a distance had appeared like flesh. Yet being so close she notices the too-smooth skin plastered over half of a metal face with the back of the skull fused to the inner wall. His opaque white glass eyes with black irises dart in all directions.

"May I help you?" he asks in a voice stilted and unhuman.

A paper sign taped to the inside and facing out lists items and prices. A cool treat might subdue her throbbing head.

"A cherry ice, please," she says.

The machine-man pulls his arms in and fiddles with a compartment under the glass. He removes a packaged ice cream bar, cold steam rising from it, and opens the chrome door, instructing her to pay twenty cents. She pushes two dimes through the glass and he hands her the ice, then immediately retrieves his arms back in the tubes and continues walking.

Sarah tears off the white paper wrapper to snack on the cool cherry ice, while wandering along the less boardwalk where a meager wooden fence painted with three blue graffiti V's protects against drunkards falling over the side and into the murky water. Though Seagulls idle in the upper air as others perch upon the fence posts resting, they call to each other in a cacophony bouncing from sky to shore. She stops for a moment, resting a hand on the fence, to finish the ice bar, hoping it will calm her. She had not given much thought to how a modern city would affect her when she left home, but the bustle agitates her more than she expected.

12

Finishing the sweet, she tosses the stick in a nearby trash container. Her mind somewhat settled, she realizes that she ought to find Penny. Scattered along the wooden-planked docks are small storefronts. Through the glass windows with "Oliver's Fish and Chips" written in gold letters, she can see workers on their lunch breaks and others waiting in a line outside the door for their turn. Following the building edge are numerous shop faces, each crafted in the similar style of a rectangular frame covered with long wood panels and heavy timber columns. One in particular stands out among the others with its two brightly painted totem poles steadfast before a storefront.

Sarah loiters at a toy shop window next door, marveling at the contraptions. They are nothing like the wooden blocks or airplanes that sat in the general store of her Alaskan town. Here there are floating metallic insect mechanisms rotating by a means that she does not understand. Wrapped around a fabric mannequin head is a necklace with a flat glass pendant the size of her palm. Inside flickers a trapped storm of lightning bolts emerging and fading. When the door opens, a noise within causes her to pause, breathing in deeply the moist wood and salt that veils the air. School children, some in matching blue uniforms and others in street clothes, yet all clasping book bags, search shelves where sample toys lie waiting to be touched and others are coveted by the odd child who refuses to relinquish their turn to another.

"There you are!" Penny calls from a few feet in front of her as she shoulders past a pair of teenage girls, ignoring their shouted insults. She links her arm with Sarah's, chiding, "You shouldn't wander."

*

"Let me," Penny says, taking Sarah's brown cowhide suitcase and leather violin case at once. Penny pays the driver, who takes the payment with appreciation before driving away slowly. With Penny walking on ahead, Sarah follows her to the door, taking in the cozy Tudor Revival home painted an oyster white with ocean blue cross gables, roof tiles, and archways. Surrounding the length of the front yard is a white stone wall, waist-high, where moss clusters gather in the creases, stopped with a short black iron fence with sharp spikes to keep birds away. Through the empty holes, roses peek through along with their thorny fingers. Opening the gate, a small squeak emits as the damp hinges rub against each other, worn down from constant rain. The yard is a lush green, so far removed from straggly bits of tough grasses that grow around her family's home in Alaska. Sarah bends down to press her hand against the damp lawn that is as soft as flannel. Lifting her hand, she finds a veil of moisture shining on her skin and rubs her fingers together. After enjoying the sensation, she wipes a hand on her sleeve to walk up the wooden stairs that creak hollow beneath her feet.

"As soon as I got your wire, I made room—don't you worry."

The wire Sarah sent a few days before was an impulsive, frantic message that called for a place to stay. She was desperate for sanctuary, even if it would be with a spoiled girl no older than sixteen. Every wicked thing that that girl had done suddenly comes rushing into her mind. All the things Penny had done. She beats the grim thoughts back. Sarah has to get reparations in some way. The only city where they have the citizen's salary, one hundred and twenty-five dollars a month, she remembers, that each is entitled to so long as they have the papers for it. Once Sarah can get a salary for herself, she will never have to work, and with a nice bundle of the money that she can shake out of Penny, send back plenty of to her family with enough left over to start an independent life. She can find her own way.

"Can't believe how hot it is today," Penny says, exhaling a puff of warm breath as she puts her hand on the brass door handle. "I hope you like cats," she says as she opens the door. Sarah faintly recalls her cousin's partiality to cats.

"Not the one from the camp?" Sarah asks.

"It is! You remember him, right?"

"Only the fall."

She grimaces at the memory of how Penny coaxed her away from class recess to catch a rough-looking kitten hidden in the center of the narrow space between their barracks. Penny on one end and Sarah on the other. The kitten, wide eyed, frightened, and so skinny that his ribs were visible and his hip bones protruded. Penny tossed a pebble near his feet to encourage him to move. Whenever he did, Sarah was ready to catch him up in her skirt. Another pebble mistakenly hit his nose and startled him. Skittering off, he rushed towards Sarah with such speed that when she scooped him in her skirt she lost her balance, falling to her side on the dirt. More concerned for the animal, Penny called, "Did you catch him? Is he all right?" Sarah callously handed her the kitten, happy when it scratched her arm when searching for a place to cling.

That kitten caused too much grief.

"I didn't think you'd still have him."

"And why not? Bruce is a good boy."

15

The door opens and Sarah is bombarded with an over-fresh smell that must have come from the glade air freshener can that rests on the bottom shelf of the coat rack. She appraises the main room, decorated with a variety of styles as if no one person could agree on aesthetics as evident by the large white sofa with a pink floral pattern and a yellow-and-blue afghan quilt draped over the back. Along the center wall separating the living room from the kitchen is a fireplace with perfectly cut logs stacked inside that seem to have never been lit. Next to this is an end table with a large bronze whippet statue sitting alert as the base while a glass surface is secured on its head and on this sits a radio. There are also two wing back chairs, oyster-pink, in a semicircle facing the sofa. Pinned to plaster walls are a poster of Etta James singing, a long wall scroll of cranes in a pond, and several small, unframed scenic paintings.

"Your room is over here," Penny says.

Sarah follows her through the ghastly living room to the hallway where she sees three doors. Across from them is the very small kitchen consisting of a sink, a small refrigerator, a few cupboards, and a stove on which a teapot rests.

"And down the hallway, up the stairs, is George's house," she says, flipping her free hand dismissively towards a doorframe at the end of the hall with a steep staircase leading up to another shut door and the second floor behind it. Sarah can hear the bustling footsteps typical of a family; heavy shuffling followed by feathery patters. Soon there is a whine from a baby that quickly rises to a throaty scream. Seemingly unperturbed by the noise, Penny points to the first door on the right. While her family had been joined with Penny and her mother at Minidoka, George's had been placed elsewhere in Manzanar. What she knows of him is

16

little beyond a few anecdotes and though they share a family name, he is as familiar to her as a stranger.

"This is my room. The next one is yours, and then down there is the bathroom. Although after six the hot water runs out so be sure to wash up before then."

She opens the door to another room. Smaller than Sarah had hoped for.

"Here we are," she says, walking in and putting the things on the quilt spread on the bed. "You still play the violin? It seems a bit light."

She takes a few steps into the plain room. There is a single bed on a wooden frame underneath a window with open curtains, a closet, and a disheveled writing desk on the opposite wall with a stool tucked under it. Over-filled bookcases a few inches shorter than her line around the room, one next to the other. Books that did not fit into the cases were stacked on the desk and furthermore on the floor next to the legs, arranged in a tower. Whatever space there once was on the walls had been filled with family pictures and posters, one of which was a small cameo picture of Penny on an advertisement for The Birdcall Lounge.

"It's just the case," Sarah finally answers.

"Ah," Penny says. "Well, now you're here in the city you can buy one for yourself, eh?"

"Yes."
Suddenly there is a rumpus of pounding footsteps. Sarah glances to her cousin who shrugs.

"They can make some noise up there," she says, opening the carpet bag and takes out one of the wrinkled dresses and throws it over her arm, going to the closet to fetch a hanger.

"What church are you going to now?" she asks as she hangs up the dress.

"If ever I had a day off on Sunday, I went to First Presbyterian in Anchorage."

Penny returns to the bag, going back and forth hanging up clothes.

"Yes? Well, you can always come to church with me, even though I'm Protestant. But, Christian is Christian, isn't it? I've been going since Mom and I came back from Minidoka. Actually, Pastor Wade came to visit the church shortly after. You remember him, don't you?"

Penny had always conveniently disappeared on Sundays to meet the pastor just behind the secondary fence, along with the other church-goers eager to see him. The small group walked with the gentleman. Sometimes they gifted him with little trinkets. Penny once made him a poor handkerchief from a square of hemmed cotton on which she had tried her best to embroider a strawberry but which resulted in what looked more like a squashed tomato. He was kind, she remembered, he could have brushed the gift aside but took it with a smile and often used it to mop his forehead during service in the cramped canteen with the muggy summer heat still in the air.

"George brings his children sometimes. You could come too."

"What does George do for work now?"

"He's a dock worker down at the waterfront."

"At the docks?" Sarah asks, unimpressed. Having been under the impression that George was well-off, she stares right at her cousin, eyebrows raised.

"Is something wrong with that? Besides, there is *more* than enough money in it," she says with a smile, "what with Sinclair Industrials shuffling cargo in and out."

"Here, sit down," Penny offers, "and tell me about the trip."

18

Sarah stand, proclaiming, "Actually, I'd like to unpack."

"Oh, yes," she says, "I'll make us some tea, then."

"How can you live here?" Sarah asks.

"It's my house. Don't you know?"

"*You* have a house?"

"Yes. Since Mom remarried. She gave it to me before the wedding. Deed and all."

The unfairness that Penny should have so much and she so little.

"Where is she now?"

"Oh, Los Angeles. She's convinced that she'll meet some movie stars down there."

"When is she coming back?" Sarah asks, worried that she might encounter her aunt in the near future.

"When the summer's over, might be."

A flickering of multiple lights pierces through the curtains.

"Are those the lights?"

She does not hear the answer, too mesmerized by the balloons in the air raised up higher than the towers, spiral illuminations emanating from them so that the streets below are lit white. She was used to the Alaskan night sun that shone above in the summer. A yellow white hue as comforting as a low-burning candle. These lights, however, blared from the base, penetrating with artifice.

"That's right," Penny says, snapping her fingers. "That's Sinclair that did it for us, him and his companies. You must have seen the big sign by the port and the reactors just outside?"

Sarah nods.

"Don't know how he does it, but it gives us all this electricity here. Of course, he owns half the city now. All the better for it, I say." She shrugs. "I always forget about

Alaska. Why doesn't your family move here? I wrote about it years ago."

"We'd have to sell everything and move."

"That didn't seem like such a problem the first time. And this is a surer thing. Come on, things are better now! Just wait until you see the city, you'll have a riot. I thought we could see a matinee together. But, oh, you might want to look for work though. I suppose you can do that in the morning, what do you think?"

She inhales sharply at the thought of work. She must have misheard.

"What?"

"Work. I mean, that's why you came here."

"I—I wasn't thinking of working right away," Sarah says, stifling her shock.

"Goodness, what else are you going to do?"

"Well. . .Why can't I just spend time here?"

"How else are you going to pay rent?" Penny lets out a huff. "I'm not your mother. If you want to stay here, you have to contribute in some way. Besides, it'll help you get on your feet. Best to be busy."

She considers arguing against it, but bites her tongue, remembering that it is best for her to act cordial for the time being. A silent understanding washes over her as she watches Penny take one of her paisley blue and purple blouses from the trunk and refolds it, placing it on the end of the bed. Sarah considers immediately packing up her things to find a place to stay in the city. Yet, she knows no one. Penny might be unreasonable, but she offered to keep her when others may have refused.

"You can go upstairs and say hello to Catherine. If she's awake, that is."

Sarah looks over at Penny who works her way through the suitcase, folding clothes and arranging them according to color. She is about to ask who Catherine is until she deduces that the only woman in the family she has not met is George's wife. Instead, she questions,

"Why wouldn't she be awake? It's the afternoon. Aren't her kids out playing?"

Penny rolls her eyes, explaining, "She doesn't go out anymore and, unless I volunteer for the task, neither do the children."

The last pair of trousers folded, Penny sucks in her breath as if suddenly remembering an idea that was once forgotten.

"Oh, but let me show you the back garden. Ojiisan might be there now."

It takes a moment for Sarah to remember the man who Penny refers to affectionately in the Japanese word for "Grandfather". From what little her mother told her over the years, this man is her uncle, but, like George, she had never met him before. Had it not been for the internment camp, she doubts she would have met Penny either. Penny takes Sarah's arm and coaxes her away, past the bathroom to a white door with a diamond-shaped window. Through it is a slim sun room just wide enough for a gardener's work table cluttered with tools and purple morning glories growing up the table legs from a pot underneath.

There are two staircases, one on the left leading down and another on the right leading up. At the top is a windowless locked door. She can hear children playing behind it. An adult's voice is clearly absent. There are shouts and happy screams. The windows draw her closer to a view of the backyard. Deep evergreen grass grows thick as a

21

carpet, barred only by fenced garden plots set along the farthest side of the back fence. Bushy radish tops and cucumber vines curve over each other, clambering for space. Penny opens the door, having to jiggle the round handle before it relents.

"Ojiisan! Sarah is here."

She lets go of her cousin and jumps down the three wood steps to the wide slate stone which must be for stomping off dirt from shoes. Penny's heels click against the slate and then swish on grass as she walks to a wide garden shed with a single window and a door kept open by a heavy rock propped against the bottom. A figure passes by the window, approaching the entrance, Penny calls again while Sarah remains on the top step, surveying the wide yard which must be at least half an acre of vegetable plots. There is also a great length of raspberry bushes held in place by thin wood posts set in a single row next to the radishes with a stone path separating them. At the front-most plot are three raised mounds in continuous lines, the stopping point marked by a dowel rod painted red at the tip. Narrower bits of newly-tilled soil edge along the house and there are fruit trees a few inches from the side fence. An overloaded kiwi tree reaches with one of its thick branches held up by a post set from the ground to the base.

Penny draws Sarah's attention to the old man coming nearer whose strong steps plod against the ground, causing the tops of his wide rubber garden boots to slap back and forth against his calves as he walks. He is not as large as she might have imagined. If he could stand up straight, he might equal her height. As it is, his shoulders slump forward and his upper back is curved so that he reaches just below her

22

shoulder. He wears a simple pair of worn blue overalls with mended holes in the knees and the handles of pruning shears sticking out of his left pocket. A rusty orange and white checked button shirt had been rolled up at the sleeves from the wrist to just under the elbow. On his head a straw hat with a hole worn at the front and the brim frayed so bits of fine straw poke out. A clean shaven, wrinkled face smiles at her and he holds out a hand to shake. She obliges.

"*Konnichiwa,*" she says, assuming he cannot speak English.

He responds in quick English, saying, "Welcome, welcome."

"Let's go," Penny says hurriedly after checking her watch, "There's a movie I want to see. By the time we walk there, the movie will just about start." She tugs Sarah by the arm, leading her back inside. "Come, we'll get our coats and hats."

"I don't have a hat."

"Really? Oh, you'll borrow one of mine."
She puts on the only jacket she has, which is a rough spun wool necessary for the Alaskan spring but far too warm for the mild city weather and a hat from Penny's closet and Sarah walks down the hill with Penny, who takes her arm.

"A fine movie it should be. *Une si jolie petite plage.*"

"A French film?"

"*Oui!*" she exclaims.

"Now, how am I supposed to know what they're saying?"

Penny pulls away from her in surprise. "No?" she questions, shrugs, and holds her close again. "I would have thought that Oniisan taught you as well."
Sarah guards her emotions at the mention of her own father, replying with a curt, "No, he didn't."

23

"Shame." Penny says. "Well, here we are."

She motions just down to a strip of the street lined with all manner of boutique stores, a grocery, a café, and a theater marked "Admiral."

"Grand, isn't it?" Penny notes as she lets go of Sarah, going towards the ticket box.

A quick exchange of money for paper and they both enter the theater.

It is as quaint as a neighborhood theater should be, yet much grander than the simple one in Anchorage. This theater has a concession stand without a server. Instead, the popcorn churns on its own inside the glass. A penny coin slot and the push of a protruding button releases a paper bag down a chute under the glass as it fills up the bag with buttery popcorn. The candy is purchased from a machine much like the one she had bought cherry ice from earlier, only this one has a mechanical face that offers thanks as it spits out her chocolate bar through a narrow slat in the window. Penny rushes her into the theater that is already dark as the title crawl plays, and tiptoes in. Penny hushes Sarah as she scurries to the middle row seats, but with so few people inside, it would hardly have bothered anyone if they had come in screaming.

A dreary film, Sarah thinks as it begins and plays through. Dull. When she turns to see Penny munching on popcorn, her eyes fixated on the screen, she knows they must be seeing two different films. All the French takes her back to a cramped room in the Minidoka camp, forced to hear Penny reciting French to her father who relaxed on one of the cots with his back propped up against the wall and one leg extended in front of him, the other bent so he could rest his

24

elbow on his knee. Penny sat on the bed next to him, writing in her notebook. She spoke aloud, of which her Uncle was thankful, but Sarah was not. A rustling of books and papers.

"So, I'll read the story again for practice. I know I should do my verbs, but this is more fun. Ready?"

Oniisan nodded, half listening while he smoked a cigarette, flicking the ash to the cold ground, listening with more attention than Sarah had seen him give anyone.

"*Maître Corbeau, sur un,*" she paused, silently pronouncing it first, "*arbre perché. T--tenait en son bec un fromage.*" A breath. "*Maître Renard, par,*" she rolled over the word four times until "*l'odeur alléché. Lui tint à peu près ce langage.*" She wetted her lips as she glanced away from the page to Oniisan, his glossy eyes fixed on the wall. "*A ces mots—*" she begins, at which a heavy sigh came from him. A signal of frustration.

"Read it again." He commanded and drew on his cigarette.

A shake of the shoulder alerts a dozing Sarah. The theater lights rise to a glow as the end credits appear on screen.

"Poor thing, you must have been tired from the trip," Penny says as Sarah stiffens her back.

It might have been a quick walk back to the house if Penny had not detailed the movie to her as they went, though Sarah ignores most of it. Still drowsy from waking, she mistakes the balloons in the sky for evening clouds.

"You go on and change while I make supper," Penny says once they return. "If you don't have a dress, you can use one of mine. Oh, you like liver, don't you?"
Silently, Sarah retires to the room to rest her head for a time until she is startled by footsteps coming down the stairs. A deep voice follows, slightly muffled by the racket of

Penelope cooking. Sarah attunes her ear to the kitchen beyond the door. Inaudible speaking that breaks with George's stubborn voice.

"Why is she still here? I thought she was staying somewhere else. Get rid of her."

Penny lets out a throaty giggle that sparks of impertinence. "She *is* my cousin. Where else would she stay? It's the right thing to do. Besides, she's going to work in the factory."

George sucks air in through his teeth and mumbles, "*Mendokusai.*"

The door clicks open. Behind is George and Sarah finds herself without words. Standing so near, and given that she barely reaches his chest in height, she can hardly escape the thick scent of bodily musk emanating from his pores. To properly assess his features, she tilts her head up to find his long face tipped down towards her. A face masked by a few week's growth of a beard and a moustache. Atop his head is an un-brushed mop of wavy black hair parted in as much of a fashionable style that he can manage with the natural curls and no pomade. Though skinny, his arms are defined as if his sun-toasted skin were stretched over inflated muscles, yet the only reminder of his hardships are his rough hands, short trimmed nails, and on his left hand, a shortened pinky below where the second joint should be. She dismisses this as either a birth defect or an unfortunate accident.

"Sarah, isn't it?" He takes the cigarette from his lips, setting it in the ashtray on the kitchen counter and approaches, smiling largely so she can see his yellow tinted teeth, many of which are crooked. One in particular, a sharp tooth on the left, turns inward so that all others cram together to make up the extra space.

26

"Yes." She retreats a step back, finding his smile and demeanor unsettling.

"Yes, I know. Penny has told me about you."

It is then that she notices his deep, smooth voice does not match his crude appearance.

"All good, I hope."

He sits down, picking up his cigarette from the tray where is rests, emitting a single line of smoke into the air, to press it between his lips. She stares at him for a moment while standing in the entryway. Here he is, real, not just a picture or a passing mention, and too familiar to another man she knew before.

"Please sit down," he says, pointing to the dining room table. "You must have had a long trip. You'll want to rest."

"Why, thank you, but I'd rather like to wash up first, you see."

He shrugs, making an indifferent frown. Penny slides next to him and they whisper together, and she laughs--she always laughs--and once in a while Sarah hears him join in. Rather than washing her hands, she finds that her appetite has waned and she helps herself to the tea kettle sitting on a burner, fills it with milk found in the refrigerator, and heats it.

She waits, shutting her ears to her cousins' bawdy conversation that makes her shirk from their company. Placing her palm on the side of the pot, she decides it is warm enough. The burner off, she pours the milk into a floral cup from the cupboard. It takes her a minute or so of searching until she finds a glass bottle of maple syrup to pour into the milk, stirring the contents with a spoon until it turns a warm brown. This treat she takes to the privacy of her room.

27

2

Penelope
Gifts of Morning

A click of the unlatched door and her weary step imprints on a stack of mail beneath her foot. Penny lifts it to gather the letters in her hand, sifting through them as she shuts the door behind her and kicks off her shoes. Sandwiched between an electric bill, two bank statements, a paper-wrapped package and the morning newspaper is a standard white envelope. She stares at the looped cursive addressed to Sarah, then brings it to her nose to find the faintest smell of fish. It must have seeped into the paper from the writer's hand. Penny knocks on Sarah's door, which is answered after a few moments of waiting.

"Great news!" she starts, then pauses. "You look glum. What's wrong?"

"Just a letter." Sarah shakes her head. "Some family news."

"Serious?"

"No."

"Let me see."

Sarah hands her the letter. Penny skims it, frowning at the written Japanese

"But it's in *kanji*," she complains.

Sarah takes it back. "Too bad for you."

Sarah tears open the fold from behind, as Penny watches, withdrawing a pink letter written in *kanji* with a small, compact script that she holds close to her face, reading through it twice. Sarah jerks when Penny touches her shoulder with the tip of her forefinger.

"What do you have?" she asks in an exceedingly curious voice.

When Sarah ignores her, Penny takes the package bound with white butcher paper marked with dirt and smudges. Written on the front is Sarah's name and the sender's address lists a Mr. and Mrs. Louise Darrington. There are post stamps on the far corner reading Air Mail.

"It's from your sister," Penny pushes it out towards Sarah who still holds the pink letter. "Open it, won't you? You're lucky. I never get packages."

She places the object on the floor, settling it down on the yellow carpet. Sarah crumples up the letter, stuffing it in her pocket. Picking at the tape, she unwraps the paper to reach the cardboard box beneath. Lifting the lid, she sees an oblong object wrapped in brown paper with the words "Bullocks Wilshire" stamped on the front. She tears this open as well and finds a pair of brown leather kid gloves and a mink stole to match. Puzzled, she takes these up. They are nothing like what she would wear or would ever have the occasion to wear.

"Look at that! Aren't these swell?"
Sarah lets them fall back into the box.

"You're not going to try them on?" she questions, following her to the kitchen.

"No," she says, pushing the box down into a full trash can.

Penny lingers on the package in the trash can, wondering what must have happened to make Sarah refuse such a gift, and tears her eyes back up.

"Are you hungry?" she asks then goes about preparing breakfast before getting an answer.

She puts a small dented copper pot on the stove whose two wooden handles are so worn that they are nearly white. She takes out a large Chinese cabbage from the refrigerator and shoves it towards Sarah.

29

"Chop some of this, won't you?"

When Sarah begrudgingly follows her instructions, Penny gathers half a *daikon* radish and a white and green tub of *miso* paste as they work silently side-by-side in the kitchen. As the mixture cooks, Sarah breathes in deeply.

"It's been awhile since I've had this. In Alaska, there aren't any stores to buy *miso* paste and *dashi*."

Penny smiles at her, then steps out to turn on the radio, returning to find Sarah with her face over the pot, eyes closed, savoring the smell.

"Done?" Penny asks, flitting into the kitchen.

She turns off the burner, takes a bowl from the cupboard that she immediately brings to the pot to scoop up the savory soup, then wipes the edges with a tea towel hanging from the stove handle. Opening a small drawer under the counter, she then grabs a blue cloth napkin that she uses to pick up a pair of well-worn lacquer chopsticks with mother-of-pearl inlaid at the blunt end. Carefully carrying these and the bowl of soup, she strolls out of the kitchen, down the hall, and up the stairs to the second floor.

Setting the soup on the top steps for a moment, Penny removes a key to unlock the door. With a double click of the latch, she turns the handle gently, pushing the door as she picks the bowl back up and enters into a living room whose curtains muffle the morning sun. The only open door is to the kitchen while the three others remain firmly closed. Nearest to the entrance is Ojiisan's room, then on the opposite side of the flat are those of George and Catherine, separated. On her side of the door she hears a clacking of typewriter keys, a welcome change from the usual scratches of Ojiisan's pen on paper. He has finally relented, it seems, to use the Semaphore Typewriter that Penny installed months ago. A sleek

30

invention modeled after the Nickerson Automatic No. 3 that communicates messages by wire. She lets herself in, surveying the conditions of the room. A well-used desk, it is stripped of colors in patches that creates a pattern of polished surface intermixing with worn unfinished wood. Books of all lengths and widths clutter the workspace. Three head-high bookcases cover every wall space, leaving slivers between them to peek at the pastel seafoam green wallpaper behind them. Trinkets sprinkle the small crevices left in his room; past mementos kept either out of respect or the inability to part with possessions.

One such accoutrement sits atop a low bookcase amongst other minuscule trappings: a voluptuous hourglass held in a wooden casement, its white sand flowing down, filling the hollow base. On the hour, a high-pitched *ping*! sounds and the hourglass turns of its own accord, leaving the full top to fall. A single revolution at every hour. Any light that comes in filters through sheer blue curtains covering the sizeable rectangular window before the desk which overlooks the pristine garden in the yard below. Settled on the windowsill is a ticking mantle clock in which his small reflection is cast in the glass face.

"Good morning," Penny says cheerfully, walking through the door, setting the warm *misoshiru* on a clean space on the desk.

He flicks from a thin stack of pages to the keys, his head turning from side to side, typing at a slow pace. His own letters emerge from the top and when a response comes, the keys move independently to record the incoming message after the words "ATTN" on a separate line.

"Let me," she offers. "I can do it quicker."

He stands up, relieved, with his back remaining curved from sitting for so long, and gathers the bowl enthusiastically to eat while standing. Beginning with the sending and receiving address, Penny skims over the dry black-market business correspondence about the products that were slipped through the docks under George's oversight. The keys, winding, pinging of the typewriter noises are joined by Ojiisan slurping the soup.

"Koike-san needs some acts to fill the night." She keeps her fingers steady, ensuring that she does not pause in trepidation. The Dime Theater is the old club. One of Ojiisan's first dealings. Perhaps before the war it was spectacular, but it has since faded from a once-renowned vaudeville theater to a windowless slum dive.

"Well!" she says, seeming excited. "Tell me how you got that deal, by the by, I've been curious."

His face lights up. "My big opening!" he says. "After I joined, Koike-san and I were set up together by Oyabun— before the camps and the war, you know—to get the club as a side business. Back then, the owners didn't care about us Japanese. We had the money and were among the biggest men in the city. There weren't all these different gangs then running around picking the wings off each other." He clicks his tongue against his teeth and murmurs, "Entitled youngsters." He sips at the soup broth. "If only my fool of a son were as ambitious. Or even that wife of his." He sighs, focusing his gaze on her for a moment. "Never mind," he says, digressing. "I told Koike-san you'd be there for Friday night."

She presses her lips together, ensuring that she keeps her remarks contained, and gives a complacent nod. In a quiet restitution, she finished her task while Ojiisan did

32

likewise with his meal. There were only the languid sounds of typewriter keys hitting paper. A beautiful relaxation lay on Penelope's shoulders and oozes down her spine, a sensation that is broken with the inevitable waking of children.

Finishing the soup, her uncle drops it on the desk and looks over Penny's shoulder as she completes the letter and then taps her shoulder as either a sign that he will take over or as a dismissal to help with the children. With the last key punched, she sighs and relinquishes the chair to Ojiisan. Wordlessly, she recovers the empty dishes and exits the room, closing the door behind her and announces her arrival by shouting a morning greeting and hears it reciprocated from the living room. She follows a narrow hallway to the kitchen that is only big enough to hold a stove and a sink pressed up next to each other to rest the dishes on the stovetop. A few tiles separate the kitchen it from the carpet covering the rest of the house. She finds George's wife, Catherine, sitting on the floor with her son, who is making loops on white poster paper with a green crayon. Though the boy is past toddler age, she has rarely heard him speak more than a few words. He prefers instead to make word-like sounds and gestures. It is abnormal for a child, she knows, but to bring attention to it is futile. There is nothing to be done for it.

She has long since become accustomed to a certain family quality among them in which one ignores the uncomfortable and refrains from exposing themselves to a semblance of vulnerability. The newest baby, a girl named Rose, lies on her back on a quilt spread on the floor, chewing the top of a wooden rattle. Penny settles cross-legged on the floor across from the mother who lifts her head. Penny

33

reaches into her purse and slides a small unmarked tin container across to the young woman, some years older, but with her unwashed hair pinned up into a bun and being wrapped in her nightgown in the middle of the morning, she looks decades older. Inside are the white tablets, Bennies, much stronger than the regular brand that can be bought at a pharmacy, the ones that make men psychotic if one is not careful enough. The ones that need a prescription. Yet this doesn't stop the heavy flow of them through the black market. Since George handles the trafficking of these white cures, she has an open door to however much she wants.

"You're swell!" she says, taking the flat tin and clasping it in her hand. "With Timothy and the new baby it's been so busy. I feel so tired that coffee doesn't even get me up."

"Why not get a prescription?" she asks.

"I wish I could," she pauses at the cry of her newborn cracks on her ears and slices through the walls only to continue, "if I could ever leave this house alone."
It is difficult not to sympathize with the woman. Even safe behind these walls, there are outside eyes. As a wife to Ojiisan's son, she has to be protected anytime she steps outside the door. It had also long been established that there would always be members of their group living in some of the neighborhood houses to keep a secure presence.

"No. It's much easier and cheaper for you to come here. I don't want to bother my husband unnecessarily. Besides, he much prefers you."

Penny dismisses the comment, instead, she removes a tiny brown gift bag from her purse and places it on the table. Catherine, seeing it, perks up and pulls it towards her by the handles. She pulls a polished silver chain from within,

34

pulling it up until a large glass ball pendant appears, catching the light from the window. She gasps, immediately cupping it in both hands. Hearing the excitement, her son rushes up to her, climbing onto her lap to glimpse the treasure. Inside the glass, an iridescent pygmy seahorse propels itself about its small water habitat that it shares with a few blades of seagrass growing from a bed of sand. Timothy whines, trying to grab it from his mother who pulls it back close to her chest, slipping the chain covetously around her neck. She sits up quickly, letting her son slide away. But rather than tending to the baby rolling around red-faced on the floor, Catherine pulls on the brass handle of one of the slim white drawers of the glass cabinet to remove a different brand of cigarettes along with a box of matches.

"Would you like one?" she asks without looking. "I have too bad a headache to stand the Firelites just now." Bringing the cigarettes to the round side table beside a teal lounge chair, she disregards the child again, to relax on her chair, pulling out each slim tube from the black pack with shiny green cursive lettering whispering "Golden Crane" over two gold leaf cranes, one mirroring the other, with touching wingtips. She lays them down parallel and produces a match and then does something curious. Catherine lights the cigarette away from her mouth, letting the flame linger on the end until finally bringing it up to her lips to inhale and blowing out the burning match.

"I never could bring a burning flame right up to my face. Something about the heat and that one gust of wind and, poof, there goes my hair."
By now the baby's cries have become raspier and more desperate.

"Do you mind. . ." she inquires, motioning towards the baby, "Is she all right?"

35

"What?" Catherine sounds surprised and looks to where Penny had mentioned. "Oh, don't mind her, she'll cry it out. She does get into awful fits." Catherine pushes out some smoke from the side of her mouth, her cigarette pinched firmly between her middle and ring finger.

"Are you sure?" she prods, attempting to sound as unjudgmental as possible.

It had been little more than two months since Penny retired from sharing a room with the new mother. Catherine had been too weak and too lonesome, despite the assistance of the white tablets, to tend to the tiny and often-fussy baby Rose by herself, leaving Penny with the responsibility of a newborn and the older brother. Yet, Catherine's eventual recovery caused the inevitable separation of the physical closeness Penny had shared with the children. A bodily memory that aches with each of Rose's cries.

"Oh, yes," Catherine crosses her legs, her nightgown rising at the knee to reveal a fine stubble from ankle to calf. "Give her a minute or so."

Before, Penny would have soothed the child immediately but now she knows that Catherine has that privilege. With neither the cause nor impropriety to act, she finds it difficult to remove herself from the seat on the floor where Timothy has made a game of spinning her cigarette tin of Firelites around in a circle on the carpet, watching the light catch on shiny metal.

"Is your mother having a good time?" Catherine asks, raising both eyebrows slightly as if to address an unsaid secret, then relaxes her face and taps the spent ash into a cup sitting on the tabletop, filled with the remains of George's morning coffee.

"I'm not sure." She shrugs a shoulder. "She hasn't sent a postcard."

Penny is about to tell her that she has to go but then there is a dying down of the wailing and the mother gives a victorious grin.

"See," she says, standing, "she cries it out. You have time for a game, don't you?"

Catherine goes to the glass cabinet to open the drawer and brings a worn deck of cards to the table. Sitting down, she lets out a small moan as if in pain. Though not busy until the evening, Penny never enjoys staying long in the main room. It has the smell of sour milk and old rags. Still, she finds herself unable to refuse Catherine's pleading demeanor.

"Just a quick game, won't you?"

Catherine shuffles.

"We haven't played gin in some time." She proceeds to deal out the cards. In fact, they have played gin. They play it nearly every time Penny visits and while she doesn't much care for cards at all, George's wife has few friends of which Penny knows little.

"I have the worst bellyache. I'm sure it's the flu." She grimaces, convinced of an illnesses.

"Why not go to the clinic?"

"*Tsk*. Those doctors don't know anything. Last time I went there, all they did was send me off with a brown syrup that made everything worse. And I don't ever want to go there again if I don't have to, not after all I went through." Penny ignores the complaint. She had been with Catherine at the time, escorting her to the clinic, only to find that the ailment was an early miscarriage.

"And how is George?" Penny asks after the husband. Since she is here, she might as well discover what George has been up to since she last saw him.

37

Catherine fusses with the cards, fanning them out before her and reordering them.

"He stopped drinking beer," she announces.

"Did he?"

"He's onto vodka now."

"Ah."

"Says it's healthier for him, since it's clean and clear."

"Still. . ." Penny mumbles, remembering the internment camp with a sickening turn of her stomach and how her uncle often drank in the mornings before breakfast. The bottles were so prized in their shared room at the internment camps that they used them as garden dividers in front of the barracks. His body always had a stale smell from the alcohol escaping his skin. Without the facilities for a daily wash, his stink built up on him in layers. In good weather, the window could be opened and the fumes dissipated. Yet winter posed a different problem. All the money he made working and half of it ran through him from stem to root.

"He did promise to not drink on Sundays," Catherine says, pulling Penny from her memory, "but his mood is so much better when he drinks that I almost want him to keep on. He's much friendlier."

As she says it, she looks to the window covered by white curtains that shut out a harsh light. She shows her cards and says, "Gin" without mirth.

"You talked to him?" she asks with hope in her eyes, gathering up the cards.

"I did."

"What did he say?"

How to put this gently? Penelope wonders.

"It seems that you'll be on your own if you want to go home."

Her fingers freeze at the notion and then after a moment, they flex. "I can't even take Rose?"
Penny's eyes shift to where the baby girl sleeps. "No."
She deals the cards once more. "There was a time," she says with her eyes fixed firmly on the cards, "when I thought he loved me."

"You never told me about that." Penny forces a smile.
"No."
Penny waits, hoping for a story of emerging romance. None came.

"I'll help you any way I can," Penny offers while wanting to both embrace her and shut her away behind a door.
She exhales, about to open her mouth when Timothy whines for a yellow crayon from the pack that sits next to her. She wordlessly hands it to him.

"It was a small chance," she says wistfully. "If I didn't have my babies. . .well, it's too late for that. I thought he might at least let me have her, after all. . ."

After all, Penny finishes, *she was a girl*.

Catherine had thought, wrongly, that George would not care about a daughter. His children belong to him, Penny knew, he had said so more than once. The situation is not helped by the fact that there are only certain hospitals that ensured that a child would be born a citizen. They are expensive, costing more than a working-class man could make in a year. even if he never touched a cent. The investment of paying for a citizenship ensures that George will never willingly part with his children. It was difficult at first for her to believe that George had much sensibility beyond the practical until the birth of his son.

When Catherine huffed and moaned, Penny had been there to take her to the Pacific Citizens' Hospital, a three-story structure in the West Hills. Unlike the public hospitals, this one was often empty of waiting patients. Flat wooden benches along the interior walls shone with polish, having never been used. Behind a marble-topped counter sat an automaton nurse painted white with a red medical cross on the chest. When she approached, the synthetic voice asked, "How may I help you today?"

She gave Catherine's name and condition. Soon, a voice came over the loudspeakers, asking for a maternity assistant to arrive with a wheelchair at the front counter. A nurse of similar stature in a rosy pink uniform dress pushed the wheelchair into the front room. She spoke softly, easing Catherine into the plush leather seat while Penny followed, her left hand carrying a purse and an overnight bag. chattering pleasantries to the nurse, and requesting, twice, that George be contacted immediately.

They stopped at an elevator door where the nurse slid a brass screen from the left to the right. She pushed one of the large black buttons with the number three in polished brass. It rose with ease to the topmost floor and stopped and she opened the screen, pushing the chair to the first maple door in the hall. Inside, the room was made up with a wide, single, flat mattress on a white steel frame arranged with clean white sheets. A brown suede loveseat sat adjacent to it just to the side of a floral curtained window where Penny set the bags. Framed paintings of landscapes hung on the pastel-green walls. One, Penny noticed, was of a deep blue lake in which a bevy of swans swam in the shadow of grassy hills under a clear sky.

"Please change into the gown," she said, gesturing to a folded pink dress on end of the bed. "I'll be back with the doctor."

Normally, Penny would have looked away, but with Catherine's heavy breathing, the difficulty of her movements, and then a clear, "Help me." She did not hesitate to assist.

*

When the nurse returned, it was with a tall man in a white coat, followed by a soft whirring as a medical mechanized nurse followed behind. Catherine was shocked by the bulky machine forged together with metal rungs supporting its center. A heavy steel circular frame painted white with a glossy finish hung about its waist and to it was attached a long, thick, white cotton skirt. It had arms without hands and where appendages should have been were adaptors for various tools. The head was a mass of tubes, wires, and metal all twisted together and topped with a white panel at the forehead with a red cross in the center. Its face was a panel of glass with a looped projection of a serene woman who smiled and never blinked. They spoke to her, though she was too fixated on the strange mechanized woman in the room that the hospital doctor and nurse barely noticed. Penny stood by, scrutinizing as the nurse attended to Catherine, sticking needles into her, the machine instructing her movements, its voice unwavering.

The ensuing hours consisted of the constant clamor of the few people in the room, Catherine's body half upright, her legs bent obliquely at the knee, determined breathing indicative of labor, on forcing a small being out of herself, to meet the doe eyes of her longed-for child. Though Penny held her hand and gave encouragement, she had to force down a frantic fear that squirmed deep in her belly that was not eased by the sight of various instruments being used to assist in the labor and the unemotional face of the mechanized nurse.

"You don't need to worry," Penny reassured, their fingers threaded together; bright pink from squeezing so tightly.

Catherine could not speak; every muscle dedicated to a single task that she had none to spare. Every now and then the doctor, sitting in the space between her open legs, gave instructions, but as the labor wore on and the newborn yet unseen, his concern led to intervention in the form of a suction hose. Penny placed a hand on Catherine's shoulder only to be reproached with a biting, "Don't touch me." that made her jerk away. The hose had a soft rubber cup attached at the end when she saw it move from its place on the nurse to the area below Catherine's gown. The doctor pressed a button on the side of the mechanical nurse's body and a sharp, airy sound emerged from the hose.

It seemed to be only a few seconds in the time it took for the sound to stop, replaced with the unmistakable first wails of a newborn, and Catherine's entire face was absolved from the pain that was etched into it before. Penny watched in awe as the doctor lifted the red-faced baby to present him to Catherine. The child, whose skin was pasty and splattered with blood and mucus, had a moist tuft of stringy black hair, and a thin face that held his button nose and pouting lips. His tiny fingers were clenched inward so his fingertips touched the palms of his miniscule hands. Perfect but for the raised bulge atop his head where the suction had been.

It was only after the post-labor care that George was allowed into the room, disheveled, excitable, and smelling strongly of cigarettes. Catherine rested, entrusting Penny to watch over the hospital bassinet holding the sleeping newborn wrapped in a loose blanket. Without a word, George approached, towering over the small boy. He stood, eyes fixated on the child, and then, very gingerly, he stretched out his arms, leaned his chest over the edge, cupping his hands under the baby's body so that the head slid easily into the crook of his father's arm. The movement roused him awake and he began to whimper, a sound that jerked Catherine's attention, but once she saw her husband, fell back into her pillow. George lifted the baby, his back straightened, and soon the boy was quiet. Had she not been so attentive, Penny would have never seen the small drops of tears welling in the father's eyes.

The door clicks, interrupting their game. The boy jumps up, shouting, "Papa, Papa," following the giant legs that he tries to catch. George pays no attention to him. In a desperate attempt to draw his father's attention, Timothy pats an open palm on his leg and George pushes past him, making the boy stumble.

"Penny," he says, then asks suspiciously, "What are you doing here?"

"Just visiting."

"I'm hungry, want to eat somewhere?"
Penny looks from him to his wife, wondering to whom he is speaking. She picks at her fingernails uncomfortably.

"I'll leave you two alone, then," she decides and stands up.

"No, no," he says, correcting her misunderstanding. "*She's* fine here. We'll go."

"We?" she asks, waving a finger back and forth between herself and George.

He nods. Penny glances towards Catherine who is bent over at the waist, struggling to pick up her daughter with one arm while keeping the half-spent cigarette in her other hand. After successfully gathering Rose into her arm, she shoves the cigarette back between her lips. With a wave of her hand, she permits the two to leave. Passing through her home, empty except for one of George's associates waiting patiently at the front entrance, and Bruce following her at the heels, she retreats to the living room to gather her purse, slips on her shoes. Before withdrawing out the door, she says a quick farewell to her cat who sits comfortably on the sofa, swishing his tail back and forth.

*

At the edge of the city where the slums begin stands an incongruous building at odds with the ramshackle homes and shining city on either side. The theater is an unclean white brick where black grit and damp moss spread across its face. Inside, round tables set with over-used velvet tablecloths, some of which have small round burn marks left by cigarette ash, are scattered around a wide-open floor., whose leftover bolt holes can be seen on the hard ground where there had once been theater chairs. Crossing the main floor, Penny finds a man with a telephone receiver at his ear who sucks on a toothpick sticking straight from his lips. She recognizes him well. A slender man of forty-two with eyes as wide and round as a newborn's. His age shows in the skin

44

hanging in folds around his thin neck, his elbows. He speaks too little and too softly. In the years she spent with him sending letters from one point to another, they had, cumulatively, perhaps one conversation. Yet whatever ill feelings he rouses in her, she is sure to keep a kind demeanor. As a man, Penny knows him as Koike-san, but he has another, more sinister, name. A moniker taken from old folk tales that she vaguely knew. *Namahage*. The Japanese *yokai*; a demon whose human-like features are hidden under long straw capes and a frightening mask with protruding ogre teeth.

"Ojiisan sends this," she says to him, passing the sealed envelope, "and says that you might have an opening for me tonight."

He takes the note, stowing it immediately into his shirt pocket, nodding once with a "*Hai*" and returns to his telephone.

Brown leather kitten heels take the young singer outside the closing nightclub. Night lights dim in anticipation of the rising sun. On the boardwalk is a mechanical woman inside a glass box. Her metal skeleton covered by black rubber skin and horsehair that flows around her plaid shawl-covered shoulders. She holds her hands out in the air around a glass ball. When Penny slides a dime into the slot, the lights from the top of the box shine blue and white. Simultaneously, the inside of the glass ball glows orange and on the table in front of her, four panels turn over and from under appear four playing cards: a Queen of Hearts, the Suicide King, an Eight of Clubs, and a Two of Spades. She has played this game often enough to know what she will get for each suit. The gypsy woman moves her hands and her head in motions meant to mimic those of humans. There is a click and a

45

muffled tumbling. Penny leans down to the brass door under the coin slot, reaches in, and withdraws a pack of regular-strength Firelite cigarettes that has a card stock fortune adhered to the back. As she smokes one, she can feel a buzz emerging, thrusting alertness into her body. It makes her hands shake already, the right worse than the left. Before slipping the pack into her purse, she skims through the fortune with a few enlarged words bellowing "A Starlight Journey." She considers tossing it into the waters rippling underfoot but instead folds it in half, sliding the paper between the clasps of her purse.

The nearest sky train runs from King Street Station, a fair walk from the brick alley near the waterfront. Morning skies are grey with a light fog settling over the tops of buildings so that when the sky train passes overhead all that can be seen is the flat base pummeling through the mist. As she trods up the concrete hill approaching the station, the streets are bare but for the dozing homeless, the hungover passersby stumbling wearily towards some point of transportation, and the curving backs of the street cleaners, men and women in tough cotton working shirts tucked into brown trousers kept fastened with a belt, their heads protected by wide-brimmed straw hats. At a quick summation, Penny guesses there must be more than a hundred on this stretch, sweeping the sidewalks, gathering bits of trash into large canvas bags, washing store window fronts, while others squat to dig out dandelion sprouts growing up from between the cracks in the concrete with a thin flat tool. More still by square garden plots along the sidewalk, picking weeds from the dirt surrounding saplings or flower clusters. In these mornings if she takes to stroll the dawn sidewalk, she usually takes care not to linger on their

46

sad figures Yet, in a brief respite, one stretches his back, twisting it left and right so that Penny is simultaneously drawn to and repulsed by the gentle, warped face of the institutionalized. Her eyes focus on the movement on the old tracks by the silver building. Electric blue bolts rise from below. A prank, she thinks, not uncommon for the V gang, perhaps, or even the Patriots. Unconcerned, she continues up the sloping sidewalk to the sky train station.

*

Upon reaching the front door of her house, conversations tumble down from the second floor. Though quiet to her ears, the voices bear egregious words soon followed by clomping steps and a slamming door. Another door unlatches, revealing Sarah who gives Penny a start. Sarah is visibly startled to see the platinum hair that now covers Penelope's head in an attempt to mimic the *Belle Voix*, or, perhaps more desperately, to assimilate. Acting as if nothing is amiss, Penny gives a brisk morning greeting before passing the kitchen to the back stairs leading up to the epicenter of the dispute. Unlocking the door that divide their houses, she tiptoes up the stairs and into the nearest room that is Ojiisan's hospice. The desk is covered with all manner of papers, an overflowing ashtray, books rising in towers around the surface as well as on the floor around the legs and the sleeping typewriter. In the empty square space, he writes on a sheet of white paper.

"What was that row?' Penny asks. Ojiisan snorts.

"George has the idea that one of his *kyodai* should chaperone you from now on."

47

She chortles, insulted at first but then suddenly overcome with a ray of self-importance which is at odds with the annoyance at having a minder to follow her along.

"He worries too much about trivialities."
Ojiisan looks up, stretching his neck from side to side, then leans over in his chair to peer out into the garden where trickling rain falls from charcoal clouds.

"Still," he says at length without taking his eyes from his writing, "I did hear a rumor today about a famous singer."

Penny sits on his bed, her legs crossed together at the ankle.

"Someone I know?" she asks teasingly.

He chuckles. "Not you, I'm afraid, at least not yet. No. I thought you could go over to a certain nightclub and confirm it for me. One of our lackeys works there as a waiter part time. I spoke to him. He'll leave the back door unlocked for you."

"*Our* lackeys?" she ponders on the inclusion of her in their grand family.
At this, Ojiisan pauses to reiterate, "Isn't that right?"

"Oh, yes. And—do you smell that?" Penny asks, "Lord, Sarah must be baking. I forgot how good her bread is."

Penelope rushes quickly down the stairs to a place in front of the stove, appearing as if she were just checking on her baking. Penny enters, sliding on the smooth floor to the oven window, then cracking open the door, smelling.

"Nearly done," Sarah says, closing it.

She counts to sixty, then removes the tray with a towel placed over the lip and sets it on the stove top. Penny breathes in deeply, her nose almost touching the hot tray.

"I made this one special for you."

Sarah points at the etched roll. Without hesitation, Penny grabs it, blows the heat away and nibbles on the edges. It is nice of her to make such a gesture, making Penny think of a way to reciprocate. She gives a congratulatory nod, snatches another, and disappears upstairs to Ojiisan who she finds finishing the letter and folding it in half. Holding the warm gift to him, he takes it with his thumb and three fingers, sniffs twice appraisingly, then takes a large bite with his buttery-yellow teeth. Satisfied with the taste, he finishes it, wiping off some crumbs from the sides of his mouth. The short respite is interrupted by the pinging hourglass that follows its rotation to resume the hourly counting of the sands.

Stiffening, Ojiisan takes the cleanly-folded letter, slips it into an envelope, the seal closed and purposefully left without identification. A letter for her to deliver. While the typewriter is quicker, he distrusts it with important information and prefers a more personal approach to communication. When she first began as one of his couriers, he told her that a young lady was less conspicuous than a man in a suit. Passing letters, dossiers, and whatever else he gives her is dull work, but it was their arrangement that she would do it so long as the family persuaded clubs to take her on as a singer.

"The Candy Apple Pub and The Dime."

He pulls a bottom drawer to sift through stacks of envelopes until he finds one, lifts it out, and shuts the drawer with a quick push. He holds out the letter which carries a golden stamp of an innocuous peony.

3
Sarah
Luna Park

Penny knocked on the door that morning to wake her up for a surprise. Sarah had not been a guest for long and already she became weary of Penny's unabashed emotional needs. Annoying though it was, Sarah sought to use it to her advantage. If Penny was desperate enough for friendship, it might be easier for Sarah to coax her into relinquishing part of the inheritance.

The ticket booth is the same as the one for using the train. Sarah approaches a box-hatted automaton that takes five cents and gives a rectangular paper ticket while Penny slips through the ticket gate with a red plastic stub that she pushes across the counter. Seeing this unfairness irritates Sarah in that Penny is allowed to ride freely. A few men wait on the benches by a café stall, one of them smoking a thin brown cigarette and checking his watch, the other chatting with the stall worker. With a great riveting whistle, the train pulls towards them. As it slows into the station, the driver appears through the curved windows in his blue suit and silver buttons. It is not like a train at all. The shape of it is like a bullet, a long cylinder pinched into a cone at the front and hooked onto the overhead rails and moved along by wheels at the top. The entire thing seems upside down.

"Just wait until you get on. It's a real hummer," Penny says, pushing open one of the wooden doors with the brass knobs.

The platform under the train serves as a catch if anyone falls, but drops off at the edge into the city below.

The train hooks onto the rail from the tops of the cars. The tracks are a crosshatch of metal and cables, stretching off into the misty sky so she would never see where it ends. She remembered coming into the port seeing the swerving tracks through the towers.

"Oh, don't worry so. It's as sturdy as a charging rhino; never had a drop," Penny says.

"Can't we take a normal train?" Sarah asks.

"How dull! All the old trains run through King Street. That's a half-hour away. You want to go by that, get along walking."

Two doors open sideways from the inside. Penny rushes in, stepping wide over the open crack in between the yellow caution line and the inside of the car. Peering down, she sees the tops of the buildings. A schoolboy bumps past her, jumping clear over the crevasse. A wrong step and he could have fallen, breaking his back or worse. Not wanting to be showed up by him, Sarah passes over and into the steady car. Penny shifts aside, steadying herself with her hand clutching one of the dangling leather loops on the horizontal aluminum bars on either side of the car close to the roof. Sarah sits on a free bench rather than risking standing. The doors close. An announcement rings:

"This is the number four line to Pioneer Square. The stops will be: Lincoln Park, Alaska Junction, South West Avalon Way, and Pike Street Terminal."

A screech signals the beginning movements of the train. It rumbles free of the locks that hold it in place at the station. A quick and steady run down the massive rails that snake through the city. Though no faster than a city bus,

51

Sarah holds onto the side bar. Penny smirks, telling her that she should look out the window. A glance is enough to satisfy Sarah's small curiosity. Once the locomotive slows to a stop, Sarah hurries to the door to escape, and is relieved at once when the air hits her face. Rushing after her, Penny catches her hand, pulling her in a different direction.

"I want to show you over here first."

"Can't we just—"

"Come on, it'll only take a minute."

She guides Sarah through several alleyways that she loses track of as Penny drags her by the arm. In an unimpressive location on the brick wall is a poster, the same one that she had seen before in her room.

"It's the newest one," she says with an overlarge smile. "I'm singing here three times a week. You should visit me, you know. You haven't yet."

"Yes, well," Sarah says, uninterested.

She stops, distracted by another poster a few paces down. "What's that?" she asks, breaking away from Penny's arm.

The poster shows a woman, or what seems to be a woman, melded with glimmering machinery parts. Crystal-encrusted cogs, wires, clockworks, extend from her neck and down her exposed upper chest, her mouth frozen open as if in song as she holds a microphone before her. Large monochrome capital letters announce, "The original Belle Voix at The Fortune Follies."

"That's Kate Page," Penny says with a tinge of envy.

"What's on her face?" Sarah asks, mesmerized by the metal on skin.

"It's fashion, mostly, and she got her vocal chords done up so she can sing in all sorts of tones."

Grinding echoes against the alley walls, signaling the approach of a great Iron Boy, a machine as tall as a man with a body of metal. Sarah expects it to squeal at the seams as it moves, but it walks in silence except for the sound of its artificial steps on the ground as it walks away, presenting a poster plastered on its back that shows a laughing red skull and the words: "BEWARE THE RED DEVIL. REPORT SUSPICIOUS ACTIVITY."

Ignoring the propaganda, she recalls one morning in the internment camp canteen. Papa had brought the newspaper to their side of the long picnic table where they ate together under a barracks ceiling. He spread out the pages so that Sarah could read the English out loud for him. Emblazoned on a section was a picture of a great mechanical man with a machine gun affixed to its chest standing amongst the allied soldiers. She hadn't remembered the words, just the picture of the new machine that would quickly end their time in the camps through sheer numbers and force. Once the war was over, they would let them all leave. As the old Iron Boy passes—outdated though it is—she feels indebted to it for doing what live men could not: ending the war quickly without bombs or needless death.

As quickly as they glimpse the poster, Penny pulls her away and back toward the station, through the ticket gates and another jump onto the sky train. Pulling out, the train rushes smoothly along the track while some advertisement jingles play from bell-shaped speakers hanging above the doors. Penny nudges her cousin, telling her to look out the window. On the opposite side of Elliot Bay, a roller coaster rises from a wooden boardwalk that extends out into the sea. Nestled at the edge are bright yellow buildings with orange rooftops. On the top of each are colorful red, white, and blue flags that flap in the salty wind. Surrounding the white front walls is the entrance marked by two square columns with conical spires each with a shiny golden orb at the top and a line of carnival flags tied between them. An over-arch settles between the towers where the name "Luna Park" is etched in giant blue letters. Giddy screams come from a group of three children, no older than ten or eleven, who press their faces against the window glass, each one pushing and pulling to get the best view.

As soon as the train locks into the station, the young ones rush out to the park entrance with Penny following shortly after, guiding Sarah along with a tug at her hand. Carnival waltz music and hints of sweet confections waft from inside the amusement park to the white cobbled streets leading to the ticket booth.

Again, the booth is manned by a hatted automaton dispensing tickets through a glass window and again Penny passes through with a wave of her citizen's card across the turnstile leaving Sarah to buy herself a paper ticket. The mechanical man spits out the rectangular admission from a slot in the window and says, "Thank you, enjoy your time at Luna Park." in a monotone voice. She inserts the ticket in the turnstile ticket punch and pushes through the rotary bars. Sarah looks over the scene, searching for her cousin who she finds admiring the central forum. In the center of a concentric circle garden stands a bronze statue of a genderless child wearing a cowl in the shape of a crescent moon whose smooth edges curve forward. The child's face is slightly upturned to gaze at the sky while sitting on a dais incised with stars of all sizes. At the base of the pedestal is a clear pool fed by trickling streams spreading out from each corner. Beneath the water are pennies, a few nickels, and even a dime or two, that glint when the sun breaks through the clouds in the sky. Spreading out from the center are five rings, each potted with different flowers, beginning with Allum, then Night Flox, followed by Candytuft and Dianthus, and ending with Snow in Summer.

"You took your time," Penny remarks when Sarah finally gets through, then holds out her gloved palm to reveal two shiny pennies. "Toss one in."

Obliging, Sarah takes one, thinking quickly and flicking it into the pool at once where it lands with a *bloop*. In contrast, Penny holds her coin between thumb and forefinger, pressing the metal just to her lips as she whispers to it inaudibly. Once finished, she draws her arm down, then raises it and when she releases the coin, it hits the statue's underfoot with a chime and falls into the water. She lets out a sigh, then turns to Sarah.

"The games are here," Penny says excitedly, pointing to a road just before them lined with colorful booths. Sarah follows in slow, reluctant steps. After all, it had been her boisterous cousin who woke her that morning with the idea of the amusement park. Penny, seeing her unenthusiastic accomplice, takes Sarah in the crook of her arm to walk past a line of carnival games. A ball toss, balloon and darts, and what interests her most: a shooting gallery.

Disappearing from Penny's side, Sarah approaches the wooden stand where four BB guns lie on their sides, waiting to be picked up. Already, two boys are firing at the red targets. In the red center, numbers ranging from one to fifteen correspond to the prizes displayed alongside the counter. The boys speak excitedly about the top prize: a bolt gun. A pistol shape of dull black lacquer with a winding spool on the chamber and a yellow lightning bolt painted on the side of the grip. Like the boys, she decides to win it. The vendor, in a bright red-and-white striped shirt tucked into orange pants gauges her gullibility and flamboyantly waves a hand and bows, causing his long beard to momentarily catch on the top button of his shirt.

"Come, come, I see the young lady has an eye for this," he gestures at the prize with an open palm and as he speaks she notices a deep mark on his tongue as it flicks. "The newest brand from Cosmo Toys"
He picks it up from the display and holds it steady in his left hand while the boys watch in awe as he aims at the nearest target. With a pull of the trigger, the spool begins to spin, making a high buzz that lasts mere moments before ceasing, letting loose a stream of blue and white that connects with the red target.

"Double-click the trigger," he advises.

A line of sparks burst from the end of the shaft. The youngsters let out shouts of delight, shooting until the cup of brass beads for their BB guns empties with Sarah following their juvenile fervor. It should be easy, and she becomes frustrated that she is unable to hit any target. Another cup, another nickel and still no closer to the thirty points she needs. She generously empties her pocket of silver coins, going so far as to put down a dollar bill. It is in this state that Penny finds her, quickly threading an arm around her waist.

"Here you are! Boy, don't you manage to slip away easy," she says cheerfully, then looks to the vendor. "You'll have to excuse my sister." Sarah, indignant at the word, breathes in sharply. "It's her first time to the city and she's blinded by the lights."

The man appraises Penny from her hat to her handbag. "You look like someone I might know."

"I daresay you should!" she exclaims, holding out her hand daintily to shake his. "Ms. Penny Morgan. You might have seen me singing at the Birdcall Lounge?"
Sarah huffs at Penny's bragging. She was always one to embellish.

"No, I don't think so. It was one of those workman's clubs by Sinclair's." He scratches his neck where a fly had landed and flown away.

"Where the best men are, of course," she says, hiding any offense behind a careful smile and playful gaze. "If you'll excuse us, there's more of the park to see," she says pleasantly, and when out of earshot, advises her cousin that, "There are better ways to spend money."

It seems odd to Sarah that Penny should worry about how she spends money, given that Penny has plenty to spare. The thought is temporarily displaced as Penny takes Sarah by the hand to guide her from the man and the games to a circular building in the center of a sea-pool as wide as a lake where two-person paddle boats round the edges of the pool, each one a rainbow skimming across the surface.

Penny pulls her cousin towards the domed building as the amusements buzz past in swirls of colors. Inside are blooming greens seen just touching the top. An arboretum of orchids and heat. Rising tropical trees that perspire just like the ladies in their dresses. Bright pools in glass tanks where brighter fish swim. In the center of the garden, a tall glass column juts up from the base to the ceiling. Sliding up the inside glass is a rusty skinned octopus with thick tentacles, suckers firm, rolling up and across the tank. Penny presses her face close to the glass, oblivious to her cousin becoming

57

ill at ease in the growing crowd. She turns, calling for Sarah, and grabs her by the hand to pull her towards the exhibit, bumping into several passersby to peer into the giant eye, a horizontal black slit surrounded by dusty orange skin. Peering down into a pit of grey sand with natural sea rocks and algae taken from the ocean. A sharp in-take of breath from Penny ends with her quickly announcing that she wants popcorn. Not wanting to follow but also not wanting to get lost, Sarah once again joins her cousin while frustration burns in her chest to returning to the bright outdoors where seagulls drift overhead. From the whitewashed sidewalks rolls an unassuming black marble that Sarah suspects is a child's lost toy having fallen from a pocket.

A short whistle sounds, piercing the ears of each pedestrian whose hands rush to cover ears as some begin running while others, stupefied, remain with eyes fixed on the object. Colorful smoke rises upwards and outwards from within the sphere along with whizzes and pops that remind Sarah of fireworks in a nighttime summer. Those who remain cover faces with their hands, shirt hems brought up to shield noses and expose bellies, or handkerchiefs held tightly against skin in a kaleidoscope of patterns. A rough tug on the back of her waistline that nearly topples her over is followed by a sharp grip on her forearm from an overly calm woman. In the haze, Sarah's eyes water to blur the daylight into streams of whites and yellows.

Overcome by instinct, Sarah wriggles free from Penny's grip to run. Every muscle shouts at her to run. In the struggle of Sarah wringing to free her hand and Penny fighting, cursing at her, to hold on, she manages to throw her sleek frame against her cousin, causing them both to fall to the ground with Sarah hitting the back of her skull against a wall. Sarah breathes raggedly. Her vision worse, burning, she tries shaking her head to focus. Already steady, Penny waves about a pink and purple kerchief all the while speaking and yet her words are muffled. Frustrated at her cousin's unresponsiveness, Penny shoves the cloth onto her cousin's face and ties the ends behind her head to cover her face from the bridge of her nose to her chin. Waiting, alert, Penny crouches over Sarah with on hand pressing firmly on her collarbone. The smoke lifts thickly in the air, traveling on the breeze to spread in a frightening rainbow. Padding footsteps arrive with a strong billow. Penny straightens. Booming out are several figures all with faces covered by white scarves with three intertwining letter Vs printed on the front. Each hold a knife. Spotting the two young women, they point and in a moment saunter towards them.

The ensuing eruption is a tempest and the desire to run pummels against the refusal of her body to move. In the smoke and with her unfocused vision, Sarah finds it difficult to decipher where Penny stands. Crackling pops and red flashes are followed by hollers coming from masculine voices that rise over the whistling still emitting from the marble. When Penny returns, her breathing strained, her skin and hair are dusted with color. Her dress, a pristine powder blue earlier that day, is now a mousy grey. Though visibly distraught, Penny stubbornly remains by Sarah, gripping her arm to keep her still. Both are silent in the mayhem, leaving Sarah to linger on each frantic thought whirling in her mind. Foremost among them is the alarm to escape, to remove herself from the imminent danger. Yet, each time she jerks away, Penny holds on tighter.

*

Sarah wakes to the deep, oaken aroma of coffee and the mumbling radio. Rising, she opens the bedroom door, wandering to the smell to find Penny sitting comfortably on the sofa where she listens to a program with a cigarette in one hand, a cup in the other, and the fluffy cat settled comfortably on the back roll of the sofa brushing his tail back and forth. Seeing her, Penny smiles and gives a cheerful, "Good morning."
Still drowsy, Sarah blinks several times and clears her throat.

"You stopped me from running," Sarah blurts, her mind having turned over the events of the day before.
Penny stares at her for a moment, searching for meaning, and then, suddenly realizing, clicks her tongue against her teeth.

"Of course, I did. Running is the worst thing to do when a whistle goes off. It was the V gang." She pauses to draw on the cigarette. "They toss one of those to scare everyone off. Either the sound or the smoke does it." She flicks ash into the nearby ashtray, keeping the stick between her index and middle finger. "Then people run out and they shank them one by one." She draws again. "Usually they're careful not to kill anyone but mistakes have happened."
Penny nods at the disgusted look on Sarah's face.

"Why—" Sarah begins to ask.

Penny taps the cigarette ash into the tray and, giving a left shoulder shrug, says, "For a laugh."
She sips on her drink, then stands, her face lightening.

"I have something for you before we go."

"Go where?"

"To get you a job, of course!" she says, her cigarette firmly between her lips.

60

A job. Sarah takes a slow breath at the mention of work. Before her arrival, she supposed that this would be a restful transition from her old family life to a new, unknown one. Gazing from the coffee cup, the cigarette, and Penny in her morning wear strikes Sarah with the sudden awareness that this is a sixteen-year-old girl.

"Don't you have school?" she asks.

Penny chortles. "What would school give me that I don't already have? And how could I sing at night if I had to worry about getting up for class?"

Placing her cup down by the radio, she moves to her room and back in quick motion.

"A present," she says, holding out a thin rectangular white box. "I thought it would suit you." Opening it reveals an object wrapped in tissue paper. Pulling at the seams, she picks up what is sitting inside. A wallet or what appears to be one, for it is crafted of a black metal that refracts the light, creating a rainbow array upon the surface like dancing fireflies on a night pond.

"Turn it over."

Doing so shows the clear back wherein turning gears are seen in perpetual motion encircling a square frame containing a small clock with the winding dial set on the right edge.

*

Down a sidewalk, a young woman stands, fliers in hand, her bushy brown hair pulled up into a braid. She extends an arm out to people, her hand grasping a leaflet emblazoned with a bright American flag on the front. Sarah tries to read it, managing to catch the words "Liberty" and "Rally" before Penny picks up her pace, pulling her gently by

61

the arm. At the gate a crowd of people wait in knots on the left side while others enter through the gate door on the left in a single line. These people, the workers in solemn colors, some in white coveralls, others in blue, still more in brown. Penny makes uncomfortable eye contact with one—a large woman with a plump mouth and brittle hair. She wrings her chapped and crooked hands together, sometimes pulling at flaking skin.

"Have you been waiting long?" Penny asks cheerfully.

The woman glances over and lets out a bawdy laugh.

"For two weeks I've stood out here every morning, even Sunday, and each day I get turned out. Maybe there will be an accident today and I can finally get some work."

"I see," she says and nods, beginning to walk off.

"Oh," she remembers, stopping. turning her attention to Sarah, "and telephone if you need anything."

Penny taps away on her high heeled shoes to catch a bus down the street. Abandoned, Sarah remains with the crowd intending to stay just long enough that, upon her return to the house, her cousin will be convinced that she tried to find work. She waits with the patchwork crowd, a mix of women, unfortunate youths, and children that can pass for working age, all with the same grim expression made worse by their sallow skin. The war took most men before the machines tore through enemy skin and bone with their strong arms and unrelenting force, leaving those men who survived with the marks of travesty. There are a few of them standing near her, some with scars and others prematurely aged by war.

Sarah watches for a moment as workers shuffle through. Each pass under a glowing green circular lens

overhead. Whenever the door shuts between workers, the color turns yellow and the worker waits until it changes to let them pass through. None of the people around her speak loudly. They whisper or murmur to each other. All are in a state of tension, men and women alike. She catches someone to ask, "What's the wage today?" and then spies a hanging chalk board tacked to the gate showing, "$1.23".
The crooked-hand woman mumbles, carrying on a conversation with herself that seems devoid of reason.

"Aw, shut up over there," a gruff woman says from a few steps away.

She hides half her face under a wool cap, leaning against the gate as she nibbles on a blueberry muffin wrapped in a napkin.

"You're always complaining. I keep telling you to try the fishery, but you won't go."

At the comment, Sarah looks closer at the woman's hands where from her pinky to her ring finger bend inward at the joints.

"I'm not spending my days in fish guts."

"At least there you might find some work instead of hanging around here every breakfast. Ah, here he comes." She wraps up the muffin and slips it into her work pants pocket. "Let's see how our luck is today. Stand up straight, now, and show them you've got life in you."

She pushes her cap back to show her face and pushes her chest out as if she is a soldier awaiting an order. The older woman hides her hands behind her back as a figure comes towards them. A muscular man in workman pants held up by suspenders and a brown collared shirt tucked in with the sleeves rolled up to his elbows. His rubber boots crunch against the gravel.

"Good morning," he says as cheerfully as he can manage as he nears the gate. "Quite a crowd today." He lets out a chuckle as he places his hands in his pockets, rocking back on his heels.

"I know you're all looking for job vacancies today, and there's luck. Two workers are out sick, so I need a cover for their shifts. Welding. Easy work. Anyone up for it?"

Once he finishes, everyone raises their hands, all shouting over each other to gain the man's attention. Though it does no good as the man peers through the crowd and points to the ones he wants.

"Oy!" says the capped woman as the man turns to walk away. "What about munitions? Thought you always needed people there."

Copper shells painted at the tips one by one as they passed down the line. Sarah could never forget the scent of metal and fingers that she willed steady because one twitch might knock the explosives down. Sinclair had brought work to them while they waited for freedom in the camp. Sinclair's Wartime Munitions, they called it. A way to earn money, but they had been no better than indentured servants. Even if there are jobs there, she will never bring herself to stand on the munitions line again.

The day free, everyone disperses. Some curse, mumbling to themselves, while Sarah tightens her lips against a happy disposition. And the next day is the same, with Penny escorting her to the fence, leaving Sarah with the apprehension that she may have to concede to the idea of working. Labor has been such a significant portion of her life that the inevitability of it easily changes her initial despondence. It is not a terrible situation, in any case; money always seems to make life easier. Before departing, Penny shoves a small flat orb covered with a soft blue and red flannel pouch in Sarah's hand.

"What's this?" she asks.

"It's supposed to be cold this morning, so it's a heater.

Funny little thing, though, don't leave it on too long or they're known to explode. Sometimes, that is. I'm sure you'll be fine. In any case, I'll be gone when you get home, so I'll leave the back unlocked—oh, and don't forget to wind your watch!"

Sarah takes the sky train by herself, brave enough this time to stand on her own for a time until a sway of the car causes her to give up and sit down. She departs at port side and gets off at the Sinclair factory. This time she is early enough that the crowd has gaps yet to be filled. The two women from the day before stand there again, hoping that today will be their turn, along with several ragged older men with the type of sallow faces caused by malnourishment and physical labor.

"You look fresh today," says the woman with the crooked hands.

"She ought to," comes another.

It takes Sarah a moment to recognize her without the cap.

"Nice to meet you," she says, popping up to offer her hand, which Sarah shakes lightly. "I'm Ruth."

The woman with the crooked hands mutters something to herself. Ruth glances in her direction, then rolls her eyes, ignoring the comment.

"Never mind that old marmie, she's just upset that she's being looked over. Though I don't blame her." Ruth sighs. "I've picked up some shifts before. A few months in

65

packing, some weeks and days here and there doing this and that around parts and manufacturing, you know. It is quick work, easy, anyone can do it. . .well," she flicks her eyes over at the others, "most anyone. What I really want is to get a full-time job, or at least part-time. Maybe today is my day, eh?"

Sarah wraps her arms around her chest to warm from the sudden chill coming off the sea, then, remembering, takes out her wallet for a moment to wind the slowing clock, then finds herself staring at a lady who has a pair of gloves covering her hands. The woman seems lost as she keeps her eyes locked through the gate bars. Sarah switches from Ruth, who shrugs her shoulders dismissively, and back to the woman.

"Excuse me," Sarah prods, a little louder.

The lady turns her head and then looks surprised to see someone looking back at her.

"Oh, hello. How ever did you get here?"

"I—don't you remember me?"

A blank stare meets her, then a flicker of acknowledgement. She gains her composure, her milky eyes searching for a focal point, saying, "Yes."

Sarah hears a stomach grumble from one of the men nearby. Workers begin filing through the gate and shortly thereafter comes a foreman. This time it is a stocky woman in white coveralls with her short hair pushed back and tied with a white bandanna to shield her face. She takes one glance and points to Ruth.

"You can fill in today."

She opens the door, which Ruth dashes towards, as the stocky woman leaves without another word, letting the new worker follow. Ruth gives a thumbs-up in her direction, disappearing into the gargantuan red brick building. Ten minutes later, an accident picks Sarah from the crowd. The foreman returns, saying they need five people in packing and distribution. A tawny finger points to her and she rushes to the gate. Glancing back, she sees the crooked hand woman still waiting behind the bars. Sarah follows through the metal door leading inside, the same door she had seen workers file through every morning. The hall inside is tile floor and brick walls. They near a cross that flows to three separate halls, each with an iron cast sign bolted at the center that reads "Packing and Distribution" to the left, "Repair" in the center and "Parts and Manufacturing" to the right. She and four others follow her squeaking rubber boots down the left corridor in what seems like a half an hour walk to a locker room un-separated by gender. With a grumble, the foreman pulls down spare brown coveralls from inside a locker. These he passes out to each person along with pairs of black boots.

"Get dressed quickly and come out the door when you're done," he says, leaving through a door marked "OUT."

Sarah glances at the others who quickly kick off their casual shoes and slips into the used workers' clothes. Now Sarah understands why Ruth always wears pants. It is much easier than trying to fit a dress skirt into the coveralls, even though the size is so large that she has to cuff up the ends of the pants and sleeves. She leaves her shoes under the long center bench as she'd seen the others do, though she worries about leaving them, new as they are. Following everyone else, she passes through the door where the man waits just outside.

"Here's the front," he says, gesturing to the left where lines of workers in coveralls stand, their heads bent down, as packs of red fly down the belt. "You check them to make sure there are eight in each pack and that nothing is damaged: no cuts, scrapes, slanted prints, or nothing out of the standard. After that, they go down here." He moves to the right where still more people pick them up and place them in boxes. "and pack them to the top of these boxes. See where the boxes get stacked into crates?" He points to the cardboard boxes that are taken by other workers outside the lines and put into wooden crates that they then load onto push carts. He eyes every one of them. "They take those to the loading dock and keep doing that until the trucks get here. When they do, the crates are put on the trucks. Any questions?"

"When do we get off work?" Sarah asks boldly.

"If you don't want the job," he says without emotion, "I'm sure there are others waiting outside eager to take your place. Now, get moving."

When she lowers her head in submission, he points to Sarah, the other woman, and one young boy who may very well be under fourteen years old. Almost everyone moves at once, though Sarah hesitates at first, making the foreman leer; she quickens her pace as well as she can in the over-sized boots. She takes a place next to the skinny girl and watches as she gracefully slips the packs of cigarettes from the belt and into the empty boxes waiting at his feet. Sara tries to emulate the movements of those around her. She picks each box up, placing it level in the box, one by one, like dropping pieces of chocolate into a pan. The belt moves too quickly or else the other workers' hands are robotic. As fast as she can go, it was not enough. She peers over to the skinny woman who has already filled two boxes while she has barely completed half of one.

"You're good at this," Sarah says, a little loudly as the foreman gives her a warning look.

"Keep your eye on your work," the woman warns in a low whisper.

The foreman shouts. A moment of panic shoots through her, but it is the skinny woman, stoically continuing her work, who he taps on the shoulder, pulling her off the line. He makes no obvious order beyond the simple gesture. Sarah snaps her sights to the conveyor belt. All day the product slides down in a cascade of rectangles for her to catch. The pace is quick, much more than the cannery, and it takes all her attention to keep up with the moving track. There is no pause, not even for her to use the restroom, which she needs badly but is too afraid to ask. Stand and work. Until the bell. She can identify the regulars by the abruptness of their ceasing and their shuffling feet that are too tired to completely lift from the floor. Walking off the floor with them she asks one how long for the break. The reply is a terse half hour.

Sarah rushes to the restroom, relief in her bladder and her legs when she sits. She leans her head against the wall of the stall to rest, her eyes rolling to the poster tacked to the inside door. This one shows a man in overalls sitting on a tree branch with the word "Productivity" carved into it holding a handsaw marked "Strike" as he saws through the wood. As her eyelids begin to close, she startles when the bell sounds. Hungry, thirsty, tired, she returns to the floor for the same routine until the bell rings once more to signal that her first shift is over.

"Come back tomorrow," the foreman says, a little too cheerful for her liking.

4
Penelope
High Night Life

At the opening of the door, Penny meets Sarah in a twinkling evening dress, her hair freshly curled, and make-up smoothly adorned.

"Let's go out, get dinner or something."

"I just finished work," she says flatly, "and I really need to clean this," she adds, pointing at the collar of her work wear. Penny seems to catch a whiff as she scrunches her nose, then relaxes.

"Come on," she pleads, rolling her eyes. "Let's go. I'm tired of being stuck in here all the time."

An insulting thought passes through her head, but she holds her tongue.

"I have to work in the morning and—"

"Work, work, work. It'll be fine. We won't stay long at the club."

"I don't like clubs."

"I know, but Kate Page is going to be there, and I want to meet her."

"Isn't she *famous*?" she asks, implying the impossibility of such an event. "Won't there be someone at the door?"

She passes her hand across her face dismissively.

"Don't be silly. The strongmen don't come until two o'clock."

"How do you know that?"

She lets out a mock gasp,

"I'm surprised at you! *La Belle Voix* is my idol. Don't you think I'd know everything about her?"

Sarah scratches behind her ear.

"Wait," she says, closing her eyes in thought. "Won't the doors be locked?"

"To customers. Doors usually don't open until late evening. We'll go through the staff entrance."

"Oh, so you've performed there already."

"No."

"Then how?"

She smiles, pressing a finger to her lips, saying, "Top secret." and lets her hand falls gently to her side. "Don't worry about it. Just come with me, won't you?"
She widens her eyes like a child asking her mother for a puppy. It produces the exact result she desires.

"All right," Sarah relents.

"Well, let's go then. Get out of those things. Come, pick something from my closet. I'll wait," she says while guiding Sarah through her bedroom door.

Bruce lifts his head from his comfortable place at the center of a well-made bed to mew at her once before settling back down where Penny joins him, petting his head and staring off into the distance, humming, now and then peeking over at her bewildered cousin.

Seeing Kate Page may be the push she needs. A few good pointers from a well-known singer, maybe even a recommendation, and Penny can become popular herself. It is only a matter of time. To be a famous, talented, singer was always her dream.

"Where did you get that?" Penny asks, accusingly, seeing Sarah now changed into a conservative off-white dress with flat Mary Jane shoes.

71

"Looks like something my mom would wear," she comments, looking down at Sarah's bare legs. "Good golly! If you're going out like that, at least put some stockings on." Penny tromps to the dresser and pushes a pair of peach colored stockings into her hand.

"Let's go," she says and leads her outside where her bicycle is parked against the curb. Sarah slumps her shoulders.

"Am I going on that?" she asks in disbelief. She recalled the first, and only, time she accompanied her cousin on a bicycle. When Penny borrowed a rusty old banana-seat bicycle from their school teacher at Minidoka. It had not been fit for one person, let alone two. She took them halfway around the barracks before crashing over from displaced balance and into the dry dirt.

"Yes! Come on, I won't crash this time. I'll go slow," she says reassuringly. Sarah glances at her cousin distrustfully and takes hold of the bicycle.

*

Rushing down hills with their skirts flowing at their calves, Penny giggles at the wind in her face and slows only when approaching a stop. The glowing orbs in the sky brighten the streets, lessening the chances of running over the odd pebble as well as showing the road ahead as clear as the dawn. Winding and turning, Penny takes them down cobble sidewalks and through narrow alleys until she brakes hard to park in front of a blue building with a marigold yellow door and a porthole window at eye level.

"How are we going to get in?" Sarah asks. "The lights are off. The front door is locked."

Regardless, she follows Penny around the back side where the dumpsters sit. Sarah puts her hand to cover her nose from the rotting food smell.

"Here," Penny says as she strides towards the back door without windows. "Let's see."
She twists the handle, pulling gently. It opens.

Although it is bright outside, the club is so dark that it takes several moments for her eyes to adjust, immediately drawn to the high dome ceiling of a midnight sky with stars and a crescent moon projected onto it. As she watches it in awe, the sky changes to a purple as deep as blackberry juice. The moon disappears into a soft glowing sun, the stars evaporating into blue skies with billowy clouds, brightening the room to where she observes a large circular fish tank holding brightly colored fish swimming in and out of coral decorations. So large is the aquarium that she spots a striped shark gliding by the other fish. A thick platform stage sits atop it, set with electric bulbs while a curving staircase winds around an aquarium pillar leading to a balcony floor overlooking the stage.

Within it the water glows a crystal blue where jellyfish bob up and down. Ascending the stairs, the entirety of a back wall is another giant aquarium. In this are sea turtles and yet more unidentifiable fish, tall live corals and bubbles rising from a hidden vent under the sand. Low undulations follow a slim mechanical mermaid in the shape of a teenage girl and the false skin and hair of an automaton whose small propeller tail whisks it past the front most glass. Echoes of voices come from the stage floor where waiters and stage hands prepare for the night. Penny peers down. There she stands. Kate Page. A petite woman whose blonde

73

hair curls perfectly around her jawline. A soft silk scarf is wrapped around her neck with the ends falling down the front of her winged collar dress.

"Good evening," Kate says, her voice carrying over the noise through some ventriloquist's trick. She looks up at them, then walks towards the stairs to meet the two young women. "They commissioned a special automaton from Sinclair months ago. A swimming mermaid. Waterproof. Squint and it looks human."

To compare the glamor of her picture in the street poster and the woman herself leads to the assumption that they are strangers. All the images of her that she had seen never showed the wrinkles on her forehead, or her yellow tinted teeth, or the thick makeup smeared over her face like a mask. Like a baby seeing its first pinwheel spinning in a breeze, Penny's eyes brighten as she approaches the majestic woman, clasps her hands and shakes them two vigorous times before letting go.

"Marvelous," is the word Penny manages to conjure. "You *are* quite marvelous."

"Naturally," the singer replies with a pleasant smile. "And, glad as I am to meet fans, how, may I ask, did you get in?"

"Early tickets," Penny lies quickly, leaving Sarah visibly astonished. "To make sure we got good seats." Whether Kate Page believes it or not, she cannot tell, but she lifts her arm at the elbow, flitting her hand in the air with a wry grin.

"I daresay you will. Come, have a drink. It's been a long time since I've had some female company."
A polished curved bar with fixed stools cushioned with black and grey velvet is where they gather.

"Have a seat." She motions, then, turning her head, calls out, "Toby!"

A young redhead jogs in from an unseen area as if appearing from the walls. His sleeves are rolled up and a black apron is tied at his waist.

"Make us some drinks, would you? Sherry." She doesn't bother to ask what any of them want. His only protest of the order is in a tightening of his lips as he ventures wordlessly behind the bar, serving her the ruby liquid.

"Thank you, Toby, you can go."

"So," she begins after taking a drink, "tell me about yourselves."

"I'm a singer, too, at some nightclubs," Penny blurts.

"Are you?"

Penny blinks a few times, seemingly insulted.

"Small clubs. Not as grand as all this, of course." She looks up at the high ceiling and around the trappings of the room.

"Don't be ashamed of small clubs. We all start somewhere. You might be surprised at some of the places I started. At least this city is a might clean. Try the row bars in San Francisco. I'd have to go on after the tease shows—a desperate business, that—or shoddy magicians with skimp magic tricks."

Penny lets out a giggle.

"I do have to follow some mediocre magic performers."

Kate Page smiles too widely, patronizingly.

"It happens to the best of us."

"What—I hope I'm not too forward—what suggestions can you give me?"

"Take risks. Without doing that I wouldn't be here. During the war I thought it was finished. All the men went

75

off and you can bet that it wasn't their wives who would come to see me." She sips her drink. "I had nothing else to fall back on—I only made it up to sixth grade—and I'm too proud to go back to my parents. All I had was my voice. Singing on corners for change.

Eventually I got a job as a backup for some vaudeville. Then I had an idea when I saw all those automatons being made for the war and even after. Now you can find the tinkers anywhere but back then I had to raise high water. After a few years, I suddenly became very popular." She sips once more. "Well, let's have a look at you," she says, appraising Penny at once. "The dye job isn't bad. It makes your face brighter. But try a different color. This one is too severe for your skin. It might work for Marilyn Monroe but not for you. Use a good blush onstage. The lights wash you out. It looks like a lot of makeup up close," she gestures at her own face, "but up there it looks natural."

After a few silent moments, she says, "Sing for me."

Without hesitation, Penny begins *A-Tisket, A-Tasket*.

An animated songstress, moving her shoulders, her arms, bopping in an act that she seems to have perfected long ago. As she sings she smiles here and there, her eyes drawn to the mechanized mermaid swimming in clear water.
Once finished, the famed singer lets out a dispassionate hum. Under the table, Penny clasps her hands together, pushing her left thumb cuticle back with her right forefinger.

"I see," she says flatly. "Old music. Not a bad voice."

Penny contains her disappointment as well as she can.

Though Sarah can make out her fading smile, the folds recede into a stern line.

"These old songs," Kate continues, "are for old soldiers; young cats want faster beats and a tune to match. That's why I got this." She pulls down a silk scarf wrapped around her neck, revealing the moving gears embedded in her larynx so deeply that in between rounded metal and springs is her raw cartilage. Even now they rotate gently inside her neck. "Expensive to do, but I can sing the highest, lowest, or any note I want without ruining my voice."

"That's how you can do so many shows." Penny realizes, her tone low, heavy with displeasure. After seeing so many posters of the songstress with the gilded throat before, she assumed it was superficial. Such an adaptation relies on technology, not talent.

"Why, yes! No need to rest or practice; perfect pitch every time."

When she adjusts the scarf back in place, Penny catches sight of a flash of a blue bracelet with a single white star and eagle wings on either side on her wrist that had been covered by her sleeve. She leans back, resting her elbow on the chair.

"If you want to be successful, you give the audience what they want, no matter what it is." Stretching, she shifts her peripherals to the watch fastened over her right sleeve since there are no clocks to be found anywhere.

"Now," she says, rising. "The next you'll see me is on stage. And you," she puts the tip of a fist gently beneath Penny's chin, "get to see *La Belle Voix*."

Turning her back, Ms. Page disappears behind the stage leaving Penny to swallow her drink bitterly with a grimace that fades as soon as her empty cup hits the bar top. Sarah lets out a groan. "I don't want to stay so late. I told you—"

"I know. You have *work*," she says irritably.

77

"And I really need to wash my clothes and—" she stops abruptly, realizing that she has yet to see an actual laundry room in the house, or indeed, any clotheslines in the yard. "—wait, Penny, you do have a laundry, don't you?"

"*Golly*, are *you* worried about such a little thing. Yes, of course, there's a washer machine at the house. A nice, sturdy, Sinclair Home Wash-o-Matic. I just never use it." She smiles, getting some of her cheer back. "No point! I never do wear the same clothes twice; a star can't be seen to be out of fashion."

*

Once the hour seeps into night, illuminations from hidden places shine as colorful stars in the dark, the aquariums glow a clear azure, the fish happily darting to and fro, at times their paths interrupted by the mermaid swimming smoothly through the water and the club fills with patrons of all sorts. Yet there is a clear divide between the men and the women. With few exceptions, the men are citizens made plain by the flash of their cards to the host at the entrance to gain free fare while the women, mostly young and donned in high fashion, pay cash for entry. Penny is completely overcome with excitement when the lights turn to the stage while Sarah has to strain to keep her eyes open in the narrowest of slits, often shutting them unknowingly only to startle and widen them when a shiny tin automaton emerges from a curtained alcove near the stage. A spotlight turns on it and low conversations turn to silence.

"Welcome," it says in a strangely human voice from its mesh mouth, "to The Fortune Follies!" the audience claps lightly. "Our first act tonight is a rambunctious group. Please welcome the Harmonica Rascals!"

The main curtains part. To the left side are six lean men all sitting on rattan chairs of varying heights. Each man wears white slacks, white shirts, black cardigans, and matching black pork pie hats. Harmonicas in their hands, they begin playing a quick rhythm that is soon accompanied by ladies in silver brassieres with matching hip skirts. The skirts are decorated in the back with fluffy blue feathers forming a long back train so that when they spin to the music, the fabric swishes around their legs. Light catches on the sparkling stones set within long feather headdresses that push back their hair to better present each plastered-on smile. Amidst the dancing and singing, the audience is served drinks by the numerous waitresses amid a low murmur. Some minutes pass until the act finishes and a pleasant applause signals the end.

There is silence from the stage to allow preparation for the next performance. In this intermission, a young camera girl flits about each table in red high heels and the club mini-dress uniform consisting of a tight red bodice kept up with a halter strap fastened at the back of her neck, leaving her upper back exposed, and a skirt that stops at the middle of her thigh, pleating to reveal golden stripes when she moves. Around her wrist is a thick silver bracelet with a flat container kept closed with a latch. When she takes cash from various tables as she makes her rounds, she opens the box to deposit a bill or two before closing it again. Once she passes by the two cousins, a cheerful persuasion and a quick money exchange is all it takes for Penny to agree to a photograph. She cozies up to Sarah, prompting her to smile, and after a short countdown there is a bulb flash which leaves spots in their vision.

"Make sure to get your photograph at the door before you leave!" she exclaims.

Penelope moves back to her original spot with her sights fixed on the aquarium stage, taking her eyes away for a moment to remove some money from her purse.

"I'll get us some drinks," she says.

Though not particularly wanting any alcohol, it is an excuse to relieve her earlier disappointment. Keeping the greens in hand, she winds through the thin pathways that surround each full table, pausing to admire the enormous aquarium and marvel at the Mechanical Mermaid, then approaching the crowded bar to wait her turn for a drink order. The bar man, Toby, hurriedly mixes and crafts colorful alcoholic beverages with the help of a few other rough-looking men marked with scars and premature wrinkles. Waiting her turn, she fixes her gaze on the back of the bar. Now that the nightclub is in full bloom, each cylindrical glass tap is alight from within by a phosphorescent glow. On the stage, the automaton reemerges to announce the next performance by a pianist named Horace Villanueva.

A handsome Filipino gentleman clad in an immaculate pinstriped suit appears sitting before a grand piano. A short round of applause from everyone and he begins to play a soft rendition of *La Mer*. Pulling Penny away from the melody is a bar man ready for her order. Unlike Toby, who is young and unspoiled, this man bears the etchings of turmoil in the lines of his face. When he speaks, his voice carries a raspy kindness like a boy calling against a freezing gale.

Not caring about the particulars, she tells the bartender to make anything he wants. A nod of understanding and the man turns away from her, taking two flute glasses between the fingers of one hand to fill them with a deep red liquid from three separate taps, returning to the bar to set them down. "Devil's Tail." he says with half his mouth upturning into a wry smile. From behind the counter he brings up a sliced lime, squeezing the contents into the mix. As he does, his collar pulls away from his neck, allowing her to glimpse the upper designs of a swallow in flight. Embarrassed at finding herself staring at the naked space between his shirt and throat, she turns her attention back to the drinks which are now complete with two orange rinds sitting on the edges. She hands over her money and pockets the change. As carefully as she can, she grasps the two flutes in each hand and returns to Sarah, placing the drinks on the table.

By now the pianist ceases his playing and the announcer then riles the audience with the name of the diva who is eagerly awaited, rousing the audience to fervor dampened only when Horace Villanueva begins the first bars of *Rum and Coca Cola* soon joined by a few secondary instrumentals including maracas and a guitar. And then she appears. A curvaceous body draped by a golden dress, making even her skin glimmer. Her voice is a choir of seraphim singing in polyphonic rhapsody, reaching the vibrating hearts of the audience.

5

Sarah

A Banner for Patriots

Sarah lines up with the others in the morning and files
through the employee entrance gate on the Eastern side of the
building. Calls from the unemployed shouting at the fence
are difficult to ignore. Squinting, she sees a woman waiting
at the gate with her knobby hands hidden in her pockets.
Sarah waves to her, her arms sore from using the washing
machine this morning, having had to wake up especially
early so as to properly clean and dry her work wear. The
machine was easy to use, the hulking white metal box on four
thick legs ran on electricity, and the motorized internal
workings did the hard labor. Yet, she still had to wring the
water from the clothes using the mangle built into the top of
the machine, leaving her upper arms sufficiently fatigued.
She waves again. If the woman sees it, she chooses not to
return the gesture.

Though she had not wanted to take up work so soon
after arriving, she since finds herself enjoying the habit,
giving her a semblance of normality. The second day goes
faster, though her arms are sore from the day before, working
in industrial rhythm. It is easier than when she worked at the
cannery in Alaska. Packing fish. Cut chunks of Pollock and
Salmon she scooped into round cans, placing the top over it
and pulling the canning lever to seal it closed. Sliding tins
approaching over and over until the work bell rang. At least
here she does not have to worry about smelling like the
underside of wet seaweed. She smiles to herself and opens
her mouth to say something to the lady next to her, but closes
it, remembering the rules, remembering the foreman. At the

end the shift, she is relieved when the foreman tells her, "Come back tomorrow."

As Sarah leaves the great factory, Ruth catches up to her.

"Here," she says, handing over a pack of cigarettes with a cut off label. "Slipped them in my pocket before we left."

"I don't usually. . ." she starts, but finds herself unable to refuse the gift, ". . .but I guess it wouldn't hurt. Thank you."

She takes them from Ruth's stiff hands and stores them in her purse. She learned that it was always better to say thank you when receiving a gift, even if it was not welcomed.

The brusque woman furrows her brow.

"Ain't you gonna smoke?" she teases.

"Oh," Sarah lets out, then obligingly rustles in her purse for the gift.

After opening it, she slides a single thin cigarette from the pack to hold it between unsure fingers. Smiling at her innocence, Ruth slips a matchbox from her pocket, lights one for herself and then for Sarah, telling her to inhale. She coughs immediately, not from the act itself, but from the prickly texture it leaves on her tongue. At times, Ruth chuckles at Sarah's failing attempt to smoke gracefully as the young girl makes low coughs at each inhale. After several points of instruction, Sarah manages to consume the cigarette without issue, finding herself acutely alert after a few rounds of ingestion. Across the street, she notices an automaton, the same one that she bought a cherry ice from. It keeps on up and down its set path. In the fading light, his face shines even lighter even in the spiral illuminations that hang under the clouds at night.

"Ah," says Ruth after a few puffs. "Faster and stronger than coffee. Whatever they put in it sure works."

"Sounds like a commercial."

She smirks and answers, "Yeah, it does. Been smokin' these too long."

Sarah stops at the bus station, relieved to be able to sit on the bench to rest her tense calves from standing for so long and to steady her body, which begins to react to the strong effects of the cigarette, unlike those typical of tobacco, making her suddenly alert and invigorated.

"You're going to the orientation, aren't you?"

"What?" She jostles her head to focus, then remembers the leaflet that had been given to her on her third day that she had balled up and tossed in the trash. "Oh. I didn't plan to—"

"—You oughta. After it's done they give everyone a double pack of the *strong* Firelites. Free. I've probably gone through it about a dozen times. Bet I could recite the whole tour for you."

"I think I'll be fine. What else is there to know about filling boxes with junk?"

Sarah shrugs, searching the bus times plastered to the nearby streetlamp post.

"It's a horrible place, isn't it?" She tosses away her spent cigarette and is already lighting another. "But we work there because there's nowhere else."

"Shouldn't the bus be here by now?" she asks, still looking over the schedule.

"Oh, they don't run after two. No need. Everyone takes the sky train."

Sarah rises slowly from the bench, mimicking Ruth's manner of disposing of the Firelite.

"I'll see you in the morning," she says but then lingers as if mulling a thought over. "Unless. . ." she begins, taking the cigarette from her mouth as she comes closer with her mouth in an upturned half-smile, "Want to come to a swell dig?"

*

On a sky train from the Industrial area, they pass a row of clubs and bars that so many workers stop at after work before going home to spend their hard-earned wages on drink and entertainment, the sort of places she imagines Penny frequenting.

"It's a little after-work party. We usually get together about once a week," Ruth says. "Just a few friends. Thought you might like to meet some people since you're new. And don't worry—they're nice."

The train is fairly crowded when they enter and thins out at each stop until she and Ruth are the only ones in their car apart from a young boy in rough overalls and banged up shoes who curls up asleep on the floor with his arms folded across his chest. In between pockets of lights from the hovering balloons are dim roads. There were only small lights in Alaska. Pinpoints of yellow in the wild darkness. But that was a country meant to be open and dark; this is the city. The train speaker announces their upcoming destination at which the boy, suddenly animated, springs up and hurries to the door to grab the inside handle in anticipation. The slowing motion of the train and the shanty homes that pass by make her uneasy. A jolly seven-note chime signals their arrival after which the boy slides open the door, disappearing. Sarah follows Ruth onto the empty platform separated from

85

the outside by an iron gate. A single automaton stands behind a dirty glass window box to dispense tickets. As they exit, it crackles, "Nice have a day." from an old, un-repaired voice box.

In the air are the ever-present balloons floating softly in the dusky sky. As it darkens, each one throws a spreading beam of light onto the streets, forcing her to take in the large expanse of slums with tattered shacks, each in its own progression of dilapidation, smashed together like too many bread rolls in a basket. Outside the doors to the wood plank homes are second-hand clotheslines made from whatever the families found available: cord, wood, twine, thin pieces of plastic, or wire. Worn and faded clothing hang to dry. The smell fuming through the ozone of the slum is of fetid sewage, rotting vegetables and sodden garbage: the stench of poverty. It seems ludicrous that a short ride away lies a city imbued with a glass skyline. In the crooks and cracks of every stone surface grow tufts of deep green moss, some sprouting blades of grass.

A mewling cat forces her attention to a blue tarp roof, catching sight of short, billowy woman who carries a whining baby in one arm, holding open the door just wide enough to let the calico inside. She smiles widely at Ruth, revealing crooked teeth tarred with brown cigarette film. Sarah instinctively moves closer to Ruth, resisting the impulse to hold her hand as she might have done with a close friend. Their destination is farther down, to an old brick house with fading plaster and an unkempt yard with blades of grass clawing at the bottom edges of dirty windows. A low clunking echoes from within. Ruth tries the rusty round door knob; fiddling with it as it sticks, refusing to let them in. She curses, sighs, then gives it a hard twist, freeing it from the latch.

The room is set with a printing press churning out pages to be bound in a thin magazine called the Portside Gazette. A young woman stands at the end, gathering the pages as they spit out. Within the pages are the lesser-known stories that larger newspapers and publications ignore. Whistle-blowing reports about the work at any of Sinclair Industries' many factories or insider reports on congressional corruption. Stacked in cardboard boxes next to the door are leaflets waiting to be distributed. Over a picture of the American Flag, a title reads "Stand up for Liberty at the Harbor Steps" with a date at the bottom.

"Ruth!" Shouts another woman who jumps up from her seat at an ink-spotted writing table where she had been at work on a typewriter and claps Ruth on the shoulder. "Didn't expect you so soon."

The thin blue rope bracelet, knotted around her wrist in a chain sinnet, slides down to her mid forearm. The woman nods to Sarah. Despite her gruff posture, she is quite short, nearly the same height as Sarah who merely has to lower her chin to meet the woman eye-to-eye. This close, Sarah can smell the *lustre crème* coming from her straight mousy brown hair that hangs down to her shoulders. The neckline of her cotton blouse unbuttoned down past her collarbone frees her neck.

"And this is?"

"Sarah," Ruth answers for her, eyes darting from her to the woman, "This is Florence, and there," she points a thumb at the skinny woman working the printing press, "is Alma."

87

The silence between them is enough to make Sarah straighten her spine as if to prove herself more than a small girl in a big city.

"Sarah can help. You've heard of her cousin, Ms. Penny Morgan?"

"That nightclub singer?"

Sarah nods once, keeping herself reserved among strangers, preferring to observe.

"I had hoped she could mention the protest at her next show. Bring some fliers."

"At a jazz club?" Ruth blurts. "Not the best place to advertise this kind of thing. Besides, Sinclair sponsors most of the clubs and half the patrons work at one or another of his factories."

"If we get everyone—especially Sinclair—to notice us, then more people will help."
She shoves her hands in her pockets.

"No one looks at those fliers. They take them, sure, and once they're down the block they toss them on the street. I've told you before; people need to see action, not some complaints written in a self-printed magazine. We announce that we put up the flag and then see how many people come to a protest."

"You do it this way," she says, pointing at the printing press, "or you can leave."

"Hear me out," Ruth continues. "We have people who agree with us—they're out there complaining that someone should do something—all we need to do now is take that next step. Just doing this," she waves a hand to the front page of the newspaper, "won't solve anything."

"The war is still fresh in every one's mind—not to mention the mess with the October Strike—People are tired of fighting. What they want is a peaceful way of reform."

"Well, what they want and what they *need* are not the
same. If you want to make some real changes, you can't sit
back. You have to stick your hands in the mud before you
can wash them clean."

"Read the papers. They're saying we're communists,"
she exhales sharply after saying the word as if to expel it
from her body. "Getting rough'll make things worse; it gives
them a reason to push us down, so that's not the way it's
going to be done. We can't just be moral, we have to be
popular," she says with finality.
Ruth crosses her arms, saying, "Fine." as Florence turns
away.

Two of the women wear blue caps of a similar kind to
the ones many Sinclair employees wear, only these have a
white star with two wings sewed on the front.

"We're the real patriots," Florence states, mulling
over a ledger on the table. "Not those rats on the hill. They
were given their citizenship because of luck. It's workers,
non-citizens, that make sure they're comfortable. Why can't
they all see that? Why is it so hard?"
She leans back on the brown suede chair, crossing her legs,
resting her elbow on the armrest, her knuckles in a fist set
against her mouth and nose. She looks to Ruth and the wary
girl following behind her.

"I got picked," Ruth says, to change the subject.
Florence lowers her arm, her eyebrows rising when she asks,
"Honest?"

"Honest. They either forgot what I look like or they
don't care." She sighs and looks over to Sarah, who she
announces to the room as "a fresh hand."

"Glad to see that," she says, then turns to Ruth. "She
coming with us?"

"Why not? She's swell. She's new here. Could be a good way to make friends."

Florence thinks for a moment, then nods once.

"Well then, what news from inside?"

"More of the same," Ruth says, going to the table and flipping through a ledger. "They got me in P and M making all kinds of their Iron Boys. Foreman said that the daily quota this week is five per worker."

"And what about you?" she asks Sarah in a tone that seems to question her legitimacy.

A shrug and a hint of defensiveness. "I'm in packing; putting Firelite boxes into bigger boxes."

"Firelites, huh? Now I can see why Ruth is so keen on you," she says, going to the table to take the ledger away from Ruth.

Sarah manages a smile. At least she seems to have made a friend.

"We're building our own replacements," Ruth says suddenly, factually. "The only thing is for Sinclair to fall."

Florence shakes her head. "Impossible. For too many workers—and me—it's the only place takin' non-citizens."

"That's why it's important to get as many supporters as we can. Ruth," she turns to Sarah, "and your friend, you can talk to more people around your neighborhood."

"No way," Ruth says, nodding her head to Sarah, "Not *her*. She lives on the West, up by Luna. Not even the V gang goes up there."

Florence's eyes dart to several spots on Sarah's face, searching for any secret she might reveal.

"And you're not a citizen?"

Sarah folds her arms across her chest, "I just got here from Alaska. I'm staying with my cousin."

"Your cousin, the singer?"

90

Florence gazes down at the floor, eyes searching for something. When she looks back up, she meets Sarah and smiles.

"Well, you're very fortunate," she says warmly. "Most people who come here to work don't have such sturdy roots. They end up in Sinclair's work housing, like Ruth, or in one of these places. Very few neighborhoods want non-citizens."

Flicking her eye to a clock on the wall, Florence tucks her shirt into her waistline and says, "Let's go."

*

Another sky train to an unfamiliar station. Looking out, Sarah can see the pier even in the middle of the night. The glowing Sinclair Industries sign stands atop the red brick factory, the backside of the ever-reaching mermaid statue that sits on the edge of the docks, and the balloons illuminate the waterfront, the lights dissipating as the train rolls onward. Sarah holds her head down. Even at this distance, she worries that the foreman might see her, and her job will be given to another desperate mongrel.

The train slows, stopping at the covered platform at the same height as the roof of an art-nouveau building with a clock tower pointing to the moon overhead. King Street Station. Chimes. Florence slides the door open. Sarah stays close to Ruth, tagging along with the group as it saunters through the station's marble floors, empty except for the odd sleeper waiting for the morning trains, and down the stairs to the old train lines on level ground covered by an oxidized copper canopy frame and a roof with geometric stained-glass patterns shattered in places. Although the platform is unlit, a constant glow from the hovering lights allows her to discern only the brightest colors, reds and yellows. Taking out her wallet, looking at the clock, she finds that the silver face brightens in the presence of light, allowing her to read the time even in this dark place.

A red flag unfurls. Against the backdrop of blood, a large black shoe lifts above faceless figures who hold their arms up in surrender. In the negative space of the shoe sole screams the name "Sinclair." Florence winds nylon rope through the grommets and ties it around the columns dotting the platform. Ruth and Alma smooth out the wrinkles from the top. A clamoring sky train steals away her attention. She ducks down against the edge as the streamlined cylinder with rail wheels above speeds by on giant cables that wind through buildings. Once it fades past, she pops up and, as a final theatric before they depart, Ruth takes four smoke flares from her deep pockets.

"Catch!" she shouts to Sarah, tossing one in an arch. Sarah clasps it with both hands, following Ruth's lead by twisting the top chamber and setting them in random spots around the roof. They hiss, blowing out red plumes. Alma and Florence jump down on the tracks. Sarah nearly cautions them until it occurs to her that these tracks must have been decommissioned long ago. The unclean surroundings and wayward trash on the steel ties tells her as much. From her back pocket, Alma removes a hand-length metal capsule with a winding mechanism on the side. Turning it, the capsule elongates to reveal a glass chamber of captured lightning bolts.

"It's a Lightning Rotary," Ruth says, startling Sarah. "A toy meant for children that sets off bolts. Don't worry. It's not dangerous. Well, only if you're not stupid."

A pull of the lever. The cracking bolts are strong, lifting high into the clouds. It is a thrilling sight. Sarah turns from the satisfied faces of Ruth and the others, seeing in them a thorn bush of revolution that she does not yet want to stick her hand into, though the excitement of disobedience is tempting.

*

As Sarah readies to leave in the morning, Penny returns home and collapses on the chair nearest to the door. A brief hello. Penny is too tired and her voice too precious to waste on early chatter. Bruce creeps out of the bedroom, brushing the doorframe with his shoulder and hindquarters, and jumps up on the chair to nestle between Penny's legs. Sarah is soon out the door and buying a ticket at the station to the sky train while ignoring the man behind her who huffs as she passes through to deposit her ticket in the slot under the automatic conductor who whistles out, "Enjoy your ride on Sinclair Industries Sky Train Line!" and daring to make a citizen wait behind her as she pushed past the turnstile. So used to it now, she hardly thinks about the danger of hopping over the crevasse to the inside of the car. Any free seats are taken by citizens who pass through the turnstiles quicker, thus being first to claim them, leaving others to stand.

Every morning she watches as the red brick building comes into view. Effortless. Dangerously effortless. Sarah settles into her position so well that she thinks nothing of moving through the employee gate in the early mornings, changing, and then standing on the line in the same place as the day before for the remainder of her shift. She works wordlessly. Checking, packing, her hands becoming used to the motions. She might be punished for talking but with the

93

music of the factory around her, not even the foreman can hear her hum the sonatas she will play once more when she buys a violin. She wonders when her salary will come but is too cautious to ask. Although her plan is to gain some of the inheritance from Penny, she briefly considers that if the pay from this job is enough, she can very well live on her own. It is a contingency she decides to remember.

At exactly twelve o'clock, a siren rings from inside. Lunch. Thirty minutes of rest. Sarah wastes no time. Her stomach cramps, begging for food. At the siren, she jerks away from the packing line to find the only person she counts as a friend. They meet in the quiet locker room. Out of the locker, Ruth grabs a tin lunchbox. When Ruth shifts to sit on the bench, a fuzzy oblong shape falls from her pocket, swinging once from where a chain and silver setting connects it to her belt loop. Eyeing it appraisingly, Sarah notes the worn brindle fur and thin bones that make a severed rabbit's foot.

"What's that?" Sarah asks, pointing a finger at the dangling object. Ruth looks down, then pushes it back into her pocket.

"From a rabbit killed on a graveyard at midnight," she says with a grin. "That's the way to make it lucky. Even had it blessed by the priest."

Ravenous, she tears into her sandwich: two slices of white bread with a thick piece of square meat in between. Following suit, Sarah seeks out the sealed tin box that she purchased that morning from the walking automaton. Pulling the tab, she is met with a pale pink square and a sharp meaty smell that she cannot identify. This, a packet of rusk bread, and a miniature knife make the contents of her meal.

94

Shoganai. She uses the small utensil to spread the meat on each slice of tough bread.

A thought pushes itself through her lips, "Aren't you a citizen?" Sarah asks, shoving a whole slice into her mouth, chewing the bland mixture into mush.

Ruth scoffs as she wipes her hands with the napkin.

"Would be. Don't tell you that you have to be born at a state hospital. Mom didn't have the money, so she gave birth at a free clinic."

Sarah pushes the food to the side of her mouth, asking, "It's expensive?"

"Not if you're already a citizen. Mom wasn't, and the free clinic only gives regular birth certificates. So, I'm one of the 'residential citizens'. To be born a *full* citizen, you have to go to the state hospital and they notarize it there. Can't get that anywhere else. Might be able to forge one. It's popular to go through the black market to do it but it's sketchy. Have to watch out which gang you get it from; don't want to go to the wrong one."

"How do you mean?"

"You live over West, so don't go poking around anywhere you see a triple V. Dangerous, all of 'em."

"I thought this city was supposed to be safe."

"To the right people, it is. I doubt anyone'll trouble with the likes of you, not unless they're bold, or you go lookin' for it," she says, winking.

Ruth takes out two cigarettes, offering one to Sarah who takes it reluctantly. After sharing a match light, Sarah draws and feels a shot of energy at once. The fatigue that had been pushing down on her shoulders earlier subsides, leading her mind to snap up an idea.

"I've heard all about the citizen's visa," she says. "Do you know how to go about getting one?"

95

"Looking to buy into that, too?" she asks, then continues before Sarah answers. "Not surprised. Everyone does. Don't tell you until you get here that it's all luck." Ruth pauses to take out her thermos. When she unscrews the top, Sarah catches a hint of tomato. "Wish I had money to pay for the visa. Besides joining up or finding a rich man to help you through it, that's the only way."

At the mention of rich men, Sarah recalls the non-citizen girls flattering older gentlemen and feels suddenly sympathetic.

"Take more than three years to save up the cash for it, if I don't spend it on anything. Even if I can pay, it's a lottery." Ruth consumes the contents of the thermos, wiping the excess off her upper lip. "Besides, it's all a screw-job. Easier to get the folks coming in every three months to work, then send them back when the temporary pass expires, then do it all over again. Always people looking for cash. It's why we protest, but. . ." She finishes the remainder of her lunch, screwing the top on the thermos, and giving a shrug. "How can things change when we're all so desperate we'll take any scraps?"

This intrigues Sarah who has not considered such radical thinking before. Finding it endearing, she asks, "Come to coffee with me sometime?"

Ruth's sour expression fades into a smile. Unable to refuse, she nods. A siren rings again. Sarah shoves two more slices into her mouth, chewing as she gathers the remains of her lunch back into her locker. She hurries back to the factory floor to her spot to resume the mindless work where her hands move independent of consciousness. Check the packs for damage, a quick see-to, and put each face up in the box. Any dents on a pack go into the damaged bin on her left. Dull work. The work bell sounds, and the foreman bids her to

96

leave with an unemotional, "Come back tomorrow." It had not occurred to her, until just now, that he meant it: his words are her pass to work. An admonishment from any foreman can push her back past the gates and into the desperate crowd and while she may welcome the leisure time it would bring, being jobless creates more problems for her than necessary.

*

Once the end of the week arrives and the final work siren blasts, the foreman tells her to go to the cash cage. When she asks where it is, he turns away from her without answering. Frantic, she searches for Ruth who shows her down the main hallway to a barred window where there is already a line of workers forming a queue. Joining them, Sarah recalls the skinny woman who might have been receiving a salary if not for her own interference.

"What happens if you only work a day?" Sarah asks, pondering the difference between the Alaska fishery and a city factory.

Ruth reaches under her cap to scratch her head, then readjusts it. "Nothing. You get paid by week. Don't make the week: no pay. Don't make quota: no pay. Don't do as you're told: no pay."

Waiting, Sarah nearly falls asleep on her feet, her eyelids drooping despite her will to keep them open by repeated blinking.

"Oh!" Ruth blurts, startling Sarah from her stupor. "Brought this for you."

She slips a thin black cylinder from her pocket, passing it over her shoulder. Taking it, Sarah examines the finger-length object with a line in the center. Pulling it open reveals a gleaming steel blade. Usually, Sarah would accept any gift

97

with gratitude, but not one so dangerous. As quickly as she is able, she sheaths it and hands it back.

"No." Ruth refuses with a shake of her head. "It's yours. You might need it 'round here, especially today." Reluctantly, Sarah stows it.

At her turn, she approaches the window with the thin slat where she says a quick greeting to the old man on the opposite side and eagerly signs for her brown envelope of money just like everyone else and slips it into her pocket.

*

Two figures in the afternoon light with their faces open, speaking in rough slang that she does not recognize, with each wearing their allegiance tied around their necks by a white cloth emblazoned with a triple V sign.

"Give over what you have," one says before punching her in the ribs, causing Sarah to topple over to the wet concrete with a sharp gasp.

She coughs repeatedly, flailing away at any fists and feet that try to find their way to her body. From her peripheral vision, she sees feet from afar walk past. A voice escapes, her own, asking meagerly for help and they walk on. They pass, and she is caught by disbelief. How can anyone walk by violence? Don't they see her? Hands, fingers, clawing at her pockets, taking away unimportant items, including the hidden blade, to the envelope within.

Desperately, she flails like an upturned beetle on the ground. She lands a strong kick on one of their jaws, making him stumble back. Clawing to regain her stance, she weakly rushes after the figure who holds her envelope. The other grabs the back of her collar so roughly that the stitches pop. She turns, whipping her arm around, to hit the back of an open hand to his face. Her knuckles hit his ear and make him pause. With her money foremost on her mind, she turns away to the other who attempts an escape with her cache. Lunging forward, she grasps it, pulling. They tug at it. She is too weak to regain her wages and in the pull the envelope lip flips open, releasing bills to the ground.

Free, the thief flees, and she is left to retrieve the fallen money. Sore and slightly bruised, Sarah runs straight ahead, hoping to discover one of the police automatons in her stupor or perhaps to the nearest police station, rationalizing that there must be one close by in a city this large. It might be rude of her to push through the sidewalk traffic as she does, indeed more than a few people jeer or shout after her that she should mind her steps. One fellow calls her a "blue louse" in reference to her work coveralls. If not for her desperation, she might turn back to find the man and give him what-for.

Up the street, a metallic sign with the city's police badge rotates atop a round-roofed concrete building. There, a hulking machine stands waiting in the same manner as the others she had seen, standing idle with as much use as a broken compass. Once seeing her, however, its eyes brighten immediately with a blue glow and a whirring of starting gears echoing in their empty casement. With a hollow, worn, recorded voice, it begins listing several police services that it can perform. Impatient, she pushes the alert button with an open palm which begins strobing once signaled and sits wearily on the sidewalk. Those who pass her move along, though one or two cast a sympathetic gaze before continuing on their route.

Sirens reach her and the police car parks on the curb. From it emerges two broad-shouldered men in black police uniforms. In a quick assessment, one of the men glances from Sarah to the automaton, down and up the street, and, seeing no immediate emergency, approaches the still-whirring machine. Taking out a key from the inside of his brass buttoned jacket, he pulls open the glowing light to reveal an inside lock. Inserting the key and turning it to the left ceases the flashing. Taking one appraising look, he asks to see her citizenry card. Obligingly, Sarah takes it from her wallet and gives it to him. His face falls when he scans the paper, then gives it back. Gently slipping his hand into his pocket, he removes a pad and pen, asks her to explain what happened, and writes down every word spewing from her mouth, after which he hands it to her to sign on the bottom line, tells her they will do what they can, and offers to drive her home.

"What's the address?" he asks and when she gives it there is an exchange of glances between them before the officer begins driving.

With Sarah's nerves easing, she finds fatigue weighing on her eyelids and the lull of the car traveling uphill after hill puts her into a light slumber waking only with the click of the door as an officer guides her out and to the house. He leaves her to walk the path alone, watching for as long as it takes for her to reach the front entrance. A few knocks and Penny opens the front door, appraising Sarah's disheveled clothing and tangled hair.

"What happened?"

"Mugged."

She takes her gently by the shoulders, seeing the police car drive away as she closes the door, and sits Sarah on the nearest chair, ordering her to rest, only to then slip

100

away into the kitchen for a good while and return with a sweet-smelling beverage in a floral china teacup. Kneeling, Penny offers her the cup that her cousin takes willingly, drinking the wonderfully warm milk and maple syrup concoction.

"What happened?" Penny asks again, a prying concern thick on her voice.

"I went to the police."

"The police? You should have called me straight away. Coppers do all they can but, well, a city with troubles like this ignores little inconveniences like theft."

"They could have done something," she says, after a pause.

"And what would that be?" Penny asks, reaching out to run her fingers through her hair to straighten the tangles only to have Sarah bat her hand away. Penny withdraws her hand into her lap. After a few silent moments, she rises to sit before the semaphore, and switches it on, waiting a moment for it to sound the monotone beep signaling its connection to the telephone line.

"Do you know their names? Do you remember what they look like? "

Sarah furrows her brows, "Shouldn't the police—"

"—This isn't Alaska where police can go around and search every neighbor. Now, on the other hand, that's one thing *we* can take care of. Tell me what you remember."

"We?"

Penny looks at her wryly. "Surely you know by now what work this family does?"

Hesitant at first, she does not speak. Not only is she opposed to any act that may cause her to become more indebted, she also resents her younger relative playing the part of a concerned parent. The right thing to do would be to leave it to the authorities. Then she remembers their irritation towards her and a vague promise of justice. In a city of thousands, is it even possible to find a few common thieves? Ruth had mentioned gangs before, and if it is as Penny insinuates, perhaps this is the most direct route to retribution. The thought of some form of justice is appealing.

6

Penelope
Retaliation

On Sunday, the church is an icon of fellowship in the surrounding copse, a clean white plaster structure with a large red cross calling out from the steeple. There is a main court lined with the many flowers that grow and are tended by the church ladies who sell bouquets in spring and summer to raise money. Penny cares nothing for the bits of charitability nor for any sense of community that the other ladies may enjoy. Her sanctum is in song.

When service completes with a lengthy "Amen.", Penny files out of her spot in the choir loft, removing her cotton robe along with the others, revealing her bright cherry-red dress underneath. She departs with cheerful farewells to the other church ladies, some of whom smile politely, while others roll their eyes over her from toe to head and merely respond with a tart goodbye. Outside into the graying skies where the early afternoon sun begins to peek out in slips of golden threads, she waits by the open entrance door where Pastor stands to shake hands with the departing congregation. George appears, holding onto Timmy's hand while clutching a sleeping Rose in his other arm. Taking the initiative, Penny takes several long steps to meet George with a sweet demeanor. She gently takes Rose, who gives the smallest whimper of protest but quiets when she snuggles into Penny's arms.

Looking down, she greets Timmy as the boy squeals in delight and jumps up and down. When Penny looks up again, she notices a stranger standing next to the family. A man whose lean frame is dressed in a cream long sleeve shirt that is tucked into chestnut brown slacks and buttoned at the wrists and high to the collar where a maroon and white plaid tie is knotted comfortably snug against his top button. Fitted over his shirt is a finely knit wine colored sweater vest to further ensure that every part of him is fashionably covered. Everything, that is, except for his smooth, taut skin emblazoned by a permanent raspberry shade and in between spots of flesh about his hands are thick, cutaneous scars. The strip of skin on his exposed neck show the blotchy brown scars that trail up half the width of his throat, across the left side of his face in a scaly mass, deepening gradually into a thick, slanting scar cutting through his brow, pulling the flesh down around his eye, and disappearing into his cleanly-parted hairline and finishing with a tip missing off his right earlobe.

"This is Abraham Shimamura," George introduces, grinning.

Doing her best to avoid lingering on his mangled features, she defaults to giving him a pleasant greeting, but the meeting is cut short by the rest of the congregation filing out, eager to shake the pastor's hand, while the children push and pull to wiggle away to play. Together, they walk to George's car. Cautiously, Penny asks Abe one of the many introductory questions she has used in the past to engage others. His answer is the removal of his wallet and flips it open to present a black-and-white wedding portrait of a couple so close to each other as if they are molded together seamlessly. Abe, suited in a tuxedo and smiling widely, stands next to his wife with an even wider smile that plumps up her full cheeks.

"You can't tell," he says with a twitch of his mouth as if to hold back a smirk, "but she has red hair."

"She's lovely," Penny offers, admiring, with a hint of envy, the obvious love between the two. "I envy you."

"You don't have a beau?" he asks, more a statement than a question.

She bites back her initial retort, unsure of whether it is a genuinely innocent inquiry or a prompt to uproot any admission of a connection to George beyond the familial. She flips her hair back with a toss of her fingers, "I dare not!" she exclaims teasingly.

*

She sits, hidden in the back seat of the car, Abe in the front seat behind the wheel, skimming station on the car radio as Penny watches from the partly rolled down window as the old man and three of his young *kyodai* arrogantly strut the downtown streets in the darker spaces of the balloon blind spots, confident that their reputation as the ruthless Shizuka gang members will protect them. Ten minutes as an outsider in V gang territory is all it takes for several adolescents to approach confidently in their matching jackets and bandana masks, each one gripping a switchblade, understanding precisely who four Japanese men in black suits could be.

"Run off, gramps. You all's stumbled on the wrong road."

He shakes his head once.

"My name is Namahage," he says.

In a turn of hands, bullets crack from each Shizuka gun, connecting with body parts, leaving two youngsters wounded but alive and writhing where they fall on the street.

105

Some moan in pain, some are in quiet shock. The old man removes a clean, freshly sharpened knife from within his jacket. A nod cues the *kyodai* to grasp the remaining survivors by the scalp and jerk upwards, forcing each face to see the punishment awaiting them. Namahage thrusts a free hand into one of the hooligan's mouths, pulling on a wet tongue and pinching it between his fingers. In several swift motions, the blade cuts a symbol into flesh. Regardless of protestations, they are all given the silent mark on once-virgin tongues.

Watching the violence souses her with a mild unease as they are now writhing on the street, clutching their mouths, the suited men return to the vehicle. One takes the passenger's seat, letting the old man sit next to Penelope, passing her a torn envelope full of several single dollar bills. She scoffs at the amount.

"How much they take?" one of the *kyodai* asks as the car pulls away.

"Horsefeathers," she says, "but that's not the point."

"Then what is?"

"What would you do if someone stole from your family?"

He laughs before saying, "I'd cut out their tongue."

*

As soon as she arrives at the house, and is greeted by Bruce who meows and rubs her leg, she lets herself into Sarah's room to leave the envelope on the nightstand.

"What are you doing?" she asks, but he is gone upstairs before she is able catch him. He moves faster than she does since he is in comfortable loafers and she in high heels. How can she properly chase him? Furious, he runs upstairs to Ojiisan's room. Penny takes big strides to get to him, her skirt swishing against her calves and then stops before the doorframe separating the stairs from the flat. A thunderous quarrel pounds against the walls like storm waters bashing on boulders. *Jishin, Kaminari, Kaji, Oyaji,* she remembers. Earthquake, Thunder, Fire, and Father; those which always deserve fear.

She withdraws, preferring to wait at the point where their argument began until she hears his returning stomps. He turns to her, looking from under lowered eyelids, his cheeks burning red.

"What exactly was that?" she asks, baiting, her hazel eyes boring through him.

"Don't worry about it."

"I'm not worried," she answers as he escapes out the front door.

Going to the driver's side of his car and opening the door, he finds that she has followed him. Careful to smooth the backside of her skirt in the passenger seat, she is about to speak when George lets out a gruff sigh that causes her to pause, assessing his emotionless face.

Finally, he shouts, startling her, "How come you can disobey!?"

This is a beginning and she won't let it go so quickly. Her response is a hearty laugh.

"Because I'm not his son." She lets out a sigh. "What they did to Sarah they do to us. Let it go and the other gangs will think they can do whatever they want. We have to pull them out at the root."

Without a reply, George puts his key in the ignition, bringing the engine to a rolling rumble. In an impatient impulse, Penelope gets out and rushes to her bicycle. She pedals furiously, not stopping until the spiral lights give way to old electric lampposts, beyond the central city area. The streets are dimmer, easing her eyes.

Looking up, she tries to spot the starlight that is always hidden by the city. It seems that here, too, those winding lights still block the twinkling sky. Penny passes the brick buildings, many of them empty and boarded up—old businesses that Sinclair Industries made obsolete. Tacked onto the boards are advertisements, one a poster of a uniformed officer saluting an American flag with one hand and holding a citizen's passbook in the other, the caption reading "Serve your country. Become a Citizen." Another is a portrait of Robert Sinclair in a blue suit and red tie, his face tilted upwards just enough so that it seems he looks down on her. In his arms he holds a healthy white baby. Underneath his deceptively kind, clean-shaven, soft face is written: "Sinclair Industries is working for you."

Yet the only poster that gives her pause is of a woman, a microphone next to her smiling mouth while her eyes look to an invisible spot. Platinum-blond curls pinned up to show off curvy red lips. Sky-blue eyes. Kate Page. "Live every night at The Fortune Follies." Penny does not bother looking around when she takes down the poster, folding it into quarters and hiding it in her purse.

On the corner between Chikata Drugs and the
Tazuma five-and-dime, both of which had closed hours
before, stands an electric sign fixed on the corner of the
building. The oval sign, now lit, flashes red and blue art
nouveau letters "The Black and Tan Club." She passes the
front door to the alley, a narrow descending staircase leading
to the basement side entrance into the old club. Spying
Florence at one of the tables, she taps her shoulder, causing
the woman to jerk in her direction to see Penny and her hair
in tight curls.

"You made it after all!" Penny says to her, sitting
down quickly. "I was beginning to think you didn't receive
my message. Now, I don't have much time, you know, I'm
going up on stage." She takes the glass on the table to drink
and sets it down again. "I only wanted to clear up some fuss
about your Patriots. I happened to visit Ms. Page recently."
This catches attention. "And couldn't help but notice a
trinket." She draws a line around her wrist with a finger.

"I'm sure I don't know what you mean."

"Certainly not," she teases.

Suddenly, Penny moves her head sharply to the
opening front door. Instead of the person she hopes for, it is a
woman she doesn't recognize. When Florence turns to see,
she waves.

"Love to chat," Florence says and gives a languid
grin. "only I'm not here on social matters."

"I'm sure it's nothing, then," Penny says. "Well," she
stands up again. "it's been some time. We should have a
drink after and catch up."

"No, no," Florence refuses quickly, "I came here just
to answer your call and ask a favor."

Penny straightens, rolling her eyes, "Oh?"

"You're a performer," Florence says, gesturing with her palms open. "If you put your name to our cause, maybe speak out at a rally, or even make an announcement before you sing, we would get more supporters. Here." She withdraws a leaflet from the purse hanging on her shoulder. On its clean white front typewritten letters spell out, "Rally for Liberty presented by The Patriot Liberty Union of Seattle" at the top with the Smith Tower in black ink and a red- white-and-blue striped star above it with eagle wings. She looks from it to Florence.

"I won't. And you'd be wise to get these out of here. Look around," she says seriously. Her sights rolling over the people ordering drinks, those sitting, and finds that almost all are wearing either blue or brown overalls. "Sinclair workers are my biggest audience. They wouldn't have any work without Sinclair. You think they'd want to hear me sing if I made speeches criticizing the hand that feeds them?" Florence lets the hand holding the leaflet fall.

"Excuse me. I have to get ready," Penny states. The woman sits down next to Florence, a petite girl wearing a too-bright green dress who is about to introduce herself when Penny whisks away.

The lights illuminate the modest stage. From a trap door beneath the black vinyl floor, just behind the row of lightbulbs around the front of the stage, emerges an automaton, the top half a body, the bottom a thick post covered by a black velvet cloth that matches its tuxedo jacket. A metal face with soldered-on triangle nose, and brown circular eyes of polished acrylic. The head is a tin cylinder wearing a beaver top hat that must have been secured to it somehow since it does not fall whenever the machine jerks. With a round speaker for a mouth, it announces in a human voice, "Please welcome for her debut at The Black and Tan Club, Ms. Penny Morgan."

The lights move to the curtain. The machine descends. Out she comes in a tight-fitting dress that pulls in at the waist, giving her a round hourglass figure. She smiles with her big pink lips, and the band behind her starts to play. As she sings, her body moves, her shoulders thrust forward. Having the presence of a performer, she captures the audience's attention with her movements and her classical voice, not often heard. Florence watches grimly as Penny moves to the bar near the end of the song, tapping on a man's cap flirtatiously as the song ends. Once the band is between sets, Penny appears at the bar where she meets the two suited men and is given a cigarette by the serious man who lights it for her. Penny feigns happiness as she pours herself a glass of liqueur. When she drinks, it stings her throat just a little, then her body warms from the inside. She does not notice how much she has drunk until Florence pokes her from a stupor to tell her that they will leave.

"Why?" Penny asks. "I'm singing again in an hour."

"Maybe you forgot," she says, being purposefully vitriolic, "but we're rather busy, and having so few people, Ms. Morgan, we have more work to do."
Penny furrows her eyebrows. She puts her drink down, keeping her lit cigarette between a thumb and two fingers as one of the suited men watches her interaction.

"If you're overworked, then perhaps it's best to quit before a disaster," she advises. "I have my reputation and you have yours. We can't muddle *those* together, now can we?"

"No, I suppose we can't." Florence does not take her eyes off Penny. "But which reputation would that be?" She moves a pointing forefinger between herself and the surrounding men, as if there must be some speck of filth on them.

"We're contemporaries," Penny explains. "What else can we do but be ourselves?"

Without saying any more, Florence departs. Penny lets out a disappointed breath, then turns back to continue a conversation with George.

"Go on, then. Give me a Japanese name. I've never had one."

"Ah, it's too difficult," he says, tilting his head to the side in thought.

"Do it anyway."

She leans against the bar, resting an elbow, and nestling her chin on the back of her hand.

"I know one for you," Abe says with an infectious smirk. "Himeko."

Little Princess. Her response is a wrinkling of her nose, making Abe chuckle at her youth.

"Why not choose one for yourself?" George asks as if Abe had said nothing.

"Why? Because I don't know any Japanese names."

"Think of one. You know yourself better than I do."

"But that's not the game!" she admonishes, slapping her hand on the side of the bar and he smiles. "What you choose tells me what you think of me, just like what I choose for you."

"Pe-ne-ro-pi."

Abe lets a throaty laugh escape, which George reacts to with a light snicker.

"No! You can't cheat like that."

He turns to her, his mouth forms as if he's about to say "What?"

"A *Japanese* name. Penelope is not Japanese."

"It is if I say it like Pe-ne-ro-pi."

Inserting himself into the spar, Abe teases George with, "And now you see why so few enjoy your company, with remarks like that."

Smiling thinly, she remembers a bitter drink and a nostalgia covering her as prickling as ice. Like many nightclubs, this one has an extravagant décor with a color scheme of golds and silvers in a distracting art nouveau style that tests her attention.

"There's something to love in everyone," she says, thinking of *Oniisan*. "We just have to find it. Isn't that right?"

She searches the emotionless slate looking back at her, concluding that what he needs most from her is friendship, even if he will not admit to it. His face breaks with the twitch of one eye, and he shies away, but she follows his line of sight to one of the waitresses walking past who for a moment turns her head slightly to their direction as if to divine what a Japanese man is doing with a woman like Penelope.

"Yes, it's beautiful. For me, I don't need it; I don't care. You should try not caring about it and things won't bother you. Forget about memories."

"Memories make us who we are," she retorts, "and most can't help but be reminded of them every day, like our brother Abe here."

She waits as George ponders to himself, shifting his gaze over to Shimamura-san, and back to Penny.

"At least Abe had a chance," he says, regret heavy on his tongue.

Finding it difficult to choke back her ire, she blurts out, "A chance!? To do what? Fight or die? And *if* you live to come home from hell, what then?"

As the club is all noise and rumpus, the reaction to her outburst is reserved to the two men near her with Abe looking away to ignore the argument.

"You see?" he challenges. "You're mad because of memories. Forget it, don't worry about it."

"I know why you always say that," she says, putting out her cigarette in the complementary ashtray set at the bar and rising, then takes a breath sucking through her teeth, "It's a lie."

His answer is a shrug of his shoulders and him pulling himself up from his slouch, back straight. She glances at the clock above the bar, ready to dismiss herself.

"You'll stay for the rest, won't you?" she asks abruptly.

Without waiting for him to answer, she slips off into the shadows. The audience is more crowded now when she re-approaches the stage after the introduction to sing one of her favorites.

*

Heavy makeup remains plastered on her face as they walk up the stairs out of the muggy basement club into the stagnant early morning heat. The streets are empty but for the occasional sky train overhead or the clanking steps of the patrolling iron policemen that they pass on the sidewalk, a hulking box-like man made of metal plates bolted together. Large round metal spokes on its hips connect with gears that make its legs and arms move, a large police symbol painted on its back. As Penny passes it, a voice asks, "Do you need assistance?" Looking back at it, she finds its chest alight—a beacon in the dark recess—its open speaker mouth serving as a two-way radio to the nearest police station. All one has to do is push the red button marked "call" above the light and it connects by wire. The yellow button next to it is marked "Emergency" for situations of extreme danger, such as a robbery or severe injury. Press it, and police officers arrive at the destination in moments.

Penny eyes George, matching his quick pace so they can make it to one of the late departing sky trains.

"So," she says, bringing a subject up again, "if you don't love your wife, why did you bother getting married?"

A long pause is his answer.

"Don't you love her at all—even a little?" Penny asks, low and concerned.

An electric sign reading "Jackson Street Station" is their destination. The sky train passes through a steel structure. They walk together up the steps to the ticket booth run by an old automaton similar to the one in the club. Not having to pay because of her status, Penny and George continue to the platform, passing a bit of graffiti painted on the wall that had Sinclair's name written in red and a large X slashed through it. She is surprised it is still there, it ought to have been cleaned by now. Then again, this section is outside the citizens' area. When he stands by her. He refuses to look at her, at the smile that cannot be meant for him. He squeezes his eyes shut, tilting his head to the right, and crosses his arms in front of his chest, shaking his head once. The arriving train interrupts her and they step in, sitting down where they pleased. The train was nearly empty except for an older man sleeping with his head resting back against the window.

"Why not let her go back to Japan?" she queries carefully.

"If she wants to go she can go by herself."

A husband and wife should be as one, she recalls the pastor teaching, her heart softening.

Once, Penny sang to herself as she lay on her stomach on the outdoor picnic table. A box of crayons that she brought with her was set just within reach. With a green crayon, she drew on a discarded newspaper plastered with war stories she wanted to ignore: an arching rainbow in the corner, thick beams evaporating into multicolored hearts. In the center she wrote in large cursive letters "*L'amour toujours.*" The light was fading, and it was getting colder. The Idaho cold. She would stay out as long as she could until the cold forced her inside. Her baby cousin was darling, but he slept lightly. The enclosed space had long since grated against her, with its suffocating air that hung with the musk of bodies, unwashed hair, and now all the unpleasant odors that babies make.

Shuffling steps stopped at her. A loud scoff made her turn. Uncle stood there in his dusty coveralls, face dappled with sweat and grime. He was late coming back. The farm workers had come back three hours before. She had seen them coming back in through the gate as she finished her work shift. She stuck out her tongue at him childishly, expecting him to shake his head at her and return to the barracks. He thrust forward, grabbing her pink tongue with his workman's fingers that tasted of dry soil and salt, pinching his short, dirt-caked nails into it.

"You a foul girl," he said in his best English. She brought her hand up to strike his wrist as many times as it took until he let go. She spat out the taste of him. He remained there, looking down on her like a principal at a student. "Like *Shitakiri Suzume*. I cut your tongue, maybe." At home, she pins the stolen poster on the back side of her door, smoothing out the creases.

7
Sarah
Walking Mechanizations

Approaching the gates on a rarely clear morning, Sarah
sees the jobless waiting before the bars and a foreman
reaching up to the chalkboard. He pulls it down, wipes it
clean, and writes a disastrous "45¢" for the daily wage with a
bit of chalk.

Sarah hurries in, passing employees whispering
grievances to each other regarding the changed rate. Ignoring
them, she begins her routine on the work floor in a steady
motion that ceases only when the lunch bell sounds.
At the end of the line, she and Ruth meet. They hold their
conversation until they reach confines of the locker room for
fear of a foreman shouting, "No talking on the work floor!"
At the locker room door, Ruth takes Sarah by the hand
playfully and guides her through another door.
        "Come this way," Ruth says with mischief in her eye.
"Lemme show you the real digs."

Ruth leads her through the door, down a hall to
another door where ear protectors hang on hooks. Ruth takes
two, shoving one into Sarah's chest. Already, the grinding
and shrieking from the other side makes her slip on the
hearing protectors. As she opens the door, the lights are the
brightest she has seen so far in the factory, though daylight
comes in through the high, thin windows that are there only
to satisfy the minimal state safety regulations. Ruth guides
her through the corridors. It is the foremen's lunch break; two
hours they are given to do as they please without having to
clock out – a small privilege for being citizens. Without them

118

and their watchful eyes, she and Ruth are free to wander. Immediately, Sarah is drawn to the racks upon racks holding metal bodies. Some she recognizes as the walking food dispensers while still more are forms she has never seen. Arms welded together. Staring out from sockets of rounded steel heads are eyes so real they might be human, though glossy and with red veins connecting from behind the open sockets.

"Here's what I do all day. Look," she says, hefting one of the bulky arms fitted with a type of single barrel gun before letting it fall. "This one's just a repair. One of the police automatons, see." She points at the silver badge welded to the machine's metal chest. "It came in earlier with BB gun bullet dents all over it and an arm missing. Kids like to use them for target practice after school. I fix up at least five of these a week. But that's not the best part."

She walks away, leaving Sarah to follow her to one of the racks at the end of a long line. The metal bodies are polished to shine like silver. Like a man, they have arms and legs. Yet unlike a man there are the bolt guns welded to forearms, the thick industrial metal encasing the inner springs and gears. A high collar protects a skeletal neck holding up a heavy skull without a mouth or nose, but with two overly large empty eye sockets.

Sarah gawks, reaching out to it, her fingertips following her elongated reflection in the polished steel to the wires in the collared neck.

"Like the ones in the war," Sarah says, remembering a long-ago newspaper photo of the clunky steel machines fighting alongside American soldiers.

"But these are much newer. Will they be used for. . ." she trails off, noticing Ruth nod once.

"Might use these strongmen for the military or who knows what. Hope they do. Maybe then men'll stop dying in jolly wars." She shakes her head, jutting dirty hands into her pockets.

Sarah flicks her finger against the carapace then pulls away from the inhuman object.

"There's a little get-together I'm having next Saturday. You working?" Ruth asks abruptly.
"I work every morning. Foreman said to come in every day at six."

She grimaces briefly, then her face lightens at another idea. "After work? I was really hoping you'd come; I'd like you to be there."
Instead of outright refusing, she says, "Maybe," which seems to satisfy her friend.

Checking the time, Sarah returns to the work floor where the daily movements have become so ingrained that she is no longer conscious of her body parts. It is like a focused dream that causes her to forget much of what occurs outside the immediate task of putting products into boxes, waking only when the bell sounds.

*

First day, second day, third day, fourth. Packing cigarettes, so many that the tobacco seeps into her skin, causing Penny to complain when Sarah comes home, immediately nagging her to take a bath. After a week, she returns to the window with the steel bars that separate her from the old man. After giving him a closer look decides that he isn't that old. Much older than herself but not to the point of retirement.

120

His brown hair, sprinkled with gray, had been combed back with pomade. Even in the dull lamps overhead, his hair glistens.

"Oh, yes, I remember you," he says cheerfully, looking up from the giant ledger opened on the other side and a receipt book next to it. "Don't see too many Japs working here."

Sarah decides to ignore the comment. If she talks back, he might refuse to give her pay. Men in charge often do as they like. He opens the thick receipt book to a new page and with his pen he fills out her name, the date, and her weekly salary. She follows his script closely as he writes the amount. Again, it is less than she earned in Anchorage, but here she doesn't have to share it. Her mother won't be able to take it from her and hide it in the family account; it is hers to do with as she likes. He passes her a brown envelope that she takes greedily. A slam of the old man's stamp in the ledger and she disappears, quickly stepping from the factory to the sky train.

*

Downtown, she speeds past food shops and toy stores and an unskilled street guitarist until she finds a window with instruments sitting on the other side. Some are traditional, and others are infused with moving gears, the latter having a standing poster set next to them reading "Sinclair Industries presents: The Vota Series! A clearer, stronger, melodious sound from the best craftsmen around the world." She thinks of the cheap materials used in the factory manufacturing and wonders how much truth there is in the advertisement. As she pushes the door open, a bell chimes that announces her entrance to a black-bearded salesman behind the register and prompting him to ask, "What can I do for you?"

"I want to buy a violin."

He twitches his lip into a sardonic grin.

"Buy? Maybe you should start off with something easier—"

"—I already know how to play," she interrupts.

He nods, his expression softening. He raises his arm, pointing to the rightmost wall, "All the stringed instruments are there."

Sarah appraises them quickly. Rows of violins, from child-sized up to adult. Cheaply-made violins that seem glued together next to quality crafted ones. Towards the end are a few violins set by a back wall of cellos. In a locked glass case are the mechanized Vota instruments. She passes the case, noting the four instruments. She runs her fingers lightly over each of the remaining instruments, testing the smoothness, making sure the fingerboards are straight. Pushing her face close to the wood she scrutinizes the inlaid purfling, the decorative edge set in the top plate of the instrument.

Unbroken grain lines mean it has been painted on; a cheap tactic to save money and sacrifice quality. On the back of the fingerboard, the wood is bright brown and not the ebony it should be. Rather than wasting her time picking it up, she lifts it slightly at the bottom to feel the weight and exhales sharply from her nostrils like a bull displeased with its given mate. It was too heavy and poorly carved. The next is of slightly better workmanship and the one next to that even better – older, slightly battered, and with a molasses varnish. Left with two options, she takes the final violin, holding it up. Her arm extends, nestling the base at her neck, turning her head so her chin nearly touches the tip of the wood. With her finger, she plucks at the strings. Too flat. She tightens the pins until the sound eases into tune.

She turns to the salesman, "Do you have a rosined bow?"

He twists around behind the register where several bows hang, takes one, and holds it out to her. Sarah pulls it from him with delicate fingers. Her wrist loose, she sets the bow to the strings and begins to play. It is as if the music never left her.

She pays in cash without looking at the price, realizing how expensive it is when she sees only a few dollars left in the envelope. Her regret lasts only a short while, dissipated by the weighty case while returning to the house on the hill where the lights are always on. Penny asks the usual questions the moment Sarah comes through the door then stops when she notices what Sarah holds in her hand.

"What's that?" she asks, her voice carrying a tone of disapproval. "You didn't buy a new one already? Well, in that case, it looks like you got paid. Do you have the rent?" Sarah ignores her cousin's nagging by looking down at the case.

"Want to see?" she offers.

Penny's face suddenly brightens, so easily distracted by anything to do with music.

"Yes! You'll play, won't you?"

Sarah takes a seat, putting the case on her lap.

Opening it, she first removes the bow and the rosin. After scratching marks in the hard amber with a nail file, that Penny eagerly fetches for her, she prepares the horsehair by sliding the top of the rosin across the bow, dusting the strings with yellow amber. Once it is thoroughly covered, she rests

123

the solid sap back in the case's alcove. Lifting the curved wood, she holds it against her shoulder and chin, turning the pegs, fine-tuning, plucking chords, until the tone is perfect. She takes it by the neck, puts the case on the floor, stands up with the bow in hand. Penny kneels, looking up with her penetrating eyes, anticipating a performance.

Sarah puts the bow to strings, at once seeing the notes in her mind, hearing the music.

Yet, the sound it emits is wrong. Her vision drawn to the eyes staring at her instead of the strings. Concentrating as best as she can to hold the bow steady, it moves loosely, causing her to miss the chords she means to catch. Frustrated, she stops, putting it away in the case, dismissing herself to her room, telling Penny she is too tired to play. She rests the violin on the bed, slamming the door closed. The truth was too terrible. It had been so long since she last played. She tries to remember the last time. Before the internment. Before 1942.

They were given tags with numbers to pin on their shirts.

The soldiers gave Papa a white card with a number, which the young girl caught a glimpse of. The man said nothing, only pointed to the big square building ahead. She and all the many bodies shuffled together into the single-story building made of a simple post frame with boards nailed on to provide thin protection. While she stood, she could peer through the gaps to the outside wasteland.

"Welcome," said a man at the front she couldn't see. "I hope you all will be able to live here in a comfort as close as possible to your life before you arrived."

Penny hissed to Marge. She looked over, surprised. Penny

made her hand into a mouth, moving her thumb up and down and rolling her eyes. Marge tried to hold back her amusement, but a chortle escaped. Auntie looked down at Penny, glaring at her.

"There are many occupations available," the man went on as Penny squatted down on the dirt floor to draw patterns with her index finger. "Some farming work, work fashioning war rations and work in the camp munitions factory contracted through a new contract, should you wish to apply."

After drawing a star pattern, she tapped on Sarah's pony shoe when Auntie wasn't looking. This time Sarah ignored her. Penny whispered her name, too loudly. Auntie heard it, bent down and pinched Penny on her hand. Startled, she stood straight up. The motion alerted her mother who looked down at her daughter rubbing a pink mark on the back of her hand. She turned from Auntie and back to the man speaking who finished his speech, thus allowing them to begin their lives within the fences. They soon found their lodgings. Inside was an apartment that was scarcely as big as their own living room at home. It had two green starched cots in the center with folded wool blankets on the ends, and between the cots was a little heating stove. It must have been a mistake, she kept thinking. Papa must have felt the same, as he said.

"I'll ask one of the soldiers if we have the right room." At the same moment, Mama put her suitcase down and went to the heater.

"Sarah, Louise, put your things away and move one of these cots to the other side."
They both moved without speaking, as if in a dream.

She woke to the cold. Lying on the cot next to Mama, her eyes opening to the dark room, she thought that she must be in the wrong place. Why else was Sarah using her overcoat as an extra blanket or sharing this narrow bed instead of being in her own, warm room. When she tried to turn over to get comfortable, Mama was there so she couldn't move. Feeling a body against her own was strange. She hadn't been so near her mother since she was small, and it felt so foreign. Papa was somewhere away from her eyes but could hear the snoring and Mama's whistling breathing magnified and became part of her own. When she wakes up again on the single bed scratching her arms from the itchy wool, it doesn't seem right. She knows she must be moving-- she can see her legs bending at the knees then her body turning over, though it turns some second shadow and another shell remains to follow the first and connect with the rest of it. This wasn't her home. It was wrong. How quickly they had to pack their treasured possessions and all they had to leave behind.

"You can't bring it," Mama told her. "You might be able to play it for a while but then the strings will break and where will you get new ones?"

"It'll be fine," she said defiantly.

"Think: if we sell it we can use the money," she continued as if she hadn't heard.

She took the case and set it next to her one bag of luggage by the door and looked to Louise, hoping that she might come to her help, but instead she busied herself covering the sofa with one of the peony-printed bed sheets that had come from Mama and Papa's bed. For a moment, her head turned to her little sister and she thought she might say something, but she had turned to pick up another sheet from the floor to cover one of the chairs next to the sofa. Desperately, she calls loud enough for her and even for

126

Mama to hear but she ignores her, smoothing the sheet out on the upholstery.

"It's mine," she said pitifully.

Yet her attempt to soften her mother's heart failed. With tightened lips and a swift grasp, Mama reached out to take the treasure. Panicked, Sarah lunged at it, pulling the case towards her.

"No, Mama—I can't!" she screamed.

"We talked about this," Mama scolded while struggling to tear the object from her daughter's grip. "We can't bring it, so we should at least get some money for it."

"No, I won't!"

"Sarah, do it now," she said.

She would sell it one way or another, Sarah knew. But she couldn't let it go without a fight. She held the case tighter, her tears wetting the leather. Mama pulled it loose with a sharp pull and Sarah let out a yelp that sounded like a dog whose tail has been stepped on.

"No, Mama!" she cried. "Please, don't!"

Sarah reached out to capture it, then Mama pinched her fleshy arms and hands so that she would let go. But she didn't, so Mama started to slap, making Sarah cry harder. Finally, weak from the pulling and beating, Sarah felt her arms weaken and stood there, defeated, eyes still running, stunned that her very soul was removed so easily.

That violin had been in her life for seven years, it was as much a part of her as her nose or lips, and she could not believe how easily it had been amputated from her body. All she could process was that her life had been taken from her and where would she be able to buy another now if they had no money and only the clothes on their backs? Her music, her songs, her heart. What would she do with her fingers now?

"It's done," she said sternly. "Wipe away those tears."

Sarah squeezed her eyes shut to the darkness around her to sleep again, not wanting to wake into this alien place, the constant foreign chirping from mysterious insects infested her mind and refused to let her descend into a dreamless sleep. When there were moments of silence in the deep, she pleaded to the night to let the silence remain so that she could sleep even for a moment.

No matter how she shut her eyes and body to the alien world around her, she could not settle her mind against it. Mama's breathing beside her was deep and rhythmic. It amazed her that she could sleep so soundly while the whole of nature sang loudly in the night. Then there was Louise snoring. Her mind wept in frustration. Reaching her hands up from the warm womb of her bed, she fluffed her pillow against the rough cot and in doing so, caused the corner of the blanket the slip away from her left leg. She shuddered at the brisk sensation of her exposed skin in the freezing air.

Speedily exiting the sky train station, Sarah brushes past an old man foraging through a trash can for a discarded newspaper. The corridor is full of posters tacked up on the wall, one with half a globe painted on it, the United States and Asia and the Pacific Ocean between. The heading reads "Seattle Nearest and Fastest Route to Orient. The Fastest and Finest Terminals on the Pacific." A glittering flash catches her eye to one young girl whose skin glimmers. Looking closer, her skin is adorned with gold flecks that display the frivolities of youth.

It is a short walk to the little café on Virginia Street is a cozy shop framed with engraved maple wood columns in the Urnes-Romanesque style and Nordic knot carvings with hidden folk creatures set amongst the twisting curls that spiral up each pillar. Inside, she finds that Ruth is there already, reading a newspaper in front of her on the table. She lifts her head to drink from a cup and, seeing Sarah, waves her over.

"I ordered you a black coffee. I hope that's okay."

"Oh, yes," she says, sitting in the empty chair made of cheap chrome and a plastic cushion, in front of a white mug set on the blue table.

She drinks little as the coffee is too strong and thick for her liking. In her line of vision, she notices an average man staring at them just long enough for her to catch the grimace on his face.

Ruth shrugs and offers, "Some people can never move on. It's not your fault."

"Did you see the newspaper?" Ruth asks, already through with her coffee and ordering a refill.

"I never read the newspaper."

"Oh," she tries to hide her disappointment, "well, you've seen more of the protestors, some of them Patriots, haven't you? They always loiter around work."
Sarah nods.

"They've tried to get Sinclair shut down for years. Imagine if they manage it! Anyhow, that singer, Kate Page was seen 'round with one of them, going to a meeting of some sort."

Sarah dismisses the subject with a shrug.

"Well, her career is over. Look here," she notes, pointing at a black-and-white photo spread open in front of her in the newspaper. The singer she recognizes, despite a handkerchief covering her head and tied under her square chin, speaking to Florence at the back porch of a house.

129

"How did they get the pictures?"

"What?"

"The pictures. It looks like they're at her house and it's so close. Wouldn't they have noticed a cameraman there?"

"The balloons."

Sarah looks at her quizzically.

"The balloons. Don't you know? They have cameras and recorders. It's all part the worry over communism. First it was Nazis and now it's communists. . ."

Ruth keeps talking, but Sarah blanks it out, disturbed at the thought that she had been watched every time she left the house, walked down the street, picked her teeth, or blew her nose. Floating cameras. Memories rush back of her first attack when thieves shoved her to grab what money she had and the police doing no more than patting her head as though she were a sulking child. A molten anger runs from the apex at her heart to her extremities at the realization that they could have done something.

"Does everyone know about this?" she interrupts.

"Kate Page? I'll bet they know it now!"

"No, no, the balloons. That they're watching, spying."

"Oh, yes," she says dismissively, sipping her refilled coffee. "It had to be voted in, you know. I even built a few of them myself. They're Sinclair manufactures, too—like everything else in this city."

As soon as she had placed her feet on the waterfront docks, she had been watched, devoid of personal privacy. Then there is her association with the Patriots. As minimal as it may be, how much trouble will it cause? She does not want to be associated with communism of any kind. Sarah suddenly becomes overwhelmed with a terrible unease, taking several quiet moments, supplemented by Ruth sipping her coffee contently, for Sarah to recover from the initial surprise.

"Why didn't you tell me they were communists?"

Sarah pries, incredulous at Ruth's lackadaisical attitude.

"The Patriots?" she asks, laughing to herself. "Don't let them fool you with this propaganda." She gestures at the newspaper with a pointing finger. "Wanting worker's rights doesn't make us communists."

"Well—well, aren't you worried?"

She shrugs. "Why should I worry when I don't have anything to hide? They went after Kate Page because she's famous. They won't waste their time on schlubs like us."

While Sarah says no more on the subject, relegated to drinking her coffee as Ruth complains about her work, the news of the balloons nags at her until she arrives back home.

"That singer we met before at that club." Sarah says to her cousin as soon as she comes through the door. "There was something about her in the newspaper."

"There was." Penny says, a hint of epicaricacy in her words, and turns to the Semaphore Typewriter and prints off a fresh line of news. There is the picture of the singer, in everyday clothing but still recognizable, speaking to a woman that Sarah swears she has seen before. "I told you that group was a bunch of dissidents." The headline over the picture reads "Is local celebrity a communist sympathizer?"

"I'll read it aloud," Penny offers quickly. "Here we are: 'In late morning on Monday at her home on Fifth Avenue, local singer Kate Page was found *collaborating*'— what a suspicious word that is—' with Florence McNamera, organization leader of the Liberty Union of Seattle, a group suspected of sympathizing with communist ideas and association with the notorious Blue Cap gang.' There's more

131

but I've read enough. She'll blacklisted from every club around here."

"But she didn't *do* anything."

"She spoke with a Patriot," Penny says seriously, focusing on Sarah's bewildered expression. "So, you better be sure not to get *too* close to those sorts either. It could be bad for me."

"Don't you care?"

"About what?"

"Something other than yourself." As soon as the words leave her mouth, she regrets them. No matter how true they may be, it is rude of her to say so.

"And you think these dissidents have it right, do you? They could use their time and effort to help people; work at charities, volunteer. No. Instead they stand on the sidewalks shouting and causing ruckus. What good is that?"

It's something, she thinks and opens her mouth to say it, but stops. It suits her better not to argue with her cousin for now. Instead, she decides to thank her for retrieving her stolen envelope.

*

On the many days when George and his wife are in a stream of arguments, Sarah finds work an appealing alternative to listening to needless sparring and shouting, followed sometimes by a high-pitched scream. At times, it disturbs her to the point of considering getting an apartment, until she thinks of the cost and decides it is safer to stay put with family no matter how disgruntled.

Preferring to remain clear of any verbal bullets, and it being a Sunday, Sarah waits outside the door of the house, trying to remain comfortable sitting on the porch banister

132

reading a magazine she found by the sofa, her mind at times drifting to the inheritance money and how she might retrieve it. After some time, the house is quiet, until Penny's heightened laughter from the dining room, coupled with the whispers of a man's voice, constantly snatches her attention from the page. When she cocks her head back, she can spy them through the door frame. Her cousins look strange. Penny leans against the wall smoking one of those red-rimmed cigarettes and George is next to her with his hands resting behind his back. Unable to make out their conversation properly, she can make out Penny's high giggle and certainly he reciprocates because she catches him smiling.

Sarah finds her feet guiding her to them, unashamed of interrupting--actually, she rather hopes to.

"*Sumimasen*," she calls to grab his attention and make sure Penny sees how different they two are. One stern glance and he leaves with such rapidity that it seems he has been waiting for someone to give him an excuse to depart. Once gone, she chastises, "It doesn't look right."

Penny shrugs. She is as young as a freshly opened package of *mochi*, the crisp plastic wrapper opening to emit a sharp aroma of sugary sweetness. Penelope wipes her hand across her face in a downward stroke as if brushing rainwater from her skin. She tears her wandering eyes from the floor to meet Sarah's accusing face, her black pupils dilated and worn.

"George? Shouldn't he be with his wife?" Sarah asks bluntly.

"Isn't it a little early for you to be up?" she asks, clearly annoyed.

"Penelope, you're not—"

The nail marks on her collar bone, she surmises, are from his fingertips.

She chuckles with a loathsome glare, "Don't be such a pole cat. It doesn't matter."

"It doesn't?" she asks, repulsion clear in her voice. Worse than being related is Penny flirting with a married man. "Aren't you a Christian woman? Don't you feel bad?"

She puts a hand on her waist.

"And why should I feel bad? I'm not doing anything vulgar."

She clicks her tongue against her teeth, "Besides, *Jyu nin to iro.*"

Ten people, ten colors. An old proverb meaning "To each their own."

Sarah scoffs at it, doubtless as to why she chose such a permissive saying.

"*You're* not Japanese."

She blows smoke to the side, smirks at the insult, then saunters to her spot on the sofa, turning up the radio as an announcer introduces Jack Benny. The music and audience roar, she unpins her cap, laying it on the armrest and unties her shoes, slipping them off and placing them at the edge of the couch, lifting up her legs to bend at her side. Sarah abandons the issue for now, seeking shelter in her room as entire house seems to bend inward to crush her under its own weight. Standing, alone, her arms crossed, she considers packing her bag and leaving, but is reminded of her purpose.

All she has to do is convince Penny. She should not have argued with her, however wrong her actions. It is far better to be on her good side, though her cousin makes it increasingly difficult. Taking to her bed, she curls up in the fetal position, half listening to the sketch of two men

134

imitating Bing Crosby and Bob Hope. Every now and again she checks the time on her wallet watch, winds it a few times, letting the soothing ticking lull. Although her eyes close, they flicker when she hears the laughter of the audience mingled with Penny's high titter.

She must have slept for some time. When Sarah wakes, the light in her room is a glowing orange like a candle flame swaying in a burning oil lamp. The radio is quiet now, playing *Big Road Blues* while Penny sings along intermittently from the bathroom. Pushing up from the quilts, ignoring her full bladder, Sarah follows an impulse and sneaks into Penelope's room, though there is little reason for her to tip-toe. Penny will be in the bathroom for hours getting ready for whatever night gig she has arranged.

Careful steps take her to the half-closed bedroom door. It feels as if she is stepping into a cordoned room. The air is warm from the sun coming through the window, bathing the surroundings in a soft yellow glow. It is a strange room, decorated with the trappings of a young woman's tastes among hints of the previous owner's belongings. Nightclub posters tacked next to framed photographs of her ancestors. Popular magazines sitting on an heirloom table. Handmade quilts spread over store-bought sheets. A frosted glass lamp set on a well-worn dresser, where hairpins and ribbons lie in a tray next to it. A man's scarf sits tousled on her unmade bed. Slipping over, she sits down on the folds to touch the keepsake, unwillingly reminded of her own father. Looking away, she is drawn to the chest of drawers, the top covered with photo frames of her smiling face next to a solemn white man with a tawny face and thin body—her father. Though there are a few pictures of him smiling fully, this one seems to be at a carnival. Penny has her arms around him and they look at each other, not the camera. Comparing them, she notes the same facial structure and identical smiles.

A creak of the door makes her jump. Her mind struggles to come up with some excuse should she meet Penny, but when she looks to the door there is no one there. It isn't until she lowers her gaze to the floor that she sees Bruce swagger through, swishing his puffy bob tail as he comes around the bed, jumping up to find her hand and beg for her to scratch his chin. Her lip twitches in amusement as she complies to the cat's selfish gesture.

Glancing about, her fingers rubbing Bruce's dense fur, she realizes why the room seemed so odd to her before. In contrast to Penny's modern demeanor, the bedroom is decorated in the most traditional way, from the patchwork quilts, polished wooden furniture, colorful circular knotted rag rugs scattered everywhere. One frayed rug in particular that lay by the bedside is clearly Bruce's favorite. She rushes, quietly pulling out drawers, looking under folded clothes, searching for evidence of the inheritance or, even better, actual cash. Stealing is not a habit she prefers becoming familiar with, but it is increasingly emerging as a necessity in her life. She rationalizes it not as stealing, but as retrieving what she is owed. As she rifles through her cousin's belongings for any hint, all she finds are personal letters and, hearing the bathroom unlatch, sneaks out of the bedroom with the frustrating realization that getting any money from her cousin may be more difficult than she originally expected.

8
Penelope
Looking Through Windows

Drizzling rain streams down the living room window. There are the daily rumbles from upstairs that does not disturb Penny's determination. She emerges from her bedroom in a robin's-egg day dress, a wide-brimmed hat, and a shopping basket on her arm to interrupt Sarah, who relaxes on the couch next to the radio listening to the low murmur of a broadcast of a Sherlock Holmes story while enjoying a cigarette.

"Come with me to the supermarket?"
Preening, Penny brushes some strands of cat hair from the front of the dress. Being Sarah's day off, the idea of any physical labor awakens sore muscles.

"I'd rather stay in."

"Are you sure?" she asks, her eyes taking on a mossy green from the diluted light coming through the window.

Meeting her gaze, Sarah nods. Her cousin takes the refusal with a shrug, then, remembering a forgotten task, she says, "It's been a month." When Sarah does not respond, she clarifies, "Your rent."

From what she knows of Sarah, Penny considers that there are two options are at odds in her reasoning: refuse, which will doubtless lead them into a scuffle and drag her into an argument with her cousin or hand over the cash and continue her day in peace. The latter is the more appealing as it allows her to finish her morning ritual unimpeded. In fewer than twenty steps, Sarah goes to her room, Penny following, and to the closet where she stores the useless violin and the carpet bag she arrived with. It is there she keeps her remaining stash of earnings; a mix of crumpled bills and

137

stray coins. This she brings to Penny who waits in the same spot, one hand on her waist and the other raised to her line of sight, fingers spread out to check the fineness of the nails.

"You keep all that here?" Penny chastises at the sight of Sarah with a handful of dollars. "Don't you use a bank?" Sarah exhales sharply.

"A bank? I don't need that," she says, thinking on her residency card. "I probably couldn't get an account if I tried."

"Well, how else will you keep your money safe?"

"What money?" she mumbles, which Penny ignores.

"Here," she shoves the bills forward, which Penny takes gently in her groomed hands.

Appeased, Penny leaves her. Taking out her red bicycle, she speeds down the hill to the market, passing a billboard of a happy-faced pregnant woman standing over a platter of scrambled eggs and bacon with the caption: "Now she can cook your breakfast again. . .with Noxedyn!"

The quickest way is through Windhurst Residential, a housing community for some non-citizens created for charity by a generous rich man. The homes are nice if the residents take care of them. The outsides are a patchwork of fading paint and dilapidated pipes. Penny had often heard about the neighborhood's problems in the chatter amongst nightclub audiences. Too eager to sign a mortgage in a prestigious area, safe, far from the central ghetto where most of the non-citizens live, they did not discover how shoddily the homes were built until after they moved in and it was too late. If they had had the money and if a lawyer would ever choose to defend a non-citizen, some families might have taken it to court. But they are stuck.

138

Each time she rides through the shortcut, the homes appear consistently more dilapidated. On a whim, she cycles to the waterfront, passing children as they walk to school. One is a ruffle haired boy in long brown trousers and a blue shirt carrying a BB gun over his shoulder and a Hopalong Cassidy lunch box. Coming up to the docks, she slows down to see a recognizable figure who keeps his head low even to the other workers as he moves down crates. George in rolled shirtsleeves accounts for the incoming cargo, the man beside him with scars on his face nods after George leans his head over to make a comment.

Passing by, she is assaulted by a memory of having once walked within the center of a yellow chalk line along wire fences. Whenever she saw a guard looking in their direction, she would blow a kiss. The spires rose higher than any of them could climb; she had tried it on a dare. The guards didn't watch so closely in mid-afternoon when they changed shifts. As she hoisted up her dress skirt, Penny glanced over to make sure that Sarah was doing her part as lookout. Waving her on, Penny put the toes of her saddle shoes into the fence gaps, gripping with her fingers as she crawled higher towards the tower. There were no barbed wires. They assumed no one would try anything so rash with armed soldiers watching.

Touch the base of the crow's nest, she thought, *that'll be high enough.*

At the top of the fence, she pulled herself up, balancing her feet on the bar and keeping one hand on the side of it. She reached up. The edge was nowhere near her. Still several feet higher than her head. She might be able to jump.

Then came a chickadee whistle from Sarah. Startled, Penny wavered. Catching her hands on the bar she managed to steady her bones. Turning gently, she faced her cousin who looked up at her to mouth inaudible words. Risking it, she jumped down the height. Though landing on her feet, the impact was steep, and she twisted on her right foot, falling hard on her side. When Sarah glanced up to check if they had been seen, the guard atop the tower looked down at her as if she were as miniscule as spider skittering along the grass and soon took his eyes away. It would have been great fun if not soiled by Sarah's pestering conscience. Penny had not seen much of her own mother's temper when they were home, before the war, when things were safe and happy, but inside the wire fences, without her husband, it was the first time Penny had been struck by her mother's sharp punishment.

Penny follows the cobbled street up a low slope to the red market sign. Being so early, there are plenty of spaces to park her bicycle. While some storefronts remain closed, others have pulled open the shades or put out produce in crates on raised wooden platforms. The morning market noises make a tempo that she adds to her rhythmic steps. Within the covered market where fishmongers settle fresh catches in ice-filled boxes, she finds a familiar vegetable stall where an unassuming elderly man sells various greens, chief among them being radishes.

*

The following morning, side by side the three walk down the interior of Pike Place Market, winding through the cross-cutting paths and pockets of crowds to the Café 1894, a white stone front and a marble sign above the door with raised golden lettering. Despite the grand exterior, inside is a rustic appearance. Wood floor panels are discolored from where so many feet have tread. The timber columns supporting the ceiling have a dark varnish that fades towards the base along with dents and scratches where people have damaged them. The windows, while clean on the inside, are dirtied on the outside by rain marks and seagull excrement. The state of the café serves a greater purpose in that George wants a place where any social class can enter without reprimand, as he explains to Penny when she asks. And when she complained earlier when told to join them, the reasoning as to why they needed her presence was that, "A young lady makes people behave."

While there are many tables set on the main floor, there is a secluded room waiting for them near the bar whose walls are separated at the top by a run of stained glass windows. Inside is a booth with a table fixed to the floor and a window overlooking Elliot Bay.

First through, Penny pulls off her coat and hangs in on a brass hook, revealing the evening gown she never changed out of from her nightclub gig the night before, which sparkles in clear contrast to the daywear of those around her. The waitress emerges in a pair of gray trousers with a red blouse tucked into them. Her chin-length bob brushes against her neck as she moves, holding three menus in front of her chest as if she were walking with schoolbooks. These she places on the table, one for each.
Once the waitress departs, George holds up a miniature brown envelope in hand.

"Something for you to do," he says, handing it to her.

"And what might that be?" she retorts, jerking her arm away from his touch.

"A little task," he says, causing her pause, "at the Atelier Lounge."

"Ojiisan usually tells me the place."

"He's busy."

The impunity is a lightning crack against a blue sky. Who is George to tell her what to do?

"Give this to the owner, Mr. DuPont, and you have a place on stage."

Her mother's voice seeps into memory, "Apologize out loud, curse in silence. Say, 'Yes' and when their back is turned, do what you want. "

She takes the envelope obligingly, storing it safely in her purse. If performing menial errands helps her towards singing fame, she will not refuse.

As the hours wear on, all sorts of people come and go from the sheltered room. She pays only a little attention to their pleas or grievances, preferring instead to read one of the magazines she borrowed from Catherine before having left the house. From what she does hear, she gathers that the Shizuka have more influence than she originally suspected, and that George and Abe have been doing this for some time, judging by a comment one older lady makes about having had their protection for three years. In between the small meetings, they are served drinks according to the hour. Early on it had been coffee and now into the afternoon, stronger spirits fill glasses on the table, and George having consumed the most has cheeks the shade of pink roses.

Tearing herself from George, she smiles at Abe, Penny exits to the market floor, turning by the radish stand where one of the gang members watches over the merchandise. As she passes, he nods, greeting her briefly. Fire bursts stinging on her ankle where a wayward ember remains resting in an orange glow. Inhaling sharply, she flicks it off. Looking up, she finds the culprit, an electrified sphere no bigger than a ball bearing, and follows it as it rolls away down the street. By the time she turns her head, she finds the atmosphere a smoky haze, her sight so blurry she can see no more than a few feet before her. Rambunctious shouts mingled with laughter come from the smoke.

Inevitably there are pained screams from citizens who have been sliced by V gang knives, including the *kyodai* who had been managing the stand. Pushing to the edge of the building, Penny flattens herself on the sidewalk. Footsteps hurry by. She risks thrusting out her hand. A hard smack on her elbow forces the stranger to stumble. As the smoke dissipates, Abe is soon by her side, assessing the struggling body Penny holds firmly by the legs. With a twist of the edge of his mouth, he in turn wrestles with the young man's flailing arms.

Penny glances sidelong at the chaos, wondering for a moment which gang is responsible for the display. The answer is revealed on the boy's jacket. With Abe keeping a strong hold on him, as they curse at one another, Penny lets go of his legs and stands, blinking away her dizziness at rising too quickly. Like a twisting record, a static bolt blazes across storefront windows, turning the area an azure blue. Manufactured lightning strikes every hard surface, pulsing up walls and sidewalks. By now a small crowd has formed and numerous policemen section off the street from a mechanism that continues to sputter lightning. Together, Penny and Abe push the hooligan forward to the police who eagerly capture him in manacles and depart before being bothered by authorities.

Leaving the scene, Penny runs through the event once more and realizes that someone is missing.

"Is George alright?" she asks.

Abe smirks. "Oh, sure he's alright. He slipped out and told me to check on you."

She takes offense at George ordering someone to look after her but keeps the upset to herself. Strolling together to calm their excitement, they find themselves along the shore where a sweet sea breeze from the ocean freshens their skin. Nearing a pier, far past the welcoming mermaid, Penny stops to sit on the edge and let her feet dangle over the water.

"How was it where you were?" she asks Abe. "When you were in the camp, that is?"

He tugs up on his trousers to squat next to her, "Like hell. Was yours any better?"

"Not by much, I don't think. We were six of us in one room." She draws an imaginary square in the air. "And the winter was so cold there was nothing to do to get out of it. Sometimes I can't believe I was there for two years."

He makes a little grunt of acknowledgement, "One of the reasons I volunteered."

"In the Army?" Penny asks.

He nods. Overcome with excitement and relief at the small similarity, she asks, "What regiment? My father was in the Twenty-Fifth Infantry."

Abe sucks in a sharp breath at the revelation. Like any soldier, he knew of the invasion on the shores of Japan beginning with the peremptory Operation Downfall, and the numerous offensives thereafter to bring down the Imperial Army with as many American soldiers as could hold a rifle.

"I was in the Four-Forty-Second."

"You'll have many stories, I'm sure!" she says in awe, taking her eyes from the water to the horizon. During the war fighting, anyone who could read a newspaper knew of the hardened, most highly decorated, all Japanese-American, 442nd Regimental Combat Team.

"It's good that you came back. Your wife must be pleased." She smiles tenderly at a childhood memory of her parents watching her play on a park slide while they sat next to each other on swings, laughing together. "You can always tell in the little things."

Snapping open her purse, she finds her cigarette case and matchbox. Removing two, she offers one to Abe, who takes it, and settles one in the corner of her mouth. Lighting a single match, she passes the flame between them then tosses it to the spume.

She takes a drag, pushing out smoke in a single line that fans into the air, "Will you tell me something about the war?"

"Whatever I have to tell is not for a young lady to hear."

She looks at him, crosses her legs, and leans her weight on a hand pressed against the wood planks. Taking a deep drag off the cigarette, Abe blows it out while making the slightest motions with his jaw to form smoke rings.

"How the devil do you manage that?" she asks, delighted.

"Curl your tongue inside your mouth while you blow."

He draws again, demonstrating, allowing Penny to follow suit. As she does, all she manages is a terrible sputtering that emits nothing more than a few weak puffs. Chuckling, he says, "Well, it may take some doing." After clearing her throat, she flicks the ashes from the cigarette. They stare out at the water together, taking turns smoking, tapping the ash down into the rock crevices, and letting the sea breeze cool their skin.

"I'll tell you one thing," he begins, ruminating, "I've never seen a better sunset than in Anzio Harbor just after a rain."

Abe curls his mouth into a slight smirk that only appears untainted on the unscarred portions of his face. The scars remind her of explosions, recalling the pandemonium at Luna Park and the many unknown hazards on the streets, knowing that she can defend herself well enough against an obvious threat and yet she does hold the small fear of a single blade in the dark. Penny stretches her arms above her head, prostrating, then lets them fall and pushes her palms against the rock to stand up, saying, "If you don't mind, I have an errand."

He rises with her, tossing his cigarette into the water, meeting her with eyebrow raised, giving the insinuation that he will accompany her. Upset, she claims the need to rest her voice on the way there as he walks near her side far up the slopes from the waterfront to the level ground on Pine Street is the two-story Atelier Lounge. Through the redwood exterior with a bay window open to the street, several men can be seen relaxing in leather chairs or being looked after by young cocktail waitresses. Although its iron filigree doors set on mirrored panels are closed, a dashing gentleman in an impeccably starched tuxedo stands at attention under his black umbrella, firmly gripping the curved golden handle with his white gloved hands. Penny passes him, ready to open the door herself when he stops her by putting out his arm as a barrier.

"Pardon," he says, keeping his eyes fixed on a point at the horizon. "I'm afraid no ladies are permitted inside."

"That so?" she says haughtily, while in the back of her mind knowing that she can ask Abe for help but refusing, stubbornly fixed to independence, "I'm here to see Mr. DuPont, so kindly move aside."

"Mr. DuPont is the owner. He doesn't see job seekers or waitresses."

"I'm *not* a waitress."

"If you're looking for a job—"

"—Not that either," she interrupts. "My business is strictly with Mr. DuPont."

When he ignores her, his arm remaining as a barrier, she adds, "Perhaps you don't know me? Penny Morgan?" When that does not elicit a response, she says, begrudgingly, "or does the word '*Shizuka*' sway you at all?"

At the mention of it, his eyes flick to Abe, and his jaw tightens. Where he avoids looking at her before, he tilts his head towards her, casting his gaze upon the inconsequential girl. She spreads her lips into a smile as the door opens for her to the trappings of a Victorian gentleman's club. At once she is approached by a cheerful waitress who, after whispering heatedly with the doorman, crisply leads Penny away from the open lounge where well-dressed men relax on suede sofas smoking from complimentary cigars while talking. A calm piano melody rises from an unseen stage.

"Apologies, we expected someone—" She pauses, going down a thin hallway with dim overhead lights that barely illuminate the hanging portraitures of damsels. "—a little more—well, it's always been men who come around, even the ones carrying the letters." At the end of the hall is a winding stairwell leading up, "But then, this is the first one of your folks we've had."

The stairs reveal another hallway where -costumed ladies go in and out of the many entrances that line the hall. At the end, the waitress stops next to a nondescript door and informs that she will remain until the meeting is finished. Pushing the door open, she sees the man himself sitting with his legs at a ninety-degree angle in front of a Semaphore Typewriter. Unlike the fashion of the day, his tweed suit is so stiffly starched that his shoulders appear as straight as a paper's edge. His hair, cut in a bowl style, is parted in the center and kept down with a copious spread of pomade along with two long silver clips pulling the bangs back to set them in place.

"Excuse me," she says with a tinge of annoyance at his failure to address her as soon as she walked in, "Mr. DuPont?"

At this, he turns his attention to her while continuing to type on the machine.

"Is there a reason for you to be here or are you lost?" Smiling, she removes the sealed letter from her handbag, puts on an air of confidence, and says, "From Mr. Igarashi" as she holds it out.

The name is enough to make him stop and stand long enough to walk the few paces from the typewriter to his desk and sit, scooting a chair in until his chest nearly touches the edge. From the left drawer, he removes a pair of black leather gloves which he pulls onto each hand, tugging them into place. He takes the letter and meets her stare, explaining, "Too many dangers in taking a letter with your bare hands from someone you don't know. Especially where your kind is

148

concerned," he adds under his breath while turning his attention to the envelope.

"By my 'kind,' Penny retorts with a hint of humor, "do you mean *Shizuka* or women?"

Without looking, he says, "Either."

Scanning the letter, he scrunches his nose as if he is about to sneeze. Folding it in half, he creases the fold crisply between his thumb and pinky nails, then drops it into the center desk drawer. He turns his back to her, facing the Semaphore, types quickly, then returns to the desk. Sitting, he picks the olive-green accented gold fountain pen from a floating base and holds the tip just near the open desk diary page, then glances up from beneath his pencil-thin eyebrows.

"It seems there is room for a pretty, young singer. I'll happily book you for three Fridays starting this week." He turns down, writing her name in choppy letter. "You *will* tell Mr. Igarashi directly?"

"Yes, of course, I—"

"—As for the other," he pauses, turning words over on his tongue, "stipulations. . ."

He stops, taking a clean white page from a stationary set and licks the tip of his pen before writing. Penny, deciding that DuPont takes pleasure from forcing others to wait, chooses a seat on the black leather ottoman in the corner and remains there until after the cuckoo clock on the wall sounds the hour with a wooden whistling. Once the man ceased his whirling writing of pen on paper stops, he slips the folded note into a cream envelope and he smiles, holding it out to her. At the action, Penny rises, taking it from him and stows it in her purse.

*

149

It is late morning and Penny wakes to Bruce licking the tips of her fingers with a coarse tongue. Sitting up, stretching, the cat meows at her with enough force to convince her to stand. He follows, consistently complaining, as she walks to the bathroom to use the toilet, wash her hands and face, and then brush her teeth. In the kitchen, she picks up his empty food bowl from the floor to fill it with rice porridge she keeps in the refrigerator along with a half-full can of chopped liver. These she mashes together with a fork and places the mixture on the floor before Bruce who immediately chomps on the contents.

She tosses the utensil in the sink, rinses her hands, and takes the teapot that forever keeps its place on the stovetop to fill it with water and replace it on the coils, turning the heat up. Waiting for it to boil, she goes to the mail slot, gathering the few letters, she sifts through each, keeping two in one hand while setting the others on the table by the door. The whistling from the pot drives her back to the kitchen to turn off the stove. allowing the pot to cool. To ensure privacy, she retreats to her room, closing the door softly behind. Bruce twitches one ear in her direction from his spot curled up on the floor, then stretches out luxuriously.

Taking a seat on the foot of the bed, Penny holds both letters. One from her aunt in Alaska that she opens to find a returned bank check and a letter that she skims. In it, she is thanked for her generosity, but again her charity is refused. Every year she sends them money and every year they are too embarrassed to accept it. The other letter is from "The Daughters of Charity Sanitarium" written in the bold cursive that belongs to her mother. Unable to bring herself to open it, she stows it in her dresser drawer; the thoughts of her

150

departure still fresh in Penny's mind. It had not been long after the news of her father that her mother departed from the house, abandoning Penny to an early adulthood. Eight days later came three letters. One from the office of a sanitarium informing her of her mother's whereabouts, the other a large brown envelope from the city court house informing her that all her parents' belongings had been entrusted to her, including a copy of the deed to the house, a letter of changed ownership signed by her mother and a notary with a embossed seal, and the last a bank letter in which the contents explained that an account was made in her name that held substantial amounts of money to include her mother's inheritance and her father's life insurance. Attached with it was also a letter from the U.S. Army stating that the pension fund for Army widows had passed to her.

It was well enough that she need not ever worry about finances, though she would rather have her parents. The money seemed always to be tainted and she preferred not to spend it, instead using her citizen's wage to purchase anything she wanted. Bruce jumps to the bed, licking his teeth and preening his fur, while Penny opens her closet and chooses a dress with a high-waist ivory skirt topped with a wide lace strip attached to a blue and orange polka-dot short-sleeved blouse. Properly attired, she paces back to the kitchen, fetches a cup to pour the steaming water, and makes a strong bitter lemon tea. Walking carefully with the cup in hand, she creeps up to the second floor.

Although the main floor is empty, she hears George's laugh from his room followed by Timmy's as a sign of them sharing a playful moment together, and Ojiisan's radio playing low in his room, the volume subdued enough to be

151

courteous. She knocks gently to let herself in, finding him at his writing desk with pen to diary page.

"*Ohayo,*" she greets with a whisper, placing the cup near him.

He drinks it, making a sour face.

"Tea," he says.

"Yes, tea. It's good for your lungs."

He grimaces.

"Would you rather have cough syrup?"

"No, no, this will do fine. Thank you."

Penny sits on his bed.

"What is it you're writing?" she asks, peeking at the pages written in Japanese on one line and below, an English translation.

"Some family history."

"Is that right?"

She skims the page, seeing a name she recognizes.

"Takeda Shingen?"

"Yes. On my father's side," he states proudly. "The Igarashi's come from Shingen's third cousin." She listens, as her knowledge of Japanese history surmounts to what Ojiisan tells her through story and conversation. "Well, my family, we're from the third cousin of Shingen. Same blood. Not like these other Japanese, no. Not some underclass dirtmongers. But, *dakara*, if my son weren't stupid he'd have married a better class of woman."

"Catherine is—" Penny begins, ready to defend her.

"—I know what she is. At least she was smart enough to have a boy. Well, it all won't matter in the end. I am old, and George will do what he's told." He relaxes his shoulders, breathing easily, staring at Penny. "Do you know how it was that we spread our name so quickly here?"

She shakes her head once. True, she heard the tale in quips on the streets or comments from George but never in full and she was too smart to ever ask directly.

"Koike-san and I rode the boat together from Japan. The bosses. The 'Shizuka Twins'. Ha!" he lets out, slapping her once on the knee playfully. "At that time, we Japanese had no one to speak for us. Police," he waves a hand across his face, "nowhere. The gangs were all we had and the only ones with the most power were the Chinks, the V gang, and the Skylarks—you call them the Blue Caps now— and all the little groups," at this he flutters his fingers "so who do we go to for anything? Imagine! Japanese having to ask *those* sorts for help." he pauses to drink the tea and make a repulsive face at the bitter taste, "You're too young to know the kinds of fighting that happened every day. Think it's bad now? This—" he lifts up his shirt to reveal a thick calloused scar on the right side of his chest in between two ribs mingling with nicked patterns of smaller marks etched on his skin. "was only the first time." He puts his shirt down, letting his hand fall against his thigh, "when I called a V gang boy a nance." and grins at the memory. "So, Koike-san and I thought, 'Why should they have the right to do these things? We are *Nipponjin.*' And me the same blood as Takeda Shingen!" He raises his hand in a fist with knuckles facing forward, then settles. "So out we went. It wasn't too difficult. Many Japanese were upset. They had gangs, *ne*, but all mixed up. All we had to do was put them together."

Enthralled, Penny asks, "How?"

He raises his arthritic hand as vertically as his fingers can manage, keeping it level at the center of his face.

"You have to show that you are strong; to be strong, you have to make people afraid." he lowers his hand. "Koike-san went to the East district and I went South. I wanted to get

153

the V gang back for cutting me," he says with a grin, "and I'd heard that their boss liked a certain Soda Fountain Creamery where he took his family every Wednesday. So, I went there and," he breaks into a throaty laughter, "well, he didn't expect to see me waiting."

For a moment, Penny feels as if a wad of cotton had been thrust down her throat and left there to engorge on her disgust. As best as she is able, Penny hardens her resolve and forces her lips to spread into a complimentary smile.

"So, *ne*, we took their heads and showed them to all the other little gangs. After that, every Japanese followed us, and we drove out the Chink rats. They were *afraid*—ha!—so afraid we'd take their heads, too. Instead we took their tongues."

The brandings.

"How did that begin?" she asks.

His eyes excite, "I'm sorry to say that it wasn't *my* idea but Koike-san's. One day he started cutting *Kanji* into people's tongues with a knife. Said it sent a message. It did but it also took too long. One person to hold the man down, another to pinch the tongue, and one to do the cutting." he tips his head to the side, "there's more feeling in the Kanji when using the knife." Setting the cup on his desk, "*Jaa,* after all that the other gangs wanted to settle things. Fine. By then we controlled downtown. So long as they kept their heads bowed to us, they could keep their swine-pens." He clears his throat in a low grumble. "But now, they're becoming obstinate."

The door pushes open, George on the other side with Abe accompanying him. Seeing the serious exchange of looks between father and son, Penny quickly excuses herself, soon followed by Abe, diligent in his charge to chaperone the young woman. Grabbing her things from downstairs, she leaves the house and saunters casually to the sky train station. A full car waits for her. She squishes herself in amongst suited men and women. Their heads downward looking at freshly printed news from the automated presses that sit on every other street corner.

Off the train there is a metal contraption encased in thick glass. Slipping a nickel into the coin slot at the mouth sends a single heavy arm moving, sweeping across an enlarged typewriter keyboard. The arm swings, pushing down on keys. In fewer than two minutes, a single sheet of paper spits out of a thin slot with the most recent stories. A clattering draws her attention up from the sky train platform waiting for the next sky train, about four blocks down where two groups rumble against each other. Mixed together are those wearing blue caps and others in black leather jackets with a white triple V painted on the back. Some shouts carry over to where she stands. She turns back to the printed paper, catching it when it spits out from the slot. Returning home, she sits cross legged on the floor with newspapers and printed lengths of paper scattered in front of her, searching for clubs both obscure and well-known where she can introduce herself, ask for work. She circles telephone numbers and addresses as the radio spews.

"Come visit the Daddy Cool Club," and from an announcer, "enjoy slim liquor. Experience the famous singer Kate Page live and don't forget our newest Mechanized Mermaid! See the wonders of technology and entertainment."

Soon the drama program reemerges with organ music reintroducing the show. From what she half listens to as she studies the papers, a man is uncertain of whether he wants a wife or not; two monotone male voices speaking to one another with few emotions. Voices reminding her of another storyteller. She hates to think of him but does so, inevitably, when intrusive visions show his features and there is soon a sickening retch in her stomach when she sees Oniisan with the sour face, even though he smiled often, and quickly banishes the memory.

*

The radishes cover what is underneath. Innocent shoppers buy a few ounces of the white vegetable for their supper, not knowing what lies hidden in the covered crates stacked below that hold dozens of brown paper bags. He smiles, makes cheerful conversation, asks how they find the weather that day and tells them to take care when they depart with their paper bags of radishes. It is a busy section across from the fish stall, where fresh salmon, trout and crab sit on crates of ice. The fishmongers stand behind the counter in overalls shouting to the passing customers, "Alaskan Salmon, fifteen cents! Fillets for five!"

The crowds make it too fast for others to see him pass inconspicuous bags with wholly different contents to recognized faces and for them to return a handful of cash. The goods he provides depend on the customer. Penny buys strong medicines for George's wife that most can only get with a prescription, brand-name cigarettes that are usually too expensive in stores, and all her make-up nick-knacks. She comes to him directly whereas the usual route is to make contact with one of his workers who takes the order, which is then filled by George, ready for the customer to pick it up at an agreed-upon time. Small orders can be retrieved the same day, usually the latest drug, while larger orders take days, the largest of which are the coveted citizenship papers that can be precisely forged so as to fool any authority. After all, that was how George himself procured such a document. Proper documentation combined with his father's small ambitions keep him in a comfortable stance with the ability to peddle black-market merchandise in an out of Pike Place and the influence over several areas of the city. Their modest district holdings give them respect and some small sense of control over certain nightclubs, businesses, and with modest bribes to police, protection. The profit was and continues to be remarkable, the biggest problems coming only from the smaller gangs who seek to upend his schemes.

If it weren't for the camps, peddling contraband would never have become lucrative. He started it because he was told to make money, he kept doing it to make more money. Penny had been taught this all by Ojiisan. Every morning she sat by his side, serving him breakfast, and he talked, often chastising his son either because of stern affection or sincere dislike. The first abdication came when George did what he thought was right by marrying the pregnant girl. It cost him a finger. He knelt before his own father, his mother by her husband's side, and chopped off his pinky with a kitchen knife. When he couldn't hold back his own tears, his father called him a coward. A man has to be strong, unrepentant, unemotional. Although George wears the face of such a man, she has seen cracks emerge. There are moments of vulnerability when she notices that his face softens, and his lips spread into a sincere smile when he looks at his children.

9

Sarah

Bodies in the Dull Light

April 1949

It is a late night when Sarah departs from a shift at the
factory. Too late to catch a bus to the station, she walks there
alone amongst the few couples strolling along the waterfront
under the glowing sky before the steel mermaid who opens
her arms to seafarers. Green pennies settle at the base,
flowers both new and withered, a heart locket of pure silver
speckled with age. No one dare steal it. A wooden box with a
glass window is the shrine of the sea. Behind it on red velvet
hangs pristine mermaid charms. A sign reads "The Seafarer's
Mermaid" and under it "A lucky charm for your sweetheart.
Two for five cents." From her pocket, she sticks in a nickel,
twists the knob and out roll two mermaid pendants each on a
thin chain contained in a plexiglass orb. Cracking the one
open she decides to keep for herself and clasps it around her
wrist. For a moment, she considers keeping the other and
giving it to Ruth. Deciding that it is too forward, she tosses it
instead into the chopping waters.

The old neighborhood is free of balloons. Any hovering
overhead would find the mature fir trees and untended
overgrowth a hindrance. The remains of the forgotten have
been overtaken by roots pushing up through cracks in brick
sidewalks. A safe, sheltered, space for Sarah to decide if the
Patriots are worth her personal risk. After her initial shock
upon learning of their negative public association, a
circumstance presented itself. Perhaps the best way to
convince Penny to give her a share of the inheritance is to
threaten to derail her singing career. If Sarah is seen as a

sympathizer, the connection between them may be enough to produce results.

The steps are low and wide marble leading to a pair of eagle statues parallel at the top, standing stalwart with outstretched wings despite each having significant wear as to render one with a broken beak tip and several missing talons while the other has uncountable chips along the surface. Both share layers of graffiti as if every now and then some ruffians pass through to add their marks. At the rise is a small plaza just before a white columned building with boarded-up windows, bits of trash at the edges, and two long bolts of cloth hanging horizontally down the center, just hovering above the ground. One is blue with "PATRIOT LIBERTY UNION OF SEATTLE" in white paint while the other has a pattern of red, white, and blue vertical stripes. A foldable table is set just off to the side of the stairs, watched by Alma who stands by attentively, overlooking the stacks of pamphlets, publications, blue bracelets, and a donation canister made from a tin can painted blue. Florence stands at the bottom step, on equal footing with the handful of people who decide to attend. Finding Ruth among them, Sarah approaches to witness the meager event. A desperate plea for a change that few have the rigor or the ideals to propagate. It was reckless to be around them, knowing now their supposed association with communist ideas, but she is determined to prove the contrary. Like her, the Patriots want everyone to be equal. That is not wrong, surely.

"Where we are shows a hard truth," Florence begins with a voice impassioned enough to wake the statues. "This was our city hall," she looks around, raising her arms to gesture at the surroundings, softening her tone, "A place open for all people to be heard and acknowledged. Equal and just," she lets her arms fall in a show of disappointment. "But now

159

forgotten," she pauses, gathering a deep, commanding tempo, "And where does our new center of justice sit? On the Hill with the rich and privileged, in the hands of Sinclair who fills the wallets of our civil servants with bribes; money stolen from *your* pockets and your toil. Meanwhile, every work-shy citizen gets a monthly salary for no other cause than their title." She pauses, scanning the gaggle, then points to Ruth as if seeing her for the first time.

"You there," she says, "you seem a fine worker. What's your trade?"

"Manufacturing at Sinclair Industries."

"And what does he pay you for your hard work?" Letting the question simmer, she then answers, "Going rate today was twenty-five cents."

Of the few who attend, some exclaim at the atrocity, others shake their heads, and a few nod in agreement, likely being Sinclair employees themselves, perhaps attending out of curiosity, knowing well the unfairness but so poor that even pennies are better than nothing.

"Twenty-five cents," Florence repeats., emphasizing, "Why, that's near enough to buy a lick of shoe polish."

"Never mind a citizenship," Ruth adds wryly.

"Sinclair grows wealthy on your hardship, keeping your rightful wages for his own gains."

"And what 'bout that last rumble?" a thin youngster interrupts, a baggy set of hand-me-down overalls covering the gangly frame, making it difficult for Sarah to decide whether the child is a boy or a girl. "Didn't go so well that time."

Unfazed, Florence continues, "With a strong purpose, we do better than their bullying schemes."

"That right," the kid jibes. "October was 'sposed to change it all and all's what happened were cuffs and shipping out. Didn't even fight back. Now they're sayin' you're all jus' Reds."

The two exchange challenging looks with Florence taking a stern refrain to address the audience.

"Fighting is the fuel they want. Aggression will give them a better reason to make stricter laws and push our noses deeper into the ground," she passes her eyes over the skeptical faces, and attempts to persuade them with a few last words, "To regain equality, we have to treat others justly."

At the end, the few coins left in the tin are barely enough to buy a cheap pencil.

*

Using the sky train so often has numbed any hesitation that she once had, giving way to a subtle fascination with the smooth invention much like her resolve with the many novelties that abound in the city. As the train slows into the station, she follows her usual route along the boardwalk towards the factory, taking pleasure in the seaside aroma and watching fishing boats arrive to deposit their catch. It is on this commute that she often picks up sprinklings of the daily happenings from the gossip on the train and the patchwork headlines on newspapers both instantly printed by the mechanical arm shielded in glass boxes and displayed on newsstands every few blocks. Today there is a grainy overhead picture of a group gathered in front of an old city hall with a Patriot banner clearly visible.

Twelve hours inside the factory. Six hours putting cigarette packs into cases, over and over, so that when she blinks she can see the red and white wrapping imprinted on the backs of her eyelids.

161

Speaking to Ruth for a few short minutes during their break is the only chance she has to use her voice and even that is lost when she stuffs food in her mouth. No matter how she eats, a hunger seems ever present, subsiding only when smoking a cigarette or drinking black coffee.

Six more hours until her shift finishes.

Going home on the train, the seats are taken, so she stands, and all she thinks is how she will drink a warm cup of milk with maple syrup and go to sleep. Then, when the train wobbles from a gust of wind and she raises her arm to grasp the overhead rail, she smells the day's work on her, and the thought of sleeping is pushed away in favor of giving her clothes a thorough wash.

Before finally settling in her room, she spots the old violin case still resting where she placed it at her arrival. Deciding to move it, she first opens the lid. Nestling in the rosin box of the empty violin case is a piece of velvet that she had once cut to make a secret pocket. Beneath the cloth, she lifts at the corner. Settled against the revealed brown board is a paper folded in half, perfectly flat; she lifts it up to look at the photo she knows is there. The picture is a film still of *Destination Tokyo.* In a bomber jacket with slick hair topped by a Navy Officer's cap, Cary Grant leans with his arms folded, his face serious, his eyes pointing at her. Written in pencil on the front corner is, "Don't you think this looks like him?"

Of course, he doesn't look anything like her sister's husband, then suitor, but imagines that it had been the essence of the type of man that she wished to marry. It leaves her bitter, that their sisterly bond was broken by a man. They were supposed to take care of each other as their own women, to be independent, to not fall into the cycle of marriage and childbirth. It was a promise made in the interim of their time at the relocation center. Much like the internment that would come shortly after, their days were spent amongst crowds, amongst thousands of other men, women, and children just like them. They had to wait in line to use the latrine, wait in line to eat, wait in line to wash their clothes, wait, wait, wait. There had always been a barrage of bodies all scrambling for space so that privacy became a nearly impossible luxury.

In their single, shared family room, the walls were thin, so every aspect of their neighbors' lives could be heard, and besides being inundated with the constant sights, smells, and sounds of other humans, there had been mice. Camp Harmony, many ironically called it. In much of her young life, Sarah had been relatively amiable, hardly causing trouble, or if any happened, it was avoided. That was, until, a miniscule slight caused her insides to capsize. The day was typical. She and her sister, Louise, woke to help their mother with the laundry. After waiting longer than usual, an older man walked up from behind them and shoved himself into a spot ahead. Though mama verbally reprimanded his behavior, she nor any of the others standing in line did anything. *Shoganai.*

Infuriated, Sarah shouted at him and when he refused to move, she kicked his shins, all the while shrieking any curses she knew. It took Louise several tries to pull her away, finally resorting to picking her up by the waist and carrying her some feet away. It was then that, like many tantrums, her anger gave way to sadness as hot tears poured down the sides of her nose, and tickled her lips, all the while exasperated since she tried desperately to talk, to explain everything that was wrong in her world. Louise listened, wiped Sarah's face with the back of her sleeve, and when an inevitable calm arrived, made a promise.

"When we're out of here," she said, "after all this is over, it'll just be you and me."

She stuck out her fist with only the pinky raised. Sarah met her with the same gesture, wrapping both fingers together and shaking twice.

Now with the picture in front of her, she tears the reminder in a ragged half, holding each piece in each hand. Being frustrated enough to damage but not destroy the memento, she replaced it to the hiding place only to then jam the rosin in place.

10

Penelope
Stained Spirits

Penelope walks leisurely down the boardwalk despite the darkness, passing the giant mermaid and the seagulls sitting on the lengths of her arms cackling and squawking. A lone adolescent in grubby overalls plays a harmonica, peddling for money with an upturned hat. Still farther down is one of the Patriots passing out fliers and shouting about equality. None of these stop Penny except for an automatic newspaper printer that types off as soon as the person standing before it slips their coin into the slot. The words "Fortune Follies" and "Auditions" draws her eye and she reads over the patron's shoulder:

The Fortune Follies
OPEN AUDITIONS
April 5-7 from 12:00-3:00

The most prestigious nightclub in the city seeks a chosen few young ladies for backing vocalist positions.

Branding the words onto her memory, she then flits away to her appointment at The Candy Apple Pub on the corner of Second and Virginia on the waterfront. A giant green apple in fluorescent light beams over the sign. As usual, Penelope enters through the staff door in the back alley by the trash cans. With no one there to meet her, she wanders in the quiet to find her contact in the main room, replacing a burnt-out bulb on a floor stage light that has its hood uncovered. Penny sees her first, kneeling over on the stage with a screwdriver handle in her mouth, the tip pointing

outward, a black-topped bulb sitting by her knee and the
sound of the new bulb squeaking in. Penny starts to speak
and is soon interrupted with a muffled, "Wait a tick." The
woman looks up briefly, long enough for Penny to appraise
the lady who has a fixed scowl which is offset by her bright
pink lipstick and pale makeup meant to cover the ruddy skin
that still manages to flush through. In the dim light, her
earrings glow a pale green. To keep in fashion, she wears a
pair of drop earrings of hollow glass containing a twirling
firefly that darts blissfully around inside.

"Sorry about this. None of my staff are in yet and I
noticed a bulb needing changing. You're Ms. Morgan, isn't
that right?" she asks, her gaze focusing on screwing the
light's hood back on.

"Yes," she says, taking out a note from her purse to
place it in the 's hand woman while pulling her lips back in
an attempted grin.

"Swell. So, you start your act around eleven, I think,
after Donovan's Magic Ensemble." She rises, tool and
broken bulb in hand. "I'll show you your dressing room. You
are changing, aren't you?"
Penny glances down at her new white dress, answering,
"No."

"Well, it'll be a place to hang your purse," she says as
she walks, leaving Penny to follow. Pushing swinging double
doors through the kitchen where two cooks in wide white
aprons chop vegetables, she is careful to keep her hem close
so as to not to brush against anything that smears. To the
right another swinging door that opens into a narrow hallway
stuffed to the corners with boxes, one of which is a wooden
crate with potatoes peeking through gaps. Pressed up against
the wall is a billboard that must have been the previous sign

166

as the letters that formed "Candy Apple" are weathered and the paint chipping. Here, she is shown a door.

"You can use this room," she states, "and you can make yourself comfortable at the bar until it's time for you to go on. I'll provide the back-up music for your set."
She clears her throat before saying, "Excuse me but I have to finish fixing the stage." and turns, pushing the doors open, leaving them to swing back into place.

Penny expects little when she opens the door but is nevertheless displeased by the contents; a glorified closet with the brooms and mops removed and replaced with a tacked-up mirror and a stool where she can sit before it. A nail on the wall just above the mirror is where she hangs her purse. Content with her quick survey of the room, and deciding that a drink is in order, she steps out, shutting it with some difficulty since it takes a certain twist of the knob to latch the bolt in place. Returning through the back hallway into the main floor, she finds that it is still too early for the bartender to have arrived.

Helping herself behind the counter, she draws a clean glass, settling it under the head that spouts drinking water. Cup in hand, she settles at the bar on the closest stool to the modest stage with a faded curtain just below a plain wooden overhang with a gap in between that shows the high windows on the wall behind covered with a thin layer of black paint to block out the light. Some time passes until a quiet bustle emerges in the form of the few arriving staff, half of whom wipe the tables and chairs of dust while the others prepare the stage. A small crowd arrives as the skinny young Donovan in his bright blue velour waistcoat with its three silver buttons clasping it closed, arrives on the stage followed shortly by his

167

tall sister, whose teeth are too big for her mouth, in a shimmering blue dress to match her brother's clothes, and stands in contrast from the black stage curtain behind her. Raised in her left hand is a red and white striped handled bow saw. She hands this to Donovan, keeping her arms in the air, standing straight up and down without a kink in her spine as if she is going to dive into the audience. Taking the saw, he first places it at her midsection, pressing it, slicing forward and backward. She stands still, smiling as he separates her torso from the bottom half. With a tap of his foot, her legs and lower half fall to the stage floor. She slaps her arms down. He moves up to her neck, making short work of it before it too falls to the ground along with her legs so that all that remains of her is a toothy grinning head. He puts down the saw, picking up her parts to place them together in a vertical puzzle.

It is a good trick, Penny thinks, *with terrible showmanship*.

Donovan goes through the steps without fanfare. Sure enough, the audience claps half-heartedly, most too bored to bother lifting their hands higher than the handle of their drink glass. Unimpeded, Donovan escorts his assistant off-stage, taking the saw with her. He alone stands in the center, his hands clasped together. He opens his hands, claps them once, and when he opens them again there levitates a box jellyfish encased in an orb of water. This presentation gains slightly more applause than the previous one, piquing some interest amongst the audience who wonder how he captured the jellyfish. Penny had seen a similar trick that souvenir shops discovered years before, though they had preferred small capsules of live chameleons or lizards too similar to the ones that crawled along the dry dirt in Camp Minidoka. She used to chase them. How many could she

168

catch? One time, absentmindedly following one had led her to a man.

A pungent smell of burning rubber draws her attention back to the present. Donovan has performed some trick that leaves double rings of black smoke above his head. With his act almost finished, she leaves her drink to head backstage. She waits until Donovan and his sister bow to the smattering of applause. There will be no announcement for her, not in a cheap bar like this. She merely struts out, back straight, head high. Her music accompaniment is the club owner herself playing a violin. Penny looks into the silhouetted audience, consciously blurring her vision so she won't have to look into their surly faces. Between songs, she finds a comforting face. George is at a table nearest to the stage, a mug of flat beer in hand and cream gardenias wrapped in newspaper. The early dawn haze burns through the filmy black windows, casting its dew over the golden sun while peaking rays of sunlight make the panels on the wooden stage shimmer a brilliant golden. Standing in the glow is this singer.

He positions a few feet from her, not daring to interrupt the trance she is in, song and body in a perfect union. On an upstroke, when her head moves slightly to put feeling into the note, he sees a glimpse of her face. Her eyes close in a dreamlike consciousness, absorbing every note from the core of herself and emitting it into the atmosphere while her glossy lips part slightly. With the last note, she lets out a smooth exhale and opens her eyes to meet his, which have fixated on the moment as the echo of the last note floats through. Perhaps it is a dream after all and they are both on the verge of consciousness. She bows, thanking the patrons,

169

as George meets her at the foot of the stage. Catching her breath, she greets him happily and she guides him to the broom closet. The space is just wide enough to fit them both. In her purse, she rummages to find what she was looking for, a soft square of tissue that she takes with her to stand before the mirror and pats her forehead to collect the sweat brought on by stage lights and the stream from the kitchen. Balling up the tissue, she keeps it in her fist, and pauses, frozen, staring at her pale face, at a woman with red lips and false blonde hair who swallowed a nightingale, and a shadow behind her at once shrouded and cast in light from overhead. They two joined as one photograph pasted over another.

At once, she remembers a movie that she saw when she was young called *Virginia City*. There was a saloon dancer who plastered a smile on her face as she kicked her leg high into the air, showing her white thighs and the ruffles of her skirts. That is what she pretends to look like. It is easy for her to see many futures hanging down like silk streamers. She can pull any of them and down it will come. A wide space open for her with colors raining.

Penelope shuffles in through the door of her house with beaten eyes and collapses on her sofa, not bothering to take off her evening dress, damp from sweat, to sleep off the alterations of her blood from a night at the club. It wasn't the alcohol that did it. The chain of Firelights to keep her awake are wearing off. The stage lights had been hot, the weather even more so. The cushions envelop her as she sinks into their comfort until she does not feel any part of her body. She drifts, lying on the couch pretending to sleep with the daylight peeking through shaded windows and the ticking clock on the mantle. Steps on carpet and a body snuggling beside her that she assumes is her cat.

*

When she wakes, she is alone, and has to touch her face and arms to ensure that they are her own. Whatever memories remain from the night before are purposefully repressed.

As long as I can sing, she reminds herself, *nothing else matters*.

Already there are heavy footsteps above her along with the muffling shouts she has long been able to ignore. Outside the window, a blue sky and a piercing bright sun. Penny peeks out the window to see Ojiisan pottering in the garden with his grandson close by. Removing a kerchief from his back overalls pocket, he coughs every now and then into it, releasing phlegm and mucous built up in his lungs. Penny turns to the stairs, her cat following her, then choosing to remain inside while she exposes herself to the outdoor air.

"What are you doing up?" she nags, startling the old man.

"The garden needs tending."

"And I planned on doing it tomorrow morning after my show."

He shakes his head, "It needs looking after every day."

"I watered this morning."

"You watered the *leaves* but look here." He points to the soil underneath. "It's dry. There should be enough to make the dirt damp. And here." A step toward the blueberries. "You see some new weeds grew since last time."

"Yes, yes. You come here, sit, and I'll take care of it."

171

He waves his hand away at her suggestion.

"Come here," she insists, "I can handle pulling weeds by myself."

A sigh, wanting to refuse but his lungs must be weak and his head dizzy, for he relinquishes. Penny leaves Timmy among the plants to go inside and fetch a trowel, pausing at the unusually sharp shouting tumbling down from upstairs. Sneaking in quietly through the back door, she flattens up against the door frame, tucking her skirt into her thighs so it will not puff out to reveal her hiding spot. It is no use eavesdropping. They both speak in such quick Japanese that her ears are unused to hearing. Yet she can make out some small commands from George spoken with a ferocity that she has never heard from him before.

Listening to his booming shouts make her skin jump in surprise, and his wife's miniscule rebuttals do nothing to quell him. It was then she understood what Catherine meant about distracting him and will use anyone as a way of taking her husband's attention elsewhere so that she might have more freedom.

Penny steals herself away back to Timothy. He was waiting for her where she left him under the broad leaves, trying to reach the wide yellow petals by small jumps.

"Here are the scissors," she says, walking over. "Let's get this pretty little thing."

She is about to cut it when he whines.

"Do you want to do it?"

He nods his curly head and she hands him the scissors and lifts him up. He opens and shuts them around the base. Down it falls to the grass.

George's voice beckons Timothy into the house. Hearing it, he rushes with scissors still in hand, leaving Penny to follow him. A door slams. Sitting on the carpet having dropped the scissors nearby, he cries without tears. She gently bounces him on her thigh, her hands resting on his baby stomach, singing *Oh My Darling, Clementine.* His cries soften as he looks to his father with his big eyes. There is no response from George, not even a turn of the head. In swift succession, he goes into his room, shuts the door, rustles therein, and reemerges. With a few deep whimpers, Timothy stops his crying, and Penny lifts the edge of her skirt to wipe the tears from his cheeks. He sits up, walking away to his mother's room where the indication of her presence is in the sound coming from the radio and Rose's babbling.

Hearing a pitiful meow, Penny peeks into the living room where Bruce is sitting up attentively on the arm of the couch, gazing straight at her and letting out another whine.

"You want to come?" she asks him and hefts up Bruce in her arm. her free fingers pull the key from her purse and paces up the steps to the second floor.

With Bruce held comfortably in her arm, his forelegs and head rest on her shoulder while his whiskers tickle her neck, she pushes the door open, meeting George on the other side. He is in his Sunday suit and there is a plaid fabric suitcase at his side.

Curious, she asks, "And where are you going?"

"On a business trip."

"A what?" she asks, surprised at the sudden turn of his absence.

"I'm leaving for a few days." He says, then pats Bruce on the head.

"What do you mean you're leaving?"

173

"Just that."

She nearly retorts with, "You weren't going to tell me?" and yet she hesitates, barely a twitch of a smile, and says "Take care" before pushing past him through the door, resisting the temptation to look back to see his reaction.

Pushing on, she feels a bump against her leg and finds Timothy staring up at her. He reaches his arms up, trying to touch Bruce's soft fur. Bending down, Penny sets the cat on the floor, knowing Timmy is gentle with the cat; he had never pulled on ears or even tried to pick him up, unlike his sister who reveled in chasing Bruce around, trying to grab onto his tail. Timothy squats with his hands folded on his belly, watching the cat who sits, licking his raised right paw. Penny leaves them there, venturing to Catherine's bedroom where she suspects that the woman will have confined herself. She knocks twice on the closed door. When there is no answer, she calls, "It's me."

"Oh! Come in, come in."

Opening the door, a chemical smell wafts at her, burning the inside of her nose, coming from bottle of Lifeguard Disinfectant and a used rag on the floor. She holds in a gag, not wanting to let it out and upset Catherine who sits upright on her single bed, flipping through a novel while Rose rolls around on the bed to keep herself entertained.

"Sit down," she says without looking up from her book. "I've been feeling so sick. Dizzy, tired, nauseous." Penny rolls her eyes, knowing Catherine isn't looking, but offers a concerning, "I'm sure you'll feel better."

"I will now that *he'll* be gone. I can't relax with him here."

"Never mind him, then," Penny says, dismissing the subject. "We should do something. Let's go out somewhere. Why don't you come to church on Sunday?"

"I don't think I'll be better by then," she replies quickly, keeping her eyes pinned on the book pages. "I sometimes wonder about those powders. . .The camps. That cake we mixed."

"It's still a few days away," Penny says, dismissing the sickening memories of internment and of the munitions manufacturing while they resided. "Timothy and Rose always go anyway; you should come too."
Her answer is a low exhale.

"Didn't you go to church when you were a girl?" Penny asks.

"Oh, yes. I was married in one, too, at the camp. But," she closes her book and pushes it under her pillow, "I don't suppose I'm a proper Christian, not really, since I wasn't baptized." she turns her eyes to Penny. "You were, weren't you?"
She nods.

"How was it?"

"My baptism? Oh, it was wonderful." She rests her head on her hand as Catherine reaches into her housecoat pocket, taking out a pack of Firelite cigarettes and a matchbox. She goes about removing one, lighting it, and stowing the rest safely back in her pocket. Drawing on the cigarette, she lets out a great puff of white smoke.

"We got a special pass, all of us who were getting baptized that day, so Pastor Wade could take us to the church. It was the first time in a year that I'd been outside the darn fence. Mother let me borrow her dress. It was a little big, but Mom tied one of her satin scarves around my waist for a sash." She taps the excess ash in the tray. "One of the farm trucks took us there. Hours until we got to Twin Falls. Small town but the church was lovely. Colorful stained glass, polished wood. It was a castle. Me and the others waited in the back room." She pauses to extinguish her cigarette in the tray. "In that puffy white dress, it's the closest I've been to feeling like a bride. One after the other we went through a little door that led to a kind of bathtub set in the floor a ways from the sanctuary. Usually it was hidden by a curtain. When it was my turn, I walked out and saw the pews all full—my first audience!—and there the Pastor knee-deep in water motioning for me to come towards him. Down I went. I thought it would be cold, most of the water in the camp was cold, but it was warm and up to my hips. The Pastor held me like a baby—truly—and dipped me down, straight under. No one went with me that day except Oniisan." She glances up to Catherine, offering more. "My uncle. The first time I met was in the camp. He told me to call him that, Oniisan. He told me that since my father was gone, he'd be my big brother, to keep me safe." She stops for a moment, swallowing, "Though, really, he must have been closer to thirty. My aunt was older."

"*Kin no waraji,*" Catherine explains.

The golden straw sandals. An old idiom for a slightly older woman marrying a younger man. The ideal situation that results in a woman who will care for her husband with the love equal to both mother and wife.

"I should have been so wise," remarks Catherine. "If I married a younger man, I might have more say in my life."

In the uncomfortable silence, Penny mentions Sunday service.

"Oh, now you too?" she retorts. "See how I have no choice? George tells me one thing and you side with him."

"It's not like that—"

176

"—It is. But I suppose I can be grateful. When he's gone with you, it leaves me alone to do as I like with my children. With him in the house…I can't be around him, I can tell you, not with that voice of his, the sounds he makes. I'm thankful he wants separate beds—I couldn't bear to sleep next to him every night," she says, thoughtful, "How can you spend so much time with him?"

Penny lowers her head; her eyes fix on a point on the blue table, "There's beauty in everyone."

Catherine scoffs. She lights another cigarette while bouncing Rose, trying to lull her to sleep.

"*Shoganai*," she says. "You two do as you like. Just don't leave me alone with him. Even if you two. . ." She shrugs her shoulders slowly. "*Itoko ni seppun o kyouku.*" While the songstress resolved that a marriage was not true without love, she nevertheless withdraws her body slightly, distancing herself from the wife, her attention now moving to stroking Bruce's chin.

"What does it matter? Better I know who it is instead of some stranger."

Whimpering cries come from Rose on the bed near her mother. Ignoring her, Catherine flips through the magazine while the baby rolls back and forth, kicking her feet in the air in her temper. Seeing the child in such discomfort pulls at Penny's nerves. If it were her daughter, she would heave her up in a moment to sing and soothe the girl. Yet she is not her mother and will not cross the bond between the two. After some minutes, Rose brings her fore and middle fingers to her mouth to find comfort in suckling the tips. Happy at her self-soothing, Catherine lays a hand on the girl's belly.

"But you said you can't stand him."

177

"I can't. But what can I do alone with two children? A modern woman's work does not interest me and neither does divorce. No. I'd like to be free, as I was before. It's impossible now."

She leans back, Rose now snoring in her arms.

"In a way, when I was in the camp that was the most freedom I've ever had." She draws on her cigarette as if pulling the string on deflating balloons. "Isn't that sad?" The grim expression on her face changes suddenly to a miniscule smirk.

"You know, it's silly, but," she starts, "I sometimes think about my old dreams."

Curious, Penny's eyes widen enthusiastically, persuading Catherine to continue with a sweet, "Tell me."

A relaxing exhale leaves her lips as she dampens the cigarette in the ashtray already full of half spent Firelites.

"I'd always wanted to work in a bakery. You never have to worry about mistakes when baking bread; you just start again. Tea cakes, shortbread, French rolls." She swallows down some saliva that rises beneath her tongue.

"It sounds wonderful," Penny offers, a hint of somber barely hidden in her voice from the knowledge that such a dream may have happened in better times.

She nearly suggests that Catherine try to pursue it, were it not for the woman's aversion to the outdoors and the stipulation that such skilled positions are reserved for those who possess citizenship and while George or Ojiisan can easily bestow this on anyone, such generosity had not been extended to Catherine for reasons unexpressed by either of them. Nostalgia seems to calm her as she slopes down on the bed, settling her head on the pillow and closes her eyes. Penny remains for as long as it takes to sense the deep sleep that comes with a heavy body. Shifting carefully, Penny slips from the sheets and into the living room to discover Timmy satisfyingly occupying himself with climbing atop the furniture only to jump down and repeat the game. Catching Bruce up from where he sharpens his claws on the edge of the sofa, Penny returns downstairs to her bedroom, leaving her cat free to roam. Taking the letters that she hid amongst her possessions, she replies to each, knowing precisely how she should answer.

11
Sarah
Club Crawl

"I'm going out to the Black and Tan. You should come too." Penny says in the evening shortly after Sarah returns exhausted and sweaty from work.

"I really am not in the mood to go to one of *those* clubs with your rowdy friends."

"Come anyway. You never want to have any fun."

"I have fun just fine. You know I can't stand that racket down there."

"If I can stand that violin, you can come with me. Otherwise what will you do tonight? Annoy the neighbors?" Penny crosses her arms. "Have you had supper yet?"

"No."

"Well, all the more reason to get up out of this place. Come on." She takes her hand and tugs.

*

It is a short sky train ride, then through the station where posters with Robert Sinclair's silhouette are plastered to the inner walls, three stripes of red, white and blue. Underneath reads "Proudly A Patriot." She peers at a woman in a white suit dress with a Stars and Stripes button pin on her lapel handing out pamphlets to passers-by, saying cheerfully, "Be sure to vote on the Fourth of July!".

The sidewalks are scattered with suited workers walking towards the sky train station. Penny winds around, turning corners that Sarah doesn't recognize. All the buildings seem to meld together into the same picture. She slows down as they approach a brown brick building with apartment windows above a lit sign that reads "Merchants Café." Talking and the knocking back-and-forth of doors opening and closing become louder as they pass over the glass squares in the sidewalk. As they pass through the doors under the golden number 109, they wait for a seat at the bar. The light as dim as if there were only candles illuminating the inside.

"Tell me about work," Penny says to pass the time.

"The same."

"There must be something. Are they hiring more people? I remember when you were trying to work there, the front was full of everyone looking for jobs."

"There are hardly any workers. I have to fill double the quota now. Not to mention," Sarah adds spitefully to elicit some guilt over Penelope, "the changing wages every morning" and, scowling at the memory of the fluctuating dimes and cents, she adds, "They don't seem to care. At least back home it was more regular."

"Was it?" she asks.

"They always made sure we had a day off every week. Ten hours every day. One-hour lunch, and a smoke break. Here it's twelve—more like fourteen-and a thirty-minute lunch. It's not right."

"Can't you talk to the boss--oh," she prods Sarah towards two vacant seats. When they sit, Penny orders a glass of Moscato wine for them both. She reiterates, "to get shorter hours?"

Lighting a cigarette, Sarah says, "It's not a place where you can make demands. Actually," she begins, seeing a chance, "since you mention it, if I could get a citizen's visa. . ." She let it sit in the air.

When their drinks arrive, Penny sips, seemingly ignoring Sarah.

"A visa," she repeats, thoughtfully. "that's expensive. Not to mention all the paperwork. It'll take you awhile to get ahold of one." Her tone becomes perky, eyes widening to look at Sarah, "Does that mean you'll stay here longer?"

"I—No." She considers leaving the subject as it is, but decides that this may be the best opportunity. "I thought that since you already live comfortably, that you could—"

"—That I could get one for you?" she finishes, drinking again, disapproval clearly displayed in her furrowed brows and sardonic smirk. "I *could* help you, of course, but these things cost money."

"Don't you have it?" she asks boldly, refusing to submit.

She nods once, her expression now unreadable.

"Then why not help me, help my family?"

Stage music begins, a piano player happily tapping his fingers on keys. Hearing the music seems to lighten Penny's demeanor.

"If auntie needed any money, I'm sure she would write. Let's not squabble about money," Penny says, putting an end to the unpleasant conversation. "I'd hoped you might come with me somewhere."

Sarah leans back on her chair and asks, "Why?"

At this, her face lightens as she takes her fingers from the glass to take a telegram from her purse. She holds it before her, reading, "Ms. Penelope Morgan. In accordance with your performance at The Atelier Lounge on April thirteenth, we would like you to meet with the photographer Mr. James Colburn at his studio at' etcetera, etcetera, "to have photographs taken for publicity posters." Here she stops and raises her eyebrows, anticipating her cousin's excitement. Sarah exhales, rolling her eyes, lingering on the supposition that Penny, without a job, has time to do whatever she wants at whatever hour she wants while Sarah is confined to a strict work schedule that if she breaks will lead to her unemployment and destitution.

"I have to work," she remarks. It is a lie, but after Penny's dismissal of her request for money, she has little interest in being helpful.

Penny shrugs, replacing the notice.

*

What she feared most were the detonators.
Sarah and Penny were on the line that steadily attached the mechanisms to the shells. He barely breathed, slowing his breath as if he had none. It was cruel that their shared elegance brought them here. Sarah's coveted still fingers that had been created by years of holding bow and violin. Penny's from song. Their hands should create beauty, not weapons. There was no choice. *Shoganai*. They must carry on. Auntie glued the paper on. Mama painted the tips of the shells while the baby was wrapped on her back. Papa mixed the cordite. Their eyes had tints of yellow; the tips of their hair not covered by the caps were burnt orange. Their strips of exposed skin where the boots didn't meet the tunic and the gloves didn't meet the sleeves were yellow. That awful yellow. Penny wanted to get out, as did Sarah. It was too much today. But Sarah was always obedient.

"The sooner we're done, they'll let us leave. What's the matter with you? You know how long it takes," she scolded. The foggy air was too much.

"Please, I can't stand it today."

183

Annoyed, she tensed as she lowered the shell on, her voice irritated, "Sarah—" she said.

Then it happened. She slipped. It was nothing, the movement of the fingers. As slight as a flick. She screamed and they all dropped, as they were told to do should it occur. But Sarah didn't. Fear made her and the others run in panic. And behind them came the great roar.

12
Penelope
Lights and Photography

Nerves flutter as lilly-skinned girls wait behind The Fortune Follies stage, many who prefer to avoid eye contact, instead focusing on their breathing, warming up their throats, or drinking cold water to prepare their voices. Penelope, meanwhile, matches sights with the young competitors. To her chagrin, she counts seven who have replaced their natural vocal chords with the churning gears needed to synthesize a polyphonic song. At her turn, she takes a deep breath to stymie any weakness, fleshes out her best performer's visage, and steps out, completely awestruck at the expanse. The glowing aquariums surrounding the upper balcony ripples alive where every sea creature continues their natural habits, interrupted only by the gilded mermaid swimming past, interrupting their patterns. A nervous determination steadies her resolve.

All these fake singers, she reasons, *they will have to appreciate a natural artist like me.*

At her turn, she glides from the back to the front of the stage. Her body poised, back straight, legs together with one foot slightly forward, the rounded toe of her cherry red Baby Doll pumps pointing to the center of the room. She relaxes her shoulders, pale and exposed in the sleeveless silver dress she bought the day before specifically for the way it shined in the lights. Her chin tilts up by a little to ensure that her voice will project into the audience of for two men sitting at the table closest to the stage. The nightclub seems to bend towards her as the spotlights warm her skin. In her vivid imagination, she can see her arrival on this stage

185

every night where the audience looks up at her in amazement as her words roll over them as waves on a shore.

"Name?" the first man asks, snapping her out of her reverie.

She answers, and he instructs her to sing. In her clearest, tempered voice, she sings as if she were standing among a heavenly choir, imagining herself as a seraph exalting the golden Lamb. In a beautiful moment, she revels in the joy of her song reverberating from the floors to the eaves. That time is hers that none can steal. As fleeting as plum blossoms in winter, her performance finishes as the man interrupts her song with a brusque cessation.

"Thank you," says the second man as Penny abruptly stops, and wastes no time to humor her. "You've a fine voice, miss," Penny steadies herself for the inevitable finish to the sentence, "but, a fine voice is not what we're looking for, so—"

"—if it's not too much," she interrupts, having to consciously keep a smile on her face, "what is it that you're looking for?"

"Panache," answers the first man with a wave of his fingers, "A real stunner with a singular voice—"

"—or two," the second man says in reference to the polyphonic voice mechanisms.

Penny nods once, thanks them politely for their time, and takes slow, careful steps off the stage, regretfully relinquishes her position on the stage, knowing it will be the only time she will have stood as a prima donna at The Fortune Follies. In the alley outside, she walks until the nightclub is no longer in sight, and, safely hidden, buries her face in her hands to shed years of brushed-away tears. As fast as it takes a single push from the lever of a water pump to pass a stream through the spout, her crying spills out in one trickling stream and then stops as soon as it began, leaving traces in her smeared makeup. She dabs her face with a handkerchief and glances at her pocket mirror. Composing herself, she tucks the mirror and kerchief back into her purse.

*

A clean looking brick building sits so close to the shoreline that a row of Seagulls perch on the overhanging rain gutter. When a breeze rises from the water, a few of the monochrome birds spread their wings to soar on the updraft. She walks up to the fifth floor to a room marked "9" and knocks. For a moment, she is taken aback when a dark-skinned man answers, a Firelite cigarette held taut between his lips. His short curly hair is slicked down, parted from the right, much in the same fashion as George.

"This is Mr. Colburn's residence?" she queries, unsure.

"Yes."

Any notion of shock is replaced quickly by a genteel demeanor as she holds out her hand.

"Ms. Penny Morgan, pleased to meet you."

He takes it, shaking twice.

"Yes. Mr. Mertz told me you were coming." He withdraws from the door, "After you."

She enters a small space with one window that had been painted black to shut out the sun. The lighting comes from studio bulbs arranged around a purple velvet curtain. A single table near it holds several types of cameras. A narrow door on the far wall bears a thin wooden panel hand painted with the warning, "Development Room: Do Not Open."

187

She walks in a few paces, turning to find him already at his camera table adjusting each one.

"I'm afraid this is my first studio picture," she interjects, threading her fingers together/ "I don't quite know what to do."

"Not to worry, Miss, it's the simplest thing." He closes the backing on the camera, motioning towards the curtain. "Come stand in front of the light. Now just leave your purse over there—oh—and your hat; you don't need them."

She does as she is told, situating herself in front of the velvet.

"Terrible that I can't shoot in color. Those are some eyes."

She followed his soft instructions. Smiling, repositioning, smiling again when it inevitably relaxes. The attention is a reminder of her already moderate success. It is not enough. The girls with the glimmering necks stay fixed in her memory.

A headliner is no small step, she reassures. Yet as the camera flash pops there is an insecurity pooling at the stem of her skull, threatening to flood.

*

Penny jumps from her bed, alarming Bruce who had been fast asleep, and glides to the closet to pull out a strapless dusky and white damask pink dress. The bodice is ornamented with glossy seed pearls in spiral designs, stopping at the waist and erupting into a bell skirt. She takes it to the bathroom to get ready, hanging the dress on the backside hook of the door. At the sink she brushes her teeth with the Ipana toothpaste sitting on the sink. She can't remember if it is her toothbrush or Sarah's, but it doesn't really matter. Her makeup is in the first drawer under the sink and when she opens it, her Elizabeth Arden peach-pink lipstick rolls to the front, slapping against the inside of the wood. She first pats on the foundation Pan-Cake Max Factor cream and sets it with the flesh powder, then gives her cheeks a little bit of a light blush.

Next the eyes, a thin spread of liner into a sweeping wing, careful not to make it too pronounced. She decides against putting on her false eyelashes and settles for mascara instead. She looks through the drawer for an eye shadow that will match the dress and finds a pale coral that she dabs onto her closed lids with her pinky finger. Her lipstick she leaves for last, turning to remove the curlers that she set the night before from her hair and preening them, tossing her head back and forth to decide whether she likes the way they bounce. One thread of hair on her forehead seems out of place, so she sets it back with a bobby pin. She pauses in the mirror, placing a hand at her neck, rubbing her throat with her thumb, thinking how it may look slashed open and replaced with machinery. An image unappealing.

Out of the linen closet where she keeps her undergarments, she picks out her matching brassiere and girdle and manages to wiggle into them. A pair of flesh toned stockings attach to the straps on the girdle and she covers it all with the dress, zipping it tight. Then the lipstick. Back in the bedroom, she takes a pair of daisy shaped earrings with opals for petals and a glass diamond in the center. No necklace, but she clips a simple bracelet rhinestone band around her left wrist. In her closet are her matching pink heels with a heart decal on the ankle strap. They are

189

uncomfortable in that the back often rub against her heel. She wears them anyway.

Out into the living room to gather her purse, she checks the time on the wall clock and takes her purse to her room so she can slip some money into it that she keeps hidden in her top dresser drawer in a billfold under her father's old uniforms. The space is shared with letters and old newspaper clippings kept in a shallow hat box without a lid. The topmost paper reads "OPERATION OLYMPIC" and the article explains in rousing detail the events of the final push on the war against the Axis and the Japanese Imperial Army that employed battleships, destroyers, bomber planes, thousands of American soldiers and hundreds of the iron automatons referred to as "war machines." When the newspaper had first appeared on the morning doorstep after she and her mother had been discharged from the camp, she hoarded it before showing it to anyone. Searching, hoping for any implication that her father was alive. Of course, there had been none. It was an article of facts and excitable summaries of events: a broad description of war that mentioned men as a mass of flesh set against another mass of enemies not unlike machines themselves. It spoke of patriotism and victory, of bullets and firepower, of honor and an estimated three hundred thousand dead. The ink is a steadfast reminder that death has worth.

The drawer shut, money stowed away, she stands over the gold filigree framed oval mirror tray of perfumes she keeps on her marble topped corner table. For tonight she chooses the *L'air de la Libellule*. The last gift from her father. A bright aquamarine essence captured in a teardrop crystal bottle. The stopper is a hollow sphere is a miniscule

190

dragonfly carved from a ruby stone suspended in the center. Pulling it open carefully, she dabs the droplets of fragrance from end of the stopper against in inside of each wrist and on her neck. Adequately prepared, she sits on the living room couch waiting, listening to the radio for a minute then getting up and pacing around the center from a point by the armrest, in front of the fireplace, around the chair, and back. When she clicks around the chair, she peeks out the window to watch for his car, trying not to give herself any expectations. Not until she opens the door does she notice the sprinkling rain and resigns herself to waiting on the porch, smoking a cigarette while attempting unsuccessfully to form smoke rings when his car rolls up to the curb. She straightens and swings her purse over her shoulder.

When he rolls down the window he calls, "Penelope." A tone of four syllables are low and then rise to a sweet ring. True to her request, she spies a small bouquet of four cream gardenias fastened together by a wide orange satin ribbon. Four flowers. Oniisan's voice whispers from behind, reminding her of the superstition surrounding that number; although of different *kanji* strokes, 四 is the same *"shi"* pronunciation as the word for death 死. As a result, Oniisan avoided anything that arrived in fours and advised her to do so. Quite different from Ojiisan who revels in the similarities of finding power in fear. Her sights shift from the soft flower petals to the faces of two young gentlemen in the back seat and Ojiisan relaxing between them. Delighted to see him, she gives a sincere smile, picks up the bouquet and sits in the passenger seat, closing the door.

"I didn't think you'd come," she says, lifting the flowers to her nose, inhaling gently, then laying across her lap.

"I'd hate to miss your big show."

Once more to the lounge and through the mirrored door with the flowers tucked neatly into the crook of her arm. Ojiisan settles at the bar with one of the men, leaving the others to follow her to the upstairs dressing room furnished with a well-worn burgundy velvet hoop chair sitting in front of a wooden vanity and the walls covered by pickfair wallpaper.

"Make sure you say '*Konbanwa*' to Mr. DuPont," George advises.

"But of course!" Penny cheers, removing her evening overcoat to drape over the vanity chair. "It's be shameful for me to forget that, and after he's been so kind." She finds a single iris from the bouquet, breaking it off at the stem. "I'll just go find the devil now." She says, ignoring the men who trail her steps to the office at the end of the hall.

Opening the door to surprise Mr. DuPont at his desk, she says, "Why, there you are." while reaching her arms out to embrace him at once, kissing him lightly on each cheek, and pulling back to present the flower. "I wanted to give you this," She takes his lapel in hand to push the stem of the flower through the button hole before he can refuse, "for my gratitude."

Looking past her smile, he spies the men who file in, the last one closing the door.

"Now, what is this?"

Penny backs away, letting George approach.

"The agreement?" he asks.

192

"That," he says nonchalantly. "I did make it clear in the letter to Mr. Igarashi that I am unable to breach my current business with your," he pauses, "adversaries. We can come to some other agreement?"

George nods to one of his accomplices. Catching his eye, Penny finds herself unable to tear away from the scene from both fascination and determination. This is not like watching from afar. To look away may be noticed; a subtle show of disloyalty. She does her best to dampen her disgust, but is unable to control her hands that clench together at her waist, a thumbnail pushing against cuticles as she watches one *kyodai* takes a firm hold of the unfortunate man's hair, pulling back so his head tilts up. The other forces his mouth open, one grasping onto the slippery pink muscle with a pair of pincers. A groan of protest, knowing what will come and powerless to stop it. The big band music from the stage downstairs masks his throaty scream when George presses a sharp blade to DuPont's wet tongue. At the calling of the cuckoo clock, Penny slips from the office and the smell of the sweaty ordeal, shutting the door quietly behind her.

Whatever it takes, she reminds herself, *as long as I can sing*.

Letting out a deep breath, she smooths her dress as best as she can with trembling hands, and readjusts the flower in her hair, then walks the long hall, descending winding stairs, to the stage. Bright oil lantern lights against crimson walls imbue the room with a soft blush. The main floor is set with round wooden tables with glass flower ash trays in the center, chairs set in pairs across from each other. A young girl is behind the bar counter, chocolate hair hanging flat around her head and past her shoulders. A simple wire barrette sweeps the hair from her eyes. Attendees crowd the main-floor lobby and the multiple tiers that rise from below. Bouncing off the smooth walls are the jolts of conversation from the gatherers within. Penny walks through the empty hall to the stairs leading up to her dressing room in the upper tier. Ascending the silent steps—her heels make the softest sound against them—to the second level. She holds her hand steady on the glass banister that runs the length of the center.

Nearby, she hears the delicate tune of a single oboe, and is drawn to the open door where the music beckons her. She catches a glimpse of the mahogany stage where a single man stands playing his oboe. The hum of a thousand conversations at once ascends to her ears. The sound is a toccata, spoiling the pure tune of the oboe. Every few moments a bawling laughter arises from the soft murmur, and then dissipates into the air. She watches more people emerge and join the assembly of patrons as she departs from the main room to take her place behind the stage, anxiously waiting her debut.

Whooping calls from the standing crowd to the stage where a very young Chinese girl, no older than fourteen, sweeps white ostrich feather fans over her exposed, pale skin at once covering secret parts and letting them peek through fluffy down. No ordinary burlesque, when she places the two fans together, a spark of blue fame emits from the center, growing to consume the tips, the feathers sprinkling to the ground in sequins and confetti. She stands in the center of the stage, plastic smile, her chest bare. A final theatric before she departs are the feathers disappearing into glimmering white lights that float from the ceiling to the tops of the audience's heads, some of them trying to catch illuminated flakes as the curtains close. From the side stage emerges a piece of sophisticated machinery. A man in a shimmering tuxedo with a top hat to match has a glass tube where the center of his neck should be. Within it are whirring gears and spooled copper.

"Gentlemen!" it bellows in a voice too robotic to be human. "Presenting the young lady that has been described as silky. Please welcome the dazzling, melodious siren, Ms. Penny Morgan!"

Applause as the announcer withdraws, the spotlight expands, and the curtains pull back. The high dome ceiling that can change from daylight to starry skies. When she looks out to the light she basks in the attention from the round faces watching her as she walks onto the stage to her mark behind the microphone with a performer's smile on her face. Such a moment is reminiscent of her first small recital during a talent show during her internment. At the piano, a young lady begins the introduction to *Broadway Rose* while the songstress sends out her voice across the audience. The notes drown her in a pure stream of divinity reaching a point of exuberance.

There in the center of the stage is Penny, smiling, with her platinum hair curled gently into soft rings that lay about her shoulders. Her makeup waxen on her face, rouge dusted on her cheeks, pouting lipstick lips, give no hint to her Japanese blood. The band behind her begins the set, trumpets coming in, then softening as she opens her mouth to sing *A Little Bird Told Me*. Spotlights blind her to the sitting audience; the accompanying music obliterating all thought. Penny's head sways. *Nerves, it must be,* she decides. She had a small drink while warming up and it may have been

195

stronger than she suspected. Her face is serene in the eyes that barely stray from a distant spot in the audience where she sees George and his father. On an upstroke, her head moves slightly to put feeling into the note and her curled hair bounces, swishing against her neck. Her eyes close in a dreamlike consciousness, absorbing every note from her core and emitting it into the atmosphere with slightly parted lips, showing the front of her teeth. With the last note finished, she lets out a smooth exhale and opens her eyes as the echo of the last note floats through the crowd.

Shattering. The ground rolls as summer waves. Silence and then, suddenly, panicked screeches. Bricks rub against each other, cracking, collapsing. She claps her hands around her ears as soon as the shrieking fire alarm clicks; needles in her eardrums.

Then a terrible siren from afar.

A rocking from the stage makes her stumble, falling to her knees. Looking up, she expects to see laughing faces at her blunder. Instead there is horror. The shaking becomes vigorous. Cracks emerge in the stage floor. There is a grinding from above like sandpaper on metal. Screaming concrete breaks from the ceiling to the ground. Half open to the sky, slanting and held in place by thick wires. Penny searches for live bodies. Two names flash repeatedly in her mind. George. Ojiisan. He had been in the front row that is now home to cement crumbles and blocks. She forces herself to stand, her skin throbbing against the seams of her shoes, and slides off the stage, looking at figures lying on the floor, ignoring the ones that aren't Japanese.

There.

"Ojiisan!" she shouts.

He is face down but breathing. She calls his name, shakes him. A metallic hiss that she disregards. As she pulls, there is resistance keeping him where he lies, and he makes a pitifully weak whine. His eyes are partly open. It is when he tries to move his arm that she sees it. His right arm up just above the elbow is wedged under a concrete slab. She looks around for help. A mob of heads and bodies pound against the singular entrance. She coughs, finding it increasingly difficult to breathe. Raising her head, she now sees the black smoke thickening the air. Fire. She can't wait. She can't leave him to die like this.

To burn is the worst death.

"I'll help you," she promises, crawling on her hands and knees under the smoke line to the stage in the back where she finds the glass case containing a sturdy, alarm red, emergency fire axe.

Opening it, she wavers.

It is either this or the fire.

She takes it, returning to him as he drifts in and out, groaning and mumbling. There is no time for her to say anything of comfort. Hoping he is too delirious to notice, she touches the axe blade to his arm, lining it. On her knees, steadying, she presses it into his flesh, driving it down. A terrible scream. His pain mixing with other screams of fear. She raises it again, up, down, taking pauses to wipe the blood spilling out onto her skirt, severing the meat until the bone snaps and the arm comes free. Tossing the bloody tool aside, she picks him up with ease. Penny slashes her head this way and that for any way to escape the thickening heat. There are no windows to break. The back exit through the stage is happily found.

Shoving against it once, twice, it springs open so it slams on the outer wall of the alley. The door block sits just to the side. She wedges it tightly, pulling the door against it to make sure it won't slip. Dashing across the street with Ojiisan in her arms, his blood streaming, she deposits him on the sidewalk. Frantic, she scans for the automated police. In her blurry vision, she does not see it at first, the grey gadget placidly patrolling up and down. She sprints toward it and pushes the alert button on its chest before returning to the back alley. She doesn't stop to drink in the clear air. Running back inside, she trips over a cable but regains her balance. She is confronted by shouts and frantic orders. She steadies herself on the velvet stage curtain for a moment, coughing a few times from the smoke that bloats the air. Her arms are weak. She has to find George.

The smoke. Flashing in between are knives of orange cutting up the atmosphere. As best as she can, she searches for her cousins in the dark until she can't breathe without inhaling burning ash that forces her back out into the street, now packed with emergency services and the perturbed onlookers. The emergency call had been quick to act. Already there are flashing ambulance lights, police cars, and a few of the extinguishing automatons stand before the front of the club spraying water from rubber hoses connected to full water tanks strapped to their backs. Frantically, she looks for her family, for any of them. There are no people that she can find to ask, only machines.

She passes each ambulance, opening doors and finding only strangers. At last she finds Ojiisan lying on a stretcher in an ambulance. A single emergency nurse is fiddling with a mask over his face. She sees the hack on his arm covered by layers of white gauze bandages. She can't find her voice. A pair of emergency nurses bring along a body so badly burned that its white face has turned to charcoal scales and deep crimson covers the spaces where eyes should be. Hoses protrude from a wide hole in the middle of the face. Lips blistered to the fullness of an over boiled cherry tomato. The nurse closes the door, leaving Penny alone. She glances at the mass of people scurrying around the outside of the now crisping nightclub, police guiding injured to the waiting ambulances.

Rushing to one of the policemen squatting on the curb trying to comfort a younger man whose eyes are wide open, staring at his wringing hands. Catching his attention with an "Excuse me.", she startles when the policeman shoots her at first a startled and then concerned look. He does not to tell her to go away, but she does so instinctively as if suddenly fearing such comfort. She tries to remember what George had been wearing. Black. A black suit with a blue tie. That must be right. She is drawn to the man sitting on the curb across the street, his arms crossed and rushes towards him, catching him in a hug that he doesn't pull away from.

"I didn't think you made it."

She leans back from him so he can let go. When she does, she sees that he had not been quite crossing his arms so much as cradling his left elbow. What brings her to heightened shock is that his right trouser leg is burned. She bends over to appraise his leg, ignoring any polite personal space, before he withdraws and pushes her hand away, but not before she sees his leg flushed a bright red.

Penny collapses on the street, tears spilling from her eyes.

199

"Oh, you're burned," she says, and can hear the anxiety in her voice.

The blackened skin appears through the edges of the burned sleeve, like a grotesque window looking into a bloody sea. Turning from it, she looks up at him with watery sea-green eyes. He remains, arms in front of him, peering down at the woman. It is too much. Her body shakes and she tries to muffle the sounds of her sniffling. George turns, refusing to look at anything outside a mark in the distance, showing his clear repudiation.

13
Sarah
Kaminari on the Shore

The speedy conveyor belt seems to twist. Dizziness takes over so fiercely that she risks pausing from her rhythmic work. Under her feet, the ground ripples. Above her, lights sway and machinery rattles. Cigarette cartons spill onto the floor. A voice bellows out, too gritty and panicked for her to understand but when the workers begin jogging towards the exit, she follows.

Outside in the bright sun, workers, foremen, and even office workers all stand in the yard waiting.

"An earthquake," someone murmurs.

Sarah skims the crowd for Ruth while weaving through standing workers. She asks after her and all the answers amount to "Beats me" or a shrug of the shoulders. Ruth must still be inside. She may be hurt. What if the gas main line breaks? A familiar fear propels her forward into the building despite the foreman shouting at her, through the rising and fading alarms, the darkness. A terrible memory creeps in. A booming from close and a flashing heat. No lights.

A voice screams, "Run!"

She must have moved, though she did not remember feeling her feet and soon she was in the cold, shivering. She turned over on her back, picking herself up to see the wooden slats in flames and people running out. One was half in flame and threw herself into the snow, rolling around, making a heinous snow angel. Others came, some burnt, others as clean as they'd entered. She tried to recognize each of the faces but couldn't seem to put any of the names right.

A familiar voice shouted. Sarah looked around the bleak horizon to see Papa and the other men rushing towards her. He ran past his daughter so quickly that his cap flew off like a grocer's bag in the wind. A man knelt down, his eyes wide.

"What happened?" she asked, her eyes wide with that tint of yellow.

He went from the useless girl silently, calling to the other women that had been able to escape, "Have you seen my wife?", to more familiar ones, "Do you know where she is?"

Sarah tried to pull herself up from the cold that had begun to seep through her clothes. She wanted to run into the fires, to find her mother, her baby brother. Get up, she screamed at herself, get up. But the snow had its fingertips dug into her ankles. Papa can find them. He'll do it. Then came four more from the fires. Only figures. Blue figures and a wail that even the snow couldn't mute. Two shadows leaning on each other. Papa, it must have been. An inch of hope grew.

She squinted. Penny. Penny, her outline smoky, and Papa with a blackened face, scuffling, his body hunched over, outlines in oranges and reds. Mama came behind, the baby safe under her coat. Girls screamed. She followed the mob to the clinic, trying to see. Hands pushed the unwanted away. Ripping cloth, tossed down. An arm falls and she saw it between legs. Burnt meat. Others came in. Bodies. Among them her own father. His clothes burned and what skin she could see had been as well. Black, red, and angry. What was left of his face and throat was inhuman. When he shouted it emerged as raspy groans. He shouted her name. Asking if she was safe. He ran past his own blood daughter, must have ignored his wife, his son, for Penelope. Why? Why her?

202

Sarah jogs to the door. Up the hallway. Turning around as soon as she sees the closed gates at the entrance to the hall leading towards Products and Manufacturing and a large red light above that screams at her.

She runs down the hallway, torn, cracked with one side sunken into the ground. This time, it is easy to run in the dark with the alarms blaring overhead. She brusquely pushes the locker room door with her shoulder. Flashing red lights above brighten the room. Around the corner from the toilets, there is a door with a placard reading "Parts and Manufacturing Workers Only" and she pushes it open with so much force that it bangs against the inner wall.

The floor is eerily quiet. Alarms are soft, muffled by the walls from outside the area. The sounds of swaying metal parts chinking against each other. Iron Boys from hanging racks had either fallen completely or were held up precariously by a few chain links. If she pushes them with her finger, they will surely tumble. The safety features had been built too cheaply while the manufactures themselves remained sturdy. There are spiders, people, roaming around the wreckage lost. Some toddle towards the exit, arms bruised or legs dragging behind them. Sarah shouts for Ruth. Her breath ragged, her heartbeat in her throat. She searches, tripping over cracks in the floor or fallen tools and spies a body strewn sideways on the floor with ear protectors like a halo around her head.

A massive Iron Boy on half of her. She rushes forward, falling to her knees. It takes every strength to push the mechanical giant away. When her arms give out, she sits on her backside with her feet against it and pushes until it

203

screeches along the floor and tumbles off Ruth. Eagerly, she turns the body over but draws back at the sight of black blood matted into her hair, dripping down her forehead, covering her right eye and down to red spots on grey concrete. Sarah feels for a heartbeat—low but steady—she puts the length of her index finger under Ruth's nose and finds weak exhales. Gingerly, she slaps her cheek, calls her name. Though her eyes flicker open, there is no clear response. She lifts the body onto her back, standing at an angle with Ruth's arms over her shoulders and folding her own under Ruth's buttocks. Another rumbling aftershock and she nearly loses footing. As speedily as she is able with the weight on her back, Sarah brings her out through the hallways and into the daylight.

Dense charcoal clouds are cataracts hovering above the city. Pummeling rain deafens the ear as if a thousand rattles sound endlessly only to be silenced by veins of lightning cracking across the grey.
Oniisan and his pleasant voice tumbles from memory as if he stands behind her whispering stories.
"It is the thunder god." She hears him say.
"*Kaminari*-sama, Raijin, a bat-faced god. He pounds the clouds with his giant hammers in both hands to make the thunder roll. When it comes time for lightning to burn in the sky, he wakes Raiju, the thunder beast, a creature like a weasel surrounded by lightning popping this way and that across his fur with claws as long as a bear's. When a storm comes, Raiju jumps down from the clouds, swooping from trees to bite and slash at the earth and at any child who passes by. But when Kaminari-sama stops his drumming, Raiju becomes as calm as a house cat, only to wake when the thunder god calls on his sky drums."

What had been a gleaming icon is sunken into the muck as if a giant pressed two palms straight down. So few seconds it took for the seabed to grasp the land and take it for her own. One half remains a narrow road free from destruction while the other has fallen deep into the earth where the sea has rushed in to reclaim it. It takes a few frantic moments for all the workers and foremen who are outside to arrive at the conclusion that higher ground is safer than here where the ground still rumbles, pieces of the building falling periodically, smashing to the ground, and the threat of creeping water. With fresher air now in her lungs and the shock of adrenaline, Ruth is weak but standing. The wound on her head is superficial, no more than a scrape, and despite Sarah's insistence that they find a hospital, Ruth refuses to acknowledge it except for the small admission that she requires a hat to cover it. A flock of uniforms rushing to the nearest form of transportation along with any other pedestrians that happen to cross their path. The bus stop is crowded, with a line snaking down the cracked sidewalk. Taxis are already taken or are being fought over. The gates for the sky train closed. Walking is the only option and Sarah begins up the hill. A great exhaustion trickles from her forehead to her toes, causing her vision to blur and ears to buzz, yet her feet trudge upwards. Calling, Ruth runs her down, clapping her shoulder.

"Where are you going? Not home?"

Where is my home?

"Can't be safe like this. By the time you walk half way there it'll be dark. A night like this's a dream for ruffians. You're not from a city but you have some sense, right?"

205

Sarah, unable to think with the noise in her head, stares at Ruth.

"We'll get off the street. Wait for it to stop," Ruth advises. "How much money do you have?
Money. Sarah slides a hand into her pocket, feeling at coins, removing two quarters.

"Right. Give it here. Putting ours together we can stay a night at a motel if we hurry." Grabbing Sarah's hand, they walk the opposite way up the hill. "There's a place in Nihonmachi."

Japan Town. She knows the words but not the place, having conveniently avoided any association with other Japanese. Trusting Ruth, she follows her to a skinny building smashed between two others with boarded windows. An outcropping sign flashes "Panama Hotel" in neon letters. Upon entering, an explosion of the native tongues in her ears overwhelms the remaining senses left in her mind. It is a river of languages tumbling from one wooden wall to the other. The counter on the left is kept by a young man, an actual human. It had been some time since she has had to converse with a serviceman and not an automaton that hears a command and does as asked. Oak floorboards squeal as they cross the threshold.

Ruth pushes by some others waiting in line, mostly men. Speaking quickly to the young man, Sarah finds an empty space in the corner keeping her sights fixed on the grains in the floor. Without electric lights, every candle is lit and placed in empty beer bottles, mugs, tin cans. The heat from candlelight compounded with the masses makes her perspire. The drumming blabber of the waiting men is in the many languages mixing together. A tap on her shoulder startles her and she looks to see Ruth holding a straight key without teeth triumphantly in hand. Tied to the ring is a white string threaded through a metal tag punched with a number six. How she got a room is a question Sarah saves for a quieter space, winding past the foyer to the back where a set of wooden stairs leads up and another down.

As they walk up, they squeeze against the banner to allow a mother and older child descend, both with a towel and soap in hand. The third floor has wooden panels, wooden walls, and the door marked six. Unlocking it to find a cramped room with two beds on the other side with one long window propped open to let in fresh air and two ladies tending to their just washed hair by it, letting the air dry the damp locks as they chat with each other in a mix of what Sarah gathers is Spanish, with some English words peppering the conversation.

Seeing the dirty, sweat-stained women enter makes the ladies gape.

"This is taken," the one standing says with a vague accent.

Ruth shows her key. "Seems we're sharing."

*

Together, they walk down the steps to the basement which is stuffed with women of every age. Before them are two doors separated by gender. Pushing the women's door open, the darkness is offset by multitudes of candles which, as in the foyer, are propped up in any open vessel. Immediately there is a high step up with a dirt smudged placard reading "TAKE OFF SHOES HERE" and dozens of women's and children's shoes set before it. Slipping out of

her brown leather shoes, Sarah steps up to the smooth white
tile floor interspersed with blue six-petal flowers. There is a
Greco border around the edges of the high white marble
baths and plaster walls. Humid mist hangs just below the
ceiling. Women, boys, and girls in varying stages of undress
cycle through a washing routine in a communal bath. Oil
lamps that may have once been accoutrements are now lit,
giving just enough light to ensure that she can see a few feet
in front of her. The ground rolls minutely. Sarah tenses.

"Aftershock," Ruth says, noticing. "After one that big
there're bound to be more. Not to worry."

If the children notice, they do not let it interrupt their
fun, dipping their bodies down until the surface hits their chin
and then popping back up to make the water splash, much to
the irritation of the older matrons. To the left, a long shelf
holds dry towels and under it a medley of clothing hangs
from pegs set into the walls; each outfit a display of social
class mixing together out of misfortune. Stripping off her
clothes, Ruth hangs them on one of the wall pegs leaving
Sarah to similarly undress. Besides her own family, she had
never seen another woman naked and finds her eyes drawn to
Ruth in curiosity.

Even in the dim light, Sarah can make out her sinewy
body. Her copper skin flushes in the oil light, wide scars
slash across her ribs and the back of her right thigh. A
machine made from hard labor. Sarah pulls a narrow towel
from the shelf; the cloth is enough to cover the most private
sections of the body, thankful for the darkness even though it
means stepping slowly, carefully, to both avoid the others
shuffling by and to navigate a slippery floor. Ruth squats in
front of a faucet in the wall, cleaning her bloody head with

the sputtering water before rising. With each of the three
large baths so occupied that the water splashes over the sides,
Ruth is indiscriminate when choosing and steps up to the
high platform, motioning for one of the women to make
space, then rolling up her towel around her shoulders so she
can descend into the warmth. Sitting close to her in the bath,
Sarah makes out several new scratches on her back where the
machinery must have fallen on her earlier. Ruth tilts her head
back onto the wood brim, letting out a groan.

"Appreciated, for getting me out," she says, then
closes her eyes to let the steam roll over her.
The water works into Sarah's skin, softening her numb feet
and prickling the taut muscles in her legs and back. Great
pools of hot water where steam rising to cleanse the senses.
Like the *onsens,* mother spoke of in a happier time before
war and hardship.

"I was a little girl." She remembers her mother
beginning the story in an attempt to lull her daughters to
sleep. "Maybe four, and *Okaasan* took me to an *onsen* in the
mountains. In those days it was only the well-off who could
go. Many trains didn't make the journey, so you needed a
car. My family was not so rich. The car belonged to a friend
of my mother's. A young man, I think. I don't remember
much except that he always gave me these fruit candies. It
might be easy now to get such things but when I was a girl
these sweets were very expensive and yet he seemed always
to have them. *Maa*—but he drove us there. What I remember
most were the green trees and the hot water. *Okaasan* and I
went in together. The water was so hot I remember how red
my arms became and my hair sticking to my forehead. 'Look,
Mama,' I told her, '*kani, kani*' and walked around like a crab.
She was so happy, then."

The disaster cleansed from their skin, Sarah and Ruth climb the narrow steps to the room. The Spanish women lie together on the single bed, one with her left leg crossed over the other woman's thigh.

Looking at the bed, Ruth asks, not bothering to whisper out of courtesy, "You care which side?"
Sarah shakes her head, "I'm not tired just now.", leaving Ruth to settle herself on the bed, propping her feet up on the edge of the frame without bothering to take her shoes off, placing a hand in her pocket, her fingers visibly fiddling with the charm that resides under the fabric. The narrow window lets in a cool breeze that pulls Sarah towards it. Breathing air from the window, watching the odd passerby or the few street bums settling for the night, the street invites her with its vast vacancy.

Then a strange inclination erupts from her lips, "I think I'll have a smoke."

"Got some here," Ruth offers, the humor in her voice apparent. Rustling, she fetches a pack out of her pocket, raising it in the air, and remembers to bring the knife with her on a night like this. Traversing the staircase is made more difficult with the lights snuffed out. Depending on her sense of touch, her hands pressing firmly against the walls, she takes one careful step after another.

Resting her back on the bricks, she lights up a cigarette. With the city's electricity damaged, the silence reminds her of the Alaskan summer. Yet with the lights out, Sarah keeps a hand firmly clenched around the knife handle. She sees another group in the identifiable jackets with the thick white V that reflects the moonlight overhead. Straining her eyes, she follows the shouts and physical movements of men fighting. Before a rational thought can creep into the base of her skull, a spark jets her feet forward as she whips her knife out and spits out the cigarette. Coming up behind the V jacket, she drives the blade into the flesh between the spine and shoulder blade. A high agonizing scream escapes the figure who runs away, pawing at the embedded object. Once the rush fades, she panics, shaking and escaping back inside the building and upstairs to the room. All she can think of is to run.

Her loud rustling wakes the women in the room, one of whom curses at her and then turns to the side to show her back. Ruth, waking to see Sarah in the dark, props herself up on the bed. In a tired voice, she croaks, "What in the hell are you doing?"

Without looking, Sarah chants, "I have to go." several times, clinging to the rhythm of the sentence. She leaves, descending the stairs as quickly as she climbed them, followed at length by Ruth who is unable to match Sarah's swift steps in her fatigued stupor, calling after her until she relents, surrendering to her friend's need to escape.

14
Penelope
A Fire Stoked by *Homusubi no Mikoto*

Sirens echo as Penny trudges forward. It is impossible to walk when the world is collapsing. A police car wails. Spiral lanterns flicker. She spots a deep crack, jagged, moving back and forth like broken puzzle pieces. More blaring from different sirens. A rising whistle. An up and down ringing. Bells sounding. A voice from a loudspeaker, telling everyone to take refuge, then the message echoing up the hills. The spotlights gone from the sky.

Faster, faster, Penny screams at herself. But the great earthquake numbs her body. She looks out, relieved at a moment for the sky becomes bright. Not lights. Fire. Pockets of orange dotting the waterfront.

Penny fumbles with her purse, the contents crashing to the wooden porch. Without bothering to gather up her things, she pulls her keys out. The one time she locked the door is the time needs it open. Unlock the door. Pull through with a force that could have taken her arm. On the other side, she finds brief safety. Bruce jumps onto the bookshelf, howling with his fur prickling, startling her at first and then causing her to rush towards him and pick him up, holding him close to her chest as she paces through each room. She tries the light switches. Nothing.

Bruce wriggles so she lets him down. Calmly, he saunters away into the living room then jumps back onto the bookshelf. In the dark she fondles for the candles kept in the bottom drawer of the end table. Her fingers feel over stacked fragrance canisters and a hammer at the back of the drawer where she finds the wick to a thick candle that she grasps in her hand. She finds a matchbook in her purse and lights the dust laden pillar candle. She takes it to the fireplace—a furnishing which she once thought useless but which now, in the absence of electricity, is most welcome. The ground roils in waves weaker than those before and yet strong enough that she nearly loses her footing.

Opening the glass shutters, she puts the candle flame to the wood that had always sat as decoration and keeps it there until the bottom bark of the topmost log begins to burn, growing into strong licks of fire. She sets the candle on the mantle too rushed so that a few drops of wax spit onto her thumb, causing her to recoil, rubbing the inflamed area. An instinctual urge to call her mother drives her to the Semaphore Typewriter. Flicking the switch on, off, on, off. A dull sound. She tries the radio, turning it on. Only static, static, static, and the emergency noise. Next. she tries the telephone hanging lopsided from the receiver. A strong *tap*, *tap*, *tap* as she presses down the buttons to reset the phone. She screams in frustration, slams the phone down. Silence. She laughs, still holding onto the receiver.

What kind of a fool am I? she thinks, sitting, trying to banish the barrage of recent memories to where she was thrown just moments before, unable to move. Hearing to the dreadful clamor of disaster. Too loud. Penny, muffles her frantic noises into the crook of her arm. Dots of dry blood dot her skin where before there were once sequins. Terrified of the red, she hastens to the kitchen sink where she washes it with soap and scrapes with a brillo pad until her skin braises. She finds her breath constrained and pulls off her dress, leaving it at her feet; bare except for her corselette and dirty

213

stockings. Tearing at her hair, she soaks her scalp under the icy water spewing from the faucet. It keeps her tears away. A rapping at the window startles her.

She shuts the water off. Listening. Rapping, rapping, on the back window. With the kitchen towel hung over a cupboard knob, she pats her hair from wet to damp and lets it fall alongside her dress on the floor. Peeking past the kitchen alcove, she spies a figure. A monster's body with three heads. Two arms on the shoulders, opening and shutting their hands, one against the window knocking. Scrutinizing it, she rushes towards the door, throwing it open. On the other side stands Catherine. Her hair uncombed and eyes red with Rose asleep in one arm, Timmy in the other, his head resting on her shoulder, eyes drowsy.

"My husband," she starts, her voice a whisper sprinkled with tremors of trepidation.

"I can't find him. I thought—" Penny says, peeking behind Catherine. "Is he here? I haven't seen him since. . ." It doesn't matter. Catherine takes that moment to appraise the woman with tangled hair wearing barely ruined attire.

"You said he hasn't been home?" Penny repeats.

"No."

Penny peers back inside, half expecting him to come through the front entrance.

"Come in," she says, "put them on my bed."

Catherine toes in, straight to the master bedroom to lay her children on the overlarge bed, Timmy whining as she does. He settles down soon after sinking his head into the pillow. The burgeoning fire lightens the darkness to an orange glow, enough for Catherine to distinguish the shape of her husband's cardigan hanging on the farthest bedpost. Curious that it sits there. A drape against the wood. Perhaps

214

he left it by mistake and Penny keeps it for him, intending to return it. Yet, he is particular about his clothing. Every piece he irons himself, hanging everything in his closet, wearing the same clothes for years before he will buy more.

Catherine steps closer to it and as her eyes adjust to the low light, she recognizes the pale blue color, navy blue striped at the pockets and bottom edge. The three grey buttons. She takes the cardigan into her hands, thumbing the soft knit between her fingers, only to smooth out some of the wrinkles in an attempt to similarly temper any feeling that might thaw from years of winter. Passing her children who lie peacefully unaware on the bed, she finds Penny setting more wide candles on the mantle, lighting each tip using the flame of a one already burning, steadying it in her two hands. Catherine stalks up to her, ready to drape the cardigan over Penelope's naked shoulders but hesitates. It is then that, for the first time, Catherine sees her naked shoulders, her spine that makes a trail down the center and the pale red burn scars that run diagonally from her shoulder and down her back, continuing beneath the undergarment as if a giant paintbrush swiped a red stroke across her flesh.

Gathering her senses, Catherine lays the material over the exposed skin. Knowing the feel of the cloth and the smell of the knit and the large size of a man's fit that hits the backs of her thighs, Penny pauses a moment to set the candle down, the last two unlit, turning her head so that they meet eye to eye and the smallest acknowledgement passes between them. Penny pulls her arms through the oversized sleeves and takes the candle back up, resuming her task until the rooms are alight in a soft orange glow. Then exhaustion begins to take Penny as her neck becomes too weak to steady her head and

215

the muscles behind her knees spasm. She turns with the candle in hand, wavering on unsteady legs, causing the burning pillar to spill hot wax down the side and over her fingers.

The sensation of the liquid searing her skin causes her to suck in her breath sharply and stomp one foot in frustration, leaving Catherine to respond by removing the candle, putting it with the others, and peeling the already cooling wax from Penny's fingers. Looping her arm around her cousin's shoulders, Catherine guides her to the bedroom to take refuge in the small space with the children. "Here," Catherine says, nudging her to thee bed where she obligingly rustles up next to Rose and Timothy, followed by Catherine slipping in beside her. Like a daughter to a mother, Penelope collapses a head onto her shoulder with the remainder of her body half naked and limp.

"I'm glad you're here," Penny says in barely a whisper.

With the young girl so close to her, Catherine cannot help but breathe in the terrible musk of her husband that rises from the cardigan coupled with the day's sweat on Penelope. The thought of them together brings up only a spittle of envy from an ancient spout within her that had been stoppered years ago but still leaks when the knob loosens. Much stronger is her regard for her children, for her own, personal, safety, and for her gratitude that Penelope is there to distract her husband. Once, Catherine had a spark of love for George that has since dwindled to a dying ember. Now, what she most desires is a peaceable life. Penny is family. Close enough so as to not cause competition for Catherine's welfare but just far enough removed for their actions to not be sinful in her eyes.

"I'm glad you're here, too," Catherine replies sincerely but with a tinge of sadness that lowers her tone.

"Will you sing to me?" Penny murmurs.

"I'm not very good, not like you."

"It doesn't matter."

It takes her some time to conjure a song that she remembers. Catherine never bothered singing to Rose or Timothy as Penny has been a constant presence since their birth, comforting them when their mother would not. Then, she recalls a lullaby that her mother sang to her when she was young and lets the words drift out from her unsteady lips. A soft tune called *Akai Kutsu*. It has a calming melody despite the sad lyrics retelling the story of a young girl in red shoes who was taken by a foreigner. As she holds Penny in her arms, she strokes the worn fibers of the cardigan with her thumb and an unending loneliness comes upon her as she realizes that she has been lost for longer than she wanted to realize.

A rough knock on the bedroom door wakes Penny. Ignoring it at first, she turns over onto her side. Bruce gives the smallest mew in protest of her shifting the blankets from where he had curled up comfortably. The knocking comes again, and Catherine's distressed voice comes, calling her name. She rises. Catherine only ever comes downstairs during the rare occasions when she goes shopping. It is enough to rouse Penny from her bed, knowing something must be amiss. Turning on the bedside lamp, she opens the door to see Catherine on the other side. Her hair tousled from sleep, wearing her nightgown, with blood on her fingers.

217

Looking down, she sees a blotch of fluid at the front of the slip and streaks of red down her leg. Wordlessly, she takes Catherine's hand and leads her down the dark hallway, the silence broken by a ticking clock from the living room to the bathroom. Clicking the light on, she turns the bath water faucet on hot. Bloody mucous smears glaze the inside of her slip as Penny pulls it up to Catherine's waist and carefully over her head. The bathwater splashes; drops spraying tiles like rain. Penny turns her eyes away, letting Catherine pull off her underpants and brassiere. Simple cream garments, the lace softened into fuzz from years of washing.

A lovely mother's body. Her skin soft with a stomach like a dumpling. The shape of Venus. More beautiful than Penny could ever be. As Penny handles the soap, rubbing it over Catherine's back, a spark of guilt arises. All of Catherine's complaining that she had dismissed as feigning sickness had been the early signs of pregnancy. Whatever life it may have been is lost now in a mass at the bottom of the tub.

"Don't tell George," she pleads, keeping her eyes at a point in the murky water, "please."
Pulling the robe from the hook on the door, she presents it to Catherine who steps out of the water, a towel around her body, the water pink-tinged with tiny blood clots floating at the bottom.

Penny hugs her once, releasing, and gives the natural, "*Shoganai.*" pressing her lips together, she draws a deep breath, and says, "Your time came late this month, that's all."

Carefully, Penny wraps the gelatinous mass in newspaper. A tiny body and an enlarged head with dark undeveloped eyes. Miniscule hands. Half-formed fingers. Wine skin like rice paper. There is nowhere to hide it. If she

218

buries it in the garden, it might be easily found. She knows of one way to make is disappear. A small enough fire that singes through the ink, flesh bubbling.

Hi ga hakai. Hi wa kirei.

Fire is destruction. Fire is clean. What she knew at first of the writing were few words that she was taught by her mother. Water. Rice. Child. Fire. The most basic symbols of life for a girl. Oniisan taught her the rest. Sitting next to each other at the canteen at breakfast with a bit of chalk, she copied the character that Oniisan wrote on the wooden tabletop. As straight and curved as the lines were, his were cleaner. Unsatisfied, he would erase it with the corner of her cloth napkin and make his niece try again. And again on the dirt outside, writing with a stick. And again in the snow with gloved fingers. And again the ash settled on the inner hearth. It is always fire.

15
Sarah
Upheaval

    To walk is the purest form of reflection. It reminded
her of all the hours she spent traveling to and from her old
home to the cannery with her sister. The morning air brought
the salt from the rocks up to her nose. A dampness of the
early morning evaporated into the air. A freedom. The silence
all about her but the rustling shrubbery and her breathing as
she waited for the birds to fly. All she wanted. Her own
space, unhindered by anyone.

    The disaster turns calm night streets into carnivals
for wild and stray creatures. At this late hour, a mature lady
sets out dishes at the bottom step of her house where a
number of impatient cats mew at her until she pours milk into
each one. Without the distractions of churning trains or car
motors, Sarah's once soft conscience bombards with thoughts
that sink to her gut and flutter there; the all-too familiar
feelings that rose months before when she gathered the
goshugi to flee across the ocean. She fights to dampen the
voices and images that seek to invade her mind. Flashes of
faces that sicken her with regret, others that prompt her to
anger, and still more that will bring her to tears if she lingers.
The last inevitably forces her to think of Penelope, a girl who
seems forever wedged in her calamitous memories. Still, the
safest place she can imagine is with her cousin.

    Trekking there soon takes a more serious turn as
she fights against her buckling legs and a rolling headache
that originates at the base of her skull, rising to her forehead

only to relinquish and return in quick successions. It makes an otherwise brisk stroll a punishing physical ordeal.

The house is dark, partly obscured from the street by a few cars parked along the curb. At the fence, she is met by a light shining in her eyes. Squinting, she can make out the figures of two well-dressed men, one with a hand in his pocket, the other holding a flashlight aimed at her face. There is no need for her to guess who they are.

"That's about far enough," one says "Unless I know you, you'd best hightail it."

"I live here," she replies impatiently.

"Better prove it."

Removing her wallet at once, she opens it to present them with her registration card. The man withdraws his hand from his pocket to receive it, raising it to the stream of light, shielding her in darkness.

"All right," he says, handing it back, the flashlight still in place. "Ms. Penny's been worried."

Remaining where they are, the man opens the gate, leaving her to pass in between them. Sarah rises steps with great effort, her knees weary and her feet raw. Settled in a splatted pile on the porch are the fallen contents of a handbag: lipstick, cigarette case, coins, and a folded bit of paper. Picking up the coins, stowing them in her pocket, and leaving the rest, she tests the door handle. It is unlocked, as usual. She lets herself in to a candlelit house with pockets of natural light streaming in from the purple dawn. The door to Penny's bedroom is closed firmly, though there are voices behind it intermittently overlaid by meows from a cat begging for attention. Rather than interrupt, she instead climbs the steps to the second floor. After living under it as long as she had, she often wondered what might be found there.

As far as décor, she is perplexed at the lack of personality within the home. Whereas her old home in Alaska had been spread with a type of British country pageantry as was befitting her mother's interest in royalty, and Penny's portion of the house is plastered with a collage of old furniture and modern trappings, George's tepid home contains only the necessities for living, dimly lit with emergency candles collected together in a bundle on a table. Immediately, her sights are drawn to a boy who, left to his own devices, plays with a rabble of colorful wooden blocks spread around him in various piles. Seeing the boy, she notes at once the wide spacing between his eyes that seem just slightly too large for his face. Though he has the body of a boy of five or six, the way he plays with his wooden blocks reminds her of how a toddler might fumble with stacking one object atop another. When he bumps a square shape over, he groans. Still, rather than dismissing the boy she tells him hello. Hearing the sounds, he turns his head, letting his hands drop to his lap. He must understand but does not respond. Instead, he turns away back to his toys with extreme focus.

Hearing human noise, Sarah turns to meet it, her vision beginning to blur as her headache strengthens, to assess the mother standing in the door with her doe-eyed daughter in her arms. The wife has hair cut short to her jawline and left uncurled. Her short stature makes Sarah seem a giant in comparison as there are several inches difference between them. All she knows of this woman is from Penny's assessment of her as a wife whose rapacious anxiety keeps her cowering within the blank walls. Her daughter babbles while pawing at her mother's nightgown collar with unpracticed fingers.

In a terrible moment, Sarah sees her lost sister and draws her eyes away to the white walls glowing grey in the dark. What she knows of George suddenly rushes from the back of her skull to her temple. Keeping space between them, she gathers her voice.

"If he's gone right now," she begins, pausing before she asks a question that had been in the back of her mind since she first saw the poor woman, "Why don't you leave?"

"It would be possible, except—"

"Then listen," she interrupts before Catherine can give an excuse. "The old trains might still be working."

Catherine searches her face, understanding at once.

"Go quickly. Take your children--they can always come back—" she says, pressuring as worry spreads over Catherine's face which Sarah tempers with, "this could be your only chance."

"It might," she concedes, turning to sit on the nearest chair. "I do wish it would be just as easy to walk outside or become well." She glances at the stranger. "Where could I go? Japan is no place for me alone with two children. It's impossible for me to find work in this situation. Here is not," she pauses, "so terrible."

"What?" Sarah says irritably.

"George is as he will always be. Most recently he's been. . .more content." She flicks her peanut brown eyes to Sarah's. "And here, at least, Rose and Timothy are cared for. I have an allowance. A home."

The fire pops. For Sarah, it is simple.

"You don't love each other," she proclaims.

"No."

The earth moves, weaker still. It forces Sarah away, down the stairs. She freezes, meeting two black eyes staring up at her. George.

"What are you doing in my house?" he roars at once, forcing her to retreat upstairs.

The spot where Catherine stood moments before is an empty space, making Sarah question whether the woman had ever been there at all. He approaches, suited, weary, and glowering. A demeanor in direct opposition to the figure rising from behind him whose platinum blond hair burns ochre in the candlelight. Surprised at Sarah's presence, Penelope furrows her brows and parts her lips to say something but is cut off swiftly when George repeats his initial inquiry, this time with a fiercer tone. Rather than explaining herself, she pushes her hands in her pockets in a refusal to show any of the small fear that wells in her throat at the sight of the quickly angering George. Unable to hold it in any longer, without propriety, she lets the entitlement compound with her intensifying pains, tumbles out with, "What about money?"

He looks to her with the tips of his eyebrows tight together.

"Money? What money?"

"What about your. . .your work? You must have money somewhere."

"What does *that* have to do with you?"

At the insult, she might have reprimanded him, about his sweetheart, but looking at his tired face with the wrinkles appearing deeper than before she loses her courage. It does not seem to matter to her. There is no money. No use in quarrelling now.

With a stern face that gives away nothing, Penny says, "Let's go inside."

Sarah follows, unafraid of the haughty way Penny strides inside with George following behind her like a duckling to a mother. They might bicker for a few minutes and then retire to their rooms and in the morning it will be the same.

"I'll make some coffee," Penny says, disappearing to boil a pot of water. She leans on the stove. Her hands resting on the base, spine parallel so that her petticoat blooms from the back, under the hem of her dress.

Nothing. Disregarding the tension, Sarah reclines on the floral chair with brass crimps. The pot whistles. The stovetop clicks off. The silence being too much, Penny finds Sarah resting on the chair, still in her work overalls, with her arm covering her eyes. Uncompassionate, Penny slaps her arm away from her face. Startled, her eyes snap open and she inhales sharply.

"I'm the fool, am I? Did you think you could hide this?" Penny asks as she tosses a folded flier at Sarah.

She sits up, taking the manifesto into her hands and shoots her cousin a fierce glare.

"You were in my room."

"My room. My house," she states this as sternly as her mother. "Just what is it you're doing?" Before she can answer, Penny keeps on, "never mind that this gang—"

"—It's not a gang—"

"This *gang* is always in trouble. You being a part of it in any way ruins my career. You saw what happened to Kate Page. You want that to happen to me?"

Sarah rolls her eyes. It is a shame it never got that far.

"Always thinking about yourself," she murmurs.

"Sorry?"

"Thinking about yourself," she repeats again, loudly, "I'm not some child that you can trick with your smiles. How many people have *you* hurt?"

225

Penny straightens.

"And you think joining up with these people will help? You'll ruin your chances of ever finding work anywhere else and take me along. Not just me but George and the children too! This isn't a game. This is serious."

Rumors and whispers.

"What can I say? Not being a citizen, I suppose I have nothing to lose," Sarah spits. "You've never hurt like the rest of *us*. Not in the camps, not even before. . ."

At that, Penny flares. "*You* never had to feel heartbreak. Not knowing whether your father was alive or dead." She waits, hoping her words will sting, letting her temper cool.

"You don't know how it was there. *We* stayed. *You* came and went."

The accusation so ridiculous her sole recourse is a guttural laughter. A paper blares before her memory. All the Japanese internees were presented with it. The typewritten letters still clear: "I renounce any association with Japan, be it cultural or social." Penny had signed it.

"Too right I did and would again."

"You see?"

"See what? Have you ever been to Japan?" She scoffs, closing in enough that pointing a finger at her will hit her chest. "*You're* no more Japanese than I am."

Silence is Sarah's defense. It seems to work at first as Penny withdraws to her room only to return holding a few envelopes.

"You've been lying," Penny accuses. "And I know what happened before you left." She unfolds the paper. She clears her throat and begins to read, "Dear cousin, forgive me for writing this in urgency, but it is necessary. My sister, Sarah, has run off. It happened shortly after my wedding. It is

226

unfortunate to say that we are also missing our *goshugi*. You
are the only relative nearby. If she comes to you, please send
us a letter as soon as you can—and take care of your
valuables." She holds out the letter for Sarah to read herself,
skimming the hurried writing. "Of course, as soon as you
sent me that wire, I wrote to them. They told me this." She
reveals another letter. "This one is from your mother: '*Itoko*,
I am ashamed at my daughter's behavior and am grateful that
you have let her into your house, though she does not deserve
such kindness. If she had not been so hasty—but she does not
think things through. Be careful, dear Penelope.'"

Penny gives this one to Sarah as well so that the
papers sit in her lap like condemnations. "You can see what a
puzzle that left me in; what am I to do with you? You can
only lie so many times before it catches up—"

"Tell yourself that," Sarah snapped back, which
Penny ignored.

"—and when it does, it's not sweet—" Sarah scoffs at
that. "—so, I wrote back. I said I'd keep you here, make you
work to pay off what you stole, and send it back."
No wonder she was pressured to pay rent. It all compounds,
making her lash out.

"I only needed a little," Sarah explains. "The least
you could do was give over some of yours for us—you have
enough money for a lifetime—and we need it. Everything
that happened to father—it was all your fault—and we've
been suffering for it."

The name curling on her lips does nothing to soften
either of her cousins, though she feels triumph noticing
Penny's eyes squint in anger for a moment before relaxing.
To her surprise, Penny does not argue against it. For the first
time, a sadness passes across her face.

"I know," she says.

"You have to leave," George interrupts, startling Sarah at his sudden animation.

Sarah, not expecting the last order, stands up, letting the letters fall to the carpeted floor. George picks at his hand, the only sign of his discomfort. She expects Penny to defend her, smiling, perhaps afterword quipping at her. Instead, Penelope hardened at Sarah's desperation.

"You can't mean it. Where will I go?"

Penny smirks, haughty, as an answer. Sarah bites her cheek to hold back a retort, but there is heat in her blood.

"This is all your fault," she accuses, to which Penny rolls her eyes. "Don't think I'll ever forget about that. . .You never wanted to help me; you wanted me to fail."

"No," she says. "You did that on your own. You should leave. Go get your things."

"Excuse me?"

"I want you out. Out. *Out!*"

Without hesitation, she flies to her room to stuff her suitcase as quickly as she can, having to shove it down as she does not fold her clothes. Re-emerging in the living room with the one cousin remaining, Penny, now soft-eyed, stands near the door.

"I called a taxi for you," as she says it, the black car is already seen through the window, "and this—" she thrusts a fashionable white beaded billfold towards her chest "—you should just take it. Take it and go home to your mother." Her bright gaze peers into the pitch pools of Sarah's eyes as if an unhindered summer sun burns upon a marsh pond and pecks her gingerly on the cheek. As her close kin dashes away, not looking back, she steps upon the trinkets still on the ground, down the front path and into the waiting taxi.

The taxi driver drops her at the nearest sky train, refusing Sarah's request to be taken directly to the low-income Sinclair Worker's Housing. As she approaches the station, a poster board hastily tacked to the wood frame above the ticket booth advises, "Limited Service: Expect Delays." Preferring not to wait for a train that may not arrive, she elects to cut through the station exit corridors, passing the ticket tills. Advertisements posted on the signboards announce houses and apartments for rent. Affordable, nice, and plastered with a notice saying, "CITIZENS ONLY." Scanning the board, every comfortable home shares a similar sentiment save for the well-worn box shaped homes and the Wellness Housing for low incomes. These proclaim "Non-Citizens Welcome!"

The juxtaposition serves only to incise her anger at the unfairness and, still more, at her cousins for throwing her to the streets to live as a tramp. Ducking into the passage, she descends a set of stairs carefully, unable to see clearly in the dark and while her sight prickles, to find a park entrance leading to a vast wooded area ever illuminated by floating orbs overhead that seem as *kodama* eyes waking in the night. Scurrying draws her to a lone boy in a V gang jacket who passes into the trees with a clear purpose. Following after him, she moves in, rounding the path to the left slowly to pantomime a leisurely stroll in case they turn around and see the lone woman walking amongst hand-holding couples and families with children.

To appear unassuming, every now and then she turns her head as if to admire the trees which glow with rainbow

229

hues reflecting off the leaves. Together, they climb the stone steps to join the others, similarly dressed in matching jackets, playing dice on the wooden bench. From where she views sleeping flowers, she can hear the vague mumblings of blithesome teenagers on the cusp of adulthood while one boy fiddles absentmindedly with a butterfly knife of antler bone handles and gold adornments. She curses to herself that she had lost the knife that may still be imbedded in that boy's shoulder. Impotent to act, she skulks away to wander the park. Without looking at her watch, she guesses the time by the spacious paths free of patrons and the quiet that comes in the small hours of the night. A drizzle begins, wet enough to dampen her skin and light enough that she does not feel the need to shelter herself beneath tree branches.

Having not eaten since the morning, she finds her stomach aching. The only substance resembling food that she has are the cigarettes in her pocket and lights one to stave off the churning hunger.

The scratch of tired footsteps on stones and cans tapping against each other leads her along the thin path, she passes strings of *chirimen* charms hanging from branches. Knocking through them, she bumps a charm or two fastened with bells that jingle softly.

"Who's it?" comes a sharp voice.

Searching for the voice, Sarah squints farther down the path to see the stone statue of a child and where some people reside behind it. Five figures. Two huddled together to share a forest-green army blanket that is black in the spots where rain falls on the wool. One stands, setting up a dismal shelter of a wide canvas sheet hung over a low sturdy tree branch and spread out at the ends, using large stones to fasten the ends to the soft moss ground. He stands, smoothing out the wrinkles in the sheet. The other person rifles through a bulging work briefcase to remove several odd bits of sustenance, placing them on the ground in a pile: a top rusted can of beans, three packs of wonder bread taken out one after another, and still more cans of potted meats, stews, and fruit cocktail. Following suit, the blanketed couple remove their treasures to share amongst the group. A poor supper but one that Sarah finds appealing in her ravenous state.

"You been put out?" the man with the briefcase asks. Sarah nods.

"Take a seat, why don't you?"

Not wanting to sit on the damp ground, she simply crouches near them, holding fast to her belongings. Noticing her cigarette at once, he prods, "Got any to share?" She hesitates a moment, then bargains, nodding towards the cans, "Long as I can have some of that."

The man agrees. Pulling the pack out, she passes it to him. He appraises the packaging, takes one for himself, then passes it around for everyone to take their share and return the box to her. The woman in the blanket asks for a light, which Sarah gives by placing the fresh cigarette to her burning end and handing it back. She then helps herself to the can of potted meat and three slices of bread. Ripping the tab on the can, she uses her finger to draw out the pink contents, spreading clumps onto stale bread, then folding it in half and shoving it into her mouth. She follows this same procedure until the meal is gone, her stomach satiated, and she runs her finger in each crevice of the tin to then lick from her finger.

"You work for Sinclair," the man says. It is not a question.

At her furrowing brows, he slips the single cigarette into his front pocket, and explains, "That pack don't have a product number. Must've got it from the discards." He clears

231

his throat with a hoarse cough, "I worked there too, up until yesterday. Only been two days since they laid us all off."

"They did what?" Sarah asks, baffled, her headache softening.

"Saw the chains 'round the gates myself," the man says, "and with the factory closed, they've had suits come through pulling out everyone who can't pay the rent. Says it's our fault for not saving money. The rest of 'em that stayed pooled their money to stay off the streets."

"Not like us." The woman says, shrugging her friend's sleeping head from her shoulder only to have the man completely roll to her lap. "Got anywhere to go?"

Her meager job at the warehouse was the only guarantee of a salary after being put out. Without it, she is a vagabond. Sarah remains silent for a moment under the pretext of finishing her Firelite while she hardens herself to the news that she is jobless and then extinguishes it on the sopping undergrowth.

"Maybe," she says, "over in the scraps."

"Better stay here, least 'til the mornin'. Saw some V gang louts wanderin' 'round."

A nod is her acceptance. Only when the meal finishes does the man light his cigarette while one of the others plays a tune on a jaw harp.

16
Penelope
Chrysanthemums

White walls and white floors broken by doors. The smell of pus and a strange odor like that of wet newspaper cover over every sense of hers as she walks through the door with the two men beside her. A curving metal reception desk with a half-body automaton with a button code system, each number signaling the level of emergency stands at the entrance along with a blue carpeted waiting area with few chairs set in rows, some of which are occupied by the lightly injured, and two who stand at the counter, trying to get assistance only to be refused by the automaton for not having a citizen's card. Penny seems not to mind it as she bounces along with a lunch basket slung through her arm swaying from her elbow, accustomed to sour smells. Keeping the pace next to her is the old man, Koike-san, whom Penny accompanies.

When Koike-san asks her, "What is that smell?", she answers back, "Whatever do you mean?" and so leaves it as is. The floors are an old white color except for the paths that people walked on--those were lines of pearl.

There lies a man on the hospital bed in a horizontal line of at least fifty others and no other way of knowing who he is except by his name printed on the end of the bed. His entire body is covered in bandages and draped in cloth. Only his crusted black lips stick out. Tubes flow from his nostrils and from under the strips of white, keeping him alive. His chest rises and falls gently—the only sign of life. He too has a blanket covering his legs. His right cheek is taped with a square cloth bandage. A hospital robe covers his skin but

233

leaves an opening in the back to let air touch his red skin. His stub of an arm is bandaged. His son sits next to him, not looking anywhere but at the floor. Sarah moves her gaze from George, to the father, who sits upright on the next bed with his head lowered, eyes shut, arms crossed in front of his chest. Penelope smiles as best she can at the raw eyes looking back at her. Placing the basket on the white tile floor by the bedside, she sits gently on the hard mattress, placing her hand on Ojiisan's chest. The other men who may offer tenderness to the ruined body remain far, refusing to touch the funereal air.

"I brought you something," she says, opening the basket to let the sweet scent fill the air.

The last time she ate the red bean *sekihan*, it was her mother who made them a special occasion. A morning at the Minidoka camp school. A moist feeling under her dress. The teacher sent her back to her mother who was washing clothes with the other ladies at the water pump by the bathrooms. When she whispered to her mother, she didn't keep the secret. Announcing to the other women, "*Kyo, sekihan tskutteru!*" at which their faces brightened. The barracks neighbors put their rice portions together to give as a gift so the women could cook it and mix the red beans inside. It was a rare moment when she had been treated with acceptance.

*

Leaving the polished marble steps of the citizens' hospital, Penny wraps her arm through Koike-san's, leaving her other to hold the basket, escorting him to the old railway station with Abe following close beside. Looking up, workers on pulleys repair the cracked bars and tension rods of the sky train. Some of the more daring walk across the

234

gigantic horizontal line not even needing to hold up their arms for balance. The only lines running are the old rails. The wobbling train passes what may have served as a scenic display of a seaside metropolis had it not been for the rocking axis that reclaimed borrowed land. Seagull colonies glide above emergency workers, firemen, police, volunteers and machines that mingle together sifting through the city's broken fields.

Amidst the wreckage that is the waterfront, wooden planks float amongst the scraps of destruction, clunking against the remaining boardwalk posts as currents pulse from the inlet to the edge of the sunken street where the earth had pulled the soft ground from underneath, breaking seams in the roads that slope into the water. Any buildings remaining had been torn in slashes, standing with the help of some invisible fingers pinching them together. In the array somewhere lie the splinters of what was once The Fortune Follies. Only two objects remain steadfast amidst muck and ruin—the gentle, Melusinian mermaid and Sinclair Industries.

A tunnel wipes the reality from her vision, casting her reflection on the dust speckled window. Looking away, she seeks out the Namahage's face whose steady expression eases her discomfort.

"Businesses are gone," she states. "Beggars will come looking." Koike-san rubs a finger behind his earlobe then brings his hand down smoothly to rest on his knee.

"It would be wasteful to leave them on the street, *deshyo?*" Penny says to which Koike-san ponders while rubbing a spot on his pants with his thumb.

"What better way to get support on our side?" She sits back, eyeing Abe who brushes some smut from his shoes.

235

"A dozen or so boys to volunteer cleaning up downtown. People will be out of work and we can send them towards us." she looks to the older man, querying with her bright eyes and lifted brows. A curt nod at her suggestion is all that is needed to ensure that the idea will become fruitful. "*And* now that one of the factories is closed, with us getting a riotous flux of dollars from selling off those cigarettes at an increase," she crosses her arms, smiling, pleased at herself, "it seems us *Shizuka* will do very well."

*

Snow. Falling detonators. The scratching of skin on skin. A terrible second and then the explosion that shook the frail building and snuffed out the lights, then concurrent, smaller noises of munitions sounding. Deaf in the darkness, she groped for any familiar body. Finding only cold floors, she crawled to where she knew the door would be when a flashlight beam shocks her into submission. Able hands were her salvation. The smell. The feel of his muscles. Knowing who it was, she struggled, flailed her arms, to strike him.

"Not me! Not me!" she screamed hoarsely over the bombardments, her voice cracking.

Auntie was somewhere in the very same room. And the baby. It was them he should find. He grunted as she pulled, wiggled from him. If he said anything, there was no way for her to understand beyond the vibrations of his chest.

The newspaper crinkles as she smooths it down on the carpet in a line along the edges of the wall. She had pulled the couches and chairs to the center of the room in one pile. She keeps the radio off. The idea of noise irritates her and is content with the crackling paper under her bare feet and the brush strokes on the wall, losing herself in the methodical task of making even strokes were--up, down, up, down--so that gradually the eggshell walls turn pale blue. A bright raincloud drawing across the pond. Though it is not especially hot outside--the windows are open to freshen the room from the smell of paint--she sweats through her thin dress so that it sticks to her back and under her chest. She stops at the end of one wall, rising so quickly that she is suddenly lightheaded, causing her to step back and lean against the overturned edge of the couch.

This is the first time it has been painted in many years. The last due to a letter sent to her mother, held by a soldier. She puts the brush down on the paper to make herself a cup of coffee. Out of the top cupboard she removes a lime green cup, holding it in one hand she pulls out a twisted fabric napkin that hides a tin inside. Within is her own stash of thin metal cylinders. Opening the contents, she removes two coarse slips of filament. Gingerly placing the thin papers on the counter, she replaces the napkin and put it back on the shelf. The teapot was already on the stove, filled halfway from the night before. She turns the heat up, waited by it until the water steamed out of the spout and shut it off at once. Into a clean new cup, she puts the papers, a dash of instant coffee grounds and poured the water in. After a sip, the telephone rings. Catherine on the other end asking for help, convinced she has influenza.

Bringing her cup with her, Penny walks up the stairs to the second floor. A welcome sight is Timothy running up to her, tugging on her skirt. Looking down, she sees his lips and hands covered with flour, leaving prints where he touched her.

"Oh, what did you get into?" She sighs. "Let's clean you up and find your mother."

Taking his hand in hers, she takes him towards the kitchen. Passing through the living room, a heap of blankets on the couch with a head poking out is Catherine quietly sleeping with Rose tucked under her arm. Penny continues to the kitchen sink where she notes a bag of flour on its side with the contents spilled on the green linoleum. Picking him up, facing towards the sink full of dirty dishes that emit a subtle rotten odor, she washes his hands, cupping water over his face— though he resists by moving his head from side to side—and dries him with the towel hanging on the edge. She frees him to run off into the living room while she turns to the mess on the floor, cleaning it with a broom a dustpan propped against the wall by the oven.

Penny keeps an ear towards the children playing freely as she tends to the dishes, beginning to feel the rush of energy from her coffee. The volume of bowls, pots, and plates stacked upon each other are enough for her to estimate they have been sitting for at least four days of neglect. To even begin the task, she shifts the porcelain to the countertop to reach the sink. A sharp wet rot forces her to hold her breath. In a soup pot, in a shallow basin of old water, soggy, pale white bits of pasta had molded in spots. Upturning the pot, she releases the contents, turning the faucet handle to the hottest mark. A steaming stream of water rushes straight down, spilling over the pot. The grime is tough to scrub off and the grease is burnt solid to the edges. She rinses off the flecks that she freed, cleaning her hands in the process.

As the water pours from the spout onto her softened hands, she startles at a presence behind her and then his voice, almost a whisper. Before she can try to move--though she would not have if given the chance--a body against her back so closely that it is more than mere impoliteness. Against her she can feel the buttons of his shirt pressing into her back, his belt buckle, every part of him on her as he reaches into the overhead cupboard. With a free hand he touches lightly at her waist. A reflex as she shifts her head slightly looking towards the stacked colored bowls dripping water on the drying rack, to let out a wanting breath from her lips. It takes much of her strength to keep from moaning. The mark of early summer on them both.

A turn and he is gone. She checks, peeking up. He hadn't taken anything from the cupboard after all. Immediately, the urge to leave overwhelms Penny. Shutting off the water, wiping her wet hands on a towel, she peers into the living room to see the back of George's head. She turns back to the kitchen and hastily prepares a packed meal from the contents in the refrigerator.

She calls, "I'm going."

The only reply from George is a grumble. Slipping away to her bicycle outside, rolling over the hills, perhaps a little too quickly, to the hospital.

Her mind wanders to a picture. Rough black and white. He and she in a kimono, their faces serious. His youth was plain, his hair longer by a few inches, his face less worn and scarred but no more joyful than the one Penny had seen. The wife was giddy in comparison. She had to look closely to see the smallest hint of happiness, but it was there in the crook of her mouth that turned just upwards. Her innards twist and pull outwards toward him. The heat blushing through her cheeks reveals her true intentions. She tries to forget it in the rose and jasmine scents captured in glass bottles. His hot breath prickled her neck. Anger at the forefront permeating, reaching for something, some abstract understanding hidden from her. It remains with her even as she walks into the hospital room where Ojiisan lay in his bed.

Lifting him by the armpits, she props him upright. Pouring the soup into the bowl, she takes up the chopsticks and tries using them to pick up a chopped cabbage floating in the broth. After slipping over her fingers twice and having one nearly fall into the bowl, Ojiisan groans.

"I can do it."

"No, no," Penny says, trying to steady the chopsticks between her fingers. "Let me. It's the least I can do."

He reaches for them with his full hand, "Give them here." and yanks them from her. She follows with the bowl underneath, holding it steadily close near his chin so he can eat.

"How is it?" she asks.

His answer is a nod. The slight gesture comforts her. They sit together quietly. His slurping is the only sound in the shared room until he finishes eating, puts down his chopsticks, and takes the bowl from her to drink the broth.

"It's a funny thing. I haven't thought about my wife in years." He looks up at the water-stained ceiling. "Being here, she's come back."

"What was she like?"

He shakes his head once, scratching his ear, "Ah, I forget."

Penny removes the used bowl and chopsticks from him, returning them to her basket.

"Where is George?"

An unwitting glance in his direction proclaimed an explanation. When she doesn't answer, Ojiisan slips back down, laying his head on the pillow. She stays, sometimes singing to him, stopping abruptly when an exhausted looking nurse comes to check on him and makes her leave.

*

A ride on the sky train brings her home. Putting her things on the ground by the door, she pushes in through her house and upstairs to the second floor. Early morning sounds reverberate from beneath the doors and across the floor. Rose cooing, Tim occasionally waking and screaming until he is settled, snoring from George's room. Gently, she pulls one of the armchairs across the carpet, settling it a few feet from his bedroom door, spreading her skirts and sitting down comfortably. Indecently or not, it is here that she waits for George, sights fixed on his closed door. White panels. The area around the curved handle smudged from dirty fingers. The snoring stops. Penny straightens her back, raising and lowering her hand against the threadbare armrest. George comes in smoking a cigarette, dressed in his work clothes.

"Will you visit Ojiisan today?" she asks abruptly.

"Why should I?"

"He's lonely."

George scoffs. "Good."

"George," she says gently, standing up to meet him. "I don't pretend to know your relationship with him—"

"—You don't."

She inhales deeply, smoothing all irritation from her voice.

"He's your father."

"And? Does that mean I should forget everything he's done to me?"

"No," she answers quickly, "but someday when he's gone," she swallows, the memories of her father fresher than she cares to admit, "you'll regret not settling things. *You* have a chance, at least, to reconcile."

Taking the cigarette from his mouth, he exhales the smoke into the air, finding an ash tray on the nearest table to tap his cigarette into.

"You want to know the worst thing he's done?" he asks, his cheeks tinting red. "It wasn't this," he holds up his hand, showing the stub of his finger, then lets it fall, "or even pushing my wife and me together." He takes another draw. "One day just after coming back from camp he brought me to the old part of King Street Station to an unused platform where none of the trains came through. There was Koike-san and three other men sitting on their knees with their hands tied behind their backs and their mouths held open by some bits of metal jammed in. He went to the two men, younger, with a set of pliers he pulled on their tongues and Koike-san put a rod in my hand. An iron brand. He made me push it on their tongues. Burning. They screamed. Young boys like me. I couldn't. . ." He taps the cigarette again. "The last was an old man. Father spoke to him, saying nonsense about old Japan and family. All I could hear were the boys crying." He puts out the cigarette. "That was the first time he and I ever did anything together." For a moment, he smiles sardonically, then lets it fade. "When he took my hand in his and we cut the man together. First his tongue. Then four fingers on his right hand, one by one."

Penny's eyes roll to a small action of George swirling a finger in the ash. Kanji. 静か. *Shizuka.* Quiet.

"So, of course, there's nothing I can say."

Penny meets his eyes, pleading. "Everyone still has something to love, even if it's small."

"You're a liar."

His eyes are pinned on hers in an expression of disgust. A moment, waiting, hoping he will apologize so she does not have to react. With nothing but silence, she hits him with her fist coming in sideways, her fingers tightly joined together to connect with his jawbone.

It wasn't a very good punch, she decides, but it was as good as she could manage. He responds with a reflex: a light slap to her ear and she feels his wedding ring on her cartilage. At once he lifts his hand to strike her again and just as quickly she brings up her hands to grab onto his wrist, pushing him from her.

He stops. He may try to hit her again. He stops. They are paralyzed with inaction. Letting silence fall between them, she pushes down the nervous laugh rising in her throat. The lines on his face seem clearer in the natural light; creases in smooth skin, worry lines about his eyes that are somewhat veiled by his spectacles, speckles of white in his curly black hair, the scars and freckles on his cheeks and forehead. She remembers him looking young once and it didn't suit him. His face, relaxed, looking towards the sky line.

In many ways, she wished she could love him better if only to prove that there is a love beyond what is given by children--a love apart from blood--and then she remembers Catherine with bruises on her back and a broken bloody womb. It's a shame. She smiles and releases a cruel laugh resting inside her and turns to leave him, a brusque shift of her shoulders and yet he catches her up in one harsh movement, holding her back. A palm against her neck, his fingers are firm at the back as his thumb rests on the soft flesh between her throat and muscle. It is as if a black mollusk clings to her chest, pulling and pushing on the different parts of her, leaving slime where its suctions had been.

"I *will* leave you alone," he says even while he grazes a thumb up and down; his calloused tips hard against her pulse.

He might squeeze. Her neck is thin and his hand is large. A small fear of this: If he can hit when anger flushes in his cheeks, he can strangle her if he wants.

"You see now how cruel you are?"

She struggles to keep her breath steady, yet George feels her heartbeat easily drumming on his finger. She manages half a smile, her lips curling up to the left. She raises her hand to his, softly grasping his wrist. Her mother once told her that she was like a fizzy coke bottle. Even undisturbed, the bubbles pop up on the surface, never sitting still and bumped, shaken, it bursts. George is a pallid wafer, or so he tries to display on the surface.

She sees there in his eyes a glimpse of the man behind that he so desperately tries to keep within his self-control. If he wants to kill her, all he has to do is to take a shaving razor and give her a necklace of rubies. His heartbeat a knocker rapping to a beat. Hot breath against her bare neck is enough. She lets her eyes drift to the double-pane window and sees a woman standing there; one who startles her with her waves meeting his stone. A strange woman enshrouding Penny, whom she has no conscious power over. She rounds on him, twisting her wrist violently from his grip as he struggles to keep hold while pressing his lips tighter to keep the cigarette from falling and in one swift motion an open palm meets his cheek. His eyes widen in surprise. Letting go of her, he returns the spiteful gesture and her skin flushes at the remark. Lifting upwards, she brings her forearm to his throat, pressing on his Adam's apple with a force to push him against the door.

*

Knocking wakes Catherine as she lays on her bed, opening the door at once, seeing Rose sleeping against her body with her smooth head nestling under her mother's chin, refusing to rise as Penny shouts in an orderly voice, slapping her hand against the door. Catherine turns over, slipping the blankets over her head, refusing to get up. The bed is comfortable, warm, and out there is cold—she can feel it on her nose. Yet what Penny says next makes her startle.

"Jii-chan died," she says it in a shattered voice. "Never mind getting dressed. We have to go there now." Catherine makes sure to sound sorrowful when she says, "I'm coming,"

It is enough to make her feet pass the threshold of the doorway to the outside. Still in her robe, she threads her jacket through each arm, buttoning it quickly as she can and then hefts her slumbering daughter into her arms. Neither of them says anything to each other. She has her keys in hand and her purse hanging from the crook of her elbow. Out the door, the night nips at her naked shins. The light from the hovering balloons make it seem the wrong hour. The car she drives quickly down and over the hills that surround the city. They travel from her stately home on the west side across a bridge to where those lights do not brighten. The car slows when turning into a block that she fears will be the destination. The homes are rickety sheds, no bigger than a single room and maybe a kitchen. A big gray dog chained in front of a yellow house barks at them as they pass worn homes and old brick, up steep hills until the red and white floating balls are pinpricks in the sky.

A well mowed length of hills sit naked before a white stone funeral house. Penny approaches the door first, knocking quietly as Catherine follows her into the house. Incense burns on a mantle. In the dining room, laid upon a white cloth is a body. She has to see his dead face to make sure. It had been cleaned, his thin hair combed, arms straight at his side. Chrysanthemums are laid on his chest. Through the doorframe, George sits in a wooden chair along the wall, his head low and his hands together as if in prayer. Wondering where Catherine might be, he peeks over when he hears Penelope's footsteps return to the other side of the room and sees the two of them sitting by each other, not as closely as they have done before, but just close enough that if he wants to, he can slip his hand to touch her knee just at the hem of her skirt.

"It's good, at least, that you get to see his body," Penny says, a dismal memory stitching itself on her rumination. One day, Papa was there—Penny can still see him at times when the evening light comes in the only window, his figure at the heater trying to warm—and then he was gone, leaving her to wonder if he was ever real.

"Could you make the arrangements?" George asks softly.

"Arrangements. . ." she lets the word hang in the air. "Surely, Catherine—"

At the mention of her name, her ears perk but she does not look up. Arrangements, for the funeral and then a ceremony for George to become Oyabun. Stealing a glance, Catherine finds the amalgam of sorrow and pride that she should feel in the wide, sea-flume eyes of Penelope. Any kindness Catherine may hold for him had been bludgeoned and stripped of sweetness long ago. George takes a sharp breath through his teeth and responds with a firm, "No."

17
Sarah
Carrying the Banner

Sarah opens an inner pocket of her suitcase, feeling against the silk to remove a few photos. White edges had turned yellow over time, one of a petite young woman in a slim flapper dress who is her mother standing just to the side of her father in his oxford suit. The other is a family photo where she finds herself in a long dress next to her sister. Comparing them, she finds that their noses share the same curved bridge and their cheeks a similar fullness. Pressing her lips together tightly, she slides the photographs back. Those childish times are over.

In the rougher parts amidst the rubble, the attic apartment is easy for her to find on her own despite visiting only once before. Standing in front of it, she hesitates, the words of the beggars still fresh in her mind. She has to see it, before she can move on, she has to see it. Walking the streets in these parts of the city in the day only highlighted the disaster that befell it such a short time ago. There are few men about who are picking up the bricks of toppled buildings and heaving them into a cart hitched to a green, well-used, truck. The path to the factory, though strewn with rubbish and debris, is free enough that it is faster to walk to it now than in the normal workdays when the roads had been full of pedestrians. With much of the surrounding structures levelled or sunken into the ground, the structure is made more imposing than it had ever been, standing as a lone red block among rubble.

She wants to deny the impact of the scene, but it winds its gloom around her spirit so that when she comes to the gates and sees the massive chains looped over the bars and the lock keeping them shut, she feels nothing of grief. All that remains is a whorl of anger that festers when she sees a lone woman, hunched over, pacing by the gates, mumbling, wringing her mangled hands together.

With few places to wander, and a nagging curiosity, her feet take her to a familiar road, one now strewn with uncollected trash and wayward newspapers. An image on one of the pages stops her and she bends down for a closer view, swiping away a thin layer of dust. Penny, looking jovial, stands on a pile of rubble with one foot poised on the top edge of a shovel, holding the pole with both hands. In the background are more people, some in the action of picking up large bricks or concrete slabs. Among them are many young boys, men, and in the distance, she recognizes George. In a column next to it is the headline, "Security Balloons Relocated." She reads on:

"In wake of the disaster, all security balloons have been temporarily repositioned to high-risk areas, including hospitals, banks, government installations, and select housing areas. The decision to relocate came in the wake of the April 13th earthquake after public concerns for safety."

Leaving it, she continues along to a street of hodge-podge homes that are broken, repaired, patterned in mismatched paint, or with add-ons that are clearly not city approved. Walking up the outside steps, she knocks twice and from the other side, a voice asks who it might be. When she answers with her name and association with Ruth, the door opens. Alma, the petite woman in slacks and a workman's shirt appears on the other side with a wave of heat and salty bodies rushing at Sarah.

"Quickly, quickly!" Alma snaps, pulling on Sarah's arm to get her past the threshold. The room is much changed since the previous time. Where before there were chairs and a table, with the printing press unused and off to the side. This night, the press works quietly within. A type of grand machine with long lines of paper set on a roller belt that feeds through from start to end. As if it were a typewriter, fixed above the mechanism are several rotating metal discs which each have sets of letter keys, thousands all smacking down on the paper as they churn automatically, each one punching on the page as quick as a blink. One young man stands at the start where there sits a sixty-minute clock whose hand points at five and a crank, feeding the long paper through, smoothing it out to ensure there are no creases. Another woman waits at the end, gathering the pages, pulling them to a spot and cutting them straight across with a long paper cutter affixed to the edge. Once she cuts, she slides the page into a big crate on her left. Whenever the machine slows its pace, the young man winds it to tighten the inner clockwork gears, resetting the clock to the sixty mark.

"After the first time, I thought you were done." Alma says, leading Sarah to where Florence rests on a worn velvet ottoman with several crates before her, creasing the printed pages to form a booklet and putting the completed ones in a separate crate.

"So did I," Sarah replies as Alma takes a place on the floor.

"You've had a change of mind?" Florence asks, glancing up at her. "Anything to do with Sinclair closing?"

"Something like that," she says.

Feeling useless standing in a moving room, she kneels by one of the crates to help.

"Well, everything we do here is on morals; there's no money in it."

"That's not why I came here." She replies, somewhat disheartened by the probability of her continued unemployment but it does nothing to deter her.

"No?" Florence questions.

"No. I want to help," she says unconvincingly. The truth being closer to having nowhere else to go.

Florence lets out a single "Ha!" before sitting up straight for a moment to let her spine crack before cowering over the pages once more.

Sarah stops, insulted at the laugh, and stands, "If you're going to make fun of me, then I'll leave."

Florence lets a wide grin spread across her lips. "Calm down. You don't want to help. What you want is to get back at them for treating you for what you—what *we*— are. Sometimes it takes a disaster to prove it. Just yesterday, six laid-off Sinclair workers came here looking for the same thing."

"Amazing what a disgruntled worker can accomplish," Alma comments.

Sarah kneels back down.

"You want to do something?" Florence asks, holding out one of the booklets for Sarah to take. An icon of the star with wings on the front with the word "Liberty" which she receives slightly hesitantly. "Come to the next rally." Sarah stands up once more as a thought forms.

"I don't want to start trouble."

"We're all troublemakers here."

Sarah furrows her brows, her face inquisitive.

Clanking comes up the stairs. Bursting through the door so roughly that it smashes against the wall are three of the young dissidents who Sarah recognizes from the first time she visited. Each one is in a state of astonishment, their eyes wide, mouths agape to suck in air that they spent running. A few show red marks on their cheeks and collarbones; the signs of a street brawl.

"What's this?" Florence asks immediately, her body straightening and shoulders broad.

One of them, a lean youngster looks particularly rough with a face covered in splotches and a demeanor a stern scowl. Sarah recognizes the face at once from the city hall rally.

"Damned V gang," the kid says, spitting on the floor. "They caught us putting up posters."

In two determined steps, she approaches to give a hard slap on the back of the head. "And what were you doing around the V gang?" she looks down, her hands folded. The youngster holds in a response until she pushes again with a forceful, "Hm?"

Taking the action as an insult, the kid rises, indignant, shouting, "It was them that started it. Was doing your little," a flip of the palm up and down in the air, "errand." then lets the hand fall, slapping against a thigh, voice relaxing. "Few come up giving me riff so I knock one in the eye. After that, well," the kid points at a bright red spot under the eye.

"You're about to earn another," Florence offers, her emotions carefully subdued while Kid pokes her in the shoulder, saying, "You do that, and I'll give you the same as I did to the V gang."

Putting her hands safely in her pockets, she tips her head down to meet eyes and narrows her gaze.

252

"Be glad it wasn't the Shizuka who found you," she says, letting her words settle between them, hoping that the child will absorb the seriousness. It seems to roll over the kid's head and down the back. "Then I'll tromp 'em all. I'm not letting some ass-wipes tread on *my* back."

In a single swift movement, as promised, she takes her hand from a pocket, squeezes it into a tight fist to connect against a nose with a dull smack making Kid wobble back a few steps and brings a forearm up to wipe the blood pooling under the nostrils.

"Act right," she commands. "We're not a street gang fighting every damn person who rolls their eyes at us."
"Hell with you." The kid snorts, then spits a globule of blood and mucous on the floor before Florence's shoes.

*

Sarah takes in the large expanse of slums that are smashed against each other like too many bread rolls in a basket. The smell that seeps through the ozone of the slum is of fetid sewage, rotting vegetables and sodden garbage: the odor of poverty. It seems ludicrous that a short ride away lies a city imbued with a glass skyline. From behind a blue tarp roof she catches sight of a short, stout woman in faded jeans and a flower print shirt, immediately recognizing the corrupt fingers of the old woman she first met at the Sinclair gates. The brown dirt beneath her feet is littered with tin cans and faded food wrappers. Outside the entrances are clotheslines made from whatever the families find available: cord, wood, twine, thin pieces of plastic, and wire. Worn and faded fashions hang to dry on the second-hand clothesline. A stray cat rubs against the corner of the house, then runs away startled at the deep barking of a dog. Walking on, she finds

253

the peeling paint on the apartments of Sinclair Worker's Housing barely stand on their own, hidden and sinking into the earth about a mile and a half behind the factory where she hopes to find her friend.

Each tenement holds six apartments separated by two floors, most of which now tilt forward into risen sea being the victims of shoddy craftsmanship and the shifting earth. Those that remain intact are surrounded by whitewashed iron fences, curved at the base, with round baubles on each tip, some of which have long since fallen off. The path leading up to the second-floor winding stairwell has a triangular garden patch which is overgrown by dandelion weeds and a dead cactus. Scoffing at her circumstances, Sarah realizes that Ruth never said exactly which apartment she lived in. Deciding that the best way to find Ruth is to peek in every window and listen at each thin wooden door, though there is barely enough material to cover the household noises coming from inside. From the outside, someone attempted to make it look homely by placing potted nasturtiums under the front window where sky blue curtains were closed to passing eyes. Once again, there is nowhere else for her to go and so she knocks. Relief cascades over her when she sees that Ruth is on the other side, still in her worker's coveralls.

"Sarah! What are you doing around here?" She tilts her head down to see the suitcase. "Ah, I see. Well, come on in and try to find some room. Tight in here, but there'll be a spot somewhere."

Sarah picks up her luggage, the door creaking shut behind her. A shuffling draws her eye to where Ruth pushes a rolled up knotted carpet against the underside of the door to keep the warmth in and the cold out. Inside there are three others, a young boy, a thick bearded old man whose back is permanently bowed, and a wrinkled old woman whose head is covered by a scarf of a color resembling that of an unripe pomegranate orange pulled over her ears and tied in a tight knot under her chin. It seems the only color in the dark room where they all huddle around a kerosene heater speaking in a language Sarah does not recognize, eating brown soup from big porcelain bowls of varying blue and white patterns. It seems that there is a kitchen through a slim hallway that she can spy from where she stands and a door next to it that she guesses is a bedroom.

"Go on, sit down—move over, you—Are you hungry?" Ruth says.

"Yes," Sarah answers truthfully, sitting at a cleared space next to the boy and woman who, upon closer inspection, shares a clean resemblance to Ruth. "Thank you."

Ruth turns to the kitchen and reemerges with a spoon resting in bowl, and a homemade roll in hand. Sitting, she thrusts the dish to Sarah.

"I'm starved. Just got back from scrounging the docks doing odd jobs." She bites into a hard-crusted bread roll, some marmalade spilling out of the sides that she licked up before it dribbled onto her fingers. "You heard about the closing?"

Sarah nods, filling the bowl with the hearty soup, focusing on the repeating pattern of white hearts on a blue setting.

"You don't think," she starts, a small fear emerging, knowing that without Penelope she will need a steady source of income and the cash she was given would only last so long, "it'll shut for good?"

She pulls the bowl away once she is satisfactorily full and begins to slurp, delighting in the savory flavor and soft meat.

255

Ruth shrugs. "Might do. Probably only waited so long since it's cheaper to hire us than it is to build gears to do the job. Not now, though. What happened to get you here? After you left the Panama, I thought you were staying with your citizen-cousin."

Sarah swallows, licking her lips, "I was."

"And?"

"She found this," Sarah says, reaching to her back pocket to retrieve the pamphlet, withholding the remaining truth.

Ruth's eyebrows raise, her head tilting to the side just as a curious bird would, then straighten again.

"So what? You're carrying the banner now?" Ruth says, taking it to muse over the insides. "You sure about this? Looks like they plan on it being the big push. A rally right in front of Sinclair Industries."

Sarah shrugs, holding her spoon against the inside lip of the bowl to drink the broth.

"Aren't you?"

Ruth shakes her head, giving the booklet back. "I need a job and Sinclair is the only place hiring non-citizens. He's got factories all over the city. Before it was different. They'd hire anyone who'd work cheap. Not now. Gotta work as much as I can before he replaces us with machines." She scratches her scalp under her blue cap. "Funny that. Being replaced by the thing I'm paid to make."

Ruth takes a Firelite from her pocket, lighting it with a match.

"Then you should come with me. Show him we can't be bullied."

She looks down, focusing on her shoes, knowing it is not Sinclair she wants to punish. Those she does are untouchable and even if she wants to retaliate, Penny or

George are too protected and too familiar. Sinclair is as good as anyone, and not without guilt, making him a figurehead to unleash her anger upon.

"I need to do this, Ruth," she pleads, the truth of it sinking into her stomach.

When she looks up, she meets a pair of eyes that judge her critically. After several moments pass, Ruth nods.

"That a violin?" the boy asks, nodding to the oblong case, revealing a large chip on his front tooth when he opens his mouth.

To his amusement, Sarah removes her Vota Violin to the awe of both mother and father. Not since she first handled the instrument has she felt comfort in gripping the neck with her fingertips pressing on exquisite strings while she draws her bow along the waist. A run of simple notes pours in a melodious resonance, undulating to a French lullaby she learned many years ago.

*

There is no extra space and so she shares a single bed. While Ruth falls asleep easily, Sarah struggles to find comfort on the cheap mattress and is kept awake by the snoring coming from the other occupants. She cannot turn in the bed, forced instead to lie on her side, facing a single window cracked open to let in fresh air. Outside are neighborly noises. Giggles and low conversations sometimes broken by a child's cry or a raucous holler. Whooping comes from farther up the road. Bicycle chains. Peeking out the crack, a gang rushes past. On their jackets are triple V emblems. As they pass, some throw objects indiscriminately, an empty pop bottle hits the side of the house, startling her, and all the while the vandals laugh. Her father's whispers lull her into a calm.

"In the winter when the snows and the cold were the worst, when it's so cold you can see your breath no matter how close to the fire you are, when four *hanten*—winter coats—aren't enough to keep you warm. The snows come knocking at the door. But be careful not to walk out into the white darkness. You may see a woman. A beautiful young mother. The *yuki-onna*. 'Come,' she whispers, 'come, my child. Come and sleep.' And because you are kind, you go to her. She smiles, like a young mother, and takes you into her arms, and wraps you in her long-sleeved *kimono* and for the first time all winter you are warm. You sleep. And when you do, she has taken another child for her own winter family."

With the waterfront in patches of ruins, Sarah expects no more participants than herself, Ruth, and the Patriot figureheads. As she and her companion walk the road, the life stirring along the boardwalk comes in the form of the meandering automatons, occasional workmen who clear rubble from the streets, and some people shopping at the few places open for business. Nearing the red brick factory, any sign of humanity dissipates into broken timbers settled in the muck.

Yet, coming upon the iron gates now wrapped in heavy chains, a quick scan of heads leads to an estimate of more than eighty worn-soled workers standing ready with Florence invigorating them with her vibrant optimism, tossing blue bracelets with the star and wings symbol into the air. In a clear sky, the balloons drift overhead, soon forming a wide concentric circle directly above the protestors. It is her warning to retreat. One she ignores. Young rebels hold homemade signs with slogans of "Fair Wages", "Strike on

Sinclair Industries", "Sinclair Unfair to Labor", "Protect the Workers" while following two women in the front who brandish one such cloth banner. Together they begin walking as one mass down the road from the factory and along the downtown streets where pedestrians avoid their presence. Voices roar in the hope that those walking the streets can hear them and be swayed.

Marching with others makes her feel powerful perhaps for the first time. Sarah wonders briefly that if people had protested like this before the internment, then perhaps no one would have gone. Sirens approach. Wheels burning on the roads bring a half dozen police fleet cars and a convoy of wide, silver bullet shaped vehicles, all stopping a few feet in front of the crowd. A single oversized black-and-white Fleetline with two police officers safely inside. The black uniformed officers whose buttons shine in the daylight erupt from the cars, several of whom hold bolt guns while others clutch short, thick, batons that can easily bludgeon flesh. One officer takes up a handheld radio from within the car, speaking into the mesh so his voice is amplified by the transmitter and spews out the single speaker above the windshield.

"This is the Seattle Police Department. Cease all activities and disassemble immediately. If you choose not to comply, we will be forced to apprehend and detain any and all participants."

Their answer is a sign thrown at the windshield. The square rod bouncing from the glass to the ground. Feet firm against the ruined ground, the flash of bodies are as one voice. Never has her heart been as unfettered and determined as when beating with the others in unified purpose.

259

Overwhelmed by hope and determination, she finds that her lips are spread into a content smile. She stands next to Ruth with the protestors in a single line. The gates are behind them and the police before them. In a swift move, the side doors of the bullet cars open and out roll six sturdy steel automatons. Each one is broad, five feet tall, covered top to bottom in thick steel armor, with wheels instead of legs, lining up in a barrier, enclosing the protestors between them and the gates.

Every face has the simplest representation of humanity presented in two giant black lens eyes and a thin line where two pieces of metal joined together to form a mouth. Where their forearms and hands would be are instead the newest bolt gun, another of Sinclair Industries' many manufactures, jutting out from the machine in a long barrel. A rivet wheel on the side charges the voltage, spinning and popping with electricity as a warning. There are murmurs amongst them, questioning what action should be best. Yet, they have families. What can they do against a police force? They have no weapons. Standing up to the star-badged automatons would lead to a lightning bolt fired at their heart.

Resolute, eager for violence, the ralliers keep feet pressed firmly to the ground, some screaming obscenities, others taunting, while Florence tries to calm them with rational guidance that is mute to their ears. In the ruckus, a singular action begins the chaos. From a point in the line, a workman's shoe flies sharply into the sky, landing with a *thonk* on an automaton's head. The two lines merge in a roaring clash with protestors picking up any item from the ground that can be used as a weapon. Looking frantically around her, Sarah spots an oblong red object sitting under some rubble. Grabbing it, she flies into the roaring bodies of flesh and metal with the giant red wrench in both hands, drawing it up into the air to let loose with an oblique strike where the bolts met the head of an automaton. A dull crunch is the only damage. She strikes again, coming down swiftly on its left mounted bolt gun. Sizzling, the arm falls with a charge running up and down until it disappears.

A shock at her shoulder makes her reel. The wrench weighs on her muscles as she strains to keep hold. Turning, she sees another Iron Boy the size of a grizzly. A line of them make a wall, forcing her and the others together with their back against the fence, she slips slightly on the thin bracelets that dot the ground. Sarah scans the heads, looking for Ruth among them and finding one familiar face—Florence. Her upper lip and cheek are smeared red where she had wiped away a bloody nose. Deep white streaks on her neck show where a bolt gun had struck her. Her mouth moves but in the noise of sirens, shouts, and moving metal, Sarah cannot hear.

A dense white fog covers them in blindness. Shouts warn to cover the mouth and nose. Slapping her arm over her face, still her eyes water. Weakly, she swings the wrench, desperately trying to hit any object she can until her hand loosens despite her resolve, then her fingers, and it drops. Her arms fight off hands that grab, cutting as manacles secure her wrists.

18
Penelope
Succession
襲名盃
Shyumeisakazuki
May 1949

When the camp celebrated *Tanabata*, the festivities
made the camp guards more alert than on normal days with a
flux posted in their high towers along the fence. All her
cousins dressed in homemade *yukata* from fabric ordered
from the Sears catalog. Mom and Auntie helped dress the
girls. Penny helped her Mom wrap a plain yellow obi around
Sarah's waist, contrasting with the checked blue and white
pattern of the cotton kimono. Penny held the knot firm while
Mom tied it, moving her hand out of the way when she was
told to. She would be the last to go, the other girls having
been secured into their bandages earlier.

"Where is Papa?" Sarah asked, noticing he was not
there.

Auntie did not look. Instead ordering Penny, who was
still in her western clothing to, "Find your uncle," Though
she did not want to, and would have refused as she had
always done, she desired even less to be bound up into the
tight kimono fabric.

Out in the empty spaces, there were multi-colored
paper star chains hung around the outsides of barracks
windows. Stuck into the dirt at the edge of the doors were
thin cut branches decorated from the top to the bottom with
pink, white, and yellow paper flowers. Some had written
wishes on paper and hung them from the desert trees that

grew within the fence lines. Penny and Sarah hung theirs, written in French, on the young Joshua tree next to the swing set. Most children were playing; some complimented each other on their *yukata* even though most had the same designs as everyone at the camp ordered from the same catalog. The stink of cheap moonshine was on him, the liquid hidden inside a brown Coca-Cola bottle.

"The purpose for *Tanabata, wakaru*?" he asked her.

His drunken slurs made it difficult for her to understand his broken English.

She shook her head.

"No. It doesn't matter. Auntie is looking for you."

"*Mendokusai*," he complained. "*Onna wa sugoi urusai, ne?*"

She put her hands on her hips and said, "Fine. You can stay here."

"*Matte, matte*," he said. "Wait, wait, *Suzume*."

She didn't like that he called her that. *Suzume.* Sparrow.

"I tell *Tanabata* story to you." He motioned for her to come over with a flapping hand. "Come on, *nomimasho*." He pushed the bottle across the picnic table. It stank. But she had never tried it before. No adult had ever let her so much as sniff alcohol. She went to the edge of the table yet refused to sit. Holding her breath, she sipped from the bottle. It stung her throat, made her cough so that Uncle laughed at her. He took the bottle from her, guzzling from it as a baby would with warm milk. A hollow thud when he placed it back down in front of her. She tried it again, thinking that she would enjoy feeling like an adult. This time a small dose that was a tolerable burn.

"*Tanabata*," he began. "It *kawaisou* story. English is. . . I don't know, but I say in *Nihongo*. You know, *wakaru*?"

263

Emboldened by the drink, she met his gaze directly and said, *"Jibun wa subete o wakarimasu."* in such effortless Japanese that all he could do was let out an amused chuckle.

"Shitte imashita," he said. "I knew it. So, *mukashi, mukashi,"* he started once more, "There were two great lovers, Orihime and Hikoboshi. Now, Orihime was the daughter of the Tentei, the Sky King, and she would weave her beautiful fabric by the bank of the Amanogawa. Her father loved the cloth she weaved and so she worked hard every day to become more skilled than the day before.

However, Orihime became sad that because she worked so hard for her father, she was never able to meet and fall in love with anyone. Concerned about her sadness, Tentei introduced her to Hikoboshi who worked as a cowherd on the other side of the river. Once the two met, they fell in love and married soon after." He drank again from the bottle. "As time went on, Orihime no longer wove for Tentei and Hikoboshi let his cows stray all over the grasses. Angry, the Sky King separated the two lovers across the Amanogawa and forbade them to meet. Overcome with sadness, Orihime begged her father to let her see Hikoboshi again. Moved by his daughter's cries, he allowed the two to meet once a year on the seventh day of the seventh month when the sky is clear." He looked up, pointing to the sky, "There they are." And slid the bottle back to Penny who did not drink at first until he held it to her lips. "But it is said that if it rains, the river floods and they cannot meet until next year. The rains are their tears."

*

Nippon Kan theater remains a sanctuary for the traditional Japanese ceremonies that since the war have worn away from practical memory like river water washing over stones. A dignified building on the slant of a hill near Nihon Machi comprised of the same red brick as the older structures scattered throughout the city, though not as grandiose as The Fortune Follies. Penelope, with the immense assistance of Koike-san, had undertaken every preparatory task with the utmost attention. Where the tables are set according to each ranking. One long table is horizontal, the chairs on one side with the front left vacant, overviewing the room's expanse, while the others are set lengthwise in rows. Each person's seat indicates his or her designation within the gang as evident by their proximity to the head table and to Oyabun. George now being the boss rests at the head of the table, Koike-san at his left, Shimamura-san to his right and Penny at the end. Four people. 死.

The top bosses gathered in the open hall watch as he sips from a shallow *sake* cup, holding it firmly in two hands. Subdued applause rises from the serious audience. After this, the cup is passed to the other men. First to Koike-san, then down to Penny who is the last in a line of four men with George at the head, sensitively aware of her platinum locks standing out in a mass of black, like a white koi swimming within a bracken pool. Nervous when she takes the porcelain, she controls her quivering lips to sip as George had done, letting the tepid liquid touch her soft skin, rolling over her tongue in a prickling stream. George insisted that she be there yet was not deaf to the whispers in the hall just moments before the ceremony when the Shizuka families gathered, greeted her politely, and mumbled insults in Japanese that they assume she does not understand. Half-breed. Roundheel. All insults she learned to ignore since childhood.

Sake flows endlessly. The clear rice wine appears deceptively innocent. Each time she finishes a glass, some low ranking *shatei* arrives to refill it. There being limits to Penny's tolerance of alcohol, she ceases, lifting her glass only to raise it in *kanpai* whenever one comes to congratulate the new boss. Some hours pass in this fashion until the atmosphere changes with the arrival of dinner platters in the steady hands of servers to each table place, food the like of which she has not seen nor smelled since the internment. *Honzen-ryori*, prepared by one of the old *i-sei* who still remembers the methods by which to craft its true taste. Three trays of nine separate dishes.

On the first tray in the center, each bowl a matching red with gold leaf rims and ivy patterns swirling around the outside except for a small white porcelain saucer holding chestnut brown *shoyu*, neatly made fish cakes that can be easily confused for sweet confectionaries by their pastel coloring and dainty size. On her left, a deep bowl holds a healthy serving of steaming rice that leaves thin condensation along the inside, topped with two juicy pickled plums.

Next is a teaspoon-size *sake* cup, and then a bowl of *miso* soup. In the center is a shallow plate with pickled vegetables and at the back of the tray are a variety of fresh boiled vegetables and a fanned row of eggshell white *sashimi,* raw fish. The second tray on the right has three bowls arranged in a triangle; the closest is a milky opaque soup broth with a strong scent of savory pork bone *tonkotsu,* next to it is yet another serving of vegetables but with a thick golden sauce poured over the top, and the last is a blue and white porcelain cup of raw carrots and cucumber. The final tray to the left has a single wide white oval plate dressed with a whole broiled pink salmon the length of half a forearm.

Farther up the table, George laughs, his wide smile pushes up his alcohol-flushed cheeks. Turning her bleary eyes over the heads of the crowd, she fixes on movement coming from the stage curtains. On the stage, Penny notes three ladies and two gentlemen wrapped in solemn summer kimono, in shades of blue, bright green, and purple, whose white *tabi* contrast with the kimono hem, back and forth from backstage to retrieve a long wooden instrument that appear as if someone had hollowed out half a tree trunk, stained it with a deep brown varnish that brought out the swirling grains in stark white ridges, curved in the width as narrow half-moon with a length that reaches just to the chin. Thirteen tight sinew strings reach from one end to the other, the excess gathered into two concurrent hoops. Curving from the outermost edge inwards are thick trapezoid bridges with center notches on which to rest the string.

The *koto*. A Japanese harp that the player sets horizontally on stage, kept at a slant by a thick wooden platform set under the widest point. In a moment, the five sit on their knees, their weight resting on the back of the calves, backs straight, placing hands on the strings while the right thumb, forefinger and middle fingers have black rings on the tips with flat white rectangular picks attached to make the *tsume*.

Koike-san rises, swiftly gathering attention with a single shout of *"onegai itashimasu"*. After a silence, a lady in the back hits the fabric end of the *koto* three times, emitting a hollow wood sound from the stage. A melody telling the story of a wild hawk fleeing a hunter. The dips and rising

267

wings explored in plucking strings and vibrating resonance. Each reverberating note seems to soar across the air, penetrating her skin. An ancient harmony borne from the simple harshness of life. A hawk, flying, unencumbered. The clean sky above and the sylvan earth below. Ojiisan would enjoy it were he here. Thinking of him causes her to sip from her *sake* glass; the taste bitter but effects calming. It is always in music that she can disappear. Sitting among the men, and herself in a seat of power so near to George, there is a heaviness in her stomach, as if she had swallowed a stone. that was never there before.

A child approaches. A small, inconsequential child but for the letter carried in its hand and the triple V cufflinks on the shirtsleeves. Rolling her eyes across the room, the men lurch forward, tense, with a hand determinedly placed in an inside jacket pocket or behind their backs. The child comes closer to the dais where they sit. Penny shoots her sights from George to the child, wondering whether the gang sent the child in order to appeal to George's paternal sentiments. Holding out the letter to the stern Oyabun, the child's hand trembles, perspiration forms as a mist on the forehead. In a swift motion, George rises, overshadowing the miniscule figure and snatches the letter from toothpick fingers with a strong hand that bends the edge. Too shocked to move, the child remains still. Waiting. The poor boy is unlucky. George beckons towards Abe. After whispering in his ear, Abe departs with two other *kyodai* in attendance. They are visibly friendly when they three guide the messenger out of the hall, but Penny easily imagines that such outward appearance will soon dissolve into something more sinister away from public view.

19

Sarah

Debtor's Work

A firm hold of her shackles removes Sarah from the
cage. Delirious, she holds fast to the notion that a trial will
surely free her from her predicament. Entering the small,
office-like room, the man she imagines is the judge sits
placed before a sturdy elm desk with carved filigree
moldings. Papers are set out, a pen ready in hand, and no sign
of a gavel. Besides this man and herself is the guard who, it
seems, will double as a witness.

"Yes," says the judge, waving her forward.

The guard guides her to the desk edge, made to stand
as the only chair remains behind the bar and is occupied by
the exhausted man eager to finish the docket.

"Sarah Igarashi," says the guard, "arrested on charges
of disturbing the peace, assault and battery of a member of
the police force—" Sarah holds in a retort that a mindless
automaton is given the same status as a man "—and
disorderly conduct."

"So I see."

In a lull, Sarah is absorbed by the minute sounds in
the room. Flipping papers, the buzzing light overhead, the
men breathing.

"Won't there be a trial?" she blurts, unable to ensure
the noise.

"No need." He scratches on the paper. "From today,
your Registration Card is revoked permanently, and you are
fined ninety-six dollars—" Her eyes grow wide in shock. "—
if you are unable to pay the fine, you will be incarcerated at

the Mercer Island Prison Workhouse until such time that your debt to the state is paid."

Another scratch on the page and the guard pulls her away from the room and back into the cell with the handcuffs remaining securely on her wrists. Unable to step or turn, she stands slightly hunched, staring at the floor, moving a hand only to brush away a gnat that tickles her neck, and again when a fly buzzes around her eyes and ears.

"Miss," the guard is calling her softly, gently. Shooing away the fly, Sarah collapses cross-legged on the floor with her hands falling into her lap. "Do you have money for the fine?"

She shakes her head. The fly returns, this time landing on her elbow. Twitching, the insect hovers in the air.

"Do you have any family that can help you?" Thinking for a moment, she considers Penelope. Even if they only share a drop of blood between them, they are family.

"Penny Morgan," she says, the fly landing on her palm, "my cousin."

There is a jangling of metal as the guard leaves her. In a quick strike, she brings her hands together in a clap to smash the pest into a mush of pus and guts. Satisfied, she rests her back against the wall of bars, her mind focusing on the movement of the sunbeams across pocks in the concrete. Despite there being no comfort in the grey square in which she finds herself, her body surrenders to a fatigue that arises as her earlier adrenaline fades.

*

One low shout wakes her to a low overcast morning light. Stretching her back to unkink the stiffness that took hold from sleeping on a hard surface, she looks up to meet the policeman standing on the opposite side of the bars. With the possibility of release, she pops up.

"Am I going?" she asks, yearning clear in her voice. His answer comes in a steel chain of facts. It is not until he speaks that Sarah realizes that this is not the same man as before, as if it makes any difference.

"Ms. Morgan could not be reached. The fine is unable to be paid. You will be moved to Mercer Island. If a relative can be contacted to absolve your debt while you are accommodated there, you will be immediately released." In a stupor, she is guided out in handcuffs with her only possessions being what she holds in her pockets. She realizes that her violin remains at the shanty house, along with her other belongings, and that she may never retrieve them again. Whatever rationality she has left swirls around in her skull with her other memories, unable to catch hold of anything that might resemble coherent thought as she is led into the daylight.

There is a short car ride in the backseat of a police cruiser to the docks where a white and black police boat waits for her. The policeman exits the vehicle to hand Sarah off to another officer standing guard on the dock before leaving. Upon receiving the perturbed woman, the officer guides her aboard with a steady, gentle palm at her shoulder blades. The small boat is separated into two enclosures. At the bow is the closed steering section. At the aft is a windowless room with one locked steel door. Lifting a key from his belt, the officer unlocks it, pulling the door open with a great effort that makes the hinges screech from wear and seawater.

An unimposing single floor weathered brick building lies behind a low fieldstone wall in which high black iron bars with pointed gable arches jut upwards, encompassing the entire acreage. Patrolling the length is a single Iron Boy, its giant, single lens black eyes display Sarah's meager reflection and the cloudy skies above her.

The policeman escorts her into the building and through worn steel doors to a small room with a man sitting at a metal desk and a wall of bars behind him followed by a long hallway and another steel door. Instructed, she takes out everything in her pockets, dropping the contents to the tabletop with dull *clunks*. As she stands, the painful assault of hunger followed by a hollow croaking pulls her stomach inwards. Unfazed, or accustomed to the starving, the man appraises each item, each coin and bill, then writes descriptions of each in his ledger. He stops at the wallet, removing the contents, then lingers on the metal case, turning it over in his hands so that fingerprints remain on the smooth surface. He paws the clock, passing a thumb over the glass face, tapping at it with the edge of his thumbnail. Before Sarah can object, the man pulls apart the clock with a loud ring of popping metal. Holding the ticking clock between two fingers, he tosses it in the bin, then, squinting at the open contents, shakes his head once.

"Just what were you plannin' to do with this?" He raises the maimed case, showing her the inner mechanisms.

A tuning needle attached by a red wire that connects to three half inch thin silver strips flowing out and around the circular edges. Trying to get a closer look, Sarah reaches out but is stopped by the automaton who gives her a slight shock from the lightning rod to the belly, forcing her to double over. The deep betrayal. Knowing it was Penny. She is given no opportunity to contemplate the epiphany. The man at the table nods to the policeman and points behind him with a quick motion of throwing his thumb over his shoulder and she is escorted to the land behind the iron bars. Through the second steel door she is placed in a room with a wall of metal drawers on one side and a single bright light overhead. The policeman passes Sarah to a thin woman with a kind face who tells Sarah to disrobe to her undergarments.

Stunned, she looks to her escort, hoping that he will somehow help her, but at his apathetic demeanor, she resolves to kicks off her shoes and does as told. When the clothes fall to the floor, the kind woman picks them up, turns them inside out, shakes them, then turns them out again and gives the clothes back. As Sarah dresses, the woman pulls open one of the drawers to remove a set of previously used but clean and folded blue coveralls. These she holds out for Sarah who takes them and is then promptly guided out to the next room before she can thank the woman. In this room there is nothing but a speaker on a wall with a switch next to it and a light on the ceiling. She is told to listen as the policeman flicks the switch and waits at attention. The speaker crackles alive with a calm piano melody and a cheerful announcer's voice:

"Welcome to the Mercer Island Workhouse. Here you will find comfortable lodgings and generous amenities while you work off your debt to society in a safe environment. After this orientation, you will be given a card. Be sure to keep it on your person at all times as it tracks your credit earned towards your debt as well as any that is further accumulated.

During the workday from seven a.m. to six thirty p.m., three regular meals are provided that are just as wholesome and nutritious as the home cooked fare. And if you crave some luxury, there are vending services to cater to your desires."

The speaker clicks off and she is taken through to the final room where two guards stand at a high counter. Here, the escort leaves.

"Sarah Igarashi?" one of the men asks. She nods. "Here is your work card."

He slides a thick card with her name typed on the front followed underneath by a long number. On it are rows of dots.

"Do not lose it. Every week one of the guards will calculate your money spent and earned and if you have completed enough towards your debt, one of the dots is punched, like this." He picks up a paper from the counter along with a hole puncher in order to demonstrate, pulling the paper away to show her a square with diagonal cross hatchings and then putting them down again, "While here you are expected to work from seven to six thirty every day. Any time spent idle during working hours will not count towards your debt. Meals are promptly at six a.m., twelve p.m., and seven thirty p.m. in the cafeteria. You will be helped to your lodgings. Do you have any questions?"

She shakes her head.

"If you need any further assistance during your stay, please speak to one of the guards."

The other guard walks out from behind the counter and guides her with a hand on the shoulder, guiding her through a tour of the facility. Though her feet move, and she nods her head at whatever he says, she is too disoriented to

comprehend the surrounding space. It is not until he shows
her to a room without a door that is large enough for the four
bunk beds that reside there and tells her which is hers that
Sarah is left alone. She sits on the bottom bunk bed, crisp
clean sheets turned down once at the top. At the foot are two
folded green wool blankets, that she suspects are surplus
goods from the war, and a fresh cotton pillow. Appraising the
room, she finds a large caged clock over the doorframe and a
small barred window on the opposite wall. Each bunk has
small tokens of the resident who sleeps there. Some beds are
unmade while others are tucked and cornered with precision.
One of the walls on the farthest upper bunk is tacked with
pencil sketches of seagulls in various positions of flight and
rest. Sarah turns to the card still in her hand, fixed on the
name written there, and then stows it away in the safest place
she can imagine.

*

Lying awake and silent but for the occasional
stomach grumbling. Rustling draws her aching eyes to the
woman sleeping on the bed. She remains still, sleeping while
one of the other women gingerly lifts the pair of shoes resting
at the foot of the bedroll. Sarah parts her lips, perhaps to
admonish the thief, but the woman slips away with her prize.
She stretched suddenly, retrieving her own shoes which had
been sitting just under the cot and slid   them comfortably on
her feet. Through the night until she drifted into sleep she
wondered what use a stolen pair of shoes would be in a place
like this.

As the morning breaks through the window, ships
passing the island to arrive to port cut through the dark water,

275

making rolling waves that splash against the island shore, disturbing the seagulls who rest on the rocks. Sleepers rise periodically as the sun rises from behind hazy skies, brightening the day like a glowing lamp behind a parchment shade.

A baby lets out a sharp cry, waking both mother and the older sibling whose disturbed sleep is followed shortly by an irritable whine. The mother sits upright, eyes half open, pulls the baby onto her lap to unceremoniously open her shirt thereby baring her breast to the hungry child. With a free hand, she gently rubs her other child on the back, calming her back to sleep.

Sarah gets up and shakes her head vigorously as if to rattle away drowsiness. Her stomach cramps, protesting its starvation. Since she kept her shoes on, all she needs to do to prepare for the day is to slip on the coarse coveralls. She is about to leave, eager to eat her morning breakfast ration when an exclamation stops her. The barefoot woman had woken and at the shock of her missing shoes, rummages through the meager belongings, her panic escalating as the shoes refuse to emerge. Barefoot, she asks everyone she sees if they know where her shoes have gone. When it came to Sarah, she thought of keeping her mouth closed, to avoid any retaliation from the thief, but the desperation on the woman's face makes her speak.

"It was too dark to see who, but someone snatched them."

The room remains quiet for a time, filled only by the gentle cooing from the suckling baby. It does not take long for the thief to reveal herself of her own admission.

"I have them," says the woman nursing while her toddler lazily wakes by pulling her legs up to her chest and letting out a sleepy groan.

"Give 'em back."

"Happy to," she says, pausing to gently pull the baby from her breast to place it on her shoulder and give a few strong pats to force the child to burp, "for fifty cents."

So that's why.

Sarah felt a strange mix of emotions, from a bursting anger at the arrogance of thievery to pitying the woman who needed the money and to a greater fury at the circumstances that forced them all into desperation. The barefoot woman screams at the mother, kicking the bunk frame while the mother remains where she is, unperturbed, and the aftershocks of which force the toddler into an energetic wakefulness.

"I hid them," she states, then glances at the clock in a cheeky manner that reminded her of Penny. "Better find a way to pay me before the work starts. Can't go in like that."

The woman shouted again, ripping the blanket from the bed and tossing it aside so that it whipped through the air and landed in a knot on the ground.

"Give them back," Sarah says roughly. "No one has the kind of money here."

"She does. Keeps it in a bag around her neck." The mother stares directly at the barefoot woman.

"I seen you take it out when you buy from the vending."

Sarah looks from one to the other, then at the clock. Reluctantly, the barefoot woman reaches under her shirt, fondling, and pulls out her hand to toss two silver quarters at the mother, one of which hits the baby on the head and causes it to yelp in pain. The mother snatches them up, stowing the coins in the cup of her brassier. With her baby now settled on her chest and held on one arm, she leaves, returning not two minutes later with the shoes held by the laces in her left fingers.

*

Two weeks, she determined, two weeks to erase the debt and get out and it might have been so but for the daily wage fluctuation determined by the contracts. What should earn her a dollar's pay is seventy cents. What was seventy cents yesterday is ten today. Tomorrow might be worse or better. Months of indenture caused her skin to pull tighter around rising bones. She is always hungry. A cigarette would help to stave her constant stomach pains. There are packs in the vending automaton. It would be a simple act to show her card to the machine, have it read her name, and dispense a pack of Firelite cigarettes. She resists.

"God, but you stink," says a mother at the work station next to her with a child sleeping on her back, the weight of which makes her hunch over into a narrow half-moon shape.

"That's my business," Sarah replies. "Worry about your own self."

"You stinking *is* my business."

Pulling pains in her stomach and a pressing headache give her little patience for banter.

"Do us all a kindness and buy soap. You all alone must have money to do that." When Sarah refuses to reply, the woman adds. "Gives me a headache. How can I work when I have to smell a stinking Jap?"

The word splashes across her vision as if she were seeing it once more painted on her house door.

"Shut up!" she snaps, pausing her work. "I'll use my money as I like."

At her small victory in succeeding at irritating someone, the woman grins. The open barred windows along the walls let in fresh wind with a hint of salty rocks and dry seaweed. Cawing seagulls glide above the water while others strut across the rocks. Sitting, scowling over the binding machine, she turns the crank, winding down. The plates press the book cover against the pages, holding them together. This lot is for an order of Sixth Grade Mathematics for the Seattle School District. Each crank turn is time passing on a clock. If not for the concrete walls and window bars, she might convince herself that she is on an extended vacation, but smacking bindings together reminds her that every press is a dime closer to removing her debt.

At noon, she and all the others stop for their lunch meal. Some jog away but Sarah walks casually through the halls. Besides the workstations, washrooms, and the cafeteria, there is an old walking automaton dispensing goods, a roof-head, the very same type as when she first arrived. She determined early that she would refrain from any such luxury items that might take money from her debt. This morning, after two months with no more than a rag wash, she is tempted to buy the one-dollar bar of unscented Dial soap sitting on one of the shelves next to a packaged toothbrush. She bites her cheek and resists, turning away to enter the cafeteria for her breakfast. Other women are already there eating. Some, she notices, are enjoying sweets and savories from the vending automaton.

A short line forms before a thin slat cut into a wall.

Sarah waits and when it is her turn, removes her debt card from a spot inside her shirt, places it on the countertop with her fingers pressed on the corners so that the unseen person on the other side can read it, and receives the bland sustenance in a tin can without a label. Sarah hides her card once more and finds an open seat on a bench far from any others. Opening the can takes a few moments of twisting a rectangular bow attached to a single key shaft that connects to the lip. A meager oat porridge is her reward.

As she quickly finishes her food, she rests with her back hunched over the table, stretching her legs, twiddling her toes inside her shoes and is at once beset by a sharp sting on the side of her right foot. Worried, she rises, returning the empty tin to the counter, to enter the common bathroom. Here she stands before the large trough sink set with multiple faucets and after checking either side to see of anyone is nearby, removes her shoes and socks. She lifts the ailing foot to the corner of the sink and bends to inspect it, careful to breathe from her mouth to avoid the smell, she finds her two smallest toes are a bright pink, irritated at being cramped in shoes for longer stretches than was typical, while the soles are mildly swollen with a cracked lesion where the calloused edge of her foot meets the base of her small toes.

Turning the faucet on, she lifts her foot into the basin, soaking it for a time, scratching off dead skin and smut from under the nails and between toes, before switching out to her left foot while the other steadies her body. This one is not as severe as the other, so she splashes it down hastily with the water, and turns off the faucet. As there is no towel, she shakes the water from her feet and dries them by rubbing the tops and bottoms against the opposite pant leg in a position that she suspects makes her look like a roosting crane. Once clean and dry, she grumbles to herself as she sheathes her feet in a pair of old socks only to slip them in her shoes again, fearing the condition will only worsen, yet having no other alternative. With lunch finished, she returns to her workstation, continuing the monotony until the workday ends. Another can of oatmeal is her dinner and in her idle time before claiming her bunk, she rests outside between the building and the fence line and the mechanical guards keeping watch. Here she can see the city from a distance. Ships pass by and the seagulls coast on the air, sometimes soaring down to rest on the walls near the rocky shore or on the strip of grass and stones where unruly children are sent to play during the day while their mothers work. Here she is able to feel the fleeting happiness of a pauper where all thoughts soon become regrets.

*

Five a.m. and she wakes wearing the same coveralls as she was given when she arrived. One woman quietly sobs next to the mat beside her. She came with her son but at ten he could work alone--nearly mature--and was put in the men's ward. A trip to the bathroom. A kind word for it, as it amounts to nothing more than an open room with holes in the concrete and the washing trough on the opposite side with a few faucets is the sole washing station. As she relieves herself squatting over the hole in the floor, holding her breath to shield from the smell, an elderly woman stands naked washing herself with a wet rag and a full bar of soap, recently bought, periodically re-soaking it in the sink to rinse her body. The woman starts at the sound of Sarah turning on the sink. One look and the grandmother snatches her soap, holding it close to her naked chest and brandishing a tin spoon that had been sharpened into a shiv in the other. Sarah does not waste her time and leaves the desperate woman. Many beg others for their quota if only to get a few extra cents. Most ignore her, having learned through rumor or overhearing the guards about what brought her here.

The women are by and large incarcerated for destitution, with some having their offspring with them. Children who can, will work alongside the mother and those who cannot are kept to the floor or left to roam free unless they cry. Sarah works, binding the books together in a methodical rhythm. The act itself is a physical meditation, freeing her body to reflect on the disruptive thoughts that strike across her mind; monotony forcing memories to the surface. A wall of iron bars had been her life, she deduced, in the internment camps, at the Alaska cannery, at Sinclair Industries, incarcerated at a jail, and then here, isolated at a workhouse. She had been a prisoner of one kind or another.

Leaving Alaska was an action she thought would change her life for the better but all it had done was to subjugate her further, and when she tried to fight back she had been betrayed, taken, and put here. She labors every day, starving, and for what? What waits for her after this? Sarah resolves that she will never hear an apology from her near-forgotten sister for abandoning her for some man, from Penny for throwing her out; from Sinclair Industries for stealing the wellness of herself and hundreds of workers, from Florence, from Ruth, for undelivered promises. The whole city is wrong. The protests were wrong. There is no way to trust others to change.

Schemes of revenge find their way in her mind in the minutes before sleep. Upon waking, they reemerge, forcing her to consider each in a manner of course. Penelope used her, just like everyone else. The most immediately satisfying would be the destruction of that house on the hill and all of value to her cousin. It would be impossible, however, as it would require her to pass through the protections that surround the property in the form of able bodied and threatening gangsters, and she is unsure that she ever wants to see any of her family again, even if it were for retribution. A cold trickle of pity runs down her spine. Penny is in as much imprisonment as Sarah. Ever since the internment, it seemed fastened to them like a red string; A thread of fate following each passing moment, as a snake stalks meek prey. In a spark of clarity, she sees a path to break her suppression. Above her cousin, there is one who stands paramount in the history of her familial suffering. A man she has never met but whose shoes left heavy footprints in their wake. A man to whom she must send a message.

20
Penelope
Lighthouse

A day and a night on the coast. Far enough away so
that city ears cannot decipher whispers. The purple sky
signals the spiral lamps to shut off. Already awake, Penny
dresses in driving clothes, a pair of brown trousers she
borrowed from Ojiisan's closet, each leg cuffed up twice
from the hem to stop at her ankles and a checked blue short
sleeved blouse tucked into the waist. Her carpet bag was
already packed and sitting by the front door. Anticipating the
separation, Bruce follows at her heels, complaining in short,
striking, meows. She speaks comforting words to placate his
protestations, though it has the opposite effect. If it were
possible to manage, she would bring him.

There are already shouts from upstairs, mingled with
childish whines and then cries. She keeps looking from the
clock to her nails and finally goes outside to smoke a Firelite,
leaving the door open. George plods down the steps holding a
suitcase in each hand, followed by Timmy and, reluctantly,
by Catherine who holds Rose in her arms. As he passes his
cousin on the way to the first of two cars waiting outside, he
glances at the trousers on Penny. They are recognizable but
with a slightly tighter fit, the fabric following along
Penelope's curves.

She stubs out the cigarette on the porch rail and flicks
it halfway across the front yard, where it lands in the grass.
Penny retrieves her bag from inside before shutting the door,
locking it for the first time in months so that Bruce will
remain safely inside, and approaches the car reserved for the

284

children and Catherine. Koike-san is in the driver's seat, waiting, tapping his finger on the steering wheel while George fusses with his family to get them and the luggage into the vehicle. When he sees Penny, he breaks away from his squabble to shoo her away, with brief instructions to go to the front car. Seeing Abe standing over the open engine, hood propped open, fiddling with the oil gauge, she questions lightly, "You're not coming, too?" as she tosses her bag through the back window of the front car.

"Got a problem with that?" he jests, grinning sideways.

"Well," she starts, "what about Mrs. Shimamura? I'm sure George would have let her tag along. I'm curious to meet her."

Satisfied with the state of the engine, Abe closes the hood carefully to ensure he does not pinch his fingers.

"Ask the boss. It's not up to me."

Pushing open the door and hopping out, George strides to the other car, followed closely by Penny, to immediately take his son's hand, holding Rose with his other. A bucket handle slung over his arm slaps at his side as he walks. Catherine remains in the car, curling up in the back seat, covering her head with a summer hat. Penny tears away from her, catching up to George who is already crossing the street. As they pass the field of tall brown and green beach grass, the water shines grey even in the sunlight. Stalks wave back and forth against their legs as they walk through to arrive at the shore.

Slate boulders cluster as a wall separating the lighthouse pasture from the ashen sand. At the base of each outcropping stone are patches of washed up driftwood, dry seaweed, and bits of flotsam. Excited, Timmy pulls away from George's hand to run in the itchy grass, ignoring his father's shout. Penny chases after him, following the movement of the grass and the bobbing black hair.

The ground becomes soft sand as they hurry to the open beach where the ocean waves roll. She goes to it, rolling up her pant legs to mid-calf and kicking off her shoes. Stepping in the cold water, she turns, expecting to see Timmy near her already playing. He stands frozen some feet from the water, his face in terror, rushing to him as the sand sticks to her wet feet, she asks what was wrong even though she knows he will not answer back. He points to the water, shaking his head, letting out a whimper. Arriving at last, George approaches his son. Seeing his son's distress only causes him annoyance.

A red and white changing booth stands near a strip of food vendors. Penny announces she will change, to which George merely nods, and skips to the booth. Her powder blue bathing suit fits tightly around her body, giving the sensation as if rising from the bath naked. She has nothing but a towel to cover up and yet doing so will draw more attention than she wants. In front of an audience, she is masked by lights, makeup, fine dresses, and her voice. She never has to look at the people sitting before her unless she wants to; they are in the shadows. Here, she cannot hide behind frivolities and so a smile plastered on her face hides her insecurity. Happy shouts from children meet the irritable commands of parents.

Once on the sand she runs to the sea as a hummingbird to nectar. Cool satisfaction swirls over her crisp skin in a perfume of mire. At times, George steals glances at Penelope, at the rosy burns across her soft skin.

The rest of the family settles within eyesight on a sandy patch. Having had enough of the water, Penny escapes to the shore where she lies back on one of the towels, putting her arms above her head and closing her eyes. Warm sunlight covers her as she begins to hum. Kicked sand catches her attention. She squints against the white sky, seeing Catherine, with her exhausted puffy eyes shaded with a parasol. She is careful not to sit upon the soft spun orange cloth that separates her from Penny. Her hands are covered by lace white gloves, fingers gripping the straight wooden handle tightly. She protects her body with a wide-brimmed straw hat trimmed with a blue ribbon. Her dress hangs loosely around her chest where fitted seams would have curved around her bust had she worn proper undergarments. A long-sleeved summer dress removed from a closet filled with unworn fashions.

Catherine spreads her stockinged legs out in front of her, slipping off her Lifestride flat shoes with a free hand and setting them beside her handbag before crossing her legs at the ankle. Though a strange sight to be wearing so much at a beach, Penny was impressed that she braved the outside when she could have remained within the hotel walls.

Perhaps, she thought, *George insisted that she come. But he had never forced her whenever he did so before. Maybe she just wanted to do it this time.*

Penny turns, fixing her gaze on George as he plays in the shallow water with his children. Rose held tightly in one arm and his son holding his hand. They jump together, splashing water around their feet. When waves roll towards them, George smiles openly and lets out a sincere, exhilarant, "Whooo!" which Timmy repeats in delight as both women watch the scene from the sand where the overcast sun warms

287

their backs. Rarely has Penny witnessed such jubilation from the man that it seems she is seeing a person who is altogether different from the one she knows, leading to a pleasant upturn at the corner of her mouth.

"It's nice today, isn't it?" Penny begins with an inconsequential topic; a safe question to break the silence. Catherine nods once from under her parasol. Shafts of sunbeams pierce through the sheer gaps in the brocade, bright ovals on her skirt.

"Tell me how you met, won't you?" she asks, wanting a romantic story to match the scenery.
While she knew the facts of their meeting, she still imagines a romance of finding love in imprisonment. Both young and cheerful, living together in a cramped space only to flee outside to walk hand in hand.

'What?" she asks, her face twisting as if a sour apple had been sliced open under her nose.

"You and George," Penny insists. "I know you met in the camp, but. . ." she drifts, hoping it will lead Catherine into a story.

"Oh, that," she says as she takes a Firelite from her handbag. "Grab the matches, dear, and help me light it?" she asks, not wanting to do it herself and let go of the shade.

Obliging, Penny pulls the small pink leather bag across the sand to find a book of matches that makes her pause. Splashed across the front are the words "Atelier Lounge." George must have taken a pack from the reception.

Penny pushes the thought away, refusing to show even the smallest sign of distress. Instead, she smiles, striking one of the matches and lighting the end of Catherine's cigarette. She snuffs out the spent match into the sand and replaces the matchbook. Catherine inhales deeply, blowing out putrid smoke.

"Tell me." Penny urges, relaxing on her side with a forearm steady to hold up half her body.

"It's not much of a story." Catherine stares out to where her children are playing. George bends over, splashing water at them as they laugh. "My family and his shared a room. A rotten fate that was. We could have been lodged with some other family, *any* other family, and I would not have ended up where I am. There was even a family across from ours, the Oeda's. They had three girls who were all near my age. I could have been their sister. Instead we were put with them. Mr. and Mrs. Ryoutaro Igarashi and their son, George. He had no older brothers or sisters there to keep him right, they all stayed in Japan, and by then his parents were already too old to teach him kindness."

"It's a sweet beginning," Penny offers

"It wasn't. Those parents of his. . ." She draws on her cigarette, her pace becoming quicker as the stimulants begin working itself into her. "All the things we had to go through made him soft in his age; Ojiisan was nice to you, to my son, but only because he knew he would die soon."

Penny keeps her disgust hidden behind a placid expression.

"Still, to be kind it has to exist somewhere," she reminisces, glancing at George. "Even if it's small."

"You didn't see him before," she snaps. "He was a different person when you met him. Now he's dead." She taps her cigarette to the sand, letting ash fall. "Not that it matters. *His* mood hasn't changed as I hoped it might. Though really," she gives an aggrieved chuckle, "I should know better than to hope at all."

"Should you?" She taps her pinky against the parasol handle. "What is it the preachers at church say about

289

husbands and wives? That a man and woman become one flesh?"

The two are united into one under Christ, Penny remembers from a Sunday sermon.

"Marrying was a ruse. Our parents forced us to for one reason." There was only one reason Penny could imagine for an arrangement to occur in such a short space of time. "And that reason disappeared a few months later. Pointless. Pointless. What else could I do? After the camp my parents went back to Japan. This," she gestures towards the sea with her hand that holds a half-burned cigarette, "this is the best I can make."

Catherine picks up the bauble around her neck, holding it up to gaze at the seahorse dancing about. For a time neither speaks, letting the rolling waves take their words.

"Never marry," Catherine advises.
Penny laughs once. Her arm tired, she turns onto her back and closes her eyes.

"Marriage is the quickest road to end my career," she replies, and realizes that despite her affinity for romance, it is true.

"There is no reason for marriage," Penelope said. "A man may take her money for his own or she may fall in love only to have her heart broken when he leaves. Her life will consist of what he fashions for her, and while she adores children, having one will make her a mother, not a woman. Anything that stops me from being a singer is not something I'm interested in."

Suddenly, Oniisan's voice emerges from memory, yet clear enough to her that she can imagine him talking in her ear. When he was overly drunk from the sharp moonshine fashioned in the camps, he told stories. They were the few

290

times Penny could stand listening to his voice when his breath was thick with alcohol.

"*Mukashi, mukashi*," he always began, "A long, long time ago, there lived an old man and an old woman. The old man was kind and gentle, but his wife was mean and greedy. One morning, the old man left for work in the mountains. While he was working, he heard the voice of a sparrow crying and when he looked down he saw a young sparrow trapped under a dead branch. 'Oh, you poor thing,' the old man said as he gently picked it up and left the mountain. When they arrived at home, the old man bandaged the sparrow and fed it some rice grains, but the old woman didn't like this at all and got angry. But the old man paid her no mind and worked hard to nurse the young sparrow back to health.

One day, when the old man went back to work in the mountains, he asked the old woman to take care of the sparrow. 'All right,' said the old woman. But she didn't care about the bird and left it at home when she went to the river to do the washing. While the little sparrow was left alone, it got hungry and found a bowl of starch that the old woman had made. Because the sparrow was so hungry, it began to nibble at the starch. Then the old woman returned from the river, ready to starch the linens. She noticed that the starch was missing and asked the sparrow what had happened. 'I'm sorry,' the sparrow said. 'I was so hungry and couldn't help eating it.' The old woman became angry. 'You thief!' she shouted, and she cut the little sparrow's tongue with a pair of scissors." Here he would pause to glace around the tiny room that they all shared to look on the listeners. "The poor little sparrow flew back into the mountains, crying the whole way. When the old man returned from the mountains, he noticed that the sparrow was gone. 'What happened to the little

sparrow?' He asked the old woman. 'That bird ate my
starch,' she replied, 'so I cut its tongue and chased it away.'
The old man was surprised. 'It must have hurt so much,' he
said with tears streaming down his face. He then went back
into the mountains to search for the sparrow.

     The old man went here and there in the forest, calling
out, 'Little sparrow, come back!' but the sparrow was
nowhere to be found. As he was walking further into the
mountains, three sparrows appeared before him. 'Oh, have
you seen my little sparrow?' the old man asked. The sparrow
answered and led the old man to a great *momiji* tree. When he
entered, the little sparrow came up to greet him. 'Oh, you
poor dear. Are you all right? I was so worried,' the man said,
delighted to see the little sparrow again. 'I wish I could stay,
but I must be getting home. My wife will be worried.' At
this, the sparrows brought out two wicker baskets, a large one
and a small one. 'As a gift, take whichever one you like,' one
of the sparrows said. Although he had no desire for a gift, he
accepted the small basket. When the old man reached home,
he called out to the old woman, 'I'm home. I met the little
sparrow. I even got a gift. I wonder what's inside.' The two
of them opened the basket, and to their surprise, the basket
was filled with gold."

     The childish noise grew louder until Timmy jumped
wet onto Penny's stomach. She gathered him into her arms
with a laugh as she tickled his sandy feet.

*

     Lines of yellow tape are wrapped around the seaside
town center. Down the avenue are horizontal cables every
few feet and hanging down from them are long streamers in
alternating colors of pinks and greens. A winding train of

292

people, a mix of adults and children pass through the curtains. Joining them is Timmy who laughs hysterically while spinning back and forth underneath with his head tilted upwards so the ends of the streamers brush against his face. Seeing the onlookers cast curious glances at her son, Catherine, with Rose in her usual position on her arm, hastily grasps Timmy in an attempt to pull him away.

Determined as he is, the boy refuses, screaming, on the cusp of a tantrum. Seeing the display, she looks for George and finds him ignoring the situation, to her chagrin. Frustrated at the inaction, Penny approaches the boy gently as his mother stubbornly pulls on him while balancing Rose. Pointing beyond the streamers ceases Timmy's movements. Three elephants walk in a circle, all of them tied into a shared harness that connects to a turnstile. Reaching out, Timmy takes her hand and they walk to the animals, watching at the sidelines for a few moments to let the remainder of the family find them. Enraptured by their majesty, Penelope and Timothy walk hand in hand to the line.

While the sparkle of the elephants' trussed costumes holds the singer's attention, the boy soon wriggles free only to return to the streamers, passing his mother, who rounds to chase him, with George meeting her in line. On the end, there is a three-step staircase that Penny skips towards with George joining her, holding a popsicle shaped like a watermelon slice, the top half bitten off. With a twitch of a smile, he offers it out to Penny. She takes it, closing her lips around it and giving it back to him. It is sweet, with bits of chocolate inside that crunches. At their turn, a handler steadies one of the elephants, allowing the other two a moment to hoist themselves onto the back of the great beast as Penny sits in

293

the front, creating an opportunity for George to hold onto her waist. A gesture that is easily explained by their familial closeness. Abe glances, half expecting to find a shocked reaction from those standing, waiting their turn, but the closest he finds is a young boy who squishes his face together, sticking his tongue out. Penny calls to Abe, waving as if she is in a movie serial and when the elephant moves its feet forward, she grabs onto the black and silver striped satin hat, though it is unlikely to fall off considering how slow the animal moves.

*

Sleep is an uncatchable dragonfly. The closer she comes to capturing it, a quick upwind turn of the wings takes it to elusive heights. Penny lies upon the tawny grass some way from the lighthouse, so the great burning eye does not blind the starry night. Black waves are like a mother shushing a crying baby to sleep. Overhead a bright white waning moon hovers, sometimes hiding behind the passing translucent clouds. Every star is a pinpoint in black paper, so close it seems she could pick them from the sky and thread them through a silk ribbon to craft a necklace. Here she waits, listening to the ocean, watching until the morning becomes purple, then returning to the hotel on the shore, fatigue beginning to lap at her skull.

Sneaking in through the door, careful to twist open the door handle and release the lock when it settles quietly into place with the smallest click. Grabbing a lone pillow from the sofa, she finds comfort on the Jacquard chaise lounge, hugging the cushion to her chest and wishing Bruce were with her, watching the sea, at times looking up from it

294

to glimpse the burgeoning sunrise where sailing ships and cargo cruisers dot a blue horizon meeting a yellow dawn. The hint of day soothes her into a light doze. There is a gentle push of a hand on a door, waking her. Deliberately, or in a drunken stupor, George shuffles in, gently padding to her side, squeezing into the sliver of space next to her, pulling her in close to wrap his arm over her shoulder and let one hand rest at the tip of her breast. In the dark with the summer stars blinking down at them through the window, he nudges nearer until his hot skin is against the length of her back covered by a thin cotton nightgown.

The abrupt sensation of touch churns the ambivalence resting between them. Pressing her shoulder down persuades her body to turn over onto her back. Eyes closed, his hand grazes from her collar to her navel to search the foreign parts, curving full breasts, the center channel of her stomach, the soft flesh of her thighs, and her cherub feet with their high arches curving to the round, soft, heels. Her otherworldly body at once repulsing and attracting, he finds himself with his fingers now feeling through her platinum hair, a scent of the sea in each lock.

Rotating her head towards him. Her watercolor irises, like the ocean itself, are staring back at him. A gentle smile, kind, hiding the mischief lingering behind dangerous eyes. She lifts a hand to rest on his neck, a thumb against the back of his ear to gently stroke it like a child might do to appease a wild cat. Whoever acts first is muddled in the murky dawn and the only words spoken are when the sun hovers in the center of an amber streak just below a sheet of midnight blue.

"Parfois juste être là comme cela, vous savez que vous n'êtes pas seul," she murmurs. "Will we ever be able to

tell the truth to each other?" She asks, searching for his reaction, then reluctantly accepting that one may not come. He stares to the horizon, watching the sea roil, his breathing deep and soft, the pomade scent from his hair comforting her like the sensation of an old grandfather's quilt wrapped around her shoulders.

"I don't know."

She smiles at him, a sincere, full spread of her lips. Without any identifiable expression, he slides a hand down her leg, to take her heel in his left hand, holding it as one would a crystal bowl, gently but firm, flat fingers against the underside of her arch. The other hand he spreads from her toes up to her knee. His eyes intrude with disastrous ideas infesting her mind. One breath against her neck would make her crumble as his thoughts pass over both like fingers caressing a naked body and an invasive slug pushing into her mouth. For all his hot and cold reactions, he has shown her that true secret desire, shoddily hidden, but there. She had been looking down at him during these moments, watching the water flow over her skin, his hands on her, and when he looks up she smiles, saying "thank you" to the dark eyes holding that special thing she seeks to capture, then realizing both with a hot sting of a heartbeat and a sickening twist of the stone in her stomach, that this is all there is.

*

The evening sky is a shade like bruised skin. George relaxes on the sofa within the lounge. At the table, Penny deals cards to Catherine while holding her daughter on her lap. Timmy periodically runs, pitter-pattering, around the open room. A pop of a glass beer cap raises Penny's eyes from her cards to George who locks eyes on her as he guzzles from the bottle.

"What do I do next?" Catherine asks, drawing her back to the game.
Penny shakes her head. "Never mind." She gathers up the cards, "let's do something else."

Penny rises to pass in front of George to her travel bag and takes a box of hair accessories from it across the room to Catherine. A knock on the door draws Penny to the peep hole, seeing hotel staff on the other side holding silver food trays. She opens the door, allowing the servers in who silently stride to the center table to set each tray with the accompanying paraphernalia. In efficient movements of hands, the light snack is arranged, and the staff soon disappear, closing the door behind them.

Penny resumes her spot with Catherine.

"Here, I'll do your hair," she offers, first combing through slight tangles.

Timmy grasps at the comb so she gives it to him without argument. From the box, Penny looks through, deciding what to do with Catherine's fine hair.
George rises, setting the now empty bottle on the table, to approach the bedroom where Abe and Koike-san are sitting together chatting at a corner table just offset from the door. Once inside, George shuts it firmly behind him, locking it at once.

"No, no. Not that one," she protests when Penny chooses a blue ribbon. "The yellow one." Penny puts the one in her hand back into the box, trading it for a thick yellow ribbon with white polka dots. Penelope moves gently to pass her fingers through Catherine's hair, beginning at the ends to get the tangles out and continue up to her scalp. Her gaze flickers from the closed door hiding the men to Timmy who

297

plays with the comb by scraping a fingernail across the teeth over and over to make a chattering sound.

"*Mukashi, Mukashi.*" she begins, mimicking the cadence of how Oniisan told stories, taking Catherine's smooth locks to separate them into two sections, twisting them together in a fish braid. "In the wilds of Japan, there is a great lake surrounded by bright green grass and on the plain is Mount Nantai, the man's body mountain. One morning, two lovers were walking at the base of the mountain. High atop a ridge was a *tsukimisou* flower with petals that are golden in the sunlight and purple in the moonlight.

Seeing the flower on a ridge, and deciding that it would make his lover happy, the man told his maiden, 'Wait here. I will go and retrieve the flower for you to wear in your hair,' and soon began to climb the rocks. After a time, the maiden became lovesick. Not wanting to remain alone, she placed her hands on the mountain stones and so began to climb." Penny pauses, making sure all the ends are twisted and ties the ribbon into a bow. The yellow stands out brightly in contrast to the ebony locks. "Finally, in the evening, the man comes down from the mountain with a bloom of *tsukimisou* in hand but found the maiden gone. He searches for her in the grasses, thinking she might be resting. Finding no sign of her, he turns to Mount Nantai and sees a lone *jizo* standing at the base, its face just as kind as the maiden. He cried, knowing at once that she had turned to stone." Satisfied, Penny tucks some remaining bits of hair behind Catherine's ear.

"There," Penny says, "Don't you look a picture."

Gently, Catherine reaches a hand back, smoothing her hair and touching the ribbon with a single finger. A booming echo draws the women's attention to the window. In the time it took to fasten Catherine's hair, the sky had grown dark and

298

the smoky remnants of fireworks scatter in the darkness. Drawn by the excitement, Penny rushes to the window with Timmy trailing her, leaving Catherine to comfort Rose who screams and cries in fearful surprise. Peering down to the shore below, Penny spies the origin of the fireworks. A curious machine, much like a Lightning Rotary churns, with the dials continually clicking. In one grand ignition, a whistling bulb shoots from the top of a metallic orb in wave patterns across the surface and into the sky. Rainbow shocks of light that makes Timothy howl gleefully at the colors blazing in an endless succession, lasting until the stars emerge. A song she remembers from another Sunday creeps in, and she finds herself singing. The men reappear from behind the locked door. Turning, Penny finds that Catherine is gone and the baby with her.

"And what were you fellas conspiring about?" she teases, only to be ignored in favor of the spread laid out on the table.

A feast of butter croissants toasted golden fresh presented on a porcelain platter. Jam cups arranged in a row in ascending colors from blackberry to marmalade. One large circular basket sits at the end of the table filled to the brim with summer fruit. Two pots, one tea and the other coffee, are next to each other sitting on paisley cushions. Cups are at spots around the table designating where each person should sit.

"We'll invite them all to dinner," he pauses, seeming to wait for comment and where there is none, continues, "for a peace agreement."
Already Penny is suspicious. Since when did George become inclined towards peace? It does not seem a possibility.

299

However, being the boss along with his father's death and legacy may have changed his mind after all. Regardless, she lets out an amused scoff,

"And how will anyone convince the other gangs to show? They hate each other as much as us. What honey do you plan to feed them?

"Promises. The sort no one can resist."

He meets her eyes but there is no readable emotion in them.

21
Sarah
After Solitude
July 1949

Without fanfare, she exits the workhouse and boards the boat that will take her to port. She leaves in the same clothes she came in, with twenty cents still in her pocket, and the dirt scuffs on her pant legs from the riot so many months before.

The waterfront is in a state of continual repair. The decimation of the earthquake has cleared, leaving open spaces where collapsed buildings once sank into mud and water. Fresh steel and wooden platforms contrast with the old salt-worn boardwalk. A great puff of new cut construction lumber wafts from a breeze off the sea. Hungry, exhausted, she begins walking, staring down the Sinclair Industrials building that refuses to budge despite the past upheaval. She moves past the wash of faces both flesh and tin, her steps bringing her to the downtrodden space that Ruth had once occupied. Abandoned.

A peek through the window shows no more than some rubbish on the floor and several towels laid for a vagabond's bed. It does not take much for Sarah to hazard who might be using it for shelter now that it seems Ruth has gone. Turning from it, she inhales deeply, looks up to the sky, exhales, then picks up a fallen brick from the ground and tosses it heedlessly at the shack. Frustrated at the absence of any chance to see Ruth, she begins kicking the door with her sore foot and pounding with her fists. Her anger refuses to subside. She looks for a blunt object, plentiful in this poor

area which still bears ruin from the earthquake. A thick
battered gutter pipe is her salvation. No need to worry about
the circus balloons here; there are none in this darkness. She
pounds and pounds at the sides of the shack, knocking off
chips of paint in the process. Unsatisfied with the damage,
she moves to the windows which shatter at once already
having cracks and breaks that were covered by thick brown
tape.

Crashing glass gives her as much pleasure as a brown
envelope filled with pay though not as much as if it were
Ruth's face she were beating. She continues bashing the
house on and on until a sheen of sweat turns to trickling
beads, her arms ache and her shoulders tinge. The rain gauge
bends and her rancor slows and still she continues her
destruction. Only when her breath lightens does she cease,
dropping the bashed tool. Another failure makes her seek out
the Patriot slum house where an interior light shows through
closed curtains, knocking until the door is finally answered
by Alma.

"Idiot," she says, waving her hand. "Come in, and
hurry."

She closes the door, scrunching her nose at the musky
scent emanating from the woman, and locks it behind Sarah.

"They're up there watching me," she says, though
Sarah had not seen any balloons on the way. "Least if I'm in
here. . .I'm pretty sure there aren't bugs—not anywhere I've
found, anyway."

A shock of nerves makes Sarah blurt, "I'll go."

"No! Go away now and it looks odd." She points
towards a table near the front window. "Sit." And then, "How
well can you hold your booze?" she asks, going briskly to the

small refrigerator in the kitchenette and grabs two beer bottles.

"Not well."

"Good."

From her pocket, she removes a house key hanging from a brown leather loop. With the edge of one, she pops off the tin tops. Tossing the key on the table, she hands the beer to Sarah while remaining standing.

"You don't have coffee?' Sarah asks.

"And how would that look? You coming over at near ten at night for coffee?"

Alma nods at her, encouraging, "Drink until you feel it."

Sarah sips from the round lip bottle. A raw, grainy water that makes her hack.

"I assume you're here for some reason or another?"

She leans next to the window. "Might as well spit it out."

Swallowing a full gulp, Sarah coughs as if her body tries to expel the disgusting essence. She clears her throat, giving her voice a serious tone.

"That last strike—"

"—Yeah?" she interrupts, questioning suspiciously.

"Well, we're not backing down now, are we?"

Alma rolls her eyes and finishes her drink, leaving the bottle on the tabletop.

"I'd stop that thinking there."

"What?" Sarah asks, disbelieving at once that the same woman who trotted her to a bit of rebellious destruction at the old train station now chastises her for attempting to embolden their cause.

"It's done."

"But—"

"—Nope. I've seen two failed strikes and that's enough."

Sarah, channeling some flattery, says, "Three's a charm."

"Not for me. I'm out of here on the next rig. Florence is—"

"—Everyone who managed to escape arrest won't be coming back. Those in jail are felons. You think any folks will hire the likes of us? Jailbirds and rioters?"

Sarah begins to feel a buzzing.

"To hell with that lot," she says low.

"Then you'll be a beggar."

A dismal image of the woman with ruined hands passes. An old woman at the gates pleading for work only to return to a borrowed hovel. Alma startles at the sudden laughter that escapes Sarah's mouth. A hysterical expectorant at the truth of her situation. It suddenly appears ridiculous. She came to this city to change her prospects and all that occurred has been a disaster. Two options are clear to her: stay and scratch up a living or do what she knows and leave.

"Where is that boy?" she says finally.

"What boy?"

"The one from before who you kicked out."

She thinks it over, puzzled, then relaxes her face, "Oh, that kid? Over 'round scraps about this time. Probably tossing dice by the docks."

Sarah stands at once, heading for the door.

"Don't be a fool," comes a warning.

The words like a water drop rolling across her shoulders and falling to the floor.

Unheeding the advice, Sarah departs at once. Sure enough, she finds the thin youngster crouching over a clear section of concrete behind a worn foreman's shack where a brass oil lamp hangs from a nail, casting dim light on a small figure, two broader, older boys, and the dice between them. Hearing their bickering, she calls out as she approaches. The answer is a harsh, "Whaddya want?"

"Got a job for the kid."

At this, the ruffian stands and walks over.

"What job?" inquires another, overhearing.

Shifting a head sideways, a shout orders, "Shut yer gum."

Kid must be the leader, even for such a small thing, for the large boy does as ordered and continues the game.

"I saw you a while ago with the Patriots."

"Aw, that." Kid takes a tin from a front overall pocket, pops it open, pinches a bit of chewing tobacco from it to jam behind the lower lip, replacing the tin. "Soft bellies, them. No guts fer the big risking." A pause to spit out the tar. "Last riot was a damn fool's rush. Can tell thems're citizens; never had no hard licking." Kid grins with browned teeth; some big, some baby, some lost. "Went there like a pidge to a trap—"

"—Fine," she says to cut off the beginning of a digression. "You want risking? I have a job for you, if you'll take it." She waits for an objection. When none comes, she continues, "I need help with some. . .'fireworks'."
Quizzical eyes judge her. "That right?" and moves in closer. "Jus' how much you talkin'?"

"Enough to give a fine show down at the waterfront." A mischievous grin is Kid's answer.

*

Kid had been agreeable, rooting out everything she asked for in exchange for the money she had on hand. All twenty cents. The youth had happily taken it, leaving Sarah dour at the circumstance that she is now poorer than a child on the skids. The materials bought are stowed in a ragged rucksack that she slings over a shoulder. With Kid and the other scamps following excitedly, she walks to the last place left. Her shelter is Ruth's old house that she enters through the broken window and settles on the living room floor, content to work by the floating lights emanating past the windowpanes.

"Not bad fer a shack," Kid comments, uncouthly rooting around for anything of value. Opening the sack, Sarah pulls out the contents: an assortment of wires, pocket watch faces all ticking to their own time, vinyl tape, a dozen hand heaters, and an army green steel canister. The youngster is savvier than she thought. Calling the group to her, she ensures that they sit adjacent to each other with the materials between them.

"Now, I'll show you how to make one and you can do the rest," she says, met with Kid's keen interest and goes to work.

It is simple for her to recall her time in the munitions factory at Minidoka and use those menial skills to fashion a small explosive. The careful, steady movements that remain as muscle memory allow a smooth construction. Her nerves, however, require constant attention.

Hours are a blur, as the bruised light before sunrise appears. It is not as if she has any friends to see or a purpose to rise in the morning and she finds it exciting to make some difference; some important measure. Through the long night, she breaks from her close watch on the progress to scrounge around the cupboards for any food remains, finally finding a stock of canned food in the pantry. Her glee at the discovery is soon dashed when she sees that the majority are of sour cabbage and beets. Pushing these aside, she discovers a can of green beans and another of potatoes. Resigned, she opens them with her knife, slipping at times and nicking her fingers on the point. The vegetables are watery and flavorless, but are a delicacy compared to the gruel she subsisted on in the workhouse.

The crafted explosives now stored and ready, Kid stretches out on the floor to sleep while the two others find their own secluded spots in the room. Rather than leave the wretches alone, she picks up each body, one-by-one bringing them to the bedroom. It had been stripped of anything of personal or monetary value. Only a bed frame and mattress remain. Alone, safe, she removes her shoes and socks, allowing her sore bare feet to touch the cool floor, and sits on the bed, relaxing her upper body. Lying on it, she finds it stiff. Rolling on her side, a dull pain digs into her hip. Not sharp enough to be a spring, she deduces, and down on the spot with a fist which is met with a hard, flat sensation. Getting up, she lifts the mattress. Nothing. She pushes on it again, finding the object and realizing that it is within the bed itself. Searching, she discovers a long cut at the seam. Pulling it open, she sticks a hand in, wary of the coils, fondling for the object. Gripping, she hefts it through the opening to find the leather case of her violin.

"Thank you," she says to the dark as she opens the latch to see the smooth curves of the instrument, the still-fresh strings, the silky hairs of the bow.

Putting out her hands, she nearly touches it, but resists at the sight of her blackened nails. Unwilling to place dirty skin on such finery, she finds the bathroom, keeping the door open to let in a soft glow rather than trying to switch on the light, and turns the bath faucet. The pipes clink, releasing rusty water that splatters into the basin, scaring away the few small spiders who had been hiding and now disappear up the wall. She disrobes, allowing herself to be completely naked for the first time in months, and enters the tub, squatting over the drain as she cups the free-flowing water in her hand and splashes it over her skin, then scratches the dead skin, exploring her thin body, rolling fingers over the bones of her ribcage and then rising to her collarbone.

Repulsed by her physical state, she closes her eyes and dunks her head under the now hot water. Pulling away, she runs splayed fingers through her hair, tugging at tangles, and then rubs the dripping water on her face but when the drops trickle to the sores on her feet, she winces from the pain of the scalding heat on her tender flesh. Lastly, she takes great care in cleaning her fingernails by using the thumbnail of her right hand to pick out any grime. Once finished, she shuts off the faucet and steps out, shaking herself dry out of the habit of not using a towel for so long, and slips her clothes on. Returning to the room, she takes out the bow and the rosin, carefully sliding the dusty amber surface against the tight hairs. Replacing the rosin, she picks up the violin, cradling it in her arms for a moment to smell the wooden sheen, and puts the base at her collar.
A soft, pleasant melody emanates as soon as her fingers press against the strings.

22

Penelope
Porcelain Flowers

A doorman stands by at the edge of the double door entrance decorated by oval stained-glass windows, each with a cardinal blue peacock perched on a rose branch, backs facing forward so the tail feathers fall in a cascade of azure and emerald. Penny ascended to the second-floor private room, up lime-green carpeted steps, passing a stain glass window of a singing cherub around a pansy wreath halo to a foyer marked by a wrought iron chandelier with teal tassels, reflecting on the glass table beneath. Adjacent is a set of stained-glass doors propped open an inch to let in air.

Separated by clear polished glass dividers is a private room. A secret placard where waiters in white sleeves, black waistcoats, and long black aprons to match their trousers set the table on the opposite side of the glass. A multitude of gentlemen remain in the drawing room chattering to each other in tones of reserved suspicion. Each gang affiliation remains together with few mincing words with anyone. Even a Sinclair Industrials man is there in a prim blue suit with the company logo as a monogram on the breast pocket.

After some minutes of waiting, a waiter approaches from within the glass room, props open the door, and announces the dinner service. Warily, every gangster passes through the door, some of whom hold a hand inside their jacket breast pocket to secure whatever lies beneath. Last to enter among them are the hosts, followed closely by the Sinclair man. The tall, trim gentleman overshadows George by several inches and when he looks down to meet his eye, a lock of wavy hair comes loose from his finely combed scalp to fall over his forehead causing him to habitually push it back with his index finger.

"I must applaud your scheme," he says in a low voice without a hint of amusement, drawing Penny's attention, turning her head so that the tied ends of the scarf around her tickle her neck. Confused, George furrows his brows, creating three distinct creases between them. A moment and his muscles relax, then to fib his way through understanding, says, "Is that right?"

"Certainly. Having that snake in the grass saved a generous amount of time," he lets out a pleased chuckle, "in fact, it worked better than any of us expected. After the round-up of the rioters, I doubt they'll do it again." Here he looks smug. "Enough of them are in prison—and their leader branded a communist sympathizer—to deter any more of those pesky rallies."

It was impossible not to overhear the man. She preferred not to be reminded of the trick she pulled, as it had been unintentional at first. The voice transmitter in the clock she gifted to Sarah was meant to ensure her safety. It was only when Sarah continued in her stubborn association with the dissidents that Penny thought to use it for another purpose There had not been a way to spare her cousin from retribution, as much as she wished it, without implicating herself. Approaching the man, she smiles tersely, and introduces herself while shaking his hand, hoping to change the subject quickly,

"I don't believe we've met."

"Why, no." He pushes a hair back. "Mr. Weathers, with Sinclair Industries, of course."

"Please make yourself comfortable," She says, motioning at the many open seats, then excuses herself, her

310

eyes move from the coral carpet that dampens heavy steps to the long set table to the cabinet record player next to an empty space and then a black piano free of fingerprints. George sits at the leftmost chair, leaving the head of the table clear to follow traditional Japanese custom, for god is who resides at the head.

Next to him is Koike-san who already lights a cigarette. The others find seats at various sections, though there is a short exchange of words when the V gang boss, who cannot be older than twenty-five, ventures too near another man's shoes. A waiter from the bar brings tall glasses of iced tea, sliding his arm in the space between shoulders to place each glass base on the circular white coaster placed before each plate. There is a long pause as none will touch their food, for fear of poison or in politeness, and it is not until George takes the first bite that the others follow.

There is tension in the room, dampened by terse conversations between those seated. Easing this silent discord is why Penny takes her place by a standing record player. One young waiter turns the crank on the record player with such force that there is a distinct clunking sound at each turn. Penelope's pink mouth turns into a smile and she opens it to sing. The clear space is where Penny poises triumphantly, keeping herself at arm's length from the piano. An unnecessary habit to ensure that the ambiance won't drown her out when she sings.

All are mesmerized by her voice that seems to flit upon the air in a symphonic duality. Just as she is near to complete the last stanza, she starts and her voice ceases. As her moist lips vibrate, then settle, a tilt of her head is the signal. In a single action, the waiters remove derringers from their pockets and shoot each gang leader in the back of the neck, at the base of the skull, severing stem from brain in terrifying pops. Her skin jumping as a child's does when surprised. Bullet pops crackle. The scene is one of quick blood. Too quick even for screams.

In a swift movement, each waiter pulls out a derringer from their inside waistcoat, settles it at each of the boss's temple and fires. The newly dead fall in varying positions, their weight keeling over to the floor, knocking over the chair in the process, some fall forward into their sweet cake while others hang backwards on their chairs, heads reclined, open eyes staring in a prayer for heaven. The shock of fresh death melts when the bloody perfume stings her nose. It forces her from disassociation as she tries her best to keep vomit from erupting where it bubbles high in her stomach. Those left alive are the Sinclair businessman, Koike-san, George, and the lieutenants who are scrambling to rationalize the new situation, some even shaking the bosses to confirm death. Before any man can speak, George stands, outwardly unperturbed by the event.

"This is my promise," he says, his voice as stern and steady as a marble rolling across wood, holding out his fingerless hand to gesture at the bloody carnage. "The old bosses are gone, torn out by the root." Penny chokes down her immediate terror at her past words being spoken through George. "The petty fighting is done."

Abe oversees the job of escorting the remaining gang members out. When one protests, aiming to land a tight fist in his face, another *kyodai* nearby manages a sharp punch to his ribs that pacifies him. The remaining rabble splits up with one group taking the warm bodies on the floor, dragging them by ankles and wrists to the back while the others clean up messes of blood and body parts. They do so with such swift ferocity that she realizes in horror that they must do this often. Her sights turn to George who is in conversation with Koike san and Mr. Weathers, the latter passing a thick envelope that George takes with a single approving nod. He then approaches Penny, very gingerly, to put an arm around her shoulders, pulling her away, and she follows as slowly as if she has just risen from a fevered sleep.

Walking past the table, one of the *kyodai* shifts a body that had fallen face forward on the dinner plate. When he does, the head falls back, revealing a face so ripped apart by escaping bullets that it is unrecognizable. Burst cheeks with chopped skin poking outwards, teeth shot out with some spread on the tablecloth while the few remaining give the corpse a horrible smile from cut lips. Seeing it unhitches the cap on her sick stomach. Bending over suddenly, surprising George at once who checks over her body in fear that she may have been shot by a wayward bullet, Penny spews the contents of her stomach onto the beautiful carpet, spilling bile across a design of entwining flower stems on the pink background.

Together with Namahage, they exit the restaurant to a placid street and a car waiting. Dizzy, she lies down on her side in the back seat facing towards the upholstery. The car engine rolls to a start and, instead of George taking a place in the passenger seat, he joins her, lifting her feet so he can sit down on the space underneath, and then replaces them across his lap while Penny rests an arm across her waist to comfort her clenching stomach. Sea-green eyes with an amber starburst surrounding a black pool; eyes the color of the sea

313

in a storm meet in a single smooth movement. They are the frayed strings on the ends of silken cloth.

Whatever it takes, she reminds herself, grimly.

23
Sarah
Remnant Distance

Four figures creep along the outer fence surrounding the industrial building. Only the balloon eyes dart here and there, attracted to movement elsewhere in the city. While Kid is eager, often needing to be shushed from talking too much, Sarah remains concerned of the hovering cameras, doing her best to have determination stamp out the fear that periodically spews doubt.

To get inside is the most difficult. To be safe, she sneaks to the edge of the waste area where discarded trash or broken service parts are strewn about the dumpsters along with cigarette butts scattered around the wall where workers had taken their breaks. The fences are left with gaps and a filthy gate for where the waste truck would typically come and go numerous times a day. Here also is a dim spot between two spies. The dummy cameras are in odd numbers and she waits until they pan in opposite directions. A few moments pass and Sarah clambers over quickly, pressing her body against the brick wall, looking back to ensure that the others follow her movements.

The camera meets the edge, ready to swing back and catch a wriggly figure climbing up the holes in the fence. Keeping to the wall, it seems that the courtyard is a great black sea licking the soles of her shoes. She treads gently like a gnat on a moldy wall. A steel door that is the back entrance stands to the side, the handles chained and kept together with a giant brass lock. Jiggling it, she finds there is no give. From behind there is a snicker. One of the ruffians refers to her as a "cock-eyed broad" as he nudges Sarah out of the way. From his back pocket, he removes a silver rod about the length of a pen that has two wires sticking from the tip. A switch on the side flicks up and down and up and down clicking until a blue spark comes from the wires, connecting them together in a waving stream. This he raises to the door lock, sticking it into the keyhole. There is a sizzling and then a loud pop. After flicking the switch down and stowing the object, he gives a triumphant thumbs-up. With a turn of the lever it sticks for a bit until he jostles the knob free. As they enter, she inspects the lock to find the inner workings completely disintegrated. Where the locking bar should be is melted flat against the inner steel panel.

Inside, there is all but one automaton guard moseying to and fro as a precaution. Sneaking past when the Iron Boy's back is turned, they sprint down the hallway leading to Parts and Manufacturing. The floor is dark but for the strips of city lights coming in through the thin upper windows, casting a glow on hanging racks of automaton carcasses. Shells of the automatons wait in partly finished states. Metal skeletons dangling.

"Ok," she says, whispering to Kid, passing the sack. "Have at it."

A gigantic grin is the response. Settling to work, Kid and the others scatter the round explosives, ensuring that several are set on the large crates nailed shut and labeled "Munitions."

Not wanting to stay for any longer than necessary, Sarah removes herself from the area.

Pops and whirrs from a gargantuan steel automaton. It must have heard the noise as it appears before her as a thick iron frame and within what looks like human eyes in a metal helmet. The same as what the police used at the rally, only without a badge. Instead it has a logo welded to its chest that reads "SINCLAIR INC." It utters nothing as it brings up its weaponized arm. Sarah darts, looking for anything to fight with and finds a long ball-pen hammer. A grunt and a crunch. The weight is off her and so she lifts herself up to see the sharp end melded into the side of its neck. It looks at her and then at once its eyes become cataracts and the body wriggles violently until it seems that is sleeping.

Dashing silently back the way she came; she stops momentarily when she passes an open box of packed Firelite cartons to rip it apart and slip a pack into her pocket. A swift jump and she is over the fence as deftly as a cricket. A pattering on the wood like steps. It must be rain against the trees now picking up as it prickles the top of her while she waits. The sound comes closer and there she notices breathing, though a low in and out. Then she turns.

Seventeen steps from her, a dog of a large kind that she has only seen mirrored by the feral wolfdogs that roamed around the Anchorage docks searching for the guts of salmon around the factory cannery. Its mouth open, showing its yellow teeth, some rotting, too thin as his rib bones are accentuated by the skin stretched around the patchy hair body. Coming too close, she shoos. It might bark. She can't let it. It might alert a wary automaton or, worse, a bystander. For anyone to find her here, now, so near to the factory, it will not take much for her to be shuffled to a place far worse than the debtor's workhouse. A frenzy causes a turn to mania. She picks up a piece of nearby rubble and throws it. He yelps, and it makes her pause, watching as the dog steps

317

away, shaking.

Recovering a moment, he comes up to her again and so she repeats the action. This time it seems to knock him out. Approaching the pitiful animal, she kneels by it and holds his head in her lap, convinced that she can still hear his breathing.

More footsteps, these hurried and accompanied by laughs. They meet her with expressions so hearty that she expects them to begin dancing. Concerned with moving to a safe distance, she does not stop, instead letting them follow as they banter about where to watch the fireworks. They settle on one of the abandoned train lines nearby. They walk onto the raised platform painted with V gang marks, lewd drawings, and racial slurs. As she waits, Sarah takes a pack of Firelites from her pocket, and then lights the cigarette. Kid smacks her shoulder, insisting that she share, which she does without hesitation, making sure to share her matches. Seeing them handle the substance so casually, it is clearly not any of their first times smoking. They sit, legs dangling over the side.

There is a burst from the Sinclair Industries building. The wall that forms the outside of Parts and Manufacturing explodes a hole from one side with black smoke flowing from within. Brightness illuminates the sky like morning. Giant yellow explosions burn sodium nitrate. Then the flames become bigger. A loud rupture—perhaps one of the tanks exploding, breaks a wall, spewing bricks into the water, flinging dust into the air as high as a geyser. The youngsters, in awe, clap and whoop at the spectacle as if they were children watching fireworks in the night sky.

The destruction pleases her in a way she had not
expected. For once, she controls the chaos; she is not the
victim. While she does not celebrate as eagerly as the
youngsters, she cannot restrain a smile that spreads slowly
across her lips. Moments later are engine sirens.

Sarah watches on, flicking her cigarette ashes onto the
empty rails below.

End

Made in the USA
Monee, IL
26 August 2020